It was Victor's very intensity, the way he drew up his broad shoulders and peered anxiously with his almost colorless blue eyes, that made him so attractive to Masha. She wanted to beg him to laugh, for she was only twenty-two and wanted her life to be filled with joy and merriment. She wanted to challenge him to smile, for she was young and always felt a flush of pleasure when spring arrived, and all around her the land seemed to delight in its own rebirth. But now she closed her eyes when the young Count bent toward her, his moist, feverish lips clinging to her mouth.

Masha instinctively drew back, not really knowing why. Nothing in his letters had prepared her for this, nor indicated that she was more to him than a faithful correspondent. "We can't catch up on five years in just an instant," she said.

"But we can try, can't we?"

"Then do it," she whispered. She closed her eyes, and soon felt the warmth and tenderness of his mouth against her own, the firm yet gentle way he now held her in his arms. I must teach him to laugh, she vowed. Yes, I'll take him in hand, make him cast off this ridiculous crown of thorns he's given himself to wear in the name of Russia!

FASCINATING, PAGE-TURNING BLOCKBUSTERS!

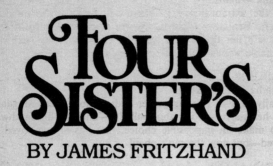

FOUR SISTERS

BY JAMES FRITZHAND

ZEBRA BOOKS
KENSINGTON PUBLISHING CORP.

ZEBRA BOOKS

are published by

KENSINGTON PUBLISHING CORP.
475 Park Avenue South
New York, N.Y. 10016

Printed in the United States of America

For my aunts, in loving memory

Henrietta Lipschutz
Norma Magelof
Florence Greenblatt

and

Harriet Meyer

Immeasurable expanses flew to meet him.

Oh Rus, Rus!

Is it you who have set the winds, storms, and snows howling across the steppe? Only hungry wolves gather in packs out there.

—ANDREI BELY, Petersburg

Life is such a ridiculous business.

—DOSTOYEVSKY

Prologue

March 1, 1881

For those who chanced to pass her on the street Sophia Perovskaya looked like the wife of an artisan, not the daughter of a former military governor of Petersburg. Dressed in a thin cotton frock, a greasy sheepskin overcoat, men's boots, and a threadbare kerchief covering her short flaxen braids, she waited outside the Manège, the riding school just off Mikhailovsky Square, anxious to catch a glimpse of the Emperor.

Alexander II was reviewing an honor guard. As soon as he left the parade and she determined which direction he was taking to return to the Winter Palace, the plan called for her to hurry to the Malaya Sadovaya, just a short distance away. Here, she would give the signal, and her compatriots would take up their new positions.

But for the moment all she could do was stand out in the cold, this girl who a few years before had shone in some of the most fashionable drawing rooms of the capital. An eternity ago, she decided, for she could hardly breathe life into the memory of her past, now that she had set herself such a monumental task. On this gray and gloomy Sunday afternoon, the world would finally learn the extent of her determination.

We have begun a great thing, she told herself. Even if it takes another generation, or another after that, it must be done. Too long the people have suffered injustice. Now, with the help of her carefully chosen circle, all that would change.

Shapeless gray clouds hung stationary in a dull and leaden winter sky. The wind picked up, and from the nearby Ekaterininsky Canal she heard the feeble rattling of the lanterns strung along the quay, those thin and grating squeaks so familiar to the inhabitants of Petersburg. Then the riding school gates swung back and she held her breath, eyes on the guard of mounted Cossacks streaming onto the street.

Riding upright so that it looked as if they were standing in the stirrups, the imperial escort was followed by a semistate cream-colored carriage, its black hood studded with gold double-headed eagles. Perovskaya was unable to glimpse its occupant, but as soon as she saw the direction taken by the four magnificent Orloff trotters pulling the carriage, she hurried off to give the appropriate signal.

Fifteen minutes later, eighteen-year-old Nikolai Rysakov saw Perovskaya blow her nose. So the Emperor was being cautious, was he. Not that it mattered, for Perovskaya had signaled him to take up a new position along the Ekaterininsky Canal. Dirty snow was piled on either side of the street. Here and there a porter's scarlet blouse lent a welcome spot of color to what was otherwise a dreary scene. It was nearly two o'clock, and the sidewalk was fast becoming crowded with worshipers returning from Mass. Rysakov lost his footing on a patch of ice, stumbled, and grabbed for the nearest passerby.

"Forgive me, Your Excellency, forgive me," he mumbled as he hurried on.

Rysakov slipped one hand into the pocket of his gray student's overcoat, then dashed around the corner. Leaning for a moment against the parapet of the quay, he tried to calm his tremulous nerves. He was terribly agitated, for inside his overcoat pocket rested a five-pound oval-shaped bomb. Having envisioned himself exploding into a thousand pieces, he now breathed slowly and deeply until at last he felt more sure of himself.

Everything was now as it should be. Perovskaya had given the signal, Perovskaya for whom he secretly would do anything. A few minutes from now the Tsar's carriage would come down the street, and Rysakov would hurl the bomb from his pocket, just as they had planned.

Rysakov walked unsteadily for another fifty yards, then stopped abruptly and looked back. At the corner of the Inzhenernaya and the quay he expected to see Timofey Mikhailov. Instead, Rysakov noticed a baker's boy, his plaited basket wobbling uncertainly atop his head. Frightened that Mikhailov might have lost his nerve, might even have decided to betray them, Rysakov looked behind him to where Grinevitsky was supposed to take up his position at the opposite end of the quay. A familiar round face, pleasant and guileless and crowned by a moth-eaten astrakhan cap, broke into a reassuring grin.

But where was Timofey? Rysakov looked back toward the Inzhenernaya, the five-pound bomb feeling much bulkier now, as if the closer the Tsar got, the heavier it became.

Perhaps Sophia got it wrong, Rysakov thought. Perhaps she blew her nose by accident, because she had to.

Again he looked toward Kotik, the nickname Grinevitsky preferred to his own. Kotik was still smiling, leaning nonchalantly against the parapet, and whistling a tune from Rubinstein's opera *The Demon.* The sad, lilting melody drifted along, carried by the sharp and bitingly cold gusts of wind blowing along the quay.

Rysakov ran his hand across his eyes. The cold stung his cheeks, and when he looked up it was to see the baker's boy put down his wicker breadbasket. Just then a contingent of Cossacks galloped into view, the furious beat of iron-shod hoofs making his teeth rattle.

Behind the mounted guard, four huge dappled gray Orloffs pulled the imperial carriage over the hard-packed snow. Mikhailov was nowhere in sight. It was up to Rysakov, and as the baker's boy began to cheer, Rysakov reached inside his pocket and curled his half-numb fingers around the bomb. He could see the imperial coat of arms adorning the side of the carriage, could see the silver-chased daggers and Circassian swords standing out against the dark blue of the Cossacks' close-fitting tunics, could see every detail of the procession as if all motion had stopped. He alone controlled the destiny of Russia, and the thought terrified him.

Rysakov hesitated no longer and threw the bomb.

Falling somewhat short of its target, it rolled beneath the carriage, smashing against the rear axle. There was a sudden explosion, a sheet of bright orange and blue flame shooting skyward. Through the oily cloud of sulphur-yellow smoke Rysakov saw with horror that the imperial carriage was still intact.

What had gone wrong? Five pounds of explosive surely should have done the job. Yet the carriage was still moving, though now he could see that the baker's boy was lying on the ground, screaming and writhing in pain, while a few yards away the body of a Cossack guard lay crushed beneath his horse.

Rough hands seized him, holding him fast. From inside the closed carriage the imperial presence made itself known with a single word, spoken in a firm and unshaken voice. "Stop!" shouted the Tsar.

Rysakov felt himself being pulled in two directions at once, a dozen or so Cossacks and police officers crowding in around him. Something warm and wet trickled down his leg. Rysakov closed his eyes, too ashamed to confront them with his sorrowful lack of self-control. The urine froze within moments, so that his cotton undergarments stuck against his skin. Unable to escape, he offered no resistance.

"Who is this man?" someone shouted.

"Search him!" came the angry reply.

Rysakov opened his eyes. A crowd of onlookers had assembled out of nowhere, filling the narrow quay with a sea of shifting, curious red faces. Never before had he received such attention. He must take advantage of his sudden notoriety, must prove his worth to dearest Sophia.

"Where is the Emperor?" he heard a voice call out.

The crowd held its breath, while a short distance away the Tsar descended from his carriage. "Thank God, I'm safe," he told his subjects.

The tyrant had spoken. Then why are they cheering? Rysakov wondered as he felt a gobbet of spit splash across his cheek. It dribbled down his face when suddenly Alexander II, Emperor and Autocrat of all the Russias, was standing before him.

How calm he looks! Rysakov marveled. He plays his part so well, like the finest actors on the stage.

"Was it you who threw the bomb?" asked the Emperor.

Rysakov tried to hold his head high. "Yes."

"Your name?"

"Glazov, artisan," he said, for that was the name he had taken months before, when Sophia had helped him acquire forged identity papers.

"Artisan indeed," said the Tsar with a look of disgust. "Where's Colonel Dvorzhitsky?" he went on as he turned away. "Ah, here you are. Come, I want you to show me where the bomb exploded."

15

The crowd of onlookers drew apart to give the Emperor room. Several yards away, Kotik, having moved up along the quay, leaned against the parapet, hands in his pockets and eyes fixed on the Tsar. Success now depended upon him and him alone. Rysakov had tried and failed. They were so close to achieving their goal that he could not let the opportunity pass, not when the Tsar was coming directly toward him.

"Was this where—?" he heard Alexander II say when Kotik pulled the bomb from his coat pocket and hurled it at the Emperor's feet.

A flock of crows, frightened by this second explosion, wheeled madly about, scattering like buckshot as they disappeared from sight. When the smoke cleared Kotik found himself lying alongside the Emperor, his cheek resting against the toe of the Tsar's boot. Where there had been snow there was now blood, a darkening crimson slush that kept spreading out in all directions. Kotik shifted position, and though he could not see the Tsar's face, he heard him clearly, the Emperor whispering, "So cold, so very cold."

Kotik too was dying, but dragged himself several inches along the snow, the better to determine if things had gone as they had planned. The Tsar had been flung against the parapet, shreds of bloody tattered cloth flapping in the wind and barely concealing the shattered remnants of his legs, one of which appeared to have been completely blown apart.

I won't live, Kotik thought as he lay there surrounded by the wounded, some twenty in all. I won't survive, but neither will he.

The Tsar's brother, Grand Duke Mikhail, pressed through the crowd, having heard the explosion from two streets away. "Can you hear me, Alexander?"

"Yes," said the Tsar, his voice all but inaudible.

The Grand Duke leaned closer. "We will get help for you, I swear. How are you feeling?"

16

"To the Palace."

"Yes, of course."

"Home to the Palace," whispered the Tsar, "to die there."

Kotik closed his eyes. Perovskaya would be pleased, and soon all of Russia would rejoice that on this wintry day the tyrant had been felled, for did not history show that the tree of freedom needed blood to quicken its roots?

Book One

1881 = 82

One

"'And then when the taboret was pushed away—'"

"What does that mean?"

"The little stool she was standing on beneath the gallows," explained Anninka. "'—when the taboret was pushed away, and the cord pressed the soft gristle of her throat and the hard verte . . . vertebrae,'" she concluded after some deliberation. "That must be the poor darling's bones. 'The *vertebrae* of her neck, she felt a sudden rush of blood to her head and her whole body writhed.'" Here the housekeeper trembled convulsively, just to make sure the two girls who were listening knew what the words were all about.

"Then what?" asked the serving girl, whose face was as freckled as a cuckoo's egg.

"Can't you let Auntie read?" complained the other girl in the kitchen; she was folding linen napkins with not nearly as much precision as the mistress had instructed.

"Now the both of you, be quiet and listen," Anninka said in her sharpest voice. "It's not every day girls like you get a chance to hear the words of Count Tolstoy his very self. So if you want to argue, don't do it when I'm reading, which took many years to learn. Now, are you ready to hear the rest

21

of it?"

"Yes," said Akulina, the girl with the freckles.

"Yes," said her friend Lyuba.

"Very well then. Now where were we?"

"The vertebrates."

"Yes indeed, the poor sweet darling's tormented bones." Anninka flicked the pages of the newspaper, marking the place with a horny and blackened fingernail. " 'Then, slowly suffocating under the black cap, Sophia Perovskaya's face turned blue and the eyes popped right out of their sockets!' "

"And then?" the girls asked breathlessly.

"And then her neck snapped like a matchstick and she died, that's what. What else could she have done, the poor frail darling? Killed the Little Father, she did, the Tsar-Liberator who twenty years ago gave me my freedom. Now back to your work before the mistress finds you dawdling."

"The mistress is upstairs in bed where she always is," whispered saucy Lyuba.

"That's why she's mistress, you impudent baggage!" snapped Anninka. "Besides, Vera Petrovna is getting married this afternoon. No wonder her poor mother is suffering so." She stopped abruptly, then lifted the skirts of her black alpaca dress, the one with the row of buttons down the front and the little white collar fastened with a cameo brooch.

"What's the matter, Auntie?" whispered Akulina.

Anninka stepped carefully over the brick floor of the kitchen. She eased the door open as silently as possible, holding it ajar as she peered outside. There was no one in the dining room, though she expected the master, Peter Semyonovich Petrov, to put in his obligatory midmorning appearance within the next few minutes.

"Good," she said, letting go of the door so that it swung back on its stiff leather hinges. She turned around and looked at each girl in turn. "Vera Petrovna is getting married," she said thoughtfully. "And from what I hear tell—"

Lyuba didn't even give her a chance to finish. Giggling wickedly, the girl raised her plump milky-white arms and held them in the air a good foot apart, just like a fisherman lamenting the catch that got away. "That's what they say," she whispered. "A prize cucumber. Isn't that so, Akulina?"

The serving girl blushed furiously. "How should I know?"

Lyuba continued to laugh. "Oh, don't pretend to be an innocent." She glanced at Anninka. "Horses don't run away from oats. They say that Simon Belinsky is as well equipped as—"

"How long has it been since you were tending the pigs?" Anninka interrupted. "Because that's where you belong, the both of you."

"But you know what he's like, Auntie. Why, every girl in the village has—"

Again Anninka cut her off before the slander had a chance to run its course. "Just because Simon Ivanovich is a healthy, lusty man doesn't mean you should go about repeating every filthy thing you hear."

"But does he love her, Auntie?" said Akulina.

"Of course he loves her," the housekeeper replied, for she didn't want to put any ideas into their impressionable young heads. "Would the master have given his blessing if he didn't think Simon Ivanovich loved his daughter? He's no fool, I can assure you. Besides, how does a body measure love, anyway?"

"This way, Auntie," and with a reckless laugh Lyuba once again showed her the fish that got away.

Of the five children who bore the name Petrov, none were as sensible as the eldest, Irena Petrovna Volskaya. She had learned the virtue of humility early on, and now as a young woman carried herself with a certain reticence. To be responsible to one's loved ones, to see to it that all around her, life moved along as smoothly as the light two-horse carriage that was now bearing her toward Petrovka, that alone was of primary importance. Too often she had heard others speak roughly and in haste, little aware of the feelings they might be wounding. Irena was not one to speak unjustly, for even as a child it had struck her that not only was silence a virtue, but also an uncommon blessing. When she did speak, it was only after she had given a great deal of reflection to what she had to say. Thus she had gained the respect and even admiration of those who were closest to her.

But now, on this warm April day, she had little doubt that her opinions concerning her youngest sister's impending marriage would meet with anything but approval. How could she tell her what a mistake she was making, and still get Vera to understand? How could she explain that Simon Belinsky was not the man he made himself out to be, when all Vera had to do was look at him and her entire body trembled?

Deeply troubled, Irena clutched the package she held on her lap, and tried to figure out exactly what she would say. The very thought drew a sigh from between her lips, one that was lost to the unceasing rattle of the carriage wheels as she journeyed from her house in Mtsensk to Petrovka, her father's estate.

The coachman, driving like a Roman charioteer with his arms outstretched and a rein in either hand, looked back with a questioning glance. His name was Spiridon, though Spirya was what he answered to, and unlike most Russian coachmen, he was not the least bit stout. Small and bony, with little bald spots on his eyebrows left from smallpox, he asked if she wouldn't mind if he took a dip of snuff.

"Please feel free," Irena said.

While the coachman busied himself rubbing the bit of snuff between his fingers, she turned her eyes on the bare fields that stretched out before her. Soon the peasants would begin to prepare the land for the summer grain, and where there was now nothing but a level expanse of earth, there would soon be endless rows of brightly gleaming rye, yellowing oats, and buckwheat.

Overhead a lark hovered in the warm spring air, trilling endlessly and ecstatically. Higher still, a long, straggling V-shaped line of cranes soared across the azure sky. Irena felt her breath quicken as Spirya turned off the highroad, the carriage lurching from side to side as they took the narrow rutted path that led to Petrovka.

Like a faint leafy smudge on the horizon, the green roof of the old yellow stone church rose above the crest of a hill. Beyond it, as yet unseen, lay the scattered tumbledown huts of Petrovka, the village taking the same name as the family estate. Nearly all of the village inhabitants, at least those over the age of twenty, had at one time been her father's serfs, or "souls," as they were called.

The mettlesome black horses, sensing that oats and water were near at hand, trotted along more briskly. They were in sight of the manor house now, built in the same Alexandrine style as the church. Petrovka's green iron-sheeted roof and yellow façade stood out clearly against the April sky, a long avenue of closely planted pollarded lime trees suddenly engulfing them, forming a dark and shadowy canopy rising above her head.

On her left, in the orchard where she had so often played as a girl, the three-note call of an oriole could be heard above the rattling of the carriage wheels. On her right, beyond the trunks of the limes, a sagging wattle fence of narrow hazel withes marked the boundaries of a meadow, while directly ahead was the two-story house with its row of white columns, pediment, and escutcheon.

"Drive around to the back," she told Spirya.

Gadflies began to swarm around the steaming horses as they followed the path that led past the kitchen garden, the servants' quarters, and numerous outbuildings. The gravel crunched loudly beneath the iron hoops of the carriage wheels as they drove into the courtyard. At one end, rude stone gates led into the fields, where off in the distance was the double row of thatched village roofs. The carriage, swaying slightly, finally came to rest in the middle of the dusty courtyard. Kolya, the stableboy, came at a run, flashing a big strong row of white teeth as he called out good morning.

"Vera Petrovna's in quite a tizzy," Kolya went on. He was a big strapping fellow of sixteen or seventeen years, handsome even by standards of the best society. Thick, wavy chestnut hair crowned his high and well-shaped forehead, and as he stood off to the side watching her descend from the carriage, he continued to smile. "Shall I take that for you?" he asked, motioning to her parcel.

"I can manage, thank you. It's my dress for the wedding."

The outer door leading into the kitchen flew back. Anninka, wiping her weathered red hands on a towel, hurried into the yard. The old woman had been *nyanya* to the five Petrov children, and now that they were grown and no longer required a nanny, she spent most of her time in the kitchen.

Irena spread her arms wide to accept the housekeeper's embrace.

"Everyone has gone mad," Anninka exclaimed. "They're all upstairs in Verochka's room, helping to get her ready. I haven't seen such excitement since your own wedding day. Such a to-do they're all making." Anninka threw up her hands, upsetting the black chenille net she wore over her neatly parted hair.

Kolya darted between them to retrieve it.

"Don't you have work to do?" Anninka asked him.

"Yes, but my stomach's been making terrible noises all morning."

"I'll be making terrible noises too, 'less you go about your business." Nevertheless, Anninka called out to Lyuba, telling her to fetch what was left of the master's breakfast. A moment later Anninka pressed a poppyseed roll into the stableboy's big, eager hand. "Now be off with you," she said, sending him on his way with a playful whack across the ear. "He's a good boy though," she told Irena as Kolya danced across the yard. "And thick as thieves with the young master."

Irena, who unhappily had already heard certain rumors to that effect, pretended not to hear, inquiring instead after her brother.

"Young Gregor should be back by now," the housekeeper told her. "Yesterday afternoon he went to pay a call on Count Durnovo. But I suspect he'll show up soon enough."

Irena followed her inside, where the long deal kitchen table was piled high with neatly folded napkins, the hand-embroidered Petrov crest uppermost on each, as well as dishes filled with all manner of sweetmeats and savories to tempt the guests who would arrive after the wedding. A myriad of delicious aromas filled the air, for atop the ancient wood-burning stove half a dozen different dishes were cooking, while from inside the oven the faint crackling of dripping goose fat could be heard above the loud and wheezy ticking of the kitchen clock.

Anninka turned to Irena, taking her into her confidence. "May I ask my sweet dear what she thinks about the wedding? In truth, I'm worried about the young mistress, if you follow my meaning."

Irena did, for she was just as worried herself. Although she knew she should have spoken to Vera weeks before, and not waited until the day she was to be married, Irena was afraid her sister would have accused her of harboring petty emotions—jealousy and the like. It had always been difficult for Irena to speak truthfully to her youngest sister, and now as Anninka admitted what she herself had come to believe, Irena felt even more anxious than ever.

"Perhaps Simon Ivanovich will surprise us," she said.

"There is surprise, and there is surprise," replied Anninka, pronouncing each in a different fashion. "They don't always weigh the same."

"Then we must just hope for the best, and leave the rest to Providence."

Nineteen-year-old Vera Petrovna stamped her pretty little foot, both of her almond-shaped blue eyes fixed on the reflection peering back at her from within the glass. "Why couldn't I have a proper hairdresser like other girls? Why must Father be so stingy? Wasn't it enough he refused to buy me the gown I really wanted? Why, I just hate this ratty old thing. Madame Ducklet's Shop of Paris Gowns indeed! It looks no more Parisian than something Irena might have gotten in Mtsensk." Vera swallowed nervously and spun around, tossing her lustrous yellow curls. "Irusha, you're here at last!" she exclaimed. "I don't know what I would have done without you."

The two sisters embraced, Vera turning her head stiffly to the side so that Irena's cheek wouldn't bear down upon the profusion of corkscrew ringlets her sister Masha had worked so hard to achieve. Holding her oldest sister's hands, Vera stepped back, the better to eye the simple gray dress Irena had worn for the brief journey from Mtsensk to Petrovka.

"What a charming frock, Irena. Though it does seem to pull a little. Right here." Vera wagged her index finger at Irena's thickening waist.

"Yes, my figure isn't nearly as girlish as yours, Verochka."

"I think you look fine—radiant, in fact," pronounced dark-haired Masha, who though christened Maria Petrovna, had not heard anyone call her that for as long as she could remember.

"But what do you think of this hideous gown, Irusha?" Vera went on. She whirled around in her little pointed silk shoes, the long stiff folds of her gown ballooning out in all directions.

Vera loved to look at herself, for Simon Belinsky was not the first man who had told her how beautiful she was. Were her chin just a trifle less pointy she would have been completely enthralled by her appearance, as she considered this the one defect she must carry with her throughout her life. But if her chin was pointy, her other features made up for it, her long golden lashes, limpid blue eyes, and alabaster skin pleasing complements to her slender waist and graceful carriage.

For the third time in as many minutes, Vera twirled around, her white silk hose revealing delicately embroidered hairlines. "Do you think my hair's arranged stylishly?" she asked Irena, who had taken a seat at the opposite end of the cluttered little pink room.

"I think you're the prettiest of us all, Verochka."

How delightful to know that Irena felt just the same as she. But then she caught another glimpse of her wretched little chin, and her smile collapsed.

"Are you sure? Are you absolutely positive?" Vera asked.

It was at this point that her sister Henriette threw up her long bony hands in disgust. She was a year younger than Irena, only twenty-four, but even in the most flattering of light rarely passed for less than thirty.

"What an annoying child you are, Vera. Shouldn't you stop parading back and forth like God knows what, and think of more important things?"

Before Vera could reply, a faint tinkling was heard from somewhere down the hall.

"*Maman* is calling," Henriette said wearily.

"That infernal bell again," Masha whispered as her sister hurried from the room. "For Henriette's sake I'd like to bury it somewhere."

"Are you certain you still want to go through with this, Vera?"

Vera, who'd been alternately glancing into the mirror and then at her sisters, wasn't sure if she'd heard Irena correctly. "I know the dress is ugly," Vera said, swallowing hard as she always did when Irena spoke to her like an adult.

"I wasn't talking about the gown, Verochka. I'm talking about you, and your future. What you do this afternoon will affect you for years to come. But you can still call it off. There's no sin."

"Call off the wedding!" Vera exclaimed. "But that's the silliest thing I ever heard."

"It's not silly when you consider Simon Belinsky's reputation. He's a gambler and a womanizer—"

"How dare you!" Vera cried out. "Just because you can't have children, doesn't mean every man is—"

Masha grabbed her chin and gave it a painful jerk. "How can you speak so cruelly, especially when you know how untrue it is?" she said angrily. "Now apologize, Verochka, apologize or I'll make things very difficult for you."

Vera pulled free, hurrying back to the cheval glass to see if her eyes were as red and swollen as they felt.

"Apologize."

"No," she whispered.

"Irena loves you, you silly fool. And she only wants you to be happy."

Irena approached her, moving with the same measured care

she took whenever she voiced an opinion. Vera said nothing until she felt her sister's hands caressing her shoulders, fixing the fringe of shiny golden ringlets that fell over the edge of her collar.

"Remember, we're sisters," Irena said in a calm, patient tone of voice. "Perhaps I shouldn't have said anything. But it's only that I worry about you, as I know you worry about me."

"Oh I do, I do, Irusha." She spun around, as graceful as a water sprite, burying her face in the soft rose-scented hollow between Irena's neck and shoulders. "Give me your blessing, Irusha. It will mean more to me than anything."

"I gave you my blessing a long time ago, Verochka." Slowly making the sign of the cross over Vera's trembling yellow curls, Irena kissed her three times, once because they were sisters, once because she could not bear the sight of Vera's tears, and last because it was too late to change anything, much too late indeed.

Two

Although the clock representing Bacchus with a barrel had not yet struck noon, eighteen-year-old Gregor Petrovich, youngest of the five Petrov offspring, had already downed more peppered vodka than he quite knew how to handle. Yet his host, Count Roman Durnovo, insisted upon refilling his glass.

"No, I couldn't possibly," insisted Gregor. "My sister's wedding, you know."

"No one arrives sober at a wedding, certainly not the best man."

"I should very much prefer some coffee, though," Gregor said, for he was having a certain amount of difficulty focusing, the dining room in which they sat swaying back and forth each time he blinked his eyes.

Gregor had arrived at Jerichovo, the Count's sadly depleted estate, late the previous afternoon. Durnovo was one of his father's closest neighbors, though neither had ever had very much to do with the other, his father always saying he had no use for a man whose entire life was devoted solely to the pursuit of worldly pleasures.

"Do you know what I intend to have inscribed upon my

tombstone? 'Here lies Roman Durnovo. No matter what anyone says, he had a very good time.'"

The Count's flabby yellow face shook gleefully, his tiny eyes getting lost in the folds of flesh that surrounded them. Although he hadn't a kopeck to his name, the Count's estate could still boast the finest plums and peaches in the district, the handsomest domestics for miles around. He maintained that he had purposely bred them that way, watching over their couplings as if they were prize cattle.

"And what do I have to show for this labor of love," the Count would say to those who found it amusing to put up with his eccentricities, "this splendid breeding program of mine? Why, the most fetching maidens and virile lads in all the province! Beauties they are, works of art, as perfect a pantheon of gods and goddesses as any who ever posed for the great Lysippus or Polyclitus. Now you may say, who is this rather jaundiced old man to make such claims? Why, it is Roman Filimonovich Durnovo, and none other! For though I may be penniless, I can still pawn the iron roof above my head, or sell my peaches in the marketplace. But never will I have to part with my mares and stallions, my Aphrodites and Apollos!"

Such was the man who sat across from Gregor, a man who had long ago given himself up to the wanton pleasures of the flesh. He had fathered but a single child, his son, Victor, who had played with Gregor when they were boys. But Victor Romanovich had long since departed from Jerichovo, for like many of the neighboring gentry, he found his father's excesses far too painful to endure. Yet these very same excesses had first attracted Gregor to the Count's sphere. Rumor had it that at night the manor house was ablaze with light, while inside the Count sat like a pasha surrounded by his harem, instructing the men and women who lived on his estate to perform for him in ways best not discussed in polite society.

"Why do you suppose they allow themselves to be used?" Gregor asked, while behind him, atop the mantel, the bronze barrel Bacchus clutched in his chubby little hands struck twelve.

"My pretties? Ah, but the answer is quite simple. They pay me no quitrent, you see. They have free use of my lands, in exchange for which they allow me to take my pleasure, shall we say."

"And the men don't object to the use of their wives?"

"Our moujiks consider a warm feather bed and a full stomach the height of the sublime." The Count took another swig of vodka, then turned his empty glass upside down, much as a peasant would do after finishing his tea. "Hercule!" he suddenly shouted. "Hercule, your master is calling you!"

The door leading from the dining room to the kitchen swung back timidly. A parchment-faced old man shuffled into the room, his deeply wrinkled face as smooth-shaven as a clerk's. Dressed in an old gray frock coat with several missing buttons and a waistcoat to match, he moved toward them with something approaching trepidation.

"The shouting hurts my ears so," Hercule complained. "And I was busy with other things, Roman Filimonovich."

"Put them aside and bring our guest some coffee."

"Chicory?"

"If I wanted chicory I would have asked for chicory!" the Count shouted.

Hercule turned slowly away, but when he reached the door he stopped and looked back. "Perhaps tea will do?" he suggested.

"Yes, yes, whatever," the Count said impatiently. He turned to Gregor. "And to think that in his youth there wasn't a finer specimen of Russian manhood in all the province. But tell me, what do you know of this Belinsky your sister is marrying?"

"He's extremely good-looking, for one." From the side pocket of his velvet frock coat Gregor pulled out his cigarette case, searching through his other pockets until he found a matchbox. "Yes, quite the ladies' man. He might easily have been your own issue, from what I hear."

"Don't remind me of how I failed. If there's one thing I don't care to discuss it's that obstinate limb of Satan who bears my name."

"Surely Victor has never treated you unjustly."

"Victor worries about the future of Russia. Roman Filimonovich worries about the future of Roman Filimonovich. There lies the disparity between father and son. He'll be at the wedding, you know."

Now this was news, and Gregor sat up in his chair.

"Oh yes," the Count reaffirmed. "He wrote to that effect just a week or two ago."

"But why? He and my sister Vera have never had very much to say to each other."

"That may be. But at one time—several years ago, if memory serves me—wasn't there talk of Victor and your sister Masha?"

"Yes, but—"

"No buts about it, my young friend. That's why he's coming. In exactly"—and here he paused to consult his watch— "forty-five minutes, providing his train arrives on time."

"Then I mustn't keep you if you're to meet him."

"Meet him?" the Count said with a laugh. "Don't be absurd. We have nothing to say to each other, and never have."

"Then perhaps I'll go instead," Gregor replied as he came a bit unsteadily to his feet.

"Hercule!" the Count shouted.

"There isn't time, not if I'm to meet him at the station."

"Of course," sighed the Count. "But first we must take a brief stroll through the gardens, for I promised you a show. And they've been waiting so patiently all morning, my dear Aphrodites and Apollos."

They went out through the French doors, then down the porch steps, the Count's backless Turkish slippers slapping slowly and rhythmically at the dust. Before them stretched a complex network of interconnecting canals and artificial pools, some circular, some square, but each and every one bone-dry. Their steep earthen sides, over six feet deep in many places, had crumbled badly, and where there had once been formal gardens and lush, flowering plants, there were nothing but thick weeds and a few stunted, prickly-headed burdocks.

Flapping his arms like a goose as he gestured at the ruins, the Count began to declaim much as an actor upon a stage. "How lovely it once was to float down these narrow waterways, to inhale the honeyed earthy breath of my peonies, the spicy brown aroma of my metiolas. Even Victor loved these gardens when he was a child. Yes, even boring, earnest Victor found them to his liking. Alas, my 'Venetian period' is a thing of the past, Gregor Petrovich. Only its memory sustains me. But look at my statuary, my gods and goddesses!"

A scantily clad Aphrodite, chalky-white down to the tips of her slender young fingers, was posed atop a marble pedestal. Several yards away, overlooking the largest and deepest of the pools, a virile youth bearing a discus in one hand stared back at them with something approaching arrogance, the statue wearing nothing but a leaf-shaped piece of cloth to conceal its sex.

A gentle breeze sprang up, and as Gregor stepped closer to admire the half-dozen life-size statues that dotted the ruined, empty gardens, the discus thrower's fig leaf was caught by the wind. It fluttered back and forth, revealing that which Gregor found most interesting. The burly moujik held the pose for another few seconds, then unceremoniously jumped off his perch.

Count Durnovo glared with apoplectic rage as the discus thrower lifted Aphrodite in his arms and helped her down. Behind them, Heracles, Dionysus, Athena, and Demeter all came to life, scampering off their marble pedestals.

"How dare you!" the Count shouted, his flabby yellow face now mottled red like an unripe tomato.

"We have work to do, Roman Filimonovich," replied the discus thrower.

The young peasant girls, some completely naked, and others with just a thin diaphanous drapery, ran off before the Count could stop them, leaving Durnovo standing in the garden with only Gregor and the angry "gods" for company.

"It's not fair," the Count said, whining like a child who's been told it's time to go to bed. "A harmless jest to amuse my young friend here. Another minute or two and he would have been gone. Now you've ruined the entire effect."

"There'll be no more posing, begging your pardon, Roman Filimonovich," another of the men spoke up, ghostlike as a result of the chalk that had been rubbed over every inch of him, even to the soles of his feet.

"No more posing? Well, we shall just see about that. You there, Hercule *Fils*," and he wagged his finger at a tall young man with a splendid physique. "I hold you personally responsible for this outrage. We struck a bargain. Now you and your friends have gone against your word. Therefore, you forfeit the free use of my land. I want you off, do you hear? You, your wives, your children, your old grannies, the whole filthy lot of you. Deny me, will you? Well then, I shall deny you."

"It's ungodly, the things you make us do," replied Hercule *Fils*.

Count Durnovo sucked in his breath, so that his baggy

checked trousers threatened to fall around his ankles. "Were the Greeks ungodly? Were the Romans? The glories of their civilizations live on, while Russia will crumble into dust and be completely forgotten. Ungodly? You are the ungodly ones, for thinking such impure thoughts," and muttering angrily to himself, the Count started back to the house.

"He's drunk," said Gregor. "Give him a few hours to sleep it off. By evening he won't remember anything he said."

"We waited out here for two hours, Gregor Petrovich," replied the heavily muscled youth they called Hercule *Fils*. "What right does he have to make us shame ourselves so?"

"He's just a drunk old man, I assure you. Beg his forgiveness, and the land will be yours again."

"And if we refuse?" said the peasant who had posed as Dionysus.

"But how can you? Who but the Count would ever offer you the free use of his land?"

Hercule *Père* brought Gregor's carriage around to the back, where Gregor quickly jumped inside and took hold of the reins. Thinking how the Count's breeding program was not without its charms, he glanced back at the sullen and unhappy-looking peasants still standing like a *tableau vivant* at the edge of the garden.

"It's the shame of it," Hercule *Fils* said again, "making us stand here as naked as babes, when all we do for him is offer kindness in return."

"But isn't it better to be ashamed for an hour or two, than to go hungry for days on end?"

"He may have owned our fathers, but he doesn't own us," shouted Dionysus, gesturing vehemently with his fist. "Besides, you enjoyed the show as much as he did. And who were you looking at, Gregor Petrovich? Me or my poor wife?"

With an uneasy smile, Gregor clucked his tongue and brought the reins down against the back of his good-tempered

bay stallion. The two-wheeled cabriolet moved briskly across
the yard, past the crumbling stone gates at Jerichovo's
entrance, and on down a narrow road no wider than a foot-
path.

Unable to get a seat in either of the two second-class carriages, Count Victor Romanovich Durnovo had been forced
to purchase a first-class ticket. Yet this added expenditure
was not without its advantages, for the tall, thoughtful-
looking man who shared his compartment was none other
than Ivan Sergeyevich Turgenev, the illustrious author of
Rudin, Fathers and Children, Virgin Soil, and numerous other
works that had inflamed the young Count's imagination.

Having left from Moscow's Kursk and Nizhny-Novgorod
station early that morning, they had spent the next seven
hours engaged in conversation. Turgenev, as it turned out,
knew many of Victor's acquaintances, including Peter
Semyonovich Petrov, whose daughter's wedding the Count
had decided to attend.

"A petty tyrant," the writer declared, speaking in a thin,
high-pitched voice that contrasted oddly with his tall and
imposing stature. "When serfdom was abolished and so many
of our neighbors were brought to the brink of ruin, let us not
forget that it was Peter Semyonovich who went from one
estate to the next, buying up as much land as he could get his
hands on."

Turgenev toyed with the gold and carnelian signet he wore
on his little finger. In his velvet jacket and waistcoat, his silk
shirt and paisley cravat, he still seemed to be breathing the air
of Paris, from where he had lately departed to spend the
summer at Spasskoye, the estate he had inherited from his
mother.

"He has four daughters, does he not?" Turgenev went on.
"It used to be said a stranger barnyard couldn't be found, not

in all the province. One girl was as silly as a goose, another as foul-tempered as a shrew, a third as placid as a cow, and the fourth . . . now, the fourth I've heard favorable things about."

"Maria Petrovna," the Count told him, for it was only because of Masha that he had decided to attend the wedding. When he had last seen her she was only seventeen. Now, five years had passed, during which time he had received his university degree and accepted an unimportant post in government service solely as a means of supporting himself.

"Then you must make sure to bring your Maria Petrovna when you come and visit me at Spasskoye," replied Turgenev. "I would be most intrigued to meet someone who has spent all her life beneath Peter Semyonovich's roof . . . and survived to tell the tale."

"Why, there you are!" Gregor cried out as a broad-shouldered young man of medium height stepped down from the train. He embraced the young Count warmly, kissing him three times in the Russian fashion so that his lips brushed against Victor Romanovich's sallow cheeks. "You haven't changed at all, not a bit," he declared as he stared at Count Durnovo's son, Victor's pale, mobile face and almost colorless blue eyes conveying both intelligence and sensitivity. Soft reddish-brown hair curled over the Count's small round ears, joining up with side whiskers of a more noticeably reddish cast.

"I hope I haven't inconvenienced anyone," the Count said, while Gregor led him from the platform. "Perhaps I should have written you, or Masha."

"It's not an inconvenience at all, Victor. Everyone will be very pleased to see you." Gregor smiled to himself, for he could think of nothing more amusing than to play match-maker. He gestured in the direction of his carriage, and

Durnovo climbed inside. Then Gregor unhitched the horse, sprung up onto the carriage step, and started not toward Petrovka but neighboring Golovlovo, the small and rather poor estate Simon Belinsky had inherited from his parents.

His bay stallion pulled the two-seater at a brisk and unchanging pace, trotting past uniformly barren fields. The April sky was mildly blue, and spring revealed itself in the short, reddish-stemmed grass that grew over much of the broad, level highroad. A distant birch copse showed itself at the very edge of the horizon, its round and crenelated tops already covered with a faint green wash.

"It's even more beautiful than I remembered," Victor remarked, intoxicated by a landscape even Gregor had to admit was lovely. "So peaceful, so—"

"Boring," he interrupted with a laugh. "And relentless. And unchanging. And the less said the better. But tell me what you've been doing with yourself these last five years, and I promise I won't make you feel guilty for never writing me, not even once."

Victor smiled.

"Politics, am I right?" he went on.

"What else is there?" Victor admitted. "I can't see just living my life solely for myself, not when there's so much misery everywhere I look. Perhaps if you'd been at the execution last week you'd understand what I mean. Had you seen that poor girl's face as I did—"

"Which poor girl?"

"Sophia Perovskaya."

"You mean you knew her?" he said excitely. "Oh, tell me everything, Victor. I want to know every delicious detail."

"There wasn't anything 'delicious' about it," Victor said with a frown. "They hanged her. She was a young woman who died for her principles. I don't think there's anything in the world more honorable than that."

"But she was a murderess, or just about. You're making her out to be a martyr."

"But she was a martyr," Victor insisted. "She was one of the most selfless persons I have ever known."

Gregor was a little frightened by all this, and he leaned over his lips close to Victor's ears, speaking in a low voice as if there were someone else in the carriage. "Were you—that is to say—did you play a part in her scheme?"

"Is that what you'd like to think?"

"On the contrary, on the contrary," he said vehemently, raising his voice. "Believe me, I don't wish to interfere, Victor Romanovich. But you'd be well advised to keep your political beliefs to yourself. My father is not what you would call an enlightened man. Only two things seem to interest him: making money, and making more money."

Victor laughed good-naturedly and patted him on the shoulder. "Then tell me what I've come to hear. How is she, Grisha?"

Gregor smiled, glad they'd put unpleasant things behind them. "Do you know the marvel of it, my friend? She's only gotten more beautiful."

Victor was silent for a moment. Then, above the steady and incessant beat of hoofs, he turned his thoughtful face toward Gregor, saying softly and with effort, "Is there anyone else, someone who claims her affections?"

"Wouldn't you prefer to find that out for yourself?"

"Be fair with me, Grisha," the young Count pleaded.

"Only if you promise to be a little less serious. Life's too short, you know."

"Yes, but is there—you have no idea how difficult this is for me, Grisha. I'm much shyer and far less sure of myself than you imagine. But is she . . . that is, is there someone else?" he blurted out.

With all the exuberance of his eighteen years, and with a

boisterous laugh that frightened a flock of starlings and sent them soaring overhead, Gregor said, "As far as Masha is concerned, there's only you, my dear Victor, only you."

A continual slamming of doors could be heard, and from the kitchen the two serving girls who usually spent more time gossiping than attending to their work were singing sweetly. "In front of the church stood a carriage, a wedding resplendent within. . . ." Their fresh young voices mingled with all the other sounds that echoed through the house, for it was nearly time for Vera to come downstairs and receive her parents' blessing.

"Are you sure the dress is suitable, are you absolutely certain?" Vera kept asking as she twisted her slender figure this way and that, trying to see what her back looked like and never quite able to catch more than a passing glimpse of it. "I'll have no neck left the way this dreadful collar chafes, and it's so hot, besides. Throw open a window, Anninka, before I faint," she went on in a petulant voice.

It had finally occurred to her that time was running out, and now there could be no turning back. In just a very short while she would become the young Madame Belinskaya, mistress of Golovlovo—that horrid little place, as she had always thought of it. How will I tell the servants what to do? she wondered. How will I be able to decide if we're to have fish one night, or fowl the next? What if Simon doesn't like me, if something happens and—

"Anninka, Anninka!" she cried. "Hold me tight but just at arm's length, for we can't wrinkle the gown. Tell me I'll be all right because I'm faint, I'm positively faint."

Anninka, her pink cameo brooch bobbing up and down against her soft, pillowy breast, rushed from the window she had just thrown open, and did everything she could to calm the frightened young bride-to-be.

"Why hasn't Grisha come home yet?" she asked. "What time is it?" though a clock stood in plain sight on her little pink dressing table, its china face and tapering bronze hands marking the hour as three o'clock, precisely.

She heard Irena reminding her that the wedding wasn't scheduled to begin for another hour, but she scarcely paid attention. It was all so confusing, so painful too. Perhaps I've made a terrible mistake, Vera thought to herself as she kept returning to the cheval glass, fixing a yellow curl, adjusting a bit of lace, calling to Anninka to brush a smudge off the tip of her little silk dancing slipper. I know what I'm supposed to do tonight, but what if—? But he's told me all about it; he's used the most peculiar words and made me promise never to tell a soul, that it'll be our very first secret. He'll touch me here and here and here and then I'll be so happy I won't know what to do, because he said that happiness like that is something only a husband and wife can experience. "But not just at night, in the dark, beneath the bedcovers," he said. "No, at any hour of the day or night, Vera, my little dove." He called me "my little dove" and stroked my awful pointy chin though he never said it was awful. Or did he?

Vera couldn't remember, but she did recall how just a few days before, on the very first day it had truly felt like spring and everything was about to come alive again, Simon had taken her hand and led her down the narrow, twisting path that wound through the orchard to the summerhouse. Father had never bothered to keep it in repair, and the wood smelled of mildew, the moist air so palpable she had brushed her hands across her face, as if she were pulling at cobwebs.

"Step carefully, my little sparrow," Simon had whispered, his voice so low and magical she remembered how she had begun to shiver in the cool, damp half-light that pervaded the summerhouse. He had said nothing else, but taking her in his arms and putting one hand on her breast and the other round her waist, he'd drawn her near, kissing her lips and eyes and the very tip of her chin. Then he had spread a handkerchief over one of the moldy green benches that stood, though barely upright, alongside a wooden table that was bolted to the floor, saying all those things only husbands and wives are supposed to talk about.

"It will be painful for just an instant," he had said, and then she would feel such pleasure, such extraordinary bliss, that she would want it to happen again and again and again, for such was the nature of the bridal couch, and such was the act of love performed between a man and a woman. Then, his hand stealing down over her shoulder, he had touched her breasts so delicately that Vera's heart had begun to pound, and her entire body trembled, for never had she experienced this before.

"But is it not supposed to be holy?" she had asked, having never spoken to anyone, not even her sister Masha, for an explanation. "Is it not an act of communion, something graced by the very presence of God?" She wanted to believe that, but Simon had responded with a laugh, and calling her "my little swallow, my sweet lovely," he'd kissed her lips so that the thick brush of his jet-black mustache had scratched her tender skin.

There in the summerhouse, in the dim, spooky half-light of the moldy summerhouse, he'd done other things as well, things that even now, days later, made her flush like a poppy as she stood before the mirror. "It's necessary," he had said in that deep and mysterious voice he sometimes used when they were alone. "After all, you're to be my wife, so it's time you learned your responsibilities."

She could still feel his fingers on her wrist, the way he'd taken her hand in his, showing her what must be done. "Oh, I'm afraid!" she whispered as Anninka made sure her gown hung just so, every pleat in place, every bit of crystal and pearl fringe evenly arranged. "What if he doesn't really love me?" she said, to which Anninka responded by telling her there was nothing to fear, that guests were coming from three provinces, for everyone knew she was going to be the most beautiful bride the district had ever seen.

Then, with Irena taking hold of one hand, and Masha the other, with Anninka hurrying on ahead to open the door to let them pass, they all went slowly down the stairs and into the drawing room.

Even before his youngest daughter came downstairs to receive his blessing, Peter Semyonovich and his wife, Sophia Mikhailovna, were waiting in the drawing room, eyes fixed on the ikons arranged on a low table in the middle of the room. The largest of these, the ikon of the Mother of God, was encased in heavy silver, and bore on the back the genealogical table of the Petrovs. On either side of it were smaller ikons, one depicting St. Mercury of Smolensk, holding in one hand his own decapitated head while in the other he clutched an ikon of the Holy Virgin, and the second representing St. Nikolai of Amchen, defender of the three virgins.

Seated upon an enormous sofa upholstered in faded blue damask, Sophia Mikhailovna periodically threw treats to the King Charles spaniel scampering between her feet. This "venomous creature," as her daughter Henriette had often been heard to declare, was named Laska, and was rarely if ever seen out of her mistress's company.

"Sweet Vyborg cracknels for my little darling," Sophia Mikhailovna would whisper as she threw Laska a bit of biscuit. For so small and seemingly delicate an animal, Laska's appetite was enormous, and the pesky little spaniel was forever sitting up on her two hind legs, begging her mistress for yet another tempting morsel.

As Sophia Mikhailovna sat there looking somewhat stupefied, for she could hardly remember when she had last left her bed, her husband paced back and forth, hunching his shoulders so that his thick, stubby neck was visible one moment and gone the next. He was a short, heavy-set man, his thinning gray hair parted somewhat off-center and kept fairly long so as to cover his ears, which nevertheless stuck out like jug handles each time he turned his head. Having recently celebrated his sixtieth birthday, Peter Semyonovich considered himself to be in the very prime of his life, so that when anyone asked after his health he would invariably say, "The old bull's horn is still hard," winking slyly just in case they missed the point.

As for his wife, Madame Petrova was a confirmed neurasthenic who had taken to her bed some fifteen years before, certain she was suffering from a terminal illness the nature of which no doctor in all of the province had ever been able to determine. Some said the milk had rushed to her brain after her last childbirth, while others prescribed large doses of potassium bromide or valerian drops for her nerves. She took neither, preferring vinegar compresses, medicinal teas, and various herbal infusions, the odors of which permeated her bedroom. Yet all her ailments did not prevent her from exhibiting as healthy an appetite as her little dog, though amazingly enough her figure had remained remarkably girlish.

This afternoon Sophia Mikhailovna had dressed with special care, and wore her hair very high, frizzed up in little curls, which fell at regular intervals across her wrinkled forehead. Her dinner dress was even more elaborate than her coiffure, for there were twice as many crystal ornaments dangling around her waist as curls upon her brow. Each time she tossed Laska a treat, the heavy satin-de-Lyon made a rather impolite sound, much like the squeaking of a corset. This disturbed her husband, though not nearly as much as

Laska's incessant yapping, or the unpleasant, dizzying effect the dress's color had upon his eyes. It was the most extraordinary shade of green he had ever seen, a green so dazzlingly bright, so insistent in its very greenness, that each time he glanced at his wife the shockingly brilliant color would dance off the back of his eyes, forcing him to turn away.

Finally, footsteps sounded on the stairs. Pressing a dainty cambric handkerchief to first one red eye and then the other, his daughter Vera stepped slowly into the drawing room.

"What on earth are you crying about?" he demanded, for if there was anything he couldn't stand it was the sound of Vera sniffling. "You begged and pleaded and made my life miserable, just so I'd give you my blessing. I should think you'd be quite delighted, now that you've gotten your way."

"I'm frightened," whimpered Vera.

"Every bride is frightened on her wedding day. Isn't that so, Sonyushka?" he said, looking over the top of his wife's head rather than subject himself to another painful glimpse of emerald green.

"If you say so, Petrushka, dear."

"Indeed I do."

"Then it must be," the woman murmured.

"So it must," he agreed, looking back at his youngest daughter. "There, you've heard it from your own precious mother's lips. So dry your tears, Vera. It'll soon be over." Impatient to get on with the ceremony, for his son would soon be arriving to announce that Simon was at the church and that Vera could now join him, he went over to the table and seized the largest of the ikons.

Vera, who seemed quite unwilling to kneel at her father's feet, sobbed even more loudly now. "Will you be unhappy when I'm gone, Papa?"

"Very unhappy."

"And will you miss me terribly?"

"Golovlovo is not Siberia, Vera. Why, even your mother could walk there in less than an hour."

"God forbid!" whispered Sophia Mikhailovna as she brushed the crumbs off her lap. "And where do you suppose is Henriette? If you're to give Vera your blessing, then all our girls must be here to witness it."

Henriette made her entrance a moment later, tall, unbecomingly so, her father had always thought, and stiffly erect in her prim, steel-gray dress. Vera slowly sank down onto her knees while Masha adjusted her train. Peter Semyonovich then held the ikon over her and began to intone the words of the blessing.

After raising his hand in benediction, and returning the ikon to its place on the table, he stepped back, waiting for Vera to come to her feet. "Today you leave your girlhood behind, Verochka," he said in a loud, businesslike voice. "I want you to be happy. That is all a father can wish for his child, that she make her way in this world without the burden of sadness."

Vera nodded dumbly and took her place on the sofa, for there was nothing else to do until Gregor returned from the church, that being the custom of the Orthodox ceremony. With a sigh of relief, and knowing that soon he'd only have Masha and Henriette to worry about, Peter Semyonovich went into the dining room to slake his thirst. Five thousand rubles for the dowry, another thousand or so for assorted expenses, seemed a small price to pay. Even if Belinsky had asked for twice as much, Peter Semyonovich still would have considered it a bargain.

Three

Peering into the cracked mirror that leaned against a wall of his bedroom, Simon Ivanovich Belinsky could not have been more pleased with what he saw. Despite the jagged line that ran through the glass, he saw before him a tall, elegant figure in an exquisitely tailored dress coat, white piqué waistcoat, and gleaming white tie. Narrow trousers of the finest black worsted were stretched over his muscular thighs, and the entire effect of his costume was one of such good taste and obvious refinement that for a moment he nearly forgot he was in his bedroom at Golovlovo, and not in one of the more fashionable drawing rooms of the capital.

"Devilishly handsome" were the words that came to mind as he stood there admiring his profile, pleased with the freshness of his complexion, and the way his thick black mustache shone like a raven's wing as it swooped across his upper lip. Although he had left the army two years before, he still preferred to remain smooth-shaven, the better to show off his dimples, and the deep cleft in his chin that was clearly visible to those who cared to admire it.

As he set to brushing his curly black hair, one of these admirers eyed him unblinkingly. Her name was Dunyasha, and she lay in an untidy heap across his bed, wrapped in a soiled sheet. When she finally looked away, for Belinsky wasn't paying her the least bit of attention, it was only to fall back against the pillows, sighing so loudly and with such exaggeration he couldn't help but gaze in her direction.

"Well, what do you think, Dunyasha? Am I respectable enough?"

Dunyasha, the daughter of one of the village elders and a girl with loose ways—green but already ripe, as they say—shrugged her shoulders.

"Perhaps you'd prefer to take Vera Petrovna's place," Belinsky went on with another self-satisfied look in the mirror. "Had your father been able to give you a dowry in kind—"

"Don't make fun of me, Senya," the girl protested. "If you were a gentleman you'd never say such things."

"But I'm not a gentleman, my little sparrow, and I never was." Having finally completed his toilet to his satisfaction, Belinsky sat down on the edge of the bed, carefully parting the skirts of his tailcoat so as not to wrinkle the expensive material. "Then again, you're not a lady, either."

Dunyasha raised her hand to strike him, but he caught her around the waist and pushed her back, nibbling at her pouty crimson lips, then sliding down to taste the salty residue still clinging to her neck and shoulders.

"You're a beast," she said without much conviction. "If Vera Petrovna only knew—"

"I'd be very careful about that if I were you," he warned. He pulled the sheet down to her waist, staring for a long, silent moment at her breasts. Vera Petrovna's bosom was still girlish, not much there to look at and even less to hold. Dunyasha, on the other hand, had full womanly breasts, each dark, swollen nipple as large as a gooseberry and just as tasty.

The girl thrust her chest forward without the slightest

51

trace of self-consciousness. "What's going to happen to me now that you'll soon be married?" she asked. "You won't be able to—"

"Oh, but I will," he told her, for he had no intention of changing his ways. Marriage was not a commitment so much as a convenience. Even though Vera might eventually prove an amusing bedmate once she was sufficiently trained, and even though he was actually fond of her, it was the generous dowry he'd already received from her father that intrigued him most of all. It wasn't that Belinsky was heartless and cold-blooded, or even particularly cruel. It was just that he believed a man must look after his own interests if he was ever to get on in this world. His father had never understood that. The elder Belinsky had squandered what had, at one time, been a fairly sizable fortune, placing his trust in men who invariably took advantage of his good nature. When, as he lay dying, he had looked in vain for all his old friends, for all the people he had treated so charitably, none came forward to stand by his deathbed and comfort him with the memory of his good works. Forced to sell off much of her holdings, Belinsky's mother had followed after her husband in less than a year. Resolved never to fall victim to that naïveté that had characterized Ivan Belinsky's entire life, Simon had set about arranging as advantageous a match for himself as possible, for it was his firm belief that there were few things in life more onerous than poverty.

"What Vera doesn't know won't hurt her," he told the girl. "Besides, you wouldn't be able to stay away very long, now, would you?"

Dunyasha's silence seemed answer enough. But before she had a chance to once again prove her willingness to please, there was a knock on the door and Belinsky came quickly to his feet.

"Yes, what is it?" he called out.

Matriona, the testy old woman who was standing out in the hall, informed him that Gregor Petrovich had just driven up in his carriage to escort Simon to the church.

"Tell him I'll be right down, that I'm almost ready." Then he drew out a worn and greasy five-ruble note and pressed it into Dunyasha's hand.

"What's this?" the girl exclaimed, feigning surprise.

"A wedding present, my little dove." And with a final glance in the mirror, Belinsky turned smartly on his heel and let himself out.

No sooner did Gregor return from the church than he threw down the reins and jumped off the cabriolet, missing the carriage step and nearly twisting his ankle. Leaving his turnout in the care of Kolya the groom, Gregor raced inside the house and flung himself against the banister at the bottom of the stairs. Breathlessly he announced that all was ready, that he had only just left Simon at the church, and that it would take him five minutes—"no, three"—to change into more suitable attire.

He had little difficulty keeping his promise, and when he rushed downstairs again Irena was already escorting Vera to the carriage. The elder Petrovs would remain at home, according to custom. They waited on the front porch as Platon the coachman helped the young bride-to-be into her seat and then got up on the box.

Seeing that all was ready, Henriette and Masha having taken their places, Platon clicked his tongue, and the old-fashioned yellow barouche began to roll slowly across the yard. Gregor followed in his light two-seater, while taking up the rear was Madame Petrova's irksome little spaniel, barking excitedly at the horses.

"Laska, Laska, my little angel! Come back before you get trampled!" Sophia Mikhailovna cried out while the servants cheered and whistled, waving their hands as the wedding procession moved at a dignified pace down the lime alley.

It was already dusk by the time the bridal party reached the church, a damp, cool smell like freshly washed linen mingling with the scent of dewy burdocks. Nearly all of the villagers were waiting to greet them, while in the courtyard more than a score of carriages clustered together.

The peasants crowded around the great antique barouche, jostling each other as they tried to get a better look. Wielding a fly whisk with a swaggering and self-important air, Platon motioned them back as Henriette and Masha stepped down, Henriette tall and severe in her steel-gray dress, holding her head so high it was a wonder she didn't miss her step and end up on all fours. Dark-haired Masha followed after her, looking strong and self-reliant, at ease with the villagers who pushed their way toward her. Again and again she extended her hand to each who greeted her, for there was not a villager among them who did not know of her good works, appreciative of the time and effort she put into the school she had established for Petrovka's children.

Then, as the church bells began to ring, Belinsky came down the steps, strutting like a peacock in his town finery. He gave Vera his arm, and as he escorted her inside, she giggled nervously. Irena heard several people say it was a good sign, that it meant the young couple's burdens would be light and their lives filled with laughter.

Irena saw at once that the church was as crowded as it had been for her own wedding a year before. The scent of flowers blended with the overwhelming sweetness of the incense, the smell of freshly tarred boots, and the sulfur dyes of the women's pinaforelike *sarafans* and the men's long cotton shirts.

A purple carpet led to the altar, and as soon as Vera stepped upon it, someone standing in the crowd—for Russian churches have neither pews nor seats—threw a handful of bright silver coins at her feet, to ensure her prosperity. It was Anninka, who had managed to sneak out of the house in the midst of all the preparations for the party that would be held later that evening. Unfortunately, Vera was walking too quickly, and not once did her feet touch the shiny coins her dear old *nyanya* had strewn across her path.

Everyone followed after the couple until there wasn't any room to move. Standing before the lectern were the officiating clergy, a priest and a deacon in heavy gold-and-silver-embroidered dalmatics. High up in the balcony a choir began to sing, the sound of the men's voices filling the church with their devotion. Irena closed her eyes for a moment, the deep, rich voices recalling the sound of wind as it rushed across the steppe, a majestic and somehow sorrowful sound, tinged with pity for the lowliness of man as he stood in the presence of his God.

When she looked up, the golden candlelight flickered as if in response, and the priest, after first blessing the betrothed, handed them two lighted tapers, and the ceremony began. Unable to find her husband, Nikolai, in the crowd, Irena kept her eyes on the young couple, her glance filled with apprehension. Vera wasn't holding her candle any higher than Simon, and if superstitions were grounded in fact, she would never have the upper hand in her household.

Her brother, fumbling in his pocket for the rings, finally found them, though one slipped from his fingers and rolled out of sight. For a moment there was absolute confusion, half the wedding party remaining where they were, the other half down on their knees, calling for additional candles to be lit so it could be located. Once it was found, and Irena heard Gregor breathe a loud sigh of relief, the priest blessed both slim gold bands and held them above the heads of the kneeling couple.

Then, as Gregor held a heavy silver-gilt crown over Vera's head, and Simon's friend Kalinovich, the police chief of the district, held an identical crown over the groom's head, the priest slowly made the sign of the cross. Speaking in a low and barely audible voice, he asked if they each had no greater love for another, and if any objection existed to the marriage.

But no one spoke up, not even Irena, who wanted to shout out and beg them to stop. But she held her tongue, and so the priest instructed the couple in the exchange of rings. After they had kissed before the tabernacle, they stood upon a piece of rose-colored satin that was laid down before them, drinking three times from a cup of warm red wine. Then, placing Vera's hand in Simon's, and tying them together with a silk handkerchief, the gilded crowns still held at arm's length above their heads, the priest made them follow him as he led them three times around the altar, so that from this day forth they would be united as they walked through life.

Seeing all this, and listening as they received communion and the priest read the parts of Scripture addressed to those about to take on the holy state of matrimony, Irena felt the tears dripping down her cheeks. The light was dim. The choir sung on in their rich, sad voices. The candles shed their soft golden light upon the ikons. The sickly-sweet odor of the incense filled the church and made her feel faint. All around her there was movement, those who had come to attend the service swaying back and forth like leaves upon a tree.

Irena stepped back, quickly brushing the tears from her eyes as the Belinskys walked arm in arm down the purple carpet that was laid along the floor, past all the friends and relatives, the villagers and well-wishers, past the sacred images and the hundred lit tapers. She followed silently after them, finding Nikolai waiting for her in the crowd. She reached for his hand, drawing strength and comfort from his touch. There was nothing she could do for Vera now, nothing but wait, and hope her fears would prove unjustified.

The young Count Victor Romanovich, his face looking paler than usual in the faint and final glimmer of twilight, stood outside the little stone church and waited to catch sight of Masha.

At last his patience was rewarded, for there she was with her lovely dark eyes the color of wet currants, her slim yet strongly knit body held gracefully erect. She walked across the courtyard with a purposeful stride, stopping now and again to speak to the villagers who approached her.

In the five years that had passed since he'd last seen her, Masha had matured in ways that were at first difficult to ascertain. It was her face, he realized at last, for he saw in her eyes something that hadn't been there before, something that spoke of the determination and youthful self-reliance he'd noticed in the way she moved. She wasn't beautiful in the conventional sense, nor was there anything coquettish in her mannerisms. Her shoulders were perhaps a trifle too large for her frame, yet he found her strikingly attractive nonetheless, so much so that he began to feel he'd wasted the last five years of his life, not having been able to share them with her.

He called out her name, his voice skipping tremulously across the courtyard. At first she didn't hear him, having turned to an unusually tall and bony-looking young woman he recognized as her sister Henriette. "She shouldn't have" and "can't argue with a simpleton" were all he could make out as the two sisters spoke heatedly to each other.

"Maria Petrovna," he spoke up.

Hearing someone call out her name, Masha looked in his direction. Even in the dim light he could see the hectic flush that sprang into her cheeks.

"What an awful man you are, Victor Romanovich, not even letting us know you were coming!" she cried out with a joyous laugh.

"Maria Petrovna," he said again, taking her hand in both of his. He'd intended to kiss it, but he was so unexpectedly shaken by their reunion that he merely held it tightly, feeling her fingers trembling like a little bird in the cage of his hands.

"Why didn't you write? Or did you want to surprise us, was that it?" Masha went on, and as she eased her hand free she stepped gracefully to the side, motioning to her sister. "You remember Henriette, don't you, Count?"

"Of course, certainly," he replied, kissing her thin, dry hand when she held it out to him. "How nice to see you again, Henriette Petrovna."

They were interrupted by a high-pitched and petulant voice. "Are you coming or aren't you?" It was the young Madame Belinskaya, calling impatiently to her sisters as she sat in the barouche.

Before they could reply, quick, lighthearted footsteps signaled Gregor's arrival. Clapping his hand over the Count's broad shoulders, he smiled affectionately to each of them in turn. When he realized Victor and Masha had already had a chance to say a few words to each other, he suggested they borrow his cabriolet while he and Henriette rode back with the Belinskys.

"Do you think it's wise?" he heard Henriette whisper to her brother. "Surely—"

"Surely nothing," Gregor replied, immediately turning back to Masha and Victor, so as not to exclude them from the conversation. "You'll take the two-seater and we'll hear no more about it. And as for you, my stately beauty," Gregor went on, addressing Henriette as if she were his dearest friend and confidante, "I shall wrap my arm around you—no easy task that, but I'll do my best—and hold you tight, keeping you safe from the demons of the night. Of which," he said as an aside, "I understand there are quite a number."

As they walked across the courtyard, Masha felt the way Victor watched her, eying her so intently he seemed to encapsulate her in his gaze. They had corresponded for many years, and now that she was finally before him she felt slightly unnerved. He gave her his arm, helping her into the stylish little carriage. The yellow hood was in place, and as Masha sat there, a shadowy half circle spreading like an ink stain across her lap, she felt the nervous warmth of the young Count's presence as he settled in alongside her.

He makes me feel so strange, so unsure of myself, she thought as Gregor's bay stallion raised its head. The horse peered back at them with a single large and glassy brown eye, then began to trot briskly along, out of the courtyard and down the road that led back to its stable at Petrovka.

White, spongy fog clung to the ground, while a faint suggestion of moonlight hovered behind the violet clouds. Off in the distance a corncrake uttered its raspy note. From the direction of the orchard, a nightingale trilled briefly, its song fading sadly away.

"How long do you intend to stay?" she said after a long and awkward silence, during which they had both sat there, eyes on the road and not on each other. "Or must you rush back to Moscow because of something dreadfully important?"

Instead of answering, the Count guided the cabriolet off the road, so that a moment later it came to rest at the edge of one of her father's fields. Though she wanted to tell him he mustn't stop, that it wasn't proper, she remained silent.

"You're cold," Victor Romanovich said when he saw her tremble. He made a move to take off his coat, but she waved aside the offer.

"I should have brought along a shawl. But I'm quite all right. It's really remarkably warm for April, don't you think?" She wondered why he was staring at her so, for now he'd swiveled around on the button-tufted seat, once again encompassing her in his gaze so that for a moment it pleased her to think he found nothing else worth looking at.

"I've valued our correspondence a great deal," Victor spoke up, "even when I thought everything else made no sense whatsoever. Here would be these wonderful letters, telling me about life as perhaps I should be living it. I've never thought of myself as a romantic, but when I read your letters my hands shook. Those beautiful sheets of rose-colored paper, decorated with irises . . ."

He went on in a shy and hesitant voice, telling her of many of the things he had written about, and those things that he dared not set down on paper for fear the authorities would find him out. Although Masha knew little of politics, and had never bothered to involve herself in issues other than that of education, she found Victor's devotion to what he termed "the cause" as romantic as the moonlight peeking out from behind the clouds.

So earnest, so devoid of humor, she couldn't help but think. Yet it was this very intensity of his, the way he drew up his broad shoulders and peered anxiously at her with his almost colorless blue eyes, that made him so attractive. She wanted to beg him to laugh, for she was only twenty-two and wanted her life to be filled with joy and merriment. She wanted to challenge him to smile, for she was young and always felt a flush of pleasure when spring arrived, and all around her the land seemed to delight in its own rebirth. But now she closed her eyes when Victor bent toward her, his dry, feverish lips clinging to her mouth.

When the young Count drew back, he began to speak quickly, gesturing excitedly, and putting tremendous emotion into his words as he told her of his numerous activities in Moscow, his involvement in the populist movement, the debt he felt the gentry owed the suffering poor for the privileges they had long enjoyed at their expense. He told her too of his meeting with Turgenev, then stopped abruptly and bent forward to kiss her once again.

Masha instinctively drew back, not really knowing why. Nothing in his letters had prepared her for this, nor indicated that she was more to him than a faithful correspondent. "We can't catch up on five years in just an instant," she said.

"But we can try, can't we?"

"Why?"

The question caught him unawares, and as he sat there he thoughtfully pondered his reply. "Because it would give me great pleasure," he shyly admitted.

"Then do it," she whispered. She closed her eyes, and soon felt the warmth and tenderness of his mouth against her own, the firm yet gentle way he now held her in his arms. I must teach him to laugh, she vowed. Yes, I'll take him in hand, make him cast off this ridiculous crown of thorns he's given himself to wear in the name of Russia. After all, it's one thing to care about one's fellow man, but not at the expense of one's own self.

Masha told him that, in those very same words, even as she continued to speculate as to why he'd come back, and what he really wanted from her, now that he was here.

When the entire wedding party had returned to Petrovka, they assembled in the brightly lit drawing room. As husband and wife, Simon and Vera dutifully took their places, for custom dictated that Peter Semyonovich once again bestow his blessing, and say a few words in defense of the holy state of matrimony.

Guests kept arriving before Peter Semyonovich had a chance to finish his little speech, so that on three separate occasions he was called upon to stop and start all over again. Finally declaring that enough was enough, and now that they were married it really didn't matter what he said, he suggested that everyone follow him into the dining room and whet their appetites.

Meanwhile, as guests continued to arrive from Anninka's three "fabled" provinces—these being neighboring Tula, Tambov, and Kaluga—not to mention Moscow and even St. Petersburg, Gregor hurriedly downed a glass of rowanberry vodka before making sure his father knew of Count Victor Romanovich's arrival. Gregor told his father that he'd extended an invitation to the young man, asking him to remain at Petrovka as their guest.

Looking at Victor from across the crowded dining room, and seeing him engaged in animated conversation with his daughter Masha, Peter Semyonovich nodded his head, then wolfed down a thick, golden slice of smoked sturgeon. This he followed with a sticky handful of pickled red whortleberries, to which he was quite partial. Finally washing everything down with a healthy bumper of vodka, he nodded once again, and gave no further thought to the matter.

"Father is delighted you can stay with us," Gregor said, going up to Victor a few minutes later.

"That's very kind of him," the Count began, when out of nowhere appeared Sophia Mikhailovna, still attired in her remarkable green dress.

"*Mon cher Prince!*" she exclaimed. "Why didn't you tell us you were coming, you naughty man?" She rolled her eyes about in a most peculiar fashion, folding and unfolding her little ostrich-feather fan. "Your charming mother wrote that you were still in Petersburg. But of course I couldn't be more delighted to see you on such a joyous occasion, Prince Voloshin."

Masha smiled patiently. "*Maman,* you're mistaken. This is Count Victor Durnovo."

"Victor? Victor who?" said Madame Petrova with a series of piercing glances, all the while looking at the Count with growing alarm.

"Count Durnovo's son, from nearby Jerichovo. He's come down from Moscow," Masha went on. She had barely gotten the words out when she had to turn away, a painful, dry, hacking cough issuing from between her lips.

"Raise your hands," instructed Madame Petrova. "It's that dreadful quinsy again," insisting Masha's tonsils were to blame, and still rather incredulous at having mistaken the Count for the Prince. "Victor, you said? Not the same little Victor who used to come and visit us? No, that Victor hasn't been here in years."

"But he's returned, my dear Sophia Mikhailovna," the Count said in a soothing and graceful manner.

Madame Petrova peered at him from under her fringe of frizzy curls. "You? Little Victor? Why, you look nothing like Victor Romanovich, nothing at all." She flicked her fan against his arm, then turned away. "Laska!" she called out as she headed toward the long buffet table. "Come, my sweet angel!" Her eyes swept anxiously across the floor, fearful the little spaniel might have gotten caught like a throw rug beneath someone's foot. "Come, my precious. *Maman* will get you a treat, whatever your heart desires."

"Are you sure you're all right?" Victor asked when they were alone.

Although Masha was still finding it difficult to catch her breath, she pretended that nothing was the matter. "I've had this cold all winter, but it's not very serious. I'll just go upstairs for a moment, throw some cold water on my face."

She hurried off before he could say anything else. Seized by another coughing spell, she managed to reach her room before anyone noticed, where she raised her arms above her head as her mother always prescribed. It did little good, for the harsh, racking cough gave no indication of having run its course. Her hands dropped limply to her sides and she pressed her head to her chest, trying to stifle the burning pain she felt in her throat and lungs.

I have no time to be sick, she told herself. There's too much to do, too much I want to accomplish. So she sat on the edge of her bed and closed her eyes, certain it was just a matter of time before she'd be all right.

Simon Ivanovich, having gorged himself on roast goose, trout in aspic, and an extraordinary *coulibiac* Anninka had set down like a crown in the middle of the table, now stood outside on the veranda, sipping a glass of champagne as he watched his father-in-law work a feather toothpick between his teeth.

"So, Belinsky, what do you think?" Petrov motioned in the direction of the ballroom, crowded with dancers trying to keep up with the erratic and clumsy beat of the third-rate orchestra. "I spared no expense, none whatsoever. Oh yes, there isn't a father in Moscow or Petersburg who could have done better. A thousand rubles, mind you. A thousand hard-earned rubles just to make my little Vera happy. But now that she's yours to look after, how do you intend to support her, may I ask?"

Having wondered about this himself, and surprised his father-in-law hadn't brought up the subject before now, never once inquiring as to his future son-in-law's finances, Simon cleared his throat self-consciously and put down his empty glass. "Seeing as how fond Vera is of Petrovka, it occurred to me that you might be pleased if I offered my services as steward, to see to your affairs, and make sure the peasants didn't take advantage of your good nature."

Peter Semyonovich peeled his lips back and whinnied like a horse, all the while manipulating the toothpick with just his tongue, and poking it this way and that around the inside of his mouth. "Come now, don't take me for a fool just because my hair is turning gray. You, be my steward? Even if Offenburg dropped dead tomorrow, and with his Prussian consti-tution that's highly doubtful, I wouldn't even give a passing thought to such a proposal."

Simon, smarting from the insult, and clenching his hands behind his back, knew better than to respond in kind. "But I assure you, Peter Semyonovich," he went on in the most cordial tone he could master, "your interests would be mine. After all, am I not a part of your family now, responsible for the happiness and well-being of your daughter?"

"That's about all you're responsible for, my friend. I want no interference when it comes to Petrovka. And by the same token, I won't interfere with you and Vera. I never approved of this match, and I still don't. But Vera is—" Petrov paused a moment, scratching at the lobe of his ear, which stuck out from his neatly parted hair. "How shall I put it and still be discreet? I would have hated to send her off somewhere just because of some youthful dalliance, if you follow my meaning."

"So I've gotten her off your hands, is that it?"

"You'd be wise to treat me with more respect, Belinsky." Petrov replaced the toothpick in its beaded case, then began to crack his knuckles, pulling on each stubby little finger in turn. "Besides, five thousand rubles can go a long way . . . providing you're clever. And if you're not—" Petrov shrugged his shoulders and went off to the dining room, where the buffet table now groaned beneath an ostentatious display of vodkas and liqueurs, glacéed fruits, jellied sweets, dishes of nutmeats, French prunes, and fancy chocolates.

Infuriated that Peter Semyonovich had gotten the better of him (for now that he was married, what were five thousand rubles when spread over a lifetime?), Belinsky was still not ready to throw in his hand. If his father-in-law wouldn't help him, there were others who would. And so Simon returned to the ballroom, not to lead his wife gracefully around the floor, but to find his friend Kalinovich, the chief of police, a man who was fully as clever and resourceful as he.

Four

There were so many things Henriette disliked, so many people she thought smug and provincial, that it never surprised her when someone remarked about how rarely she smiled. She had not always been so dissatisfied, however, and could even remember numerous occasions when as a child she had laughed and frolicked and felt quite privileged to be Henriette and no one else, not even Vera, who always got her way just because her curls were yellow and her features doll-like; not even Masha, who was probably smarter than all of them; nor sweet, patient Irena, so calm and even-tempered, so anxious to be thought of as a pillar of strength. Yes, there was a time when being Henriette hadn't meant feeling tall and awkward and unattractive, nor had it meant that when she looked in the mirror she faced a bony creature with a perpetually red nose, annoyingly frizzy hair, and two deep lines around the corners of her mouth, the better to let a frown slip easily into place.

But then she had tasted disappointment in the person of Monsieur Gautier, the French tutor her father had grudgingly hired to instruct his daughters when they were still quite young. A charming and soft-spoken young man, he had inflamed her girlish passions as no one else before. Yet for all the attention she paid him, the tender verses and billets-doux she scrawled in her childish hand, the numerous little gifts she hid beneath his pillow, *cher* Philippe had never responded in kind. Worse, he had gone directly to her father to inform on her. Peter Semyonovich had accused her not of childishness or even stupidity, but the basest of feelings, calling her names the likes of which Henriette had never heard.

Thus, over a period of several years, both at boarding school (where she was sent after her thirteenth birthday), and then at home, she had begun to notice that the girl who faced her each time she looked in the mirror wasn't the girl she thought she knew. There was something hard and despairing in the set of this other girl's eyes, something that wouldn't go away. Often she would find herself wondering what she might have been like had Monsieur Gautier never come to Petrovka, or what her life would have been had she Vera's face. But these were idle thoughts, incapable of solving Henriette's problems. Even as she had turned to God for comfort, seeking solace in the embrace of her beloved Redeemer, she had also fabricated for herself a rich fantasy life, imagining the glorious future that was in store for her.

Someday she would cause tongues to wag appreciatively from one corner of the empire to the other, for what she lacked in beauty she would make up in wit and charm. She would establish her own salon, filling her sumptuous drawing room with the brightest and cleverest and most handsome of men. She would be *une grande dame,* all of Russia bowing low in adoration for this tall and bony young woman who had elevated herself to such Olympian heights.

There was only one problem, however: How does one begin? The first thing she had to do was leave Petrovka. But how could she leave when she hardly had a kopeck to her name? She thought of this as she stood at the edge of the ballroom, eying the garish costumes of the women and the ill-fitting and foppish dress coats of the men. It was all so disgusting, all so pitiful and revolting. How could anyone bear to spend his life here, seeing the same dreary faces and hearing the same dreary gossip?

"Henriette, do stop frowning and make an effort to be pleasant. This isn't a funeral, my dear. And why aren't you dancing? No wonder you haven't found yourself a husband yet. A girl like you must do everything she can to show herself off in a proper light."

This rather blunt and unsolicited advice came from the lips of her aunt, Varvara Semyonovna Petrova, who had come down from Moscow with three large suitcases and a chronic case of dyspepsia. She was an old maid who gave off the smell of camphor, for she was as tight-fisted as her brother and invariably wore the same gowns from one season to the next—taking great pains to make them as unappetizing to the moths as possible. She had sharp, malignant little eyes and a nose to match, a faint, downy mustache, and a hairy mole on her chin.

"And why do you insist upon wearing gray?" Auntie V. continued. "It makes you look so washed-out, Henriette, if you don't mind my saying so."

Henriette did mind, but when she tried to lose herself in the crowd now swaying rather clumsily to the first slow steps of a waltz, her aunt nabbed her as agilely as a frog catches a fly.

"There's someone I want you to meet, so don't you be running off like that. See that man?" Auntie V. discreetly gestured in the direction of a tall, fat man with a tuberous nose and a distinctly egglike countenance, his smooth-shaven face as perfect an oval as any a hen might deposit in its coop. "That, my dear," said Auntie V. with a triumphant air, "is none other than General Tishin. In case you haven't heard, he's a widower who'd very much like to settle down again."

"Would he, now? What a sensible fellow."

This her aunt totally ignored as she motioned the General to join them as soon as he finished the waltz. Auntie V. was as short as her father, though built along far more graceful lines, and so Henriette had to bend nearly in half in order to make herself heard.

"Will you please leave me alone," she said. "If I wanted to meet General Tishin I would have done so long before you arrived to take charge."

Varvara glared at her sternly, then turned to watch for the General, who was already making his way across the ball-room, the long skirts of his black swallow-tailed coat flying out behind him so that he resembled a large, strange bird. Although a proper gentleman would have worn a simple white waistcoat, the General had chosen one of a light fawn shade such as only young dandies would dare affect, over which numerous red and green dots and dashes ran this way and that. Add to this a chain from which hung countless little trinkets, the entire affair slung across his prominent bay window, and Henriette knew that the sooner she left Petrovka, the better.

"*Ma chère* Varvarushka," said General Tishin as he bent forward to kiss Auntie V.'s hand. "And this must be the lovely niece you were telling me about. *Mademoiselle.*" Tishin clicked his heels and bowed from the waist.

"Apparently, I can't be all that lovely, General, not if you've forgotten that we've met before. At my sister Irena's wedding," she reminded him.

"Madame Volskaya, ah yes, but of course, of course. How foolish of me not to have remembered. But I can see why, oh yes indeed, I certainly can. You've gotten so much lovelier that I hardly recognized you. Hasn't she gotten lovelier, Varya, *ma chère?*"

"Yes, she has," Auntie V. agreed. "Why, the child is blossoming, General Tishin, blossoming as few young women can. The change has been quite remarkable." Her aunt reached back with one hand, pushing Henriette forward so that if she hadn't caught herself in time she would have fallen right into the General's arms.

"I have heard the most amusing story," General Tishin remarked. "Did you know that if you look at the moon when it is full, you see in its face an area that is actually smaller than Russia? About fifty thousand square miles are still wanting. Can you imagine? Russia, larger than the face of the moon."

"Remarkable, just remarkable," said Varvara appreciatively.

"And did you know that if one smears goose fat on one's ears," the General continued, "there is little chance of suffering frostbite?"

"Indeed?" said Auntie V. "How amazing."

"But true, but true," insisted Tishin. As if to prove the point, he tugged at one of his pendulous earlobes, swinging it back and forth like a gate. "Remarkable the number of things you discover when you read. Do you read, Henriette Petrovna?"

"Not about goose fat, no," she said dryly.

The General tittered loudly, and suggested that she and her aunt join him in the dining room, where a bowl of Siberian punch had just been set out.

"I don't think I care to, thank you," she replied, seeing this as the perfect opportunity to escape before her aunt could stop her. "If you'll excuse me." She turned abruptly away and hurried off to the kitchen, where Anninka was always ready to commiserate with her.

Madame Belinskaya, Madame Vera Petrovna Belinskaya,

chère Verochka Belinskaya, repeated Vera to herself, trying to determine which sounded best. "Madame Belinskaya," she said aloud, letting the syllables roll off her tongue. "Doesn't that sound nice, Senya dear?" She clung more tightly to her husband—husband! she couldn't help thinking. Husband forever and ever, and me his loving wife—resting her cheek against his arm as they rode through the spring darkness toward nearby Golovlovo.

Up ahead, Vera could see lights flickering like oversize fireflies, moving fretfully through the darkness. Soon they were within hailing distance of Golovlovo, and out on the sagging front porch stood Matriona the housekeeper, swinging a kerosene lantern back and forth so they wouldn't lose their way. Belinsky drew his carriage abreast of the house, jumped down, and handed the reins to another old servant who had long been a fixture at the estate.

Although Vera had been here before, seeing the house now that she was its mistress made her tremble. It seemed so bleak, everything cracked and peeling, dingy and dilapidated. Half the rotting floorboards of the porch were broken, while others were missing completely, so that dark, rectangular holes could be discerned here and there as she looked anxiously about.

Belinsky helped her down from the carriage, then instructed the elderly male retainer to take their bags up to his room. In the light of the oil lamp Matriona's skin looked so thin and transparent that Vera had the unpleasant sensation of actually being able to see the old woman's skull.

Owlet moths danced around the light as Matriona welcomed her to Golovlovo, the frenzied quivering of their wings reflected in the hovering shadows. The housekeeper set the lantern at her feet, her toothless mouth opening wide as she muttered that they were yet to perform the ceremony of the blessing on the threshold. Having anticipated what was needed, she now produced a battered metal tray on which she'd placed half a loaf of black bread and a cracked plate sprinkled with a small amount of coarse gray salt.

Annoyed that she would have to soil her gown, Vera carefully bent down, trying to hold her skirts up at the same time.

"How do you expect to get your forehead to touch the ground?" Belinsky asked.

"Must I?" she complained. "Everything's so dirty."

"You didn't expect Matriona to lay down a velvet carpet, did you? Come now, Vera, let's get it over with, because the sooner we do—" He rolled his dark-blue eyes, looking up in the direction of his second-story bedroom.

So Vera did as she was told, closing her eyes as she felt the dirt against her forehead. Three times she bowed down as Matriona held the bread and salt of hospitality over her head, making the sign of the cross, and bestowing her blessing on the union. It seemed so ridiculous, for what right had this toothless old hag to perform a ritual Simon's mother should have done? And since her mother-in-law was dead, what did it matter, anyway? But Matriona seemed to derive a great deal of pleasure in conducting the ceremony, and so Vera kept her opinions to herself, having already decided it would be wise to get on the old woman's good side, and as soon as possible.

When she came to her feet, the housekeeper held an ikon before her, the ancient face of the Virgin looking out dimly from within its tarnished and fretted silver setting. Vera kissed it briefly, then tried to conceal her distaste when the old woman embraced her warmly, her stale, oniony breath fanning Vera's cheeks and making her feel even more unclean than before.

Then, taking her in hand, and ordering Matriona to bring them the bottle of Veuve Clicquot he'd put away just for this occasion, Belinsky led her into the musty old house. The rooms were cold and dark, and a continual rustling of cockroaches could be heard behind the cracked and peeling wallpaper. At Petrovka, the house always smelled of beeswax, for the floors were polished every week, this and the faint and alluring scent of dried lime blossoms that had lain on the windowsills all through the winter. But here at Golovlovo everything had a peculiar and unpleasant odor, as if for years the house had served as a cemetery for flies and other vermin. There was no indoor plumbing, and she was afraid to ask where the privy was for fear it would only make her feel worse.

How will I wash? How will I do my toilet every morning? she wondered as Belinsky held her hand and began to lead her up the creaking stairs to the second floor.

"What's the matter?" he asked.

"It's so cold."

"We never fire up the stoves this late at night. It takes too much wood. Tomorrow you'll get right to work helping Matriona put this place in order. Not a bad little house, once it's fixed up."

Vera held her tongue. I just won't do it, that's all. I'm not a servant. That's what you hire people to do, like that old biddy downstairs. Vera was very angry now, and though she knew that was the worst mood to be in when in just another few minutes Simon would want to get down to the business of consummating their union, Vera couldn't help herself. After such a lovely wedding, all this was as depressing as it was anticlimactic. And when she took one look at his bedroom, she could barely stop herself from crying.

"What's the matter now?" Simon asked.

"The bed isn't made," she whispered.

Scowling, he crossed the room and called down to Matriona. A few minutes later the housekeeper's steps were heard on the stairs. She'd forgotten to bring the bottle of champagne, and so Simon went down to get it while Matriona helped Vera make up the bed. Soon everything looked the way it should, the soiled gray sheets replaced by new, spotlessly clean linen; four feather pillows, plump and inviting in their crisp pink calico slips; and a matching eiderdown covered in quilted satin that was also part of her dowry.

Then, laying out her bridal set and taking special delight in the nightdress whose entire front was covered with real Valenciennes lace and bows of white satin, she turned to Matriona, who stood there waiting for permission to leave.

"I know we're going to get on very well," she said, and she went on to describe all her plans for the house, and how Golovlovo could be like it was in the old days, when Simon's parents were still alive. But she couldn't do all these things on her own, and so now she was asking Matriona to help her, in exchange for which she'd make sure the old woman wanted for nothing. "Why, there's no reason you couldn't have a dozen girls working under you," she promised.

Matriona looked at her suspiciously. "And snuff?" the housekeeper said in a hesitant voice.

Vera nodded.

"And all the kvass I can drink? And honey straight from the comb? And a new feather bed for when I sleep on top of the stove? And a rocking chair?"

Vera told her she could have all that and more, provided Matriona did as she was told, and acted as an extra set of eyes, telling her everything that went on.

Matriona moved to the door, her cloth slippers like the kind they put on the dead, cut open around each big toe, so that a pair of bunions stuck out. "You're very young, Vera Petrovna," the housekeeper said, slowly shaping the words with her toothless gums. "If only it were that easy. But I promise you, I'll do my very best." Matriona backed out of the room, making sure to cross herself before stepping over the threshold and into the hall.

Simon soon returned to find her lying in bed, looking as prim and proper as a china doll. The pink satin counterpane was folded neatly across her slender waist, and she leaned back against two of the new feather pillows, leaving the other two for her husband. After they drank the champagne, Simon made sure the door was locked and then began to get undressed.

Vera had expected him to excuse himself, to disappear into his dressing room and return in a nightshirt. Instead, he stood at the foot of the bed, staring at her so openly, and with such boldness and lack of restraint, she couldn't stop herself from blushing.

"No need to be nervous," Belinsky said. "It'll be over soon enough."

"As long as you really love me, I'll be fine." She wanted to ask him please to turn out all the lights, even the stub of a candle on the bedstand. But he seemed so determined to make her aware of everything that she remained silent, blushing hotly and yet unable to stop looking at him.

What an amazing creature a man was, Vera couldn't help but marvel. How would he be able to hold her and not tear her skin off? He looked so rough, and hairy as a beast. On occasion she'd seen Gregor without his shirt on, but her brother was as smooth-skinned as a boy, whereas Simon Ivanovich's arms and torso were black with curly hair that grew right up to the edge of his thick, muscular neck.

"Turn out the lights," she whispered.

"Why?"

"Because."

"Because why?"

"Simon, I'm shy. Please."

"No." With a laugh that bounced from one corner of the bedroom to the other, he skinned off his funny-looking drawers and showed himself to her just the way she hoped God had intended.

So that was how it looked! But how could something like that give someone pleasure? Vera didn't understand it, so she gritted her teeth and slammed her eyes shut, clenching her hands into fists as she heard the bedsprings creaking ominously beneath his weight.

His big bearlike hands went right to the front of her lovely white peignoir, quickly undoing the row of little buttons that were hidden behind the panel of real Valenciennes lace.

"Oh please, don't rip it, Simon. It's the best one I have," she said, still with her eyes shut and her hands clenched anxiously by her sides.

"My poor little dove is frightened."

Then she felt his lips on the side of her neck as he undid her nightdress and eased it down off her smooth white shoulders, helping her pull one arm free and then the other. Without a single wasted motion, he went on to remove her dainty chemise, so that for the first time in her life she felt truly naked and not just undressed.

"You have beautiful breasts, my little sparrow. Look how perfectly they fit in my hands." He began to kiss them and lick them with the tip of his tongue, even as his big, rough hands with the black curly hair growing over the knuckles sought to deprive her of her drawers.

"Do you love me? Do you?" she kept asking as Simon did things to her she thought might not be proper, but that she certainly didn't intend to stop. "Do you? Do you? Am I pretty enough, Senya? Tell me, am I?"

In response, the thing between his grizzly thighs now stood stiffly at attention, so large that she drew back in alarm, for nothing he might say would convince her that it wouldn't hurt. He had told her what to expect when he'd spoken of this in the summerhouse. But talking about it, and now experiencing it, were going to be two very different things.

So she held herself as rigidly as possible, and when he climbed on top of her and got into position, she threw her hands over his shoulders and held onto his damp, sweaty back, tight-lipped and terrified that such a big and inflexible thing would somehow be able to find its way inside her. When it did, for Simon was as determined to get on with it as she was, Vera couldn't prevent herself from crying out, and tearing at his skin as she raked her nails across his back.

But though she felt pain, it was not the fierce, burning sensation she had anticipated. Rather, she began to grow aware of something else, something that filled her with such frightening desire she hardly knew who she was anymore, or what she had become. If only he would do this forever, covering her with his strength, letting her feel every inch of him as he moved backward and forward, making her shudder in pleasure.

"Oh Simon, yes, yes my darling!" she wanted to cry. But all she could do was moan and toss beneath him, not wanting him ever to leave her, or ever pull away.

"No, don't, not yet," she whimpered when he quickened his thrusts. "Oh I love you, I do, I promise!"

"And I . . . I . . ." he couldn't say it, not now, not when he suddenly stiffened and fell against her, groaning with satisfaction.

"Do it again," she whispered as his seed flowed inside her like a balm.

"I will, but let me rest a moment." He rolled over onto his back, reaching for her hand and making her hold his penis as it slowly lost its stiffness and fell limp between his blood-stained thighs.

Vera was afraid to say anything, not certain if he was annoyed at her for wanting more of him. She listened to his ragged breathing, knowing that as long as they could lie here together, everything would be all right.

"You do love me, Senya, don't you?" she asked.

"Of course."

"And even if my father hadn't given you a dowry, you still would have married me, isn't that so?"

"What a question." He made a funny snorting sound that upset her more than she cared to admit.

"But would you?"

"Certainly, Vera, of course."

"Then why do I feel so confused all of a sudden?"

"Because you're a woman now."

But what if I don't want to be a woman? she thought. What if I just want to stay Papa's little girl? Or better yet, Simon's little girl. She was afraid to tell him what she was thinking, and so she closed her eyes and snuggled up to him, pressing her cheek into the wiry nest of fur that covered his hard, manly chest.

"Will we have to wait long?"

"For what, Vera?"

"This," and reaching down, she captured him between her fingers, thinking that all she had to do was keep holding on, and the pleasure would never end.

Irena's husband, Nikolai Alexandrovich Volsky was, at the age of thirty, a man who concealed his ambitions behind a pleasant and agreeable smile, ingratiating good humor, and a general air of affability. Volsky was a *chinovnik*, as all petty Russian bureaucrats were disparagingly called. But in his position as district school inspector, he had nothing but scorn for the endless forms and regulations other civil servants found so comforting. Paperwork was, in fact, the last thing that concerned him, having accepted the position of school inspector not as a sinecure, but as the starting point for what he hoped would eventually prove a long and meritorious career in public service.

When Volsky and his wife returned home from the wedding, driving through the quiet, dusty streets of Mtsensk, the provincial backwater just an hour away from Petrovka, he saw before him not a town but a trap. There could be little hope of improving his position if he remained here for the rest of his life. But whenever he'd discussed moving to Petersburg, Irena had looked at him as if he were proposing murder. She was devoted to Petrovka, and couldn't bear to be very far away from the estate.

Now, in the bedroom of the small wooden house where they'd lived since their marriage, Volsky once again tried to convince his wife that there wasn't any future for him here, that he couldn't possibly hope to make a name for himself if he remained in the province.

Irena, seated at her dressing table, and having unpinned her long brown hair, began to brush it with slow and careful strokes, her hand rising and falling with calm deliberation and a singleness of purpose that never ceased to amaze (and occasionally irritate) her husband. Having already changed into a nightshirt, Volsky stood behind her, admiring the portrait of domestic harmony they made in the glass.

"Did you have a good time, Irusha?" Volsky asked as he bent over and kissed the top of her head.

Irena put down her hairbrush, then swiveled around on the seat. Her soft, beautifully shaped hands reached for his, and as he held them tightly, she said, "Grisha tells me Simon has his eye on being father's steward. God knows what would happen if he ever agreed."

"He won't agree," Volsky replied.

"But what if he does, Niki? What then?"

"Your father's no fool. He knows what Belinsky's all about."

"I wonder."

"In all honesty, Irena, I have other things on my mind. For one, don't you think it's time you stopped worrying about Petrovka? After all, we have our own problems."

Volsky saw how she stiffened. "What problems?" she whispered.

"It's time we had a family, Irusha. It's time we left Mtsensk. It's time we got on with our lives."

"Haven't I tried?"

"Of course you've tried. We've both tried, and we'll keep on trying. But we have our own lives to think of, and Petrovka can't take the place of that. I can't improve our position in society by inspecting schools for the rest of my life. I'm thirty years old, Irusha dear, and it's time I made a name for myself."

Irena walked slowly across the room, and climbed into the wide mahogany bed. Volsky tamped out his cigarette and got in alongside her. But when he reached over to put his arm around her, Irena remained where she was.

"And once you've made a name for yourself," she said, "and everyone knows who you are, will it make you happy?"

"I'm not looking for fame and fortune, Irena. I only want our lives to be as easy as possible, that's all. And doing good work, and being given a position of responsibility, will certainly make me happier than I am now. So you might as well know that I've already applied for a position under the Minister of Education. If he finds my qualifications to his liking, we'll have to look for an apartment in Petersburg." Now that he'd finally told her, he wished he could feel relief. But he couldn't.

"You wouldn't do that to me, Niki, would you?"

"Petrovka will get on very nicely without you," Volsky went on. "But I'm afraid I can't say the same." He leaned over and cupped her face in his hands, kissing her lips and then her eyes, the rim of each small pink ear, the tip of her gently rounded chin.

"I do love you. You know that, Niki, don't you?"

"That's one thing we'll always have, my darling."

Irena stirred beneath him, soft and yielding, helping him out of his nightshirt as he, in turn, helped her out of hers. Volsky felt a great flood of warmth then, that he could experience such a deep affection for someone, that after a year of marriage he was just as aroused by his wife as on their wedding night. That someone so outwardly calm and imperturbable, so very maternal both in outlook and appearance, could be such a wonderful lover, was something Volsky had long promised himself never to take for granted.

"We'll be all right," he whispered. "You'll see, everything will work out, I promise."

If only he succeeded in his aspirations and was awarded the position for which he'd applied. If only Irena would stop worrying about Petrovka, and her parents, and her sisters, and start thinking about herself. If only they could be a family.

The guests had gone, and Gregor and Victor sat alone on the veranda.

"How long has she had that cough?" the young Count said.

"The last few months. But I wouldn't bring it up in front of her, if I were you," Gregor advised. "She's very sensitive about it, insists it's nothing serious, and doesn't want any of us to worry ourselves."

"Then it is serious, isn't it?"

"I couldn't say."

Durnovo's face registered both consternation and surprise. "You mean she hasn't even consulted with a doctor?"

Gregor shook his head.

"But why?"

"If you lived with someone like my mother, you'd be

reluctant to deal with doctors, too. Fortunately, it doesn't seem to be getting any worse, and she tries not to tax herself, so I can't say I blame her. Tell me, will you be driving out to Jerichovo tomorrow?"

"I suppose I must."

Gregor heard himself laughing, though he wasn't sure why. "You make it sound like an obligation."

"It is." The Count said this with great sadness, but whether he was feeling sorry for himself or for his father, Gregor couldn't tell. "Perhaps you and Masha might join me. After all, you seem to be on such good terms with him. Your presence might prove salutary. And now I think I'll turn in," the Count said as he made a move to go inside. "Thank you for your hospitality, Grisha. You're a kind fellow. I'm very appreciative."

Gregor waited until he was alone, then hurried down the steps and across the garden. Keeping back in the shadows just in case that relentless old busybody Auntie V. was peering out from her window, he crept around the side of the house, then ran silently across the courtyard to the stables.

The weathered gray door was ajar, and needing no further encouragement, Gregor slipped inside. Picking his way carefully across the dung-strewn floor, and ignoring the snorting of the horses in their stalls, he reached the wooden ladder that led up to the hayloft. Taking care to scrape his boots on the lowest rung, he climbed up into the darkened loft. Here, in the far corner, he made out the sleeping figure of Kolya.

He crouched down beside him, his knees half buried in the dry, fragrant hay. "Wake up," he whispered. "I've brought you a treat." From the pocket of his dress coat he removed a napkin in which he'd tied up a raspberry tart, for like the horses he tended, Kolya was quite fond of sweets.

The brawny young stableboy turned over onto his back. When he opened his eyes and saw what Gregor had brought for him, he broke into a grin.

"See how I always think of you," Gregor went on as Kolya wolfed down the pastry.

"I thought you weren't coming," said the groom. "That's why I feel asleep."

Gregor smiled and said, "Victor Romanovich bent my ear for more than an hour, or else I would've been here sooner." He slid down alongside Kolya, resting his head against the stableboy's chest.

"Have you told your father yet?" Kolya whispered, holding Gregor in his arms as a husband would a wife.

"About Petersburg? No, but I will, I promise. You know how difficult he is to talk to. Besides, I wouldn't be able to leave until summer, so there's really no reason to bring it up yet. But don't you worry now. A promise is a promise. I said I'd take you with me, and so I shall. Besides, who else would know how to take care of me? Why, I'd be absolutely helpless without you."

He laughed softly, then found Kolya's lips, feeling neither shame nor revulsion for his sins. This was the way he was, the way he knew he had always been, for even as a little boy he was more curious about the "bunches of grapes" he saw in men's pants than what the women looked like when they went to the bathhouse. If Kolya was less inclined in this direction than he, the stableboy was at least a good sport about it, for like all healthy young animals, he never shied away from pleasure, no matter what form or expression it might happen to take.

Lies and more lies, Gregor thought sadly as he kissed the groom. But at least no one saw me come here, so that'll be one less tale to tell.

Five

The morning after the wedding, Masha, Gregor, and Victor set out for Jerichovo in a roomy four-seater. Although Count Durnovo had invited Henriette to join them, she'd reluctantly declined. Her aunt had asked General Tishin for tea, and were she not there when he arrived, she would never hear the end of it.

Masha looked especially radiant that morning in a lilac-colored dress that set off her dark hair and flashing eyes. She appeared well rested, and chattered gaily as they drove down the lime alley and into the countryside. The weather was even lovelier than the day before, and everywhere they looked, things seemed to be growing right before their eyes. Buds were swelling on the birches, sticky and swollen with sap, while faint golden blossoms were sprinkled like dust on the willows that grew alongside the road.

Overhead, skylarks in the hundreds rushed like whirling smoke across the sky, soaring and hovering as they sang their clear, liquid spring song, then plummeting earthward again to run this way and that across the barren fields. Because of the unseasonably warm weather, some of Petrovka's peasants were already hard at work, their primitive wooden plows turning over the rich, black soil. The earth itself gave off a fresh and pungent odor that pleasantly constricted Masha's breath, and she kept sneaking little sidelong glances at the Count, pleased to note the animated and joyful expression on his face.

The carriage, rounding the crest of a hill, was now within sight of Jerichovo. But where the old wooden manor house had stood, a thick column of black smoke now rose up in its place. Masha started from her seat, and would have fallen forward had Victor not caught her around the waist.

"The red cock," she heard the Count whisper, and when she fell back onto the seat and looked over at him, his sallow cheeks were even paler than usual. "The red cock is crowing," he said harshly, that being the term used to describe arson, the peasantry's favorite form of retribution.

"Don't say it until you know for sure. It's an old house. Anything could've happened. A stove might have exploded," Gregor called out from the front seat, where he was now whipping the horses on, the carriage swaying and rumbling down the narrow road toward the stone gates at Jerichovo's entrance.

Again, she tried to lean forward to get a better view, urging her brother to get them there as quickly as possible. Again, Victor caught her around the waist and hauled her back.

There was a great whoosh like an intake of breath, then a shower of sparks began to rain down on them. A piece of glowing ash the size of a thumbnail fell into Victor's lap, burning itself out before Masha had a chance to brush it off. She could smell the fire now, could feel its heat as Gregor pulled up to the crumbling gates, hurriedly jumped down, and tied up the horses. Masha made a move to follow him, but Victor stopped her with a stern and uncompromising look.

"The smoke's too thick," he said. "You won't be able to stop coughing."

"Do as he says," her brother told her, then turned and ran, heading toward the sheet of fire that had once been Jerichovo.

There were numerous peasants rushing about, but not a single one helping to put out the blaze. Instead, Gregor saw Dionysus, Aphrodite, and Hercule *Fils*, all of them in every-day clothes, struggling under the weight of immense bundles filled with the Count's household effects. Catching sight of him, they ran off in all directions, while the flames continued to soar even higher, casting their hot, reddish glow on the dusty paths that wound through the Count's sad, ruined gardens and empty Venetian pools.

Victor was calling out his father's name, and running back and forth in front of the burning house as if he couldn't decide which way to turn, or what to do. "I'm going in," he called to Gregor, and shielding his face with the side of his hand, he rushed up the moldering front steps, slamming his shoulder into the door. But it wasn't locked, and sprang back at the merest touch, while ahead the fire burned just as fiercely as he tried to make his way to the stairs.

Gregor had no desire to follow. But when he looked back and saw how his sister was standing in the carriage, and how she was watching him and expecting him to behave as fearlessly as Victor, he neither wanted to shame her by his cowardice nor to shame himself. So he wrapped his scarf around the lower half of his face, and keeping his head down as far as possible, he reluctantly hurried after the Count.

Inside the house, the heat was nearly unbearable. Shouting out Roman Durnovo's name, and trying to see through the smoke and flames, Gregor rushed into the drawing room, where the furniture smoldered and the walls were a single horrifying expanse of blue and yellow flame. Then he went on into the dining room, where less than twenty-four hours before he had sat with the Count, drinking peppered vodka and listening to the flabby old reprobate talk of his peaches and his pretties. Now the room was empty, and when Gregor looked around, he noticed that the clock representing Bacchus was missing from its place on the mantel.

So the vultures got here before us, he thought bitterly, the smoke causing tears to fill his eyes. He turned away, coughing painfully, sweeping one hand out in front of him as he staggered into the kitchen. The door swung back, his footsteps echoing loudly on the brick floor. The smoke had already permeated every part of the manor house, but here in the kitchen it wasn't nearly as thick as in some of the other rooms. Gregor paused a moment, breathing hard and trying to overcome his fear, for any second he expected the ceiling to give way and come crashing down upon his head.

It was then that he saw Count Roman Durnovo.

The old man was pinned to the door at the far end of the kitchen. Hanging upside down in a cruel and bizarre travesty of the Crucifixion, Durnovo's violated body was painted a maggoty white, save for the bloody sore marking the site of his severed genitals.

Gregor felt his knees hitting the floor, and as he wrapped his hands around his waist he tasted his breakfast, vomiting in a thick, viscous stream. Crucified, castrated, and the red cock crowing victoriously through the bloody spring morning. He could not bear to raise his eyes, for the Count's flabby yellow face—now as dead and ghostly a white as the living statues who had sullenly posed atop his marble pedestals—bore witness to the savagery with which he'd lost his life.

Here lies Roman Durnovo, Gregor thought as he wiped his mouth with the back of his hand. No matter what anyone says, he deserved better.

He backed out of the kitchen, keeping his head down and avoiding the butchered figure hanging upside down at the opposite end of the room. Victor was coming down the stairs as he started back to the front door.

"Did you find him?" the young Count called out.

"No, he's not here. Let's get out while we still can."

"But he has to be here," insisted Victor. "He didn't plan to go visiting today, did he?"

Visiting who? Gregor thought. I was the only one in the district who accepted him for what he was, who came to see him: Oh, the treachery of it, the sadism. Why didn't they just tar and feather him if they were of a mind to? Why did they have to take his life, and was he still alive when they performed that . . . that abomination back there? He didn't know, but every time he thought of it, he had to put his hands between his legs, the gesture as protective as it was involuntary. If this was what came of being different, of exercising one's prerogative for the eccentric and absurd, he knew he had to leave here, and as soon as possible.

"The kitchen," said Victor.

"I already looked."

Perhaps his eyes betrayed him, perhaps his tone of voice. Whatever it was, Victor didn't seem to believe him. Even as Gregor grabbed for his sleeve and tried to pull him to the door, the young Count wrestled free, nearly throwing him down to the floor as he raced across the front hall and disappeared into the kitchen.

Gregor called after him, and a moment later Victor staggered out, weeping as much from the smoke as the sight of his murdered father. Gregor threw an arm around the young man's shoulders and dragged him to the door, kicking it open with his boot. Behind him, the second story began to give way, and fiery beams fell across the stairs. There was gravel under their feet now, and Masha with a pail of water she'd drawn from the well.

"What happened? Couldn't you find him?" she asked.

"And who were all those people that were here? They were looting the house, weren't they?"

He made the Count drink, then dipped his hands into the wooden bucket and bathed his eyes. When he straightened up and looked back, the second floor was gone, and the fire was burning itself out like a molten heart, consumed by the very depth and intensity of its passion for the perverse.

"It's not fair," Henriette told her father at breakfast. "I have nothing to say to General Tishin, and I never will."

"You'll do as your aunt says and behave yourself."

"But why?"

"Because I'm telling you to, and that's reason enough. Do you think I enjoy seeing your ugly mug day after day? It's time you got married like your other sisters. Time you stopped being so choosy, too."

"You stupid girl," her aunt said when she left the dining room. "I heard what went on in there, every word of it. Do you want to spend the rest of your life listening to him berate you? *Ugly mug*, indeed. You're not ugly, Henriette. You're unusual-looking. And General Tishin, dear, sweet man that he is, finds you utterly captivating."

"Is that what he told you?" she asked suspiciously.

"Of course that's what he told me," exclaimed her aunt. "And if you play your cards right, soon people will be calling you *Madame la Générale*. Oh, the joy of it, another wedding, and so soon after the last one."

Something was definitely going on behind her back. But when she attempted to question Varvara more closely, her aunt said there wasn't time, the General would be arriving before they knew it, and Henriette had best run upstairs and change.

Sure enough, by the time she came down again, having changed her steel-gray dress for one of icy blue, the General's carriage was just pulling up to the front door. Not the least bit concerned what he thought of her, she sailed blithely into the drawing room, where she was soon joined by her aunt.

"Lovely, absolutely lovely," said Varvara. "Blue is definitely your color, Henriette."

"His Excellency, General Ardallion Hippolytovich Tishin," announced Lyuba the serving girl, laughter bubbling in her eyes.

Henriette began to giggle, for it wasn't until that moment that she'd heard the General's full name. Ardallion Hippolytovich sounded so perfectly pompous and inflated that she couldn't stop giggling, and had to cover her mouth with a handkerchief when the General made his entrance. Varvara gave her a withering glance, but by then it was already too late. One look at the General and she nearly fell off the sofa. His costume was fully a match for his name, for only an Ardallion Hippolytovich could have worn such an amazing suit of clothes. The General sported a yellow checkered morning coat, matching waistcoat, gloves that were even more decidedly yellow than either of these, and butter-colored trousers that were of such a smart, close-fitting cut she wondered how he'd managed to stuff his paunchy thighs into them.

"What an utterly charming room, that you two young ladies should be here," he said in French. "Varvarushka, my dear, you look quite exquisite. And as for you, Mademoiselle Henriette, I have not seen a more becoming frock in all of Russia."

Auntie V., who clearly appreciated the General's sentiments, motioned him to a seat, though it was with some difficulty that he maneuvered his tall, fat body into the delicate chair. For a moment Henriette was certain it would topple over. Instead, it merely creaked, and the four fluted legs tilted outward before adjusting to the General's considerable weight.

The General peeled off his yellow gloves as if skinning a banana, then adjusted the knot of his cravat. "I have heard the most amusing story," he began, looking for a place to put his gloves. Before he went on, he endeavored to cross his legs. Unable to swing one over the other, he had to content himself by crossing his ankles. This enabled Henriette to see the soles of his boots, and the unpleasant sight of something rather ripe and nasty that was smeared all over the bottom of his shoe.

"General," she said, for she couldn't resist pointing it out to him, "I fear you've brought something into the house that you'd probably like to know about."

"Have I?" the poor man asked in confusion. "What?"

Henriette motioned to the uptilted sole of his patent-leather boot.

The General tried to bend over to examine it, but his weight, combined with the narrow confines of both the chair and his singularly tight-fitting trousers, prevented him from succeeding.

"Allow me," volunteered Varvara. She bent forward, and when she saw what he'd stepped in, she coughed nervously and rose to her feet.

"What is it, what is it?" Ardallion Hippolytovich said in confusion, his sleepy blue eyes having come instantly awake.

"Merely a little grass. I'll have the girl bring in a cloth."

By the time her aunt returned with Lyuba in tow, the poor General was so embarrassed he was nearly reduced to tears. But when the sole of his boot was scrubbed clean, he deftly picked up the pieces of his self-respect and went on as if nothing untoward had occurred, describing in the most flowery language imaginable the beauties of spring as he alone had observed them that morning on his way to Petrovka.

Henriette was about to get up and excuse herself, having decided to feign a headache, when her father stepped into the drawing room. He and the General exchanged the most cordial of greetings, punctuated by a great deal of back-slapping and shaking of hands, as if they were friends of long standing.

"My head," she whispered, trying to convince them she was in no condition to remain in their company.

"What about it?" asked her father.

"I have a terrible headache," she announced. "I really must go upstairs." She turned to General Tishin who, for all his attempts at being charming, had only succeeded in being the buffoon. "I'm sorry you've troubled yourself to come all this way, sir, but you must excuse me. I'm not feeling very well."

"Perhaps I might call upon you again tomorrow afternoon?" suggested the General.

"I don't . . . I mean." She shot a glance at Auntie V., who was making no effort to come to her aid. "I'm not well," and she ran from the room before anyone could stop her.

"I didn't realize she had such a delicate constitution," the General remarked when she was gone.

"Oh yes, she's quite a rare flower, my Henriette," said Peter Semyonovich.

"How true," agreed his sister. "You see, Henriette is of such a modest and retiring nature, General, that naturally she's been overwhelmed by all your attention."

"But you mustn't give up so easily," Petrov advised as he poured them each a glass of rowanberry cordial. "Wear her down with flattery, General. Insist upon spending as much time with her as possible, for if you wish to see this to a favorable conclusion, you must do everything in your power to overcome Henriette's defenses."

"Then you approve?" the General asked excitedly.

"Approve?" said Petrov with a crafty grin, and he raised his glass in a toast. "Not only do I approve, General Tishin, but also I shall get down on my knees and pray for the successful termination of your suit. Yes, it will be a great day when my daughter agrees to take your hand in matrimony. And she will agree, General Tishin. Oh yes, on that you have my word. For you know what they say, General. A girl's heart is a dark forest . . . but even the most modest woman takes her clothes off when she goes to bed."

Seated in the carriage, his head in his hands and his shoulders trembling convulsively, Count Victor Romanovich wept without tears. He could find neither words nor actions to express his feelings, so he remained where he was, dry-eyed though his heart was breaking, grief-stricken though he couldn't bring himself to do anything but shudder.

When at last he raised his head and looked up, Jerichovo was merely a charred and blackened shell. "You know why they did this, Gregor, don't you?" he asked.

"I don't, honestly."

"You're lying!" the Count shouted. He began to cough, wrapping his hands tightly around his waist and shaking back and forth. "You're lying to me, but it's too late for that. Tell me why they did this, Grisha. You were here yesterday. What went on that I don't know about?"

"Nothing," Gregor insisted. "He was harmless, I tell you, a harmless old man, an eccentric; he never hurt anyone."

"Men who are harmless aren't murdered. The peasants aren't sadists. They must have had good cause. Oh Christ in heaven, there's no cause, don't you see, there's no cause to murder a man, and in such a horrible way besides." He broke down then, and was still shaking when, from the direction of the road, the clatter of hoofbeats was heard in the distance.

Masha got down from the carriage as a troika of old pinkish-gray horses drew an old-fashioned omnibus into the courtyard. Springless and stoutly built, it carried four men, one of whom she recognized as Kalinovich, the *ispravnik,* or district chief of police.

Kalinovich, wearing a dark-green tunic with gold shoulder straps as a sign of his rank, and joined by a weaselly blue-uniformed *stanovoy*, or assistant, sauntered over to them, even as Gregor greeted him by name. Kalinovich was a ruggedly built man in his mid-thirties, with close-cropped, prematurely steel-gray hair, and narrow green eyes set in an angular face. He was a friend of Simon Belinsky, but now looked at the three of them as though they were strangers.

"I thought I saw you yesterday, Durnovo, but I wasn't certain," Kalinovich spoke up, hauling Victor from the carriage without a word of explanation.

Masha started forward to stop him, but Gregor held her back, hurriedly explaining what had happened, and how they had arrived too late either to put out the fire or to prevent Count Durnovo's murder.

"Murder?" said Kalinovich, sounding not the least bit surprised. "Well, that definitely puts a different complexion on things, doesn't it? So the profligate son has returned, eh, Durnovo?" He demanded the Count produce his papers, as an internal passport was required of all Russian nationals, particularly when traveling within the empire. When Victor motioned to his portmanteau, Kalinovich ordered one of his constables to search the Count's effects. "Seems to me," the police chief went on, "that you should have registered as soon as you arrived. I don't recall seeing you at the police station."

"You knew I was here," Victor replied. "You saw me at the wedding."

While two of the constables went off to round up whatever peasants they found in the area, Kalinovich opened the Count's battered suitcase and dumped everything onto the ground, snatching a sheaf of papers he found among Victor's dirty linen. With a triumphant gleam in his narrow green eyes, Kalinovich retrieved the papers and quickly examined them.

"Last time I saw you, Durnovo, you were preaching that populist claptrap. Looks to me like you still haven't learned your lesson."

"His father's been murdered," interrupted Gregor. "Why worry about his papers when the people responsible are getting away?"

"Because nobody is going to miss Roman Durnovo, that's why."

"Why, you bastard," Victor swore. He lunged forward, but the weaselly *stanovoy* hauled him back before he had a chance to get at Kalinovich.

The police chief continued as if nothing had happened. "But as for this," and he slapped his hand against the papers he'd found in Victor's bag, "now, this is something worth worrying about, I assure you."

"How did you know about the fire, anyway?" Gregor asked.

"Yes, no one sent word," added Masha. "How did you know?"

"We happened to be driving by," Kalinovich told them.

"I don't believe you," Gregor said. "I think there's more going on here than we know about."

"I really don't care what you believe, Gregor Petrovich. Your opinions don't concern me in the least. And judging from the company I gather you keep, you'd be wise to keep your nose out of this, and mind your own business."

Secretly alarmed by Kalinovich's innuendos and unspoken threats, Gregor made a move to take Victor in tow. But the moment he put his arm around the Count's shoulders, Kalinovich shoved him aside.

"You can't take charge of my prisoner," Kalinovich said with an oily laugh.

"Prisoner?" exclaimed Masha. "What are you talking about?"

"This." The police chief waved the sheaf of papers in the air, even as the two constables returned with Dionysus, Aphrodite, and Hercule *Fils*.

"We found them loading their carts. Looks like everything they had belonged to the Count," one of the officers told his chief.

"Take them back to the village," Kalinovich said, still glancing through the papers and suddenly smiling excitedly. "What have we here, Victor Romanovich? *The Fundamental Statute of the Russian Empire.* What fundamental statute are we talking about? Freedom of speech and freedom of the press? That there shall be two law-making bodies, one consisting of local councils and the other an Imperial Chamber of Deputies. My, this is certainly very inflammatory literature you're carrying about. I suppose you planned to use it to incite the peasants. Perhaps setting fire to your father's estate was your idea, Victor Romanovich, and not the idea of those poor unfortunates."

Kalinovich motioned to Hercule *Fils* and the others, who were already being loaded like baggage onto the omnibus.

"But wait, there's more." The police chief shuffled the papers, reciting aloud, *"How the Revolutionary Question Presents Itself.* How does it, Durnovo? By killing the Tsar? And what of these—*Principles of Revolution, Some Words to Our Young Brothers in Russia?* 'Dear Brethren: Go among the people, act as midwives helping to bring about the self-emancipation of the peasants. . . .'" He stopped short and looked up at Victor. "Your father was a fool, Victor Romanovich, but in the scheme of things a rather inconsequential one. You, on the other hand, appear to be a very dangerous character, a true revolutionary." He nodded to the *stanovoy*, who quickly seized Victor and began to drag him to the wagon.

"You don't mean to arrest him, do you?" Masha cried out. She rushed up to Victor and tried to pull him away from the police officer, only to feel Kalinovich's hands on her shoulders as he forced her to release him. "But he's done nothing! Let him return with us to Petrovka. If you want to question him, he's not going to run away."

"I wouldn't interfere, Maria Petrovna. The man is a dangerous revolutionary."

"But I thought you were our friend, Mikhail Ilyich."

"Friendship has nothing to do with upholding the laws of the empire," Kalinovich said stiffly. Again he motioned to his deputy, who proceeded to shove Victor toward the jaunting car.

Masha turned to her brother and began to shake him. "Can't you stop them, Grisha? Can't you make them leave him alone?" Tears of outrage and helplessness filled her eyes. Again she tried to intervene, only to feel Gregor holding her back as Victor was thrown onto the omnibus. "But why? Why?" she kept saying. "He's done nothing. They murdered his father. He's done nothing, I tell you."

"He won't listen," whispered her brother. "You must conserve your strength, Masha."

Coughing now, she shook her head as Kalinovich joined his men on the omnibus.

As the troika of old pinkish-gray horses started past the gates, Victor called out to her. "I'll send word as soon as I can."

"But where are they taking you?" she shouted.

Victor shrugged his shoulders, then raised his hand to wave good-bye. One of the constables threw him down, and the last thing Masha saw was the side of his face, pressed up against the wooden seat and held there with the sole of the officer's hard steel-tipped boot.

Six

Although the table was laid with numerous savory dishes, the Volskys hadn't as yet sat down to dinner. Instead, Irena paced back and forth across the brightly lit parlor, trying to remain calm and yet finding it difficult to keep her emotions in check. She hated to speak rashly, and would have much preferred not to say anything at all. But she couldn't go on like this, pretending that everything was fine, that she was the happiest and most contented of wives. So at last she stopped her anguished pacing and turned to face her husband.

"Surely dinner will get cold," Volsky said. "Come, we'll talk about this later."

"Why must you make me suffer so?" she asked.

"I will not have you sounding like a martyr, Irena. My career is of the utmost importance, not only for me, but even more so for you. It's our future, dear girl, don't you see?"

"But I don't want to move to Petersburg, Niki. I'm . . . I'm not that way," she blurted out. She hurried to unburden herself of her fears, that she would have no friends if they lived in the capital, that the city would swallow them up and they'd be lost, that she was, at heart, just a simple country girl, with simple tastes, and a lack of understanding of all the social intricacies and intrigues she knew went on in the drawing rooms of Petersburg.

To this her husband responded with a hearty, good-natured laugh. Taking her in his arms and squeezing her affectionately, he kissed the top of her furrowed brow and told her she mustn't be silly, that he would always be there to look after her.

Irena knew there was no arguing with him then. After all, he hadn't even received word from the Minister yet. So she gave her husband her arm and let him escort her into the dining room, where a tureen of cream of barley soup still steamed invitingly in the middle of the table.

Volsky helped her to her seat, then rubbed his hands together as he joined her at the table. He had a healthy appetite, though fortunately his weight never seemed to settle around his waist. He was a man of medium height and build, with thick, unruly dark-brown hair and eyes that were almost Asiatic, for they were turned down at the corners. He wore his hair parted to one side, and kept his cheeks clean-shaven, disdaining side whiskers in favor of a wiry mustache. This last he left untrimmed, preferring instead to chew on the long hairs that curled over his upper lip. On occasion he would wax his mustache with *pommade hongroise,* so that two daggerlike points stood out across his ruddy cheeks. This was the exception, however, for Nikolai Alexandrovich was a man who derived self-satisfaction from his work, not from dandifying his appearance.

"This is quite excellent, Irusha. Did you prepare it yourself, my dear?"

She was about to answer when she heard carriage wheels crunching the gravel at the front of the house. "Are you expecting someone?" she asked.

"No, I didn't ask anyone to stop by, not that I can remember."

Irena came to her feet just as Katya the maid hurried into the dining room to report that Madame's brother and sister had just driven up to the house. Surprised to see them so soon after the wedding, Irena went into the entryway to welcome them, calling out to the cook to set another two places at the table. But when she took one look at her sister, she rushed outside. Gregor was half carrying Masha up the path to the front door, and when she raised her head and looked up, Irena heard herself gasp. Her sister's lips were flecked with bloody foam, and the handkerchief Masha clutched between her fingers was stained crimson.

No, she wouldn't panic. Masha would need all of her sister's strength and presence of mind. Stepping aside to let them pass, Irena called out to Katya, telling the girl to hurry upstairs to make up the spare room.

"Nikolai! Come give us a hand!" she shouted, so that a moment later her husband came running.

"My God, what's happened?" he exclaimed. He made Masha throw her arm over his shoulder, so that along with Gregor they managed to lead her up the stairs, moving sideways like a trio of crabs as Masha continued to cough, her breath rattling feebly in her chest.

As soon as they'd gotten her into bed, Irena ordered the cook to prepare linden-flower tea and vinegar compresses, then sent Katya out to bring back the doctor, who fortunately lived just a short distance away. She shooed the men out of the room, and sitting on the edge of the bed and clasping her sister's painfully limp hands, began to rub them briskly.

"*Mamochka's* here, my dearest," she said as she brushed the hair out of Masha's eyes. It was wet and slippery, as if her sister had been perspiring profusely. Irena slowly undressed her, then pulled the bedcovers up to her neck so that only Masha's pale, drawn face peeked out, lost in the plump folds of the pillows. "Everything will be all right now, Mashenka, I promise. Oh my darling, you look so weak, but you'll soon be well, I'm sure of it."

Masha's dark eyes, gleaming feverishly under their long lashes, opened wide. Her blood-stained lips were parched, and Irena poured water into a basin and moistened them with a corner of her sister's handkerchief. Masha began to toss and turn, dragging the bedclothes with her and twisting her head from side to side so that dark stains were left on the linen where her damp cheeks pressed into the pillows. She opened her mouth to speak, but could only manage the faintest of whispers.

Irena bent over her, begging her to conserve her strength and not say anything. Irena came anxiously to her feet and went out into the hall. The cook was just then coming up the stairs, and a few minutes later a vinegar-soaked cloth lay across Masha's forehead. Helping her sister to sit up, Irena urged her to drink some of the tea, but after taking just a few sips Masha's head fell to one side and she closed her eyes.

When Irena came downstairs, Nikolai and Gregor were waiting in the dining room. She urged them to take a seat, for she knew they must be hungry, saying there was nothing they could do until the doctor arrived. As for herself, she couldn't think of food now, having lost what little appetite she'd had.

Between hesitant mouthfuls, Gregor told her what had happened. Recalling that the Count had spoken of meeting Turgenev on the train, Gregor and Masha had made an unsuccessful pilgrimage to the writer's estate. But Ivan Sergeyevich had refused to be of assistance, and Masha had exchanged the bitterest of words with him. She then insisted they drive back to the village where Victor had been taken. There they learned that he'd already been sent to Mtsensk, for the town had the dubious honor of boasting a sizable prison. Although she hadn't stopped coughing since leaving

Turgenev's estate, Masha was adamant that they drive on to town. But as they neared Mtsensk her condition visibly worsened, and when Gregor saw that she'd begun coughing blood and was trying to hide it from him, he made straight for the Volskys.

A breathless Katya hurried into the dining room to report that the doctor would be arriving within the hour. Irena instructed the maid to prepare fresh compresses. Then, taking a small glass of madeira with her, she went back upstairs.

Having dealt with her mother's numerous illnesses for so many years, Irena had thought she was inured to what went on in a sickroom. But when she looked at her sister, it was hard to understand how someone so young and beautiful could suddenly be taken so ill. Again Irena took her place on the edge of the bed, smoothing the coverlets, and caressing her sister's slender and now frighteningly lifeless hands.

"The doctor is on his way," Irena whispered when Masha opened her eyes. "Do you think you can take a little wine?"

Masha shook her head. "I'll get well. I have to," she whispered.

"Of course you'll get well. It's just a bad cold, that's all. Why, it's going around everywhere; everyone I know has had it." She made do with a halfhearted smile, knowing her sister wasn't convinced. From downstairs Irena heard the welcome tinkle of the doorbell and came quickly to her feet.

"There," she said, "the doctor's here already. He's going to make you feel much better, I'm sure. It's just this terrible cold that's going around. They say it's come all the way from China. Fancy that, having a Chinese sickness." She pretended to laugh, but was afraid the sound that came out was anything but humorous. Nevertheless, Masha smiled faintly, then closed her eyes as Irena hurried from the room.

Twenty minutes later, the doctor came downstairs again. Irena, in the company of her husband and brother, was waiting impatiently in the parlor, and the moment she heard his thoughtful and measured steps on the stairs, she went to meet him at the doorway.

"Your sister is resting now," the doctor began, looking at her with something very much like pity, for such was the way she interpreted his glance.

"And?"

"I'm afraid there's little I can do for her, Madame Volskaya. You must try to make her as comfortable as possible, and see to it that she avoids taxing her strength."

"Is that all you can prescribe?" she asked in surprise.

"I'm afraid there's nothing I can do for her," the doctor said again.

"But what is it?" she asked, alarmed by his apparent unwillingness to be more specific.

"Your sister is consumptive, Madame. At the moment her condition appears to be stable, with no further indication of pulmonary hemorrhaging."

"What?" She looked anxiously at Niki, and then at Gregor, who was staring at the doctor with the same degree of confusion and disbelief as she. "Surely it's not that serious. A bad cold, yes, that I can understand. But how can you say she's consumptive? Why, that's absurd. There must be tests, or . . . or something they do to make sure. You just can't come into someone's home and make that kind of snap judgment. This is Mtsensk, Doctor, just a small town. How can you take a look at someone and say she has tuberculosis?"

Niki put his arm around her then, but she barely felt it. She was trembling violently, and felt the room swaying, the floor moving out from under her feet.

I must sit down, she thought. I'll faint if I don't.

Yet she remained where she was, Niki's arm thrown protectively around her shoulders while she stared uncomprehendingly at the doctor.

"I may be wrong, of course. But I wouldn't say this if I weren't all that certain. We have no proper facilities here, but I strongly recommend she be taken to Professor Ostroumov's clinic in Moscow."

"Professor what? I'm sorry, I can't . . . it's . . ." She looked around in confusion, allowing Nikolai to help her to a chair.

"Professor Ostroumov's clinic in Moscow," the doctor repeated, writing it down for her on a slip of paper. "There they'll be able to make a proper diagnosis, and decide on what course of treatment would be best for your sister. Perhaps it's still at an early stage, and with rest, and a proper diet, she'll regain her health. But in the interim, I would keep her as comfortable and as inactive as possible. Good, hardy fare, rest, sunshine if the weather permits, and as soon as she's able, a trip to Moscow to consult with specialists."

All Irena could do was nod her head.

"Should she be told?" she called out as Nikolai escorted the doctor to the door.

"I see no reason to keep it a secret, Madame Volskaya. But perhaps it would be wise to wait until she's a little stronger."

"Yes, certainly," she said, half to herself. Tuberculosis. The monstrous word wrapped itself painfully around her tongue, cutting off her breath. Tuberculosis. And unless it was treated quickly, it would only get worse.

It was fully a week before Masha felt strong enough to leave her bed and spend an hour outside in the warm spring sunshine that flooded her sister's garden. Irena had told her of the doctor's diagnosis, and though she insisted he could very well be wrong, Masha knew she was suffering from consumption. She didn't feel sorry for herself, however, for it wasn't in her temperament to bask in self-pity. She would fight this unwelcome visitor who'd taken up residence in her lungs. She would vanquish it with her strength of mind, and the firm belief that she was much too young to give up without a fight.

In the interim, Gregor had made inquiries at the prison, and had even managed to get word to Victor, for Masha was afraid of what he might think if he didn't know she'd been taken ill. Tomorrow her brother planned to drive her back to Petrovka while arrangements were made for the journey to Moscow. But before she left Mtsensk, she was determined to see Count Durnovo. Often she would find herself struggling to recall the sound of his voice, or the way he carried himself, or the way he had looked at her. Perhaps she was being foolish. Perhaps his feelings for her weren't nearly as strong as hers for him. Yet even though she was assailed by self-doubt, and the fear that she might be deluding herself, it comforted her to know that she cared about him, and that she was fully capable of emotions that might very well prove to be love.

So it was that a week after Victor Romanovich's arrest and subsequent incarceration, Masha found herself arriving at the Mtsensk depot, this being the designation of the prison that stood at the edge of town. It was here that prisoners were sent from all over Russia before being dispatched to Siberia, and it was here that she came with her brother, seeking to gain admittance to the grim and desolate-looking structure.

The enormous barnlike building was enclosed within a palisade of sharpened logs, so that from the dusty, unpaved street only its red-tiled roof was visible. But once past the wide gates, Masha could see what a horribly depressing place it was, surrounded by a bare and dreary courtyard, over which loomed tiny barred windows that were so few and far between she wondered how any light at all could possibly penetrate the prisoners' cells.

Once inside the prison, Masha's dread mounted. The quality of the air itself changed, and what had been fresh and invigorating a moment before was now indescribably foul, making it difficult to breathe. A guard led them down a narrow corridor, his boots scraping against the sand that was strewn across the floor. Reaching a heavy oak door at the end of the passage, the guard rapped smartly with his knuckles. A grate set high up in the door slid back, and a pair of narrowed and suspicious eyes examined them in the dim light of the corridor. Then the door was unlocked from the inside, and another guard stepped aside to let them pass.

The prison governor was seated behind a desk at the far end of the long, rectangular room. At their approach he looked up, motioning Masha to a chair.

"What can I do for you?" the official said in that haughty and detached manner that all *chinovniki* and dedicated government servants learn to cultivate.

"We've come to see Count Durnovo," her brother said in his perfect French.

"Impossible," the official curtly replied, answering in Russian and looking not the least bit impressed by Gregor's airs.

Gregor hurriedly introduced himself, explaining in a respectful and patronizing tone that they only wished to see the prisoner for a few minutes, that his sister was very ill, and that her greatest wish was to say good-bye to the young man before leaving Mtsensk.

"How do you come to know him?" the man said suspiciously.

"An old childhood friend," explained Gregor. "We all grew up together. Perhaps you know of our father, Peter Semyonovich Petrov?"

"No, I'm not from around these parts. And now, if you'll excuse me." The warden began to study the collection of official-looking papers that were strewn across his desk.

Masha glanced at her brother. Surely there was something they could do to make the warden change his mind. Gregor must have read her thoughts, for even then he was reaching into his breast pocket to remove his leather billfold. Dexterously extracting a red ten-ruble bill, he stepped up to the desk and looked down at the official with a good-natured if somewhat fawning grin.

"Surely you can make an exception, sir, just this once." He let the bank note slip from his fingers so that it fluttered through the air like a leaf, landing in the pile of government documents.

The warden flashed a greedy smile, and before Masha could see what had happened to it, the ten-ruble note was gone. "So you've come to see Victor Romanovich, have you? Well, I suppose I can make an exception. Just this once, of course."

"In the name of Christian charity," Masha spoke up.

"Yes, precisely what I was thinking," agreed the warden, who rang for the guard and instructed him to escort the visitors to the interrogation room, where the prisoner Durnovo would then be brought from his cell.

"We're terribly grateful for your kindness," she said.

The warden smiled unctuously and came to his feet. "All men are brothers, are they not?"

The interrogation room was just a short distance away, furnished with a plain deal table and two flimsy ladder-back chairs. A rather unflattering and villainous-looking oleograph of the late Tsar looked down at them from its place on the wall. Masha crossed herself before the small ikon that stood in the corner, then took a seat, her eyes focused expectantly on the door.

"Money always talks," her brother started to say when the door flew open and Victor was shoved inside.

She looked at him for a moment as if he were a stranger, for even though he'd been in prison only a little more than a week, his skin had the dead, gray pallor of someone who'd been locked away for months on end. She started from her seat, but he held out his hands imploringly, urging her to remain where she was.

"I haven't bathed," he said. "It's not a pleasant smell."

"What does it matter?" Again she started toward him, only to be stopped by the guard who'd escorted Victor from his cell.

"I'll wait outside," her brother said. He stepped past Victor, then threw his arms over the Count's shoulders, embracing him warmly. When Gregor stepped back she was surprised to see that his eyes were shiny with tears. The guard opened the door for him, then locked it and remained inside the room.

Masha could not bear to be apart from Victor. She wanted to fly into his arms, but the guard warned her to remain where she was. So she had to sit in the hard wooden chair, gazing up at him as he stood a few feet away, his pale and animated face expressing so many emotions at once that it was difficult to know precisely what he was thinking.

"I must tell you certain things right away," she said. She raised her head slightly, motioning with her chin in the direction of the guard so that Victor would know she wasn't speaking as freely as she would have liked. "Gregor intends to testify that any number of people had access to your suitcase, that the pamphlets Kalinovich found were put there by someone else to incriminate you."

Victor shook his head, and she saw how thin his neck was, how the collar of his shirt looked several sizes too large, as if the flesh had been stripped away from his bones.

"But why? That's what happened, Victor, you know that's what it was." Again she motioned with her chin, afraid of saying anything that might make him appear guilty.

"The people cry out for justice," Victor replied. "I can't betray them with a lie."

"But if they let you go you'll be able to continue your work. Isn't that what's most important?"

"It's too late for that."

She could feel her breath growing shallower as something clutched at her lungs, tighter and tighter until she couldn't stop herself from coughing.

He rushed toward her but the guard hauled him back, warning that the next time he tried anything he'd be marched back to his cell.

"It's all right," she whispered. "It'll pass." Slowly the harsh, racking pain began to subside. The blood stopped pounding in her temples. "See, it's nothing, nothing at all," she insisted. "And you mustn't be a martyr, Victor. Promise me you'll at least consider what Gregor's suggested."

"I've already admitted the pamphlets were mine," he said softly. "Tomorrow they intend to take me to Petersburg to await trial at the Fortress."

"Oh God, no," she whispered, turning her eyes to the ikon, whose lamp gleamed feebly in the corner of the room.

"So you must think about yourself now, about getting better, regaining your strength," Victor said, speaking in that earnest and deeply committed voice she'd come to associate with him. "You must forget about me, Maria Petrovna."

"Forget?" She laughed nervously. "How could I possibly forget? Look what they've done to you, Victor. How can I forget that, or what happened to your father, or how they've all conspired against you?"

He shook his head. "You must put me out of your thoughts."

Masha couldn't conceive of such a thing. "I'll wait for you, however long it takes. Don't smile, Victor. Don't look at me as if I'm a child. Don't you want me to wait? Don't you want me to follow you?"

Again he shook his head. "You mustn't wait for me, Masha," he said, putting great stress on each and every word. "If it were you who were arrested, I wouldn't stand by you. I wouldn't have anything to do with you."

She couldn't believe what she was hearing, but though she pleaded with him, Victor would not change his mind.

"There's no room in my life for love—not now, and perhaps never," he replied, his blue eyes looking right through her, as if she weren't even there. "You have to accept that, Masha. You mustn't deceive yourself into believing that I'll count the days until my release, just because I want to see you again. This is the last time, and that's the way it has to be."

Though she tried to remain calm, she was unable to, and spoke with a grasping tone, reaching out with her hands so that he would come to her.

Victor's face assumed a coarse and disagreeable expression, one that made his features almost unrecognizable. "There's too much work to be done. And there's no room for you in my life."

"No room? Then why did you come back? Why did you make me believe there was . . . something beautiful between us?"

"Don't be a schoolgirl," he said with great annoyance. "Was my father's death beautiful? Shall I tell you what they did to him?"

"I won't listen. I'll put my hands over my ears."

Victor sneered at her, and the contempt she saw in his eyes was far more painful than anything she'd ever suffered before. "If you try to see me again, I'll tell them I don't know who you are, or what you want from me, that I have no desire to see you."

"You're doing this to protect me!" she shouted. "But it

won't work. It won't work, do you hear!"

"It will work," he insisted. "because I intend to make certain that it does. I'm sorry I ever returned here. Even more than that, I'm sorry I deceived you. You mean nothing to me. Perhaps you did when we were younger, but not anymore." He turned and said something to the guard, who immediately unlocked the door so that she could see her brother pacing in the corridor.

"You're a liar!" she cried out, brushing aside the tears that had begun to drip down her pinched and sallow cheeks. "You won't protect me by doing this. I won't let you turn me away."

"It's not your decision to make," Victor replied.

When she ran out into the corridor he was already gone.

Seven

Aunt Varvara Semyonovna had arrived at Krasnaya Gorka, Red Hill, a few days after her niece returned from Mtsensk. General Tishin's modest estate, a fifty-soul affair by pre-Emancipation standards, was located some twenty-five versts from Petrovka, and even in a fast carriage took more than two hours to reach. The house stood on an eminence overlooking the River Zusha, and from the top of the steep knoll one could see for several versts in all directions. But it was not the view that had brought Auntie V. all this distance, nor was it the General's small blancmange-colored house.

Rather, she had come to discuss a matter of great delicacy—namely, the General's attempts to win her niece Henriette's hand. Not that she was suffering sleepless nights because she feared her niece was destined to remain unmarried. Auntie V. herself had never stood before the altar, and yet had managed to make quite a nice little life for herself, as she was always the first to boast. But of late Varvara had made some rather ill-advised investments, and found her finances in a shockingly depleted state. It was for this reason that she was determined her matchmaking succeed, for her very future depended upon an alliance between Petrovka and

Krasnaya Gorka.

Greeting her effusively and with great enthusiasm, and insisting that she immediately join him for tea while he told her a most amusing story, the General showed her into his dingy little parlor. Everything about the room was cold and dark, from the bare wooden floor to the marble-topped tables supported by battered chimeras and sphinxes.

"You need a woman's touch, my dear General," she said, speaking in a gentle and what she hoped was intimate tone.

"Yes, yes indeed," the General replied with a plaintive sigh. "But, as you know, I've been a widower for several years now. Managing one's servants is a full-time occupation, Varvara Semyonovna. Things were easier twenty years ago. Oh yes, life was much simpler then."

Varvara, seated in a very old mahogany armchair, folded her hands neatly in her lap and carefully scrutinized the General. Yes, he needed a wife, that was all, someone to take charge of his household, to whip his servants into shape, to see to it that everything ran smoothly and efficiently, neat and clean, and just the way it should be.

There was, of course, more to it than that, for she did not expect Henriette to be the solution to all his domestic problems. But where her niece might not excel, Varvara knew someone else who was eminently suited to the task, and fully intended to discuss this now that she had the General's ear.

"Perhaps you'd prefer to take tea outside," he suggested, rising with some difficulty from his chair.

"Yes, that would be charming, Ardalosha," and she coaxed a smile from his thick, fleshy lips, lips she decided wouldn't be at all unappetizing to kiss.

What a thought! some inner voice exclaimed, one she hadn't bothered to listen to in years. Embarrassed that she had even imagined such a thing, and wondering what the General would think of her if he knew, Varvara followed him onto the terrace.

"Ah yes," said the General, "so much could be done here if only one had the proper resources, Varvara Semyonovna, the proper resources and the proper helpmate, if you follow my meaning."

"Which is precisely why I came to see you this afternoon. In truth, I could scarcely sleep a wink all last night, just thinking how difficult this past week has been for you."

"Terribly difficult," he agreed. "Positively difficult and quite often exasperating, Varvarushka. You don't mind my calling you that, do you? I would hate to think I'm taking liberties with someone of your obvious refinement."

Varvara tittered gleefully, and even reached over and patted the General's big pudgy hand. "Your last visit was not, shall we say, nearly as successful as one might have hoped," she began, referring to her niece's sudden propensity for migraines. This had been the second occasion in as many visits that Henriette had excused herself, claiming she was suffering terribly and had to take to her bed. "But you must not forget that you're dealing with a high-strung young woman who's not used to being the center of attention. And if I may be a bit forward for a moment, for after all, we're both seeking the same ends, are we not? I'd advise you to deal with my brother in a way you may not be accustomed to. That is to say Ardaloshka, play down your current financial . . . burdens, shall we say. Ask for no dowry—"

"No dowry?" he exclaimed in a voice several octaves higher than his usual. "But that is quite another thing, Madame, quite another thing altogether. After all, if I'm to make a comfortable home for Henriette Petrovna, I cannot do it without some assistance from her father."

"And you shall get that assistance," she assured him. "But in the interim, let my brother think you are blinded by love—"

"But I am, I am indeed," insisted the General.

"So much the better. Obviously"—she curled her lips down in momentary distaste, as if to say this was as painful a subject for her as it was for him—"money must of course be of some concern. But both Henriette and my brother will think much more of you if you pretend that the needs of your heart carry far greater weight than the needs of your pocketbook."

This the General greeted with silence, finally clearing his throat and inquiring why she was taking such an interest in this affair.

It was then that Varvara took her greatest liberty, knowing that the entire success of her scheme depended upon convincing the General that she was his trusted ally, and that without her assistance he would never be able to win her niece's hand.

"It would seem to me," she began, "and please stop me if I'm wrong, that a man in your position, blessed with the attentions of a young bride, would have need of a mature, settling influence in your home."

"Settling influence, you say?"

"Settling and mature influence," she repeated with a smile that was meant to imply she was the influence in question. "Henriette is a charming girl, and as devout a young woman as any you might find. But she has little experience in dealing with servants, or seeing to the needs of a household. I, on the other hand, would—though with great regret and at considerable personal expense—give up my comfortable life in Moscow to lend a helping hand in the management of your domestic affairs."

"But why?"

"General Tishin, what a thing to ask," she said with a mischievous little laugh.

"I only mean, my dear Varvarushka, that life here at Red

Hill can in no way compare to the glittering world of Moscow."

"Moscow has lost its glitter, dear General," she replied, "for how many balls and soirées can one attend? I tell you, Ardalosha my pet," she snuck in, "it's the same dreary routine, season after boring season. But here at Red Hill, in the company of my lovely niece, I'm certain I'd be able to find the peace of mind that has so far eluded me."

"Yet surely your brother isn't turning you out."

She found his choice of words rather gauche, though she wasn't about to voice a complaint, as this was becoming more difficult than she'd anticipated.

"My brother and I are cut from the same bolt of goods, General. I fear my continued presence at Petrovka would prove an unwanted intrusion. But if you don't have room for me here," and now she rummaged through her reticule, trying desperately to bring tears to her eyes, "that is quite understandable." She dabbed at her bone-dry eyes with her handkerchief, waiting for the moment when the General would rush to her side and hold her in a comforting embrace.

"Now, now, Varya my dear friend. Now, now," whispered the General, who rose from his chair with far more grace than he'd ever exhibited in the past.

Varvara felt his hands on her shoulders and smiled to herself. "I'm only trying to do the best I can," she said with a sob. "I want your life to be as carefree as possible, Ardalosha my dear."

"And it will be, dearest Varya, oh yes, yes indeed. With you here to share my happiness, life will take on new meaning."

Varvara swiveled around in her seat, looking up at the General and smiling as beautifully as she could. "You are my savior," she whispered passionately. "Bless you, Ardaloshka my dearest, bless you." She pressed her lips to his hands, and would have continued right up to his mouth had one of the servants not intruded upon them, bearing a tray on which was arranged a delicate china tea service.

The General stepped back, a blush of boyish embarrassment ruddying his smooth-shaven cheeks. "We must now proceed with alacrity," he told her. "I shall leave it to you to arrange for my next interview with your niece."

"It is as good as done, Ardalosha, as good as done."

Reading from Vvedensky's translation of *Dombey and Son,* Sophia Mikhailovna's gentle, childlike eyes filled with tears. "Oh, little Paul's gone, gone forever," she sobbed after reading the final words of the chapter. "How heartrending, Masha. And the child was so young, too." The leather-bound volume slipped from her fingers, the gold star on its spine winking dimly in the light of the bedside lamp.

Masha closed her eyes and looked away. Her mother's voice had gotten on her nerves, and now Masha was glad the day's reading had finally come to an end. Little Paul's death hadn't affected her at all, for it had only been words, meaningless and devoid of substance. That her mother was still sobbing meant little as well. To see the tears dripping down her cheeks only served to infuriate Masha that her mother hadn't once ventured from her legendary "bed of pain" to visit her while she was recuperating in Mtsensk.

Staring at her mother accusingly, and hearing Victor's words of defiance ringing unhappily in her ears, she felt a terrible need to make someone else suffer as she had. She didn't fully understand it, this rage of hers, but she did know that she had to get some of it out before it began to consume her.

"Why didn't you come to visit me when I was at Irena's?" she asked.

Her mother's slim, girlish hands fluttered to her cheeks,

and she peered at Masha from under her fringe of frizzy curls. "Now where can my precious Laska have gone off to, do you suppose?" She looked anxiously about the room as if she fully expected the pesky little spaniel suddenly to jump out of hiding, bound onto her lap, and demand a biscuit. "Laska! Laska, where are you, *ma chère?*"

Masha sat up in bed and fixed her mother with a bitter glance. "Why don't you stop worrying about your annoying little dog and worry about me?" she cried out, only to feel her lungs respond with an angry shudder, and a series of painful bronchial coughs causing her to shake violently.

"See what happens when you excite yourself?" Sophia Mikhailovna pointed her finger reproachfully. "You mustn't tax yourself. I warned you, you mustn't do anything to aggravate your condition."

"You aggravate my condition," she said when she found her breath. Victor's voice was still inside her head. She couldn't rid herself of it, and now she stared at her mother with mounting fury, that this woman who had borne her could be so insensitive, incapable of thinking of anyone but herself. "Why didn't you come to visit me? You're my own mother, aren't you? Then why don't you ever act like one?"

Sophia Mikhailovna drew back with a start. "Maria Petrovna, what a wicked thing to say to your dear *maman.* I wasn't well, you know that. Why, even this morning I could barely drag myself from bed. The room was spinning, positively going end over end. I thought to myself, 'Sophia Mikhailovna, you must step carefully or else you'll fall on your face,' for everything was rolling about like a ship at sea. But I came to read to you, did I not, taxing my strength because I knew you needed comforting, and a little cheering up."

Masha had heard this same story, these same symptoms, even the same metaphor of a ship at sea, too many times before. She had once been tolerant of her mother's imaginary ailments, but now could no longer find room for sympathy.

"All my life you've barely been able to do anything," she said, wanting her mother to cry as she had cried when Victor had left her. "If it weren't for Irena, I would never have known a mother's love. I could lie here with blood on my lips and all you'd do is ring your hateful bell and throw treats at Laska."

Sophia Mikhailovna began to whimper like a child, and her large, timid eyes grew just as moist as when she'd read of little Paul's death.

"You don't mean that, Masha, you know you don't. I wasn't well, I swear I wasn't. I'm not well now. No one understands, only your father. I'm weak and I'm sickly and everyone makes fun of me because I'm an invalid. But I try, I try very hard."

Masha was unable to stop herself from shouting. "I'm the invalid, not you, and it's time you got out of bed and stayed out of bed. Blood on my lips and all you'd do is just pull the covers over your head."

Her mother trembled in disbelief, for no one had ever said such things to her. She came unsteadily to her feet, her elaborate silk wrapper rustling loudly as she grabbed hold of the chair. Clutching it with all the desperation of a cripple, she said, "Oh, this is not like you, Masha, this is not like you at all to speak so unfeelingly to your own mother. I've tried to do the very best for you, and this is how you repay me. But I know why. You're feeling sorry for yourself because you've not been well. But it will pass. Oh, it must, Masha, it truly must, for you can't treat me so cruelly. I won't allow it."

Masha was glad to see the tears dripping down her mother's wrinkled cheeks, glad to see her curls looking bedraggled and her hands all aflutter. But most of all, Masha was glad that someone finally had the courage to tell Sophia Mikhailovna the truth.

"You're as healthy as Anninka, yet you've managed to escape responsibility by hiding in your bed. But you haven't fooled me in the least, Mother. You're strong, and you're healthy, and you don't want anyone to know. But I know. I know your secret."

"It's not true," her mother insisted, pressing one hand to her breast as if any moment her heart would give out. "I'm a sick woman. The wedding alone set my health back irreparably. I lost a year, at least a full year, because of all the excitement."

"You didn't lose anything but Vera, and maybe you never even had her to begin with, letting Irena do your job for you all those years."

"Masha!" gasped her mother.

Masha turned over onto her side and closed her eyes. "Blood on my lips," she whispered, "and all you'd do is ring your bell. I'm tired now. Please go away, Mother. Just go away and leave me alone."

Several hours later, a shabby carriage with rattling, rusty mudguards drove into the courtyard. It was just a little two-wheeled affair, lacking a proper box for the driver, so that for the past thirty minutes Vera had been forced to endure both the smell and the company of one of Golovlovo's peasants. Although she wanted to say something to him about it, she'd heard what had happened to Count Roman Durnovo, and decided it wouldn't be wise to criticize. Instead, she held a handkerchief to her nose under the pretext that she felt a cold coming on, and was certain the dust from the road would only hasten the onset of her illness.

Once inside the house, she breathed more easily. After chatting with Anninka, and telling her how wonderful everything was, and how she was so in love her head was still in the clouds, she went upstairs to see her sister. When she knocked on the door and entered Masha's room, she was shocked by what she saw, not expecting Masha to look any different than she had at the wedding, a few weeks before. Instead, she saw a girl she hardly recognized, with pale, hollow cheeks, and eyes that gleamed with an unhealthy fire.

"Masha, what have you done to yourself? You look terrible," she said before she realized that wasn't the way to greet a sister who was grievously ill. So to make up for it, she started to Masha's bedside, only to hesitate a moment when she recalled what Simon had said, that consumption was a nasty business, and if she didn't take every precaution she might very well come down with it herself.

Masha motioned her to a nearby chair, and Vera dropped into it with an exaggerated sigh, as if she'd just come halfway around the world. Peeling off her nut-brown gloves, and complaining that all her clothes were hopelessly out of fashion, she kept avoiding Masha's eyes. It was very disconcerting to see her sister looking so poorly, especially since Masha was so young, and had always seemed to Vera to be rather pretty, though a bit too bookish and intellectual for her own good.

"So tell me everything!" she exclaimed brightly. "I'm just starved for gossip."

Masha shook her head, and a faint smile creased her lips.

"Nothing to tell?"

"It's just hard to talk, that's all," Masha said, speaking so softly that Vera was forced to move her chair a little closer to the bed.

"Does it hurt?"

"Sometimes."

"Do you feel like you're drowning, do you suppose? Is it like being underwater?"

"Occasionally."

"How boring to be sick, and you so young. Oh, I hope it doesn't happen to me. Perhaps I should hold a handkerchief to my mouth, do you think?"

"If you wish."

"Well, maybe not," she said reluctantly, sensing that all this talk wasn't making Masha feel any better. "But I have the most interesting news, just fascinating." She bent forward from the waist, not wanting to move her chair any closer to Masha's sickbed. "You'll be very interested to learn that your Count hasn't been taken to Petersburg, as was originally intended."

To judge from her sister's reaction, this piece of information was definitely as choice as she'd imagined. Masha pushed herself back until she was sitting up in bed. Her cheeks, yellowish a moment before, were now suffused with a much healthier-looking color, splotches of red highlighting her glistening dark eyes.

"Tell me what you know," Masha whispered.

"Well . . ." she began, putting as much dramatic emphasis into the word as she could, and leaning over still farther so that she was barely sitting in the chair, "he was supposed to be sent to the Fortress, but instead they sent him to Moscow."

"How did you find this out?"

"Simon and Kalinovich are very close friends," she explained. "And Simon told me that Kalinovich told him that your Count was being sent to Butyrky Prison because there wasn't any room in the Fortress. Quite full up, he said it was. I suppose that's because of what happened to the Tsar, and a good thing too, for who wants all these murderers lurking about, killing innocent people like that poor little baker's boy who died when they threw the bomb. So that's why they sent him to Moscow, because there wasn't a cell to be had in all of Petersburg."

She thought that after hearing news like this, Masha would have something to be optimistic about, for surely Butyrky wasn't nearly as terrible a place as the Fortress of St. Peter and St. Paul. But instead of looking pleased that her Count would have an easier time of it, Masha seemed to shrivel up right before her eyes.

"I don't see why you're getting so upset," Vera said as Masha rearranged the pillows and lay down again.

"How can you be so silly, Vera? If Simon was arrested, wouldn't you be upset?"

"Of course, but I love him."

"And I love Victor Romanovich."

"You don't!" she cried out. "Oh, what a thing to say. How can you love someone who wants to kill people?"

"He doesn't want to kill anybody, Vera."

"Then why would they arrest him?"

"Why don't you ask Simon that? Or better yet, ask Kalinovich."

"Well, you needn't get angry with me," she replied, not at all pleased with the way her sister was addressing her. "After all, it's not my fault they found those papers on him. I certainly didn't put them there, and I didn't ask for him to be arrested, either. I hardly know the man."

"That's about the truest thing you've ever said, Vera." Masha glanced over at the window, which was open just a crack so that fresh air could circulate through the room. "I think I hear Father's carriage. Perhaps you'd like to go down to see him. I'm going to try to get some rest."

Vera came to her feet, unhappy with the way the visit had gone, and the reproving manner in which her sister continued to look at her, as if she were the cause of Masha's unhappiness, and not Victor Durnovo.

"I should never have told you anything," Vera announced. "It's only turned you against me, Masha, and that's terribly unfair when you know how much I love you."

"Do you love me, Vera? Do you really care about me?"

"Oh, of course I do." Against her better judgment she rushed to her sister's side, and even sacrificed endangering her health by gingerly seating herself on the edge of Masha's bed. Stroking her sister's painfully thin hands, she told Masha how upsetting it was to see her so sick and unhappy.

"So you mustn't think I wish to hurt you," Vera concluded, "because it's just not so. After all, we're sisters, aren't we?"

Masha smiled faintly. "Yes, Vera, we're sisters."

"Then it's all settled," she said happily as she patted Masha's hand. "I'll come see you before you go off to Moscow. And if you're good, you silly, I'll tell you about . . . well . . . I've learned quite a bit. The most amazing things, Masha!"

"I wouldn't doubt it, Vera."

Not sure how her sister meant that, Vera blew her a kiss and hurried downstairs. Her father had just sat down to dinner, a place having been set for her at the table. After kissing him on the cheek and asking if there was anything she could bring him, she finally settled down in her seat.

"So how is married life, Vera? Everything it's cut out to be?"

"It's fine, Papa."

"Just *fine?*"

"It's wonderful, actually. Simon Ivanovich is a wonderful husband, but—" Before she could start explaining, the kitchen door swung back and Anninka, with one of the serving girls in tow, came in with the dinner.

Her father immediately dug into the sweet and peppered sheatfish as if he hadn't had a decent meal in weeks.

"Yes, a wonderful husband," Vera spoke up, desperate to pick up the threads of conversation before her father became too engrossed in his dinner. "Only we have problems, Papa, and that's what I have to talk to you about, dearest *Papochka*. I need your help."

"So does half the district," he said with a contemptuous laugh, nearly choking on a bone as a result. His face turned very red as if it were all her fault, but then he managed to clear his throat, and told her to fetch the wine.

Vera sprang to her feet and ran to the sideboard.

"Mind you, don't spill any," he warned, his little round, gray eyes peering at her suspiciously.

But she was so upset with the way he was staring at her that she just couldn't help herself. The bottle of sauterne jumped about in her hands as if it had a life of its own, and a puddle formed around the base of her father's glass.

"You wouldn't think a girl of your delicacy could be so clumsy," the elder Petrov remarked. He snatched the bottle from her hands, ordering her back to her chair.

Vera decided he was a hateful old man, that he really was glad he'd gotten rid of her, and that if he never saw her again he probably wouldn't even think twice about it. Watching him now, as he stuffed his face and slobbered and made all sorts of repulsive sounds, she wanted to shake him and ask him why he was so mean, and why he didn't love her the way he had when she was little. Then he'd laugh and lift her up in his powerful arms, carrying her about and telling her this was how the world would look when she was tall. Or else he'd have her climb into his lap, and stroking her soft, yellow hair, he'd tell her how much he loved her, and that she was his dearest little Verochka, and he'd always look after her, forever and ever.

Silly me, she thought, to have believed all that. He probably would have married me off to that fat General Tishin if Senya hadn't come along. He just thinks about himself, and all the money he's hidden away, and how to make even more, while I don't even have a decent bed to sleep in, and every time I go out on the porch I have to watch out that I don't fall through, there are so many holes.

"Well, go on, Vera, tell me how married life is treating you," her father spoke up, now that he'd made short work of his fish and was ready to start on the next course, a savory chicken-and-mushroom pie.

"It's difficult for us, Papa. If only you could give me a little more money, just to help us out until Simon gets settled."

Before he could start to object, she rushed into the speech she'd rehearsed while driving to Petrovka. Everything at Golovlovo was falling apart, she told him, and it just wasn't right that one of Peter Semyonovich's daughters, a man who was respected throughout the district, should have to live in such squalor. But with a little extra money, she'd be able to fix up Golovlovo and make a proper home for herself and her husband. "And your future grandchildren," she added, hoping this would arouse his sympathy even if nothing else had.

"What about the dowry, the five thousand rubles I gave your husband?"

Vera, after hemming and hawing for several minutes, was finally forced to admit that Simon was using the money for investments.

"What kind?"

"He won't tell me. He says the money has to be saved for more important things, that I have to learn to live as frugally as possible."

"Quite right, quite right," agreed her father. "He's obviously a man after my own heart, for he knows his priorities."

Oh, if she only knew where he kept his money she would go and take it, right then and there. Yes, that's precisely what she'd do. She'd take enough to make life bearable again, to fix up Golovlovo so she wouldn't have to be afraid to go out to the privy with the spiders and the rats and everything dark and foul-smelling. She'd never had to live that way before, and she certainly didn't intend to start getting used to it now.

"And what does he intend to do, may I ask, now that he has a wife to support?"

"His friend Mikhail Ilyich, the *ispravnik,* says the government is looking for good men, that the new Tsar needs the help of people like him, men who are loyal and trustworthy, who can be depended upon. So he's going to put in a good word with his superiors. Perhaps something will come of it."

"Oh, I'm sure it will."

She heard the sarcasm in his voice, but pretended not to notice, asking instead about the money.

Peter Semyonovich pushed his chair away from the table as if to say now that he'd finished his dinner, he'd also finished the discussion. "I've given you all that I intend to, Vera, and that's my last word on the subject."

"But we're destitute!" she cried out, and would have flung herself at his feet if she felt it would have made a difference.

"Then tell your husband to get a job. Anninka will give you some food to take home, if you need. After all, Vera dear, your papa wouldn't want you to go hungry."

There was no sense crying because the tears would only be wasted. One day I'll find out where he hides his money, she thought as her father, cracking his knuckles and belching loudly, turned away without so much as a good-bye. Yes, I'll find out where you keep it, and then you'll really be sorry, you mean, selfish old man.

She was so upset by the interview with her father that it wasn't until she was halfway home that she realized she'd forgotten her gloves, having left them upstairs in Masha's room. But since she didn't particularly care for them, and according to the illustrated magazines, nut-brown was definitely out of fashion, she decided she'd just have to ask Simon to buy her another pair. After all, what were 3 rubles when he still had 4,997?

With barely enough time to enjoy the leftover sheatfish, Simon Belinsky threw on his old army greatcoat, kissed his wife on the cheek, and hurried outside to see if his carriage was ready. Behind him the door swung shut a second time, and then Vera's irritating voice was heard.

"Where are you going, Senya dear? You promised you'd stay home, and we'd be together."

"Tomorrow."

"But I don't want to wait until tomorrow," she whined, stamping her little foot so that the rotting floorboards creaked in protest. "I'm bored, and I have nothing to do, and it's lonely here with no one to talk to. I thought we'd . . . Simon, why can't I go with you?"

"Because I have an appointment." He looked at her out of the corner of his eye, not particularly displeased with what he saw. She was a fetching little thing if she'd only learn to keep her mouth shut. He was of a good mind to tell her that, when the doddering old fool who smelled like a billy goat, and who'd been in his father's service and thus was now in his, finally brought the carriage around.

Holding the reins in readiness, the servant weaved back and forth as if he'd had too much to drink. When Simon sprang into the carriage, he seized the reins so abruptly that the old man lost his balance and teetered back, catching himself just before he was about to fall.

"Simon!"

That awful screechy voice, he thought with a shudder. Why can't she learn to modulate her tones, and coo like a proper lady, instead of yowling like a cat in heat?

"I'll be back before you know it, my little dove." He blew

her a kiss, hoping that would satisfy her and give her something to treasure until he returned. Then he drove out of the courtyard, past the sagging wattle fence, and onto the road that led into the village.

Less than ten minutes later his rusty trap stood next to a motley collection of wretched little peasant carts and skinny skewbald nags. His sorrel trotter was tethered by a hitching strap to a trough hollowed out of a tree trunk that lay in the shadow of the tavern roof. The latter extended some distance beyond where the inn itself terminated, so as to form a convenient shelter for the numerous horses and shaggy ponies snorting and whinnying in the night air.

From inside the long, low building came the steady murmur of voices, voices that grew much louder the moment he stepped over the threshold. Knowing it was the expected thing to do, and aware of the many sets of eyes that were turned inquisitively in his direction, Simon bowed and crossed himself before the ikon that hung over the threshold.

He stood there a moment, trying to find Kalinovich in the crowd. The *traktir* smelled of burned meat and cheap tobacco. It was so insufferably close, and so heavy with the fumes of spirits, that he felt a little dizzy as he passed through the dark entry and made his way into the main room.

The *traktir* was the social hub of the village, and as such was usually crowded with peasants who sat in their greasy sheepskins smelling of tallow, drinking tea when they were broke, and hard white liquor, hot and straight, when they weren't. Rarely if ever did any of the neighboring landlords venture inside, for not only was the tavern filthy and bug-ridden, but it was also the unspoken province of the moujiks, a place they could call their own, and where they could do as they pleased without having to worry about offending a member of the gentry. Thus Belinsky's arrival was certainly no cause for celebration, and he tried to make himself as inconspicuous as possible while he looked around for his friend.

A wooden counter ran the entire length of one side of the room, and served as a bar, over which drinks were sold. Presiding over the bottles and glasses was the innkeeper, whose black satin waistcoat was liberally smeared with grease, and whose entire face and beard was so sweaty that it shone like a freshly oiled iron lock. Belinsky walked up to him, and inquiring after the *ispravnik*, was sullenly directed to a far corner of the room, where, at a table covered with a filthy red cloth, his friend was waiting.

"Right on time, Simon Ivanovich, right on time," Kalinovich said, thumping him on the back as Belinsky pulled up a chair.

A bottle of vodka—the more expensive white seal, as opposed to the ordinary and barely drinkable red—and two dirty glasses were set out on the table, as well as a plate on which were heaped some salted gherkins, a couple of hunks of dried black bread, and a few pieces of herring that smelled as bad as they looked.

The *ispravnik* poured him a glass of vodka, then watched him intently as he downed half of it in a single gulp. "I must commend you, Senya. You've done an excellent job, and one that I'm certain will prove very lucrative for both of us."

"You understand I had nothing personal against him," he replied as he felt the liquor reach his stomach, immediately warming his insides.

"Of course. Business is business. Besides, the pamphlets were there, weren't they? And even if Roman Durnovo hadn't gotten what he deserved, and they hadn't set fire to his house, I still would have searched his son's belongings. Standard procedure, Senya. So you needn't feel guilty."

"Guilty?" He began to laugh, because that was one emotion he'd never had to contend with, not since he was a boy. "All I did was remind you of his past history. You saw him at the wedding, just as I did. If a man wants to do foolish things and tempt fate, I certainly can't be held accountable."

"But how convenient it is for us, don't you agree?" Mikhail Ilyich poured himself another tumblerful of vodka. The angular lines of his face softened in the dim, smoke-filled light of the *traktir*, and only the cynical expression in his eyes betrayed what he was really thinking.

For several months now, Simon had been supplying the *ispravnik* with bits and pieces of information, keeping his ears as wide open as his eyes, so to speak. He was not a police informer per se, but rather someone who saw no reason not to help his friend, particularly when Kalinovich always paid him so generously for his time. Having hoped the end result would be a position in government service, either directly under the police chief as his personal assistant, or perhaps as *stanovoy* in one of the neighboring districts, he hadn't realized that his "passion for upholding the law"—for such was the way Kalinovich jokingly described it—might ultimately prove to be quite profitable. Yet if things worked out the way they planned, Simon could very conceivably double, or even treble, his initial investment.

Because of Count Roman Durnovo's death, and the subsequent imprisonment of his son and sole heir, the State now had the right to auction off Jerichovo, selling it to the highest bidder. Behind bars, Victor Romanovich was a nonperson, afforded none of the privileges of the gentry, and deprived of all personal and property rights. There was one technicality, however: Durnovo hadn't been brought to trial yet. But as Kalinovich now explained, that could very easily be circumvented, what with the actual evidence he'd secured and Durnovo's own admission that the illegal pamphlets were his.

Thus Kalinovich now informed Simon that they should proceed with all haste, and arrange for a public auction to be held as quickly as possible. But as *ispravnik*, Kalinovich would be conducting the auction himself, as his position carried with it complete responsibility and jurisdiction over just this sort of thing. And if he chose not to tell anyone, so much the better.

"Needless to say," remarked Kalinovich, looking quite pleased with himself as he leaned across the table, "the *public* isn't going to find out about this. After all, why should they, when you and I are public enough?" He snickered loudly, thumping his fist against the table so that the all-but-empty bottle of vodka did a merry little dance.

Simon returned his friend's greedy smile. "And with the dowry money—"

"And my share—"

"We'll be able to buy up Jerichovo for next to nothing. There won't be anybody bidding against us, Misha, because no one's going to know what we're up to."

"What do you intend to do with your share of the land, once we've secured the deed?" asked Kalinovich.

Simon chuckled loudly. "Sell it to old man Petrov. What else?" he said with a laugh. "And at a hefty profit too, I might add." He found this so satisfying that he called to the inn-keeper for another bottle of vodka, determined to celebrate now that the deed was as good as his, and now that he'd figured out a perfect way to get back at his father-in-law, and beat him at his own game.

Eight

Several weeks after Masha had first taken ill, a letter arrived from Professor Ostroumov in Moscow. Cordial in tone, and with none of the standoffishness one might have expected from an eminent medical specialist, Ostroumov agreed to see her at his clinic at the Moscow University Hospital, and had reserved a bed for this purpose in one of the wards.

"Then it's settled," Peter Semyonovich announced after hearing the news. "Though why I have to pay these inflated Moscow fees is beyond my comprehension. Specialists . . . stuff and nonsense," he snorted irritably. "Why, when I was a boy, the word wasn't even invented."

If there was anything that annoyed him it was spending money on something he couldn't hold in his hands. And medical treatment was certainly not a commodity he could very easily weigh on a scale. But since everyone was convinced that Masha's health depended upon it, and even the doctor in Mtsensk seemed to have fallen under this Ostroumov's spell, Peter Semyonovich decided that despite the cost he'd best follow their advice, and do what was expected of him.

Over dinner the very same day, Gregor asked his father if he might be allowed to accompany Masha to Moscow, for surely his sister was too ill to travel unescorted.

Petrov raised his head and looked at him as if he were a fool. "You'll stay right here, you good-for-nothing, right here at Petrovka where I can keep an eye on you. Your mother or your aunt will chaperone Masha."

"Oh no, I couldn't possibly," Sophia Mikhailovna said in alarm. Though she had ventured forth from her bedroom to sample Anninka's culinary skills, the trip from the second floor to the first was as far as she intended to go. "I'm just not up to it, Petrushka dear," she told her husband. Her eyes grew wide with fright, so that Laska, sensing her anxiety, jumped into her lap and barked a warning, lest anyone say anything else that might upset her beloved mistress.

"Then Varvara will have to go," Peter Semyonovich replied as he speared a chunk of roast veal and popped it into his eager mouth. He looked over at his sister. "After all, I'm sure you're anxious to get home, aren't you, Varya dear?"

Varvara wisely chose to ignore her brother's mocking tone, and his attempt at intimidating her was in no way successful. "Are you asking me to leave, Petya?" she exclaimed, feigning surprise that he could be so unfeeling.

"Moscow is your home, Varya dear," he countered with an oily smile.

"Indeed it is. But Petrovka is my home away from home, is it not?"

Henriette, having remained silent throughout this exchange, though she was quite delighted to see them bickering, now decided the time had come to speak up. "Why can't I be allowed to go with Masha?" she asked. "The trip would do me good, Father. And if Auntie V. wants to return home, as I'm sure she's had quite enough of us, why, I suppose I could stay with her in Moscow and save you all that money."

"How could you possibly go when you're about to be betrothed?" replied her aunt.

Peter Semyonovich seemed so intrigued by this piece of news that he leaned over his plate, the result of which was a large gravy stain on the front of his waistcoat.

"Yes, General Tishin has made his intentions perfectly clear," Varvara went on, "and so I've promised him an audience with you. He's quite smitten with our Henriette. I fear his heart will break if she turns him down."

"Then I'm afraid he'd best prepare himself for the worst," Henriette told them, infuriated by the way they were discussing her future as if she weren't even there.

Her father, having been more than patient with her and her migraines these past several weeks, decided the time had come to lay down the law, and make it perfectly clear to his daughter that whether or not she approved of the match was not his concern. He now told her this, succinctly and unsympathetically, raising his voice so that even Anninka rushed in from the kitchen to see what the commotion was all about.

Henriette, determined to maintain a brave front, was nevertheless reduced to tears by her father's attack. "You can't force me against my will," she said, weeping though her eyes confounded her by remaining dry.

"Is there a new law I haven't heard about?" Peter Semyonovich turned his eyes on the table at large. "Has the Tsar decided in your favor, Henriette, is that what you're trying to tell me? Let me see the official documents, dear girl, and I'll be the first to congratulate you."

"I won't," she whispered, determined not to be victimized. "You can make fun of me all you want, but you can't force me."

"I can do whatever I please." Petrov turned to his sister. "When does the General plan to speak to me?"

"I suggested this coming Friday afternoon, if that's suitable."

"Perfectly suitable. I look forward to it with keen anticipation. So he finds our little Henriette captivating, does he? Well, that's excellent, for in time she'll learn to be captivated, too."

Alone in her room, the door locked, the curtains drawn over a sullen gray sky entirely in keeping with her frame of mind, Henriette lit a fresh candle and knelt before the three-tiered ikon stand in the corner of her bedroom. Pressing her bony knees against the wax-stained strip of carpet on which she made her obeisances, she clasped her hands to her breast and let the tears run freely down her cheeks.

Surrounded by a fretted silver ikon-cover, the gaunt and ascetic face of the Redeemer in a crown of thorns stared back at her. His hollow cheeks, blond hair, and thin, pale, pointed beard accentuated the sorrow she read in his eyes, and the desperate measures he would surely take to save her soul.

"Grant me understanding," she whispered fervently. "Shining light of the world, come and enter within me and purify me of all these frightening thoughts."

In the flickering of the little wax taper, and the blood-red glitter of the unquenchable ikon lamp, the Savior looked down at her with sadness and compassion.

"Jesus Christ, Son of God, be merciful to me, poor sinner that I am, for Thine own Mother's sake!" she wept.

Henriette closed her eyes, pressing her forehead to the floor so that the blood rushed to her temples. She began to whimper and then to sob, for she felt so alone, so abused and tormented, deceived at every side. They would use her like chattel, and cast her out when they were done with her. She was filled with irrepressible rage and longing, rage that her aunt and her father despised her so, conspiring against her while she remained powerless to stop them; and longing for someone to take her away from all this, someone like gentle Jesus, the Redeemer of all tormented souls. With sad, merciful eyes and delicate features, he would be her passionate protector, avenging the wrongs that she'd suffered, the injustices she had so long and patiently endured. He would understand the meaning of bitterness just as He understood the meaning of compassion, and after teaching her all the mysteries of love, faith, and devotion, she would then be safe forever, never again to experience anguish or sorrow.

But where was her Redeemer? Why hadn't He come for her? If only she were beautiful like spoiled little Vera, she'd know exactly how to use her good looks to proper advantage.

But I can't change the way I look, no matter how hard I try, she thought. I can't do anything. This is how I am, and this is how I'm going to stay. Wishes won't make me pretty, and faith in the Lord will only ease my pain, not make me beautiful.

She raised her eyes then, gazing at an ikon depicting the Virgin-of-the-Bush-that-burned-but-was-not-consumed. It began to tremble as if it were alive, and the halo of starlike points surrounding the Mother of God burst into flame, tongues of fiery red and yellow shooting up all around her kind and gentle face. Then the Blessed Virgin shook her head sadly, as if to say, "My poor dear child, is there nothing I can do to lessen your burdens?"

"Give me your Son," she whispered.

No sooner had she said these words than she saw Him standing before her, with long blond hair parted in the middle and flowing in fine, silken strands over His beautiful white neck and shoulders. His thin, pale lips began to move, and then she heard His voice, murmuring strange, voluptuous words that only she could understand.

Henriette trembled in ecstasy, and a delicious warmth

began to spread through her body. She threw herself down on the strip of carpet, and closing her eyes again, listened mesmerized as the voice of her Savior whispered in her ear. One day He would come for her, He said, and holding her in His embrace, would make her one with Him. Then she would never have anything to fear, for He would be with her forever.

When she looked up, everything was as it always was. The candle flickered, beads of translucent wax dripping onto the carpet. The crystal ikon lamp sent crimson shadows rushing across the faces of her beloved saints and martyrs, crowded together on the lowest tier of the ikon shrine. Henriette came shakily to her feet, making sure to cross herself before she turned away. This wasn't the first time she'd seen the Son of God, and though she sensed it was nothing more than some part of her imagination made animate by the strength of her beliefs, for only holy men had visions, and not unhappy daughters, she nevertheless felt a great sense of well-being. Seeing Him standing there before her gave her hope that one day she might indeed meet someone who would be the hero of every fairy tale, and just as in the fable of Prince Ivan and Helena the Beautiful, they would live in such harmony and love that neither could exist a single moment without the other.

When Henriette came downstairs, she found her brother waiting for her on the terrace.

"I have a plan, my stately beauty," Gregor announced, glancing behind him as if the walls had ears. "Come, we'll take a walk and I'll tell you all about it."

They started in the direction of the orchard, the gray sky heavy with the promise of rain. Along the path, clumps of stunted heartsease had taken root, while in the orchard itself there were more of the same. Here and there tall, dark-green tufts of hellebore were scattered about, looking shaggy and unkempt. The fruit trees had still not blossomed, most of the gnarled old apples disfigured by props and cankers. But the grass was thick beneath her feet, a dense, spongy carpet that lightened her step, if not her mood.

"What am I going to do, Grisha?" she asked, bending down to pluck a dandelion from the grass.

"What do you want to do?"

"I want to get away from here. I want to make my own life. I want—" She paused a moment, wondering if she could open her heart to him. "Are you as lonely as I am?" she burst out.

Gregor sank down onto the grass, leaning against the trunk of a plum tree. "Not lonely so much as dissatisfied." He drew a cigarette from his jacket pocket, and though the wind had begun to pick up, he managed to get it lit.

"Is it our destiny, do you suppose?" she asked, joining him on the grass.

"The hell with our destiny," Gregor said heatedly. "Let's worry about General Tishin, shall we? Now you're not going to marry him, that's one thing we can agree on."

"But if I turn him down, Father will disinherit me, and then I'll be worse off than when I started."

"Then run away."

Henriette laughed bitterly. "Without any money? I wouldn't get much farther than Mtsensk."

"What if we found you a position? Would that suit you, do you think?" Gregor ground his cigarette out beneath his boot, then proceeded to explain what he had in mind. Irena's husband was just the man to see. Unless Gregor was mistaken, Volsky had several valuable contacts in Petersburg, and might be convinced to arrange something for his sister-in-law.

"Father would never consent to my leaving Petrovka. And even the suggestion might convince him to disinherit me."

"Which would you prefer then, dearest chuck: being penniless and free, or having people call you *Madame la Générale?*"

Henriette looked down at her lap. What choice did she have? She would die if the General touched her, for she could think of nothing more repulsive than sharing her bed with Ardallion Hippolytovich. If she refused to marry him, her father would cut her out of his will, anyway. She had no choice but to finally do something for herself, something that would aid her in accomplishing her goals and realizing her fondest dreams.

A brilliantly lit drawing room, spacious and grand, and filled with endless variations of her Savior, took shape in her mind. She saw herself descending a magnificent marble staircase, every eye turned adoringly in her direction, worshiping glances following her every step. *La Belle Henriette,* they would call her and crowd around, basking in the glow of her sparkling wit and charm, her wickedly amusing double entendres.

"Yes, Nikolai Alexandrovich is just the man to ask," she said, needing no further encouragement. "Shall we drive over to Mtsensk right away, or would that make Father too suspicious?"

"He's with his steward. And if he asks, we'll say we went to pick up some books for Masha, since she had nothing left to read." Gregor jumped up, brushed off the seat of his pants, and helped her to her feet. "We'll make an adventure of it, Henriette. Just the two of us. And after we've settled your affairs, we'll take care of mine."

On Friday, the day before Masha and Auntie V. were scheduled to leave for Moscow, General Tishin arrived at Petrovka to ask Peter Semyonovich for his daughter's hand. Henriette was in Masha's room when she heard the General's carriage splash through the mud as it drove into the yard.

Up until this moment, she had been rather calm. But now that General Tishin was finally here, as agonizingly prompt as always, panic took hold of her.

"Oh my God, he's here," she whispered. "The fatted calf . . . oh Masha, what am I going to do?"

"Just what we discussed," Masha said as she lay in bed, smiling gently and looking better than she had in weeks. "Didn't Gregor come back from Mtsensk last night with good news? Nikolai has already sent word to his friend in Petersburg. It's just a matter of time before he hears from him."

"But I don't have time, that's the problem. There isn't any time at all. I won't marry him," she said. It took little in the way of imagination to picture him climbing into bed with her, naked and groaning, squeezing the life out of her as he pressed her into his arms. "I'll kill myself first, I really will. I'll tie a rope around my neck, or drink Paris green, or cut my throat, or . . . or something."

Downstairs, however, things weren't nearly so desperate. Varvara, presiding over the samovar, was pouring tea. When she handed a cup to the General, she smiled coquettishly as she drew his attention to the inscription that ran around the outside of the rim.

"'Cupid's dart hath pierced my heart,'" she recited with a grin.

"Apt, oh yes, very apt indeed," agreed the General, who seemed much more nervous than usual. "A charming home you have, Madame Petrova, utterly charming and captivating," he said as he returned to his place, having elected to sit on the enormous faded blue sofa, for he'd have little trouble getting in and out of it.

"It's only because you grace it with your presence," replied Sophia Mikhailovna. She was completely captivated by the General's courtly manners, and smiled approvingly at her sister-in-law, that Varvara had been so thoughtful as to introduce poor Henriette to such a dashing figure of a man.

"I've heard the most amusing anecdote," the General began, when Peter Semyonovich immediately cut him short.

"Some other time perhaps, General. I fear if we wait much longer my wife won't be able to remain in our company."

"Yes, I've not been well. It's a weakness, you know," confided Sophia Mikhailovna. "Every time I take a step it's just as if I'm cruising down the Volga."

"The Volga? How remarkable," said the General, giving her his rapt and devoted attention.

"Yes, everything sways and rolls about like a ship at sea. Or on the Volga, whichever."

"So you see," interrupted her husband, "it would be best if we got on with the business at hand."

"Oh, I agree, most assuredly," replied the General, opening his sleepy blue eyes very wide and nodding his head emphatically. "As you know—as indeed, you all must know—thanks to the kind and generous efforts of your charming sister, I've come here today to your delightful home, Madame Petrova, to your handsome and prosperous estate, Peter Semyonovich, to ask for the hand of your daughter."

Madame Petrova sighed so loudly and with such fervor that everyone in the drawing room looked anxiously in her direction. "It's quite all right," she whispered, fanning herself with her slim, girlish hand. "It's just that I've dreamed of such a day, when someone of your refinement, General Tishin, would come and sweep our dear little Henriette off her feet."

"I couldn't agree more," her husband said impatiently. "But I cannot, in all good conscience, send her to the altar without first knowing what her future circumstances will be like. Therefore, General, if you'd be so kind as to tell me how you intend to provide for her?"

All eyes were turned expectantly on the General, who flushed beet-red now that the moment of truth was at hand. Drawing an enormous monogrammed handkerchief from the pocket of his frock coat, he paused to mop his brow.

"*Mes circonstances?*" he squeaked.

"*Mais oui, vos circonstances,*" said Peter Semyonovich.

Tishin gazed at his lap, as if the answer were printed on his trousers. "Krasnaya Gorka consists of nearly five hundred acres, yielding an annual income of seven hundred rubles," he said in a barely audible voice.

It was obvious from Petrov's reaction that he had no idea the General lived so modestly. "That's all?" he asked.

Again the General drew out his oversized handkerchief and dabbed at the beads of sweat that were rolling down his forehead.

"But nothing is mortgaged, Peter Semyonovich, not an acre. And I was hoping, of course . . . that is to say, if you'd permit me to venture a guess, that perhaps when this blessed union was sanctified—"

"Come to the point, General. You want to know how large her dowry will be, don't you? Well, I've given it a great deal of thought, and I should think five thousand rubles would be quite sufficient, General, don't you agree?"

"Oh yes, yes, indeed. That would be most generous, Peter Semyonovich, most generous and gracious and—"

"Excellent." Petrov jumped to his feet, clasping the General's hand. "A glorious day, just glorious," he crowed excitedly, telling his sister to fetch Henriette and bring her downstairs.

"I told you not to wear gray," Varvara hissed as she escorted her niece into the drawing room.

Henriette held her tongue, and avoiding the General's lecherous eye, for she was certain he was trying to figure out how she looked beneath her clothes, she took a seat next to her mother.

"Ardallion Hippolytovich has done our family the honor of asking for your hand," her father announced.

"And what an exalted honor it is," sighed her aunt.

"Oh yes," agreed her mother, who began to weep loudly and copiously, calling for her smelling salts, as she felt quite faint from all the excitement.

"What do you have to say, Henriette?" asked her father.

She'd thought of her response beforehand, and having gone over it with Masha, Henriette now spoke clearly and resolutely, trying to lead them off the track by being as polite and well mannered as circumstances would allow. She said that although she was flattered by the General's offer, and grateful that he held her in such esteem as to wish to marry her, at the present time she could only think of her sister Masha's health.

"But if the General will be so kind as to wait until my sister returns from Moscow, I promise that I'll have an answer for him," she concluded.

"But why wait?" said Varvara, sounding vexed by the delay.

"And what kind of answer do you have in mind?" added her father.

"Only an answer that is fitting," she replied.

She glanced at the General, suppressing a shudder of revulsion he sat there in his foppish clothes. His waistcoat was brightly adorned with an entire meadow of little blue flowers, over which he'd barely managed to stuff himself into a grass-colored frock coat that may have been the height of fashion, but on him looked utterly ridiculous. But she wasn't angry with him, certain this was all her aunt's doing, and that he never would have looked twice at her had Varvara not insisted they be introduced.

"Charmingly put, *mademoiselle*," replied the General. Although he was greatly disappointed, he was enough of a gentleman not to pressure her for a more definite answer. "But if you'll permit me to continue to call on you, I should be most grateful."

Henriette grit her teeth. But thinking of all that Masha and Gregor had said, and the promise made by her brother-in-law to do everything he could to help her, she forced herself to look agreeable.

"Of course, General Tishin. I shall look forward to receiving you in the very near future." Now that the worst was over, at least for the time being, Henriette permitted herself to smile, and was still smiling long after the General had left.

Everything was ready for Masha's departure. Her bags had been packed and loaded onto her father's dusty old phaeton, for he insisted there was no need to harness four horses to the barouche when two on the phaeton would do just as nicely. Varvara, who had arrived with three large suitcases, was unhappily about to depart with just as many. Unbeknownst to her, her brother had made what he called "a tour of inspection." When he saw how she'd purposely left behind many of her belongings, fully intending to return, he immediately had them packed and brought downstairs.

"Look what you've forgotten, Varya dear," he said, showing her the extra suitcase she'd left in her room, and clucking his tongue in a most obnoxious fashion.

She began to protest, for her brother had been a bully even as a child, and she had no intention of letting him intimidate her now that they were both fully grown.

"Now Varya, you've had a lovely visit, and we've enjoyed every moment of your company. But you must be so tired of us by now."

Utterly incensed by the sarcasm she heard in his voice, Varvara completely lost her head. She began to rail at him as she hadn't done since the day, nearly thirty years before, when they'd actually come to blows over the provisions of their father's will.

"After all I've done for you," she said angrily, and the three little black hairs crowning the mole on her chin quivered just as heatedly. "If it wasn't for me, Henriette would have nobody!"

Her brother maintained his composure, infuriating her all the more by his refusal to raise his voice.

"We'll look forward to seeing you at the wedding," he said calmly. "Won't we, Sonyushka?" He turned to his wife, who had just entered the drawing room.

"Whatever you say, Petrushka dear," she replied, wearing that stuporous look that always remained with her after a nap.

The entire family was due to assemble in just another few minutes. Knowing this, Varvara sat herself down in a chair, gripped both arms with steely determination, and announced that she wasn't going anywhere, that they'd have to drag her from the house, chair and all, if they wanted to get rid of her.

"Fifty years ago you were a nasty little boy. And fifty years later you've grown into an even nastier man. How dare you treat me this way, Peter Semyonovich? This was my home as a child, too. Just because the laws were different then, and a daughter was entitled to just a fraction of her parents' property—"

"One eighth," her brother reminded her. "Which you subsequently sold back to me at exorbitant rates."

Varvara sniffled loudly. "One has to look after oneself, especially since I was never lucky in love." She drew a handkerchief from her mesh bag, holding it in readiness for the tears she hoped would soon be flowing. "To think it would

146

come to this, a brother who turns me out the first chance he gets. Well, I won't leave, and that's that."

"Who's turned who out?" said her sister-in-law.

"Your husband, that's who!" shrieked Auntie V. "He's sent me packing, dearest Sonya. And me, a woman all alone, with no one in the world but her only brother. If our parents only knew, they would rise from their graves that a brother could treat his only sister with such cruelty and selfishness!"

Madame Petrova's large, timid eyes opened wide, and her hands fluttered like birds trapped in a cage. "Is Varya leaving us for good?" she asked her husband, making it sound as if such a thing were inexcusable.

Peter Semyonovich's little bulldog body trembled violently. "Moscow is your home, Varvara," he said through clenched teeth.

"But Petrovka is her home away from home," chirped his wife.

"Yes it is, it is indeed," whimpered Auntie V. If she could only keep the argument going for another few minutes, she was certain her brother would have no choice but to renege and allow her to return. "Beast, to treat me like this, and with more money than you know what to do with. Here I am in dire straits—"

"Since when?"

"Since very recently. But did I come to you for a loan? No, I didn't. And did I ever ask for charity? Certainly not. I haven't shared my burdens with you at all, as a matter of fact. And I don't intend to make Petrovka my home, either. I just need a little time to get my affairs in order."

"Then why didn't you say so in the first place? A little time I can certainly give you. Not a lifetime, of course, but at least a few weeks—"

"Months," she snarled.

"All right, all right, a few months," and he threw up his

hands in exasperation.

"Oh, how lovely that you've come to an understanding," said Madame Petrova. Tears of gratitude filled her gentle brown eyes, spilling down her cheeks as her husband and sister-in-law reluctantly embraced.

Now that this was taken care of, Petrov called everyone into the drawing room. Custom dictated that they all remain seated for a moment, as it was considered unlucky if this wasn't done before embarking on a journey. So they all sat there in silence, until Peter Semyonovich deemed it time to rise. Crossing himself before the family ikons, he told Masha that he'd pray for her speedy recovery.

"Christ be with you, my sweet dear," said Anninka. "I know you're going to be all right. I can feel it in my heart."

Masha held her close, burying her face against her *nyanya's* pillowy bosom. "Look after our Henriette," Masha said softly, not wanting her sister to hear. "She's unhappy, Anninka, and needs all the love and understanding you can give her."

"Never you fear, Masha dear. You just get well. I'll pray for you every day." She reached inside the collar of her dress and removed a small cypress wood cross her own mother had worn before her, and that she'd long maintained was blessed by Seraphim of Sarov, one of the wisest and holiest of men. Ever so carefully she slipped it over Masha's head, signing her three times, so that her worn red fingers flew from forehead to breast, right shoulder to left. "Now God will be with you always, my child."

With tears in her eyes, Masha stepped outside, taking her place in the carriage and gazing for a moment at her family, who crowded around to kiss her hand and wish her luck. Then, with a nod to Platon, the carriage rolled slowly across the muddy yard.

"Maria Petrovna!" her mother suddenly cried out as they

started down the lime alley.

Masha turned her head back, able to see her mother frantically waving her hand as she stood on the porch.

"Forgive your *maman* her weaknesses!" Madame Petrova shouted. Before anyone could stop her, she rushed down the steps, slipping and sliding through the mud as she ran after the carriage. "You know how much I love you!" she cried, waving her hand again and again.

I love you, too, Masha thought sadly, though she couldn't bring herself to say it aloud, or even whisper it softly so that no one but she would hear.

Nine

Gregor, who desired to make something beautiful and stylish of his life, something that would bring him fame and fortune in roughly equal proportions, was still very uncertain as to how to go about attaining his goals. He saw his future only in the vaguest of terms. There was always a great deal of champagne, and fashionably dressed men and women who were always laughing, for such seemed to be the purpose of their lives. He referred to these handsome young people as *jeunesse dorée*, and felt a great need to become part of their world, as the gilded youth who enlivened his imagination seemed far more interesting than anyone he knew in real life.

As a boy, his fondest dream had been to attend a fashionable boarding school in Petersburg, where he would mingle with boys from only the finest and most aristocratic of families. But against his wishes his father had enrolled him in a second-rate gymnasium in the town of Orel, a school for boys of mediocre parentage, with nary a Count or a Prince among them. Here he'd learned a great many things he promptly forgot, and were it not for a private tutor his father was forced to hire for him, and with whom Gregor had subsequently fallen in love, he would never have been able to pass his final examinations. But pass them he did, as much to his own surprise as his father's. Awarded his matriculation certificate and callously rebuffed by the tutor over whom he'd suffered the first painful stirrings of adolescent passion, Gregor returned home, even more confused about his future than when he'd first left.

Nearly a year had gone by since he'd learned the meaning of unrequited love and was granted that precious document that gave him the right to enter any university in Russia without further examination. In all that time he'd remained at Petrovka, behaving very much like the "good-for-nothing" his father insisted on calling him. He'd once played the piano fairly competently. Now he rarely if ever sat down at the keyboard. Once he'd composed amusing verses, much to his mother's delight. Now he couldn't even recall the last time he'd taken pen to paper.

"Where do you suppose the year has gone, Kolya?" he asked, several weeks after his sister had left for Moscow.

He lay on his stomach, resting his head against his hands while the groom knelt behind him, rubbing him down with soap and water. The bathhouse was filled with clouds of hot, dry steam. Gregor breathed deeply, sighing to himself as Kolya scrubbed him down with a fiber sponge, his strong and agile hands working vigorously so that not an inch of Gregor's skin was left untouched.

"Perhaps I should study music, or art," he went on. "Or maybe the law. As long as we're in Petersburg, for that's the important thing. And we will be, just as I've promised. The term begins in September and I've already applied. Or should I go back to my music?"

"You've always played so beautifully," Kolya said as he jumped down from the high wooden bench and ran over to the oven.

He was as naked as Gregor, and in the dim, steamy light of

the bath, seemed to be a creature composed entirely of smoke. But what a creature! Gregor marveled.

Kolya dashed a bucket of cold water onto the red-hot stones on top of the oven. Steam billowed forth, raising the temperature even higher than it already was. The groom scampered back, and after giving Gregor another rinse, began to whip him lightly with a broom of twigs to stimulate the circulation of the blood.

Soon his skin was red and tingling, and a feeling of incredible well-being permeated his every pore. The moment Kolya put down the besom of young May birch, Gregor sat up, and with all the ardor of his eighteen years, pressed his lips to Kolya's, embracing him excitedly. Eager to get started, Gregor pushed the stableboy down onto his back, then quickly straddled him.

"You don't really mind, do you?" he whispered.

The groom smiled dreamily, showing his beautiful white teeth. He reached up and wrapped his hands around Gregor's neck, pulling him down on top of him.

"You're my precious little *barchuk*, my little master," Kolya replied. "And because you love your Kolenka so, Kolenka loves you back."

Neither Gregor nor the groom heard the outer door open, followed by the thud of heavy footsteps. The bathhouse was divided in three, with a small anteroom and dressing room separated from the bath proper by a stout log wall and a heavily padded door. Thus there was no way they could have known that someone was even then getting undressed, having already noticed their clothes piled in a corner.

They were still wrapped in each other's arms, so aroused that neither was mindful of anything but the other, when the padded door leading into the bath swung back silently on its stout leather hinges. In the faint light of the kerosene lamp that hung overhead, the two young men must have presented quite a spectacle, not unlike the utterly naked statues Peter Semyonovich had once seen in the Hermitage Museum. One look was all the elder Petrov needed. He threw his head back and began to bellow, shouting all manner of obscenities at his son.

The instant Gregor realized they weren't alone, the color drained from his skin like water from a leaky bucket, and he immediately lost his erection. With nothing to cover himself, he crossed his legs like a frightened virgin, telling Kolya that he'd do all the talking.

Peter Semyonovich's gold baptismal cross hung down over his hairy barrel chest. At that moment he too realized he was naked. But instead of exhibiting the kind of wretched embarrassment that was now Gregor's fate, he merely stood there with his hands on his hips, unmindful of anything but what he'd just seen.

Gregor slowly came down off the shelf. "I didn't know you were planning on taking a bath tonight, Father."

"Scum," hissed Peter Semyonovich. "Monster."

"Kolya was just teaching me the latest resuscitation techniques from America. We read it in an article today. That's all it was, Father. Resuscitation techniques. Straight from America."

"Reptile," said Peter Semyonovich. "Vermin, that's what you are!"

Despite the intense heat, Gregor's skin broke out in gooseflesh, and he began to tremble. "It was nothing, Father. Nothing, just boyish experimentation," he whimpered.

"You vile, degenerate creature!" screamed his father, and he ran across the damp floorboards to the oven. Gregor was certain he was going to start throwing the red-hot stones, but instead his father snatched a besom from where it hung on the wall, then rushed back and began to beat his son about the head and shoulders.

He couldn't very well hit his father back, so he did his best to avoid the old man's merciless blows, covering his face with his hands so that at least he'd come out of this without any permanent or disfiguring scars.

"Please don't hit me anymore," he whispered. "Please don't do this, Father."

In response, his father wielded the besom with all the force and viciousness of a lash, not stopping until Gregor dropped to his knees, covering the top of his head with his hands.

"Stand up, you piece of filth!"

He started nervously to his feet when his father grabbed him by the ear, yanking him toward the door of the dressing room.

"So you were experimenting, were you? Well then, we'll just have to experiment further. Get dressed, you pig."

Before he quite knew what was happening, he and his father were seated in the cabriolet. Without so much as a word of explanation, the elder Petrov set off, driving through the luminous twilight and staring straight ahead. Although Gregor tried to engage him in conversation, his father would have none of it.

They were heading in the direction of Golovlovo, though why his father wanted to go there was anybody's guess. Gregor shrank down in his seat, running his fingers nervously through his damp hair.

"You'll have to send me away, won't you?" he finally said, hoping that was what his father was planning. "After all, the shame of it, the disgrace."

"You all take me for a fool, don't you, you and your sisters both. A womanizer, yes, that I could understand, for I was like that too when I was your age. But this other business— even animals don't behave that way. And you, my only son, the only one to carry on my name. You're slime, that's all you are, just slime that lives in the mud."

Why were they stopping at the village inn?

Before he could come up with an answer, his father nearly tore his arm off as he hauled him from the carriage.

"You'll do as you're told, my little experimenter. Is that understood?"

"Yes, Father."

"Because if you shame me again—"

"I won't, I promise."

Gregor followed his father into the tavern. No sooner did they enter than every eye turned in their direction, crawling over them like insects. The place reeked of sweat and spirits, cheap shag and rancid cooking oil. Someone was playing a balalaika, while someone else was singing what sounded like a dirge. There were drunken shouts, calls for more vodka, numerous bleary-eyed moujiks staggering this way and that.

Even as his father dragged him along with him, nearly every man present came to his feet, bowing from the waist and expressing his pleasure at having the *barin* in his company. At one time, many of them had been Petrov's serfs, and even those who hadn't knew his reputation in the district.

Gregor finally managed to pull his hand free, only to be shoved into a chair.

"I'm going to find you a woman if it's the last thing I do," his father hissed in his ear. "And when she agrees—"

I'll have to perform like a trained seal, he thought unhappily.

Overhead, a silent nightingale crouched in the bottom of its cage, gloomily pecking and scattering sunflower seeds onto the table below. His father swept these aside, then suddenly smiled and waved his hand, trying to attract someone's attention. Gregor looked over his shoulder, just in time to see his brother-in-law come to his feet, bending down a moment to say something to his two companions. One of them was

Kalinovich the *ispravnik,* the other a coarse-looking woman with full, rounded breasts and stringy brown hair.

"Peter Semyonovich, what an honor," said Belinsky. He grabbed onto the back of Gregor's chair, smiling drunkenly, and accepting his father-in-law's invitation to join them.

"So you've left your Vera all alone, have you?" the elder Petrov said with a leer, his eyes darting in the direction of the red-cheeked girl who stood between Belinsky and the police chief.

"You know how these things are. A woman's place and all that," Belinsky replied, so inebriated he could barely put the words together. "And how are you, dear boy?" he went on, turning to Gregor and smiling, so that dimples appeared in his cheeks.

"He's fine," said Petrov, urging his son-in-law and his friends to take a seat, and calling to the innkeeper to bring a bottle.

Belinsky pulled up a chair, fell into it, and said, "Dunyasha, my esteemed father-in-law, Peter Semyonovich Petrov." Then he introduced Gregor, calling him "a prince among princes" and "a charmingly devilish youth."

Finally they were all seated, with Dunyasha on Gregor's left and Belinsky on his right, both of whom sat so close that every time he tried to move he came up against the girl's warm, plump thigh, or banged into his brother-in-law's knee.

His father, pouring the vodka with a surprisingly free hand, raised his glass in a toast. But Kalinovich interrupted before he had a chance to say anything, announcing that they were celebrating, and proposing they drink to good fortune.

Belinsky threw a burly arm over Gregor's shoulders and gave him a hug. "Yes, to good fortune. Don't you agree, Grisha dear?" he went on, leaning so close now that his lips were just a few inches away.

"What good fortune are you talking about?" his father asked.

"You mean you haven't heard?" said the *ispravnik*. "Why, we each own half of Jerichovo, that's what."

"But that's . . . I mean, how is it possible?" he spoke up. Surely they couldn't own land that belonged to Victor Durnovo.

"It now belongs to us," Belinsky said simply.

"But how? It belongs to Victor Romanovich."

"Victor Romanovich no longer exists," said the *ispravnik*, "not when it comes to being a property owner."

"How'd you happen to come by it?" asked Petrov.

"Auction," said Belinsky, hiccuping into his glass.

"Curious, I didn't hear about it. Do you intend to work it yourselves?"

"As a matter of fact, Peter Semyonovich, we thought you'd be interested in securing the deed," replied the police chief. "After all, the estate abuts on your own holdings. And we can promise you a very reasonable price, too."

"But it belongs to Victor," Gregor said again.

His father glared at him angrily, as if to say that in matters of business he'd be wise to hold his tongue.

After that, Gregor drank several more glasses of vodka. Soon everything was running together like letters on a damp sheet of newspaper, so that he wasn't quite certain if Dunyasha had danced for them before or after they left the tavern, or if she'd begun to fondle him under the table or at Kalinovich's house, where he found himself without even knowing how he got there.

Someone shoved a glass of weak, stale tea in his face, urging him to drink. It burned his tongue but he didn't care. Right now nothing seemed important, certainly not scalding himself and certainly not protesting when he discovered he

157

was sitting next to Dunyasha.

"Maybe he's too drunk," he heard his brother-in-law say.

"Never to drunk for a bit of tasty pudding."

Was that his father or the *ispravnik?* He couldn't tell.

"Drink the tea, you dear little angel," whispered the girl, flicking her tongue and saying other things too, such as he'd never imagined hearing from a woman's lips.

"He's done it before, hasn't he?" Simon was saying as the room tilted sideways and Dunyasha hauled him to his feet.

"Ten rubles, mind you," his father told her. Or was it still the *ispravnik?* Gregor couldn't be sure.

The dark-red floorboards were the color of dried blood. He was going to tell everyone that, for it seemed extremely important, when Dunyasha pulled aside the curtain that hung over a doorway at the far end of the room.

Gregor turned his head back, able to see things a little more clearly now. In the small drawing room sat his father and his brother-in-law, while the police chief busied himself at a writing table, rolling cigarettes. His father looked more like a bulldog than ever, his mouth turned down so that it appeared as if he'd suddenly grown a pair of jowls.

"Go on and get it over with," Peter Semyonovich called out.

Dunyasha tugged at his arm impatiently, pulled him into the bedroom, and drew the curtain shut behind her. Ahead was a high narrow bed, just like a coffin.

"You're my sweet little angel," she said as she took hold of his hands and placed them on her breasts, urging him to fondle her.

Gregor did as he was told. He would show the old bulldog he was as much of a man as anyone else. The only trouble was that he'd never been in bed with a woman, had never even seen a woman completely undressed.

"Don't they feel nice?" Dunyasha reached between his legs

and began to rub her hand back and forth, trying to arouse him.

It surprised him that it felt so good. "Have you and Simon ever . . . you know?" he whispered.

"Beast, to ask such a thing," giggled Dunyasha. She eased free of his drunken embrace and quickly began to throw off her clothes.

"Have you?" he said again.

"Why do you want to know?" She stepped out of her skirt, and stood there in her soiled petticoat, showing off her threadbare flesh-colored stockings as she hurriedly kicked off her shoes.

"I'm curious, that's all." He pulled his shirttails out of his trousers, quickly pocketing the mother-of-pearl studs before drawing the shirt up over his head. Then, as Dunyasha told him what beautiful white skin he had, Gregor slowly unbuttoned his trousers.

Untying the strings of her ruffled petticoat, Dunyasha let it drop to the floor. The arrangement of stockings and drawers fascinated him. Held up by narrow elastic bands, the stockings reached halfway up the girl's soft, plump thighs, where they stopped abruptly, giving way to bare skin which in turn disappeared a few inches higher at the edge of her drawers. These were of a very light material, not particularly clean, but so revealing that he surprised himself by stepping closer in order to get a better look.

"Aren't you making with the big eyes," she snickered, wagging a finger at him as she removed her blouse, then sat on the edge of the bed and casually unrolled her stockings.

Without removing her drawers, she slipped between the bedcovers. He watched her wiggling about like a worm on a hook. Then the drawers emerged, a trophy that she tossed at his feet before pulling the quilted counterpane up to her neck.

For a moment Gregor was embarrassed, now that it had finally come to this. But when he glanced down and saw, much to his relief, that he had an erection, he quickly shed the rest of his clothes and climbed into bed.

Dunyasha, reaching between his legs, smiled in the same dreamy and self-satisfied way Kolya had done earlier in the evening. "You're my little sweetheart," she said as she blew out the candle.

Gregor was painfully aware of what was expected of him, just as he was aware of the girl's sour, unwashed smell, and the cloying scent of bergamot in her hair. So he climbed on top of her and got into position, determined to see this to a successful conclusion. Yet as he tried to satisfy her, his flesh betrayed him, and he slowly lost his erection.

"Too much to drink?" she whispered.

He shrugged, but made no move to turn away. "So you've done it with him, have you? Is he any good?"

"Gregor Petrovich, you nasty boy," she scolded.

"Don't you like them nasty, Avdotya my pet?"

"Avdotya," she sighed. "No one's called me that in years. It's Dunyasha this, and Dunya that. They don't understand that a girl likes to be treated with a certain . . . you know what I mean, my angel, don't you?"

"Of course, Avdotya. But what's Senya like? I bet he's flabby with his clothes off."

Even in the darkness he could see her eyes opening wide. "Oh no," she whispered. She threw her arms over his shoulders, hooking her ankles around the backs of his legs. "Oh no, there isn't an ounce of fat on him. But he doesn't have lovely white skin the way you do. He's hairy all over."

Gregor closed his eyes then, trying to imagine them together, Simon pinning the girl to the bed, his big hairy body hovering over her. As long as he could keep Dunyasha talking, and get her to describe what it was like to make love to Belinsky, he'd have no difficulty consummating the act. So he continued to question her, and with each new bit of information she revealed, his penis swelled until it was fully erect.

"Oh, do it now," she urged.

"Is it very big?"

"You mean you haven't heard?" she said with a laugh. "Sometimes he even calls it by a different name, it's so large." She spread her hands apart, leaving nothing to the imagination. "'Now you behave yourself, Colonel,'" she went on, imitating Belinsky's deep, rolling voice, "'and stand straight like an officer.' And the rest of it . . . my God, you can hardly hold them in your hand."

He saw it all now, her words inflaming him in a way he would never have thought possible. Even as he kept asking her for the most explicit details, he thrust forward, grinding down against her. Dunyasha began to whimper, and then to thrash about, clinging to him excitedly as he smiled and got closer and closer to Petersburg, for such was the prize he'd earn from this experiment.

"A versatile youth," Belinsky said snidely when Gregor stepped out of the bedroom a short while later.

"But not nearly as talented as you, Colonel."

Belinsky smiled smugly, no doubt taking this as a compliment.

But Gregor hadn't meant it that way. "Yes, it must take great talent, for who else would've been so clever as to deprive his old friend Victor of his birthright."

"Strong words, my boy," warned Belinsky. "They might get you into trouble."

Rather than answer, he went over to his father, who was stretched out on the sofa, snoring loudly. "Wake up," he said, shaking him as hard as he could.

The elder Petrov sat up and rubbed the sleep from his eyes, then glanced in the direction of the bedroom. "Well, how was it?" he said, now that he remembered why they were here.

"How was it, Dunyasha?" he called out.

"You're an angel, Gregor Petrovich. An angel with a devil's horn."

His father looked at him suspiciously. "If hard-pressed, a plover can always learn to sing like a nightingale," he said under his breath so that no one but his son would hear.

I'll sing all he wants, Gregor thought, so long as it gets me to Petersburg.

Ten

Nikolai Volsky had been gone for several days on a tour of the district, inspecting the gymnasia that fell under his jurisdiction. It had been a difficult and rather unproductive trip, and now he was pleased to be home again. When he drove into the yard, the first thing he noticed was his father-in-law's groom, who immediately ran up to take hold of the reins and help him down from the carriage.

He started to ask the boy what he was doing there, when his wife came out onto the porch. One glance and he realized what a fortunate man he was to have someone like Irena to share his life. He embraced her warmly, answering all of her questions as she led him into the house. But even as they kissed, and she told him how much she had missed him, Volsky's eyes strayed across the room. A pile of letters was neatly stacked on a table in the parlor, so that a moment later he let go of her, eager to see what the mail had brought.

"I'm leaving for Moscow in the morning," he heard her say.

Volsky tore his eyes away from the mail. "Moscow?" he

said, gazing at her in surprise. "Is that all?"

"You mean you're not angry?"

"Why should I be angry, my angel? I'll just have a wretched time on my own, but . . . now, Irena, I was only making a joke. You want to see Masha, isn't that why you're going?"

Irena told him how concerned she was, not having heard from her sister in nearly a month.

"And what in the world is Kolya doing here?" he asked. Before she could answer, he recognized the handwriting on one of the letters and tore it open, curious to know if his friend from Petersburg had been able to find anything for Henriette.

"He had a little disagreement with Father. Nothing serious, mind you," Irena said vaguely. "But he's quite good at what he does, Niki, and the boy has no family, no place to go. All he requires is a pallet in the stable. He hardly eats anything at all."

"That's nice," he said, not paying much attention. He quickly scanned the contents of the letter, then turned back to her, asked her to repeat what she'd said, and then apologized for his inattention. But then another letter caught his eye, this one enclosed in a long, slender envelope bearing an impressive-looking seal. The moment he recognized the impression in the wax he nearly tore the envelope in half in his haste to get it open.

"And he won't stay with us very long, I'm quite certain of that," Irena was saying when he looked up.

Volsky smiled boldly and began to twirl his mustache, wondering if it wasn't time to get out the *pommade hongroise* and really do it up in style.

"Henriette's in luck," he began, telling her that he'd finally received word from his friend in the capital, who wrote to inform him that a certain Count Ivanov had need of a governess to look after his two small children. "The man's a widower, travels in only the best circles, and has an important position in the Ministry of Finance. Henriette must write him immediately, for my friend has told him all about her. All she has to do is explain her qualifications and express her willingness to take on the position. And—" Volsky stopped abruptly, not because he wanted the moment to assume dramatic significance, but because he was suddenly seized by the thought that his news might precipitate a very unpleasant scene between himself and his wife.

Irena drew in her shoulders as if preparing herself for the worst.

"I've been requested to appear before His Excellency the Deputy Minister of Education on the sixteenth of next month!" he burst out, no longer able to contain his excitement.

Irena spoke so softly he had to strain in order to make out what she was saying. "Do you want me to say I'm pleased for you?" she asked.

There was so much she wasn't saying, and so much unhappiness in her voice, that he didn't know how to respond.

"I've wanted this so badly," Volsky said after a long silence, during which neither of them had stirred, as if fearing to make the first move.

"I know that, Niki. I'm sorry if I can't be more enthusiastic, but I'm terribly confused," Irena replied. "One part of me is so upset by this. And yet the other part, the part that belongs to you, my darling, is so pleased for you."

Volsky brightened and reached out, grasping Irena's hands in his. "Let me tell you about something that happened the other day, Irusha dear. Perhaps then you'll understand my feelings about this."

It was one of the most difficult speeches Volsky had ever

made. But having gone over it in his head while driving home that afternoon, the words came with surprising facility, and with much more confidence than he would have thought. He told her of one of the schools he had inspected, and how he had come upon a little boy who'd been kept in a closet-sized lockup for more than two days, simply because he had tried to defend a fellow classmate who was being harassed because he was Jewish. He told her of the numerous injustices he had seen, and how education was considered a luxury, denied not only to youngsters who were extremely gifted and therefore questioned the system, but also to the children of merchants and shopkeepers, footmen, cooks, laundresses, and the like. If there was to be change for the better, men with his kind of liberal beliefs must assume a greater degree of responsibility in the Ministry's decision-making process. Only then could much-needed reforms be effected, and only by being in Petersburg could he have a chance to make his views known to his superiors.

"But what about Petrovka?" she countered. "It's part of me, Niki. I know that must sound strange, when you have no great affection for the place where you were born. But . . . I can't fully understand it myself, except that it's like the center of things—at least for me. Can you understand what I'm trying to say, or does it all sound foolish?"

Of course it sounded foolish, though he had no intention of telling her that. A year before they had argued over very much the same thing. Irena had wanted to remain at Petrovka after their marriage, and he'd been forced to tell her there wouldn't be a wedding if he had to spend the rest of his life under her father's roof.

"You can spend your summers there, Irusha," he pleaded. "Besides, why worry about it now? They haven't even offered me a post yet."

"But they will, I know it. I have great faith in you, Niki.

You know how to charm people, and be pleasant and easy-going. Besides, I don't have any other choice, do I?"

No, she didn't have a choice. But he wasn't about to tell her that—not now, and not ever.

The express train wasn't running, though in typically Russian fashion every railroad official Irena questioned had a different explanation. So instead of taking six hours, the trip took closer to eight, what with all the stops they were continually making.

At each little provincial station hordes of barefoot children held up their wares for her inspection, loaded down with bottles of cream and dishes of wild strawberries. Then, after the third bell, the train rolled onward, the white smoke from the engine blowing across the dusty leaves of the trees that grew alongside the tracks. Leaning back against the broad upholstered seat, Irena felt the train finally gathering speed, now that they were at last approaching Moscow.

Like a ribbon of iron, the train unwound its way through groves of ash and white birch. Here and there little summer cottages could be seen, with carved figures of cocks over the balconies. The long, hollow echo of the engine's hoot drifted down the tracks, mingling with the smoke and dust until the woods came to an end, replaced by scraggly rows of cabbages. Their greenish-white heads stretched far into the distance, where they actually seemed to touch the towers and gilded domes that now soared into view. When the rows of cabbages ended, other kitchen gardens took their place, these in turn giving way to untidy clusters of ramshackle cottages, and cobblestone roads along which she could hear the rumble of dozens of carts, making themselves heard above the whistling roar of the engine.

Katya had her nose pressed to the glass as she gazed excitedly at the view. With girlish enthusiasm she kept whispering. "Moscow, Moscow," as if the city were a dear friend she was about to see after too long an absence.

By the time they drew into the station and stepped onto the platform, they were nearly swallowed up in the crowd of porters and passengers who rushed this way and that, jostling each other in their haste to reach their final destinations. Irena looked in vain for a hotel porter, spotting one just as she was about to give up. A moment later she caught sight of her aunt, as well. Varvara raised her black-gloved hand, looking rather put out by the din and confusion.

"Slavyansky Bazar" read the name of the hotel, written out in gold letters above the brim of the porter's cap. He wore a dark-blue coat edged with a gold braid, and no sooner did she tell him she'd already reserved a room than he grabbed her bags and ran off. Trying not to lose sight of his back, Irena hurried after him, with Katya and an unsmiling Auntie V. keeping up the rear.

In two minutes' time they were all crowded together in a little dark-green droshky, forced to shout above the pealing of a thousand church bells and the deafening reverberation of hoofs and carriage wheels rattling across the cobblestones. The *isvostchik* haggled with Auntie V. over the price of the fare. When they finally came to an agreement the cabby took his seat, turning the copper plate that had his number stamped into the metal from his chest to his back, where it dangled on a leather cord.

The *isvostchik* drove as if his were the only droshky on the street, clattering over cobblestones as big as fists. The small one-horse carriage barely held all four of them, so that Irena and her aunt were forced to put their arms around each other, while a wide-eyed Katya sat up front with the driver, clutching his worn leather belt and trying not to tumble out.

"I still don't know why you put yourself to so much trouble, Irena," said her aunt, and dressed all in black as if she'd just come from a funeral, and wearing a fusty little hat trimmed with wilted hyacinths and smelling strongly of mothballs. "After all, your sister's condition is quite stable. Didn't you receive her last letter?"

"I haven't received any letters. That's why I'm here," she explained, greatly relieved to learn that Masha's health hadn't deteriorated, as she had feared.

Though Irena had been to Moscow several times before, she was nearly as wide-eyed as her maid. Everywhere Irena looked this city of forty times forty churches teemed with life, charming and chaotic and flooded with brilliant summer sunshine. Horsedrawn streetcars clamored past, joined by countless numbers of carts and carriages, all vying for room, and making so much noise she could barely hear herself think. The narrow streets were filled with pedestrians, while towering above them were blue domes studded with gold, bulb-shaped campaniles, red rooftops and chimney pots, and then a dazzling expanse of Moscow sky across which great flocks of rooks flew like streaks of black smoke, vanishing through the clouds.

The *isvostchik* suddenly removed his queer little hat, low and squat and with a curled-up brim, so that more than anything it resembled an inverted chamber pot. He slowly crossed himself, Varvara's gloved hand making the same circuit. Irena and Katya crossed themselves as well, for they were now passing the Iberian Chapel. One of the most highly revered places in all of Russia, it was here that the wonder-working ikon of the Iberian Virgin was kept on display.

The Kremlin sprang into view a moment later, looking for all the world like a picture postcard with its palaces and golden cupolas, its pinnacles and towers. Dominated by St. Basil's, whose asymmetrical domes took on the fanciful shapes of onions, pineapples, pumpkins, and turbans, and surrounded by a broad castellated brick wall, the most extraordinary profusion of colors danced before her eyes. Irena drew in her breath, gazing in silent disbelief at these splendid structures that rose up all around her, confounding both the eye and the imagination at every turn.

But then it all paled and she looked away, no longer mesmerized by the view. "Tuberculosis," Varvara had said, uttering the word like a curse, and repeating it just in case Irena hadn't heard her the first time. "The hemorrhaging has stopped, thank goodness, but now Professor Ostroumov wants her to go to Samara to take the kumiss cure," referring to a tonic made from mare's milk and considered of great benefit for those who were consumptive. "Afterward, he suggests Yalta until it gets too cool. Of course, there's the matter of selecting a proper chaperone."

The *isvostchik* drew up before the hotel, and a uniformed porter dashed outside to relieve Irena of her bags. Leaving Katya to unpack, and promising her aunt that she'd join her that evening for dinner, Irena quickly changed her clothes, then went directly to the hospital.

Expecting only the worst, Irena was pleasantly surprised by what she saw. Though an old facility, the Moscow University Hospital looked as if it had recently been refurbished, and there was nothing bleak or depressing about the brightly painted wards with their neat rows of cast-iron beds, the efficient bustle of doctors and nurses making their rounds.

Directed to Ward No. 6 on the second floor, she found herself entering a long, wide room perhaps twice the size of the ballroom at Petrovka. There were two rows of beds covered in immaculate white linen, and in the next-to-last bed on her right lay her sister. When Masha caught sight of her a moment later, the drawn and haggard look around the young woman's eyes vanished, her face suddenly flooded with health and vitality. But despite the shapeless blue hospital gown Masha wore, Irena could still see how thin she had grown, her bony arms just like Henriette's.

"Mamochka!" Masha cried out joyfully, sitting up in bed and throwing her pitifully thin arms around Irena's neck. "Oh yes, just let me hold you," Masha whispered, her breath warm against Irena's cheek and her heart beating so loudly it echoed in her ears.

Irena pulled up a chair, unwilling to let go of her sister's hand, even for an instant.

"I've missed you so," Masha said, trying very hard to smile, though her lips looked parched and dry. "But they've been very good to me here. Professor Ostroumov is very reassuring . . . even if it is tuberculosis."

"Yes, Auntie V. told me," Irena said softly.

"He's determined there's a tubercular process in the apex of both of my lungs, whatever that means. I suppose it's where the illness has decided to set up house. But let's not talk of that, Irena. Tell me, has there been any word from Victor?" She squeezed Irena's hand as hard as she could. "Irusha, don't you understand? I love him."

Irena had never heard her sister say that about anyone. It troubled her, for she felt it would bring Masha nothing but grief. If her sister hadn't been ill, then perhaps she'd have the strength to deal with it. But Masha was so sick, and in such a weakened state, that emotional upheavals must at all costs be avoided.

"You hardly know him," she replied.

"But I do know him," Masha insisted. "I know him better than I've ever known anybody. And I love him, Irusha. And I'm terrified of what might happen to him. I'm not a school-girl anymore. I'm not saying these things because they sound romantic. I love him, and you have to find out what's happened to him." Again, Masha clutched her hand, trying to convince her of the importance of what she'd said.

Although Irena tried to change the subject, Masha would

have none of it.

"Irena, you must do this one thing for me," she begged. "Go to Butyrky Prison, and if you can get to see him, if they'll grant you an audience, tell him that I intend to wait, no matter how long it takes, that I'll never believe what he told me. Tell him those very words, Irena. That I'll wait, no matter what."

"Of course," she said gently, deeply affected by Masha's impassioned plea. Irena stood up, fixing the pillows and promising to return the next day.

"Then you'll go?" Masha said again, as if she had to be absolutely certain she'd heard Irena correctly.

Irena nodded. "I'll go first thing tomorrow. Now you rest, Mashenka dear."

"Tell him he's opened my eyes, that I'll never see things the same way again. Tell him I love him, Irena, and that even if he gets down on his knees and begs me to forget him, I never will."

Peasant girls were gracefully pitching hay in the meadows with three-pronged boughs stripped of their leaves, for the idea of spending money on real farm tools was beyond Peter Semyonovich's comprehension. In their worn cotton *sarafans*, and with kerchiefs protecting them from the sun, they ranged across the low-lying meadows bordering the sluggish little river that ran through Petrovka.

Unobserved, Gregor watched them for a moment, seeing it all as a kind of national ballet. There was something choreographic in the way the village girls moved, pitching the still-green hay the men had already cut down with scythes.

The busy time in the fields was approaching, for after haymaking, the grain would have to be harvested, the season the moujiks referred to as the *strada*, or suffering. Gregor too was suffering, though his anguish wasn't brought on by working in the fields from dawn till sunset, sixteen and sometimes even eighteen hours a day. Seated in his cabriolet, its yellow hood raised to shield him from the glare of the hot summer sun, he finally set off again. Now that he'd made up his mind, and knew what he wanted to do come September, he was eager to have it out with his father, once and for all.

The heat intensified, so that Gregor soon felt the sweat trickling down his back. Beyond the meadows the vast expanse of yellowing rye was alive with the drone of insects, clinging to the heavy ears that rocked back and forth each time there was a breeze. Kestrels were gliding overhead, beating their wings and fanning out their tails as they hovered in search of prey.

Up ahead he made out a racing droshky coming toward him at a breakneck pace, and tugged at the reins so that the high-springed cabriolet came to a stop in the middle of the road. A moment later his father, very red-faced and perspiring profusely, drew up alongside him.

"I was on my way to find you," Gregor said. He smiled as pleasantly as he could and descended from the carriage. "I've decided to mend my ways and do something useful with my life. And with a degree from the university I know I can make you proud of me again."

His father eyed him suspiciously. "What university are you talking about?"

"The Imperial School of Jurisprudence. Or the law faculty at the University of St. Petersburg. I'm not certain which."

"You, a jurist?" Petrov said with a laugh. "Russia has more than enough lawyers as it is. But it's certainly more honorable than cavorting like a common—" His father waved his stubby little fingers in the air, rather than utter words he found so despicable. "And you've been accepted?"

Gregor nodded. "I have my matriculation certificate. The term begins in September."

"Petersburg, eh?" His father drew a greasy handkerchief from his pocket and mopped his face, then proceeded to crack his knuckles while he deliberated on what his son had told him.

"A degree is very important these days," Gregor hurried to add. "I'll be able to secure a post in government service and really make a career of it."

"That remains to be seen."

"But I can't stay home forever, Father."

"True."

Gregor couldn't believe his ears.

"Surprised?" his father said. "No reason to be, when half the district knows what you've been up to. But let's not go into that. Tell me, how much is this going to cost?"

"Not very much."

"I didn't ask you that," barked his father. "Give me figures, round numbers, rubles and kopecks."

They quibbled over the terms of his allowance, Gregor starting off with the highly unlikely sum of six thousand rubles a year, and slowly backing down until he had no choice but to accept his father's considerably lower figure.

"Two thousand a year and not a kopeck more," the elder Petrov told him. "If you don't let it burn a hole in your pocket, it'll do very nicely. And when you've gotten your degree and secured a position, I expect you to pay me back."

You'll be dead by then, Gregor thought. And if you're not—It wasn't worth troubling himself about, and so he nodded his head, agreeing to whatever his father had proposed.

Peter Semyonovich climbed back into his carriage. "Just remember, the only reason I'm doing this is because I want to put a stop to all these slanderous rumors. Rumors, hah! We all know how true they are, don't we?"

"I'll change, Father."

"Change into what, a princess?" and with a flick of his wrist he set off, leaving Gregor enveloped in a cloud of dust.

Settled. Finished. Peace and harmony. Yes, get rid of him just like you rid yourself of his sister. Children—vipers, that's all they are.

"Isn't that so?" Peter Semyonovich said to his trotter. "They're nothing but trouble, the whole lot of them. The only one who ever listened to me was Irena, and even she couldn't convince that dullard of a husband to stay on here, work as my steward, make a life of it. And Masha? A child who takes out her anger on my poor Sonyushka, who couldn't harm a fly. Oh, but my wife was a beauty in her day, remember?"

Petrov smiled to himself, then grew thoughtful again as he drove on in the direction of Jerichovo, where he had an appointment to meet his son-in-law.

Poor sweet Sonyushka, so frail, so innocent. He recalled their wedding night, and how she'd bowed down before him, promising to be a kind and loving wife. My poor frail Sonyushka, to have borne me a pack of wolves. And now the disgrace of having my neighbors talk about my son. Oh Gregor, you good-for-nothing, how did such a thing happen to me? And you, my only son, to do this to his father. Didn't I watch over you and make sure you had enough to eat, clothes on your back, and a place to sleep?

"Didn't I?" he asked the trotter. "Of course I did. Not like my own father. No, not like that poor old fool."

Semyon Petrov had been murdered by his serfs when his son Peter was just a boy. But even now, more than fifty years after his father's death, Peter Semyonovich could still see him with startling clarity. He was a short, stocky man too, despised by his servants for his brutality. A man of contradictions, he was both highly religious and totally inmoral.

Although he read ten pages of Scripture every day without fail, he nevertheless pursued a passion for very young girls, the children of his serfs, whom he would take into his bed despite the anguished pleading of their parents.

One night six of his serfs, three of whom were fathers of the little girls Semyon had sexually abused, crept into their master's bedroom and suffocated him with pillows so as not to leave a single mark of violence on his body. The doctors said his heart had given out, and that he'd died in his sleep. But Peter Semyonovich's long-suffering mother knew different, and on her deathbed she'd told her son the facts surrounding her husband's death, blaming herself, for she'd come to hate him as much as his serfs did.

Although Peter Semyonovich was only ten years old at the time, Varvara even younger, his father's image remained etched in his memory, a link to his unhappy childhood. He had determined to be different, to be loved by his own children, having always felt his father had denied him that special relationship he was certain could exist between a father and a son. But circumstance had changed all that. Petrovka was four times the size it was fifty years before. There was always too much to do, too many things to look after, for people wouldn't hesitate to steal you blind unless you kept a watchful eye.

Perhaps I didn't find enough time for them, Petrov thought. But they were babies. They had other things to keep them busy. And Gregor never liked me, anyway. Even when he was still a boy he'd run away when I came near. Oh, the shame of it, the disgrace. Why couldn't he have turned out like Simon Ivanovich? Now, there's a man for you. Vera doesn't realize how lucky she is, that she married someone who knows how to keep her in line.

When he reached Jerichovo he recalled that the Count grew the finest plums and peaches in the district. Although

Durnovo had let much of the land go fallow, there was every reason to believe it could once again be made to yield valuable crops, the market value of which would easily pay for the property in just a few years' time. As for the manor house, the pools and gardens, he'd tear down the blackened ruins, fill in the ridiculous empty canals, and plant additional fruit trees, so that in a couple of years there'd be still more fine plums and peaches to bring to market.

Petrov bent down and scooped up a handful of rich, black soil. As he inhaled the fragrance of crops yet to be sown, he saw the endless ribbons of earth unfolding behind the plows, and the promise of many bountiful harvests.

Behind him came the clatter of hoofbeats. He let the soil trickle through his fingers, then wiped his hands on his trousers and assumed a bored and disinterested expression as his son-in-law drove his carriage into the yard.

After exchanging greetings, Belinsky took him on a tour of inspection. For nearly an hour they bounced over rutted back-country roads, surveying the seemingly endless expanse of land, fields that had gone fallow, meadows already stripped of their hay, others about to yield up their rye and oats, and of course Jerichovo's famed orchards, the trees having just begun to bear fruit.

"More than a thousand choice acres," Belinsky said proudly when they returned to the ruins of the manor house.

"I've seen better. Crops don't look too good. My land yields a lot more."

"But that's because it hasn't been properly tended. With no one to pay the peasants for their labor, they've all gone elsewhere. But next year—think of the riches this land will yield."

"You know what they say, you can't heat the stove with promised wood."

"Oh, I agree, Peter Semyonovich," his son-in-law said with

a greedy smile. "Which is why I'm prepared to offer you my share of the land—and Kalinovich's share as well—with no more thought to making a profit than if I were your own son. For twenty thousand rubles you too can boast the finest peaches in the district."

Peter Semyonovich drew himself up to his full height, though even then there was no way he could look directly into his son-in-law's eyes. "For twenty thousand rubles let some other fool have the honor." He started to his droshky when Belinsky ran after him, clamping a hand over his back.

"Now what's the matter, Father? After all, eighteen thousand is dirt-cheap."

Petrov looked up at him, craning his thick, stubby neck. "Remember one thing," he said. "When your father lay dying, I was one of the few people who came to see him. So don't try to cheat me the way others cheated him. I don't need this piece of property, Simon. But if the price were a fair one, then yes, I'd consider buying it."

"I thought you'd be a little more eager than that."

"Not for fifteen thousand rubles."

"Fifteen?" his son-in-law said in surprise.

"Twelve is fair, but I'd agree to fifteen."

"Make me your steward and it's yours."

"Steward?"

Belinsky nodded.

"And Kalinovich would agree to such a price?"

"Certainly."

This put an entirely different light on things, and for a moment Peter Semyonovich remained silent, not sure what to say. He was surprised his son-in-law was amenable to such a low price, for in truth the land was worth every bit of twenty thousand rubles.

"Why do you want to be steward?" he asked. "The position entails a great deal of work—probably much more than you're accustomed to. You'd have to live at Petrovka. What would you do about Golovlovo?"

Belinsky shrugged, as if it were of no importance whatso-ever. "Golovlovo's always paid for itself. I don't have to live there to see that things run smoothly. Or I might sell it."

Although he didn't trust his son-in-law, the idea of installing him as steward and thus getting Jerichovo for so reasonable a price was very enticing. The land touched on his own. Petrovka would become one of the largest estates in the province. The Governor himself would probably come to visit, and at the next district assembly of the "Club de la Noblesse," Peter Semyonovich would surely be feted, and a dinner given in his honor. Certainly he'd be asked to represent the local gentry in the provincial assemblies, where matters of great importance, such as land reform and the like, were heatedly discussed. Why, he might even be elected Marshal of the Nobility, an honor that hadn't been bestowed upon a Petrov since before his grandfather's time. Yes, it was all very tempting, and the more he thought about it, the more tempting it became.

"If Jerichovo can be mine for fourteen thousand—"

"But you said fifteen a moment ago," protested Belinsky.

"Fourteen and a half then," he replied with a self-satisfied grin, making it sound as if he were doing his son-in-law a great favor by being so willing to compromise. "And you're certain Kalinovich will go along with these terms?"

"Not as certain as I was when I asked for twenty thousand, but I think so, yes. Shall we shake on it then?" Belinsky extended his big, bearlike hand, eager to conclude the trans-action.

Peter Semyonovich, gloating over the fact that he'd gotten the better of his son-in-law, having been prepared to pay as much as twenty-five thousand rubles for Jerichovo, smiled to himself and stuck his hands in his pockets.

"When the deed is signed," he said, "then the deed is done."

Butyrky was the central prison for those awaiting deportation to Siberia. It had been built in the reign of Catherine the Great, nearly a hundred years before. The massive stone building was enclosed within a mighty wall, with a tower at each of the four corners. The most famous of these was known as the Pugachev Tower, named after Catherine's celebrated adversary. A rebel who wanted to "shake Moscow to its foundations," he ended up being carried to the old capital in an iron cage, where he was publicly beheaded and quartered in the Red Square. The Pugachev Tower was reserved for only the most dangerous political prisoners, while in the main building some two thousand ordinary criminals prepared themselves as best they could for the hardships of exile.

It was to Butyrky that Irena came on the morning following her visit to Masha. Descending from the droshky that had taken her from her hotel to the prison, Irena stared in disbelief at the bleak gray structure that rose before her. Butyrky was located in the northwestern quarter of the city, a district known as the Sushchevskaya, and occupied mostly by the poorer classes. She felt ill-at-ease, and hurried in the direction of the prison gates, where she discovered that a large crowd had already gathered. A convoy of prisoners was due to leave within the hour, and thus all visiting privileges had been suspended for the day. Certain that an exception could be made, especially since Victor Durnovo was a "political," she went around to the side of the main building and found the offices of the prison administration.

A guard stood before the door, barring her way. No, the prison governor wasn't seeing anyone today. No, visitors weren't being permitted in. No, there was no such thing as an exception, however extraordinary the circumstances.

Irena tried to press some small bills into the jailer's hand, but he shoved them aside, saying that while he wasn't above taking "palm oil," as this kind of bribe was called, today all the money in the world wouldn't do any good. He had his orders, and he had to follow them to the letter, lest he be punished for his disobedience.

"At least let me know if my brother is part of the convoy," she replied, certain that if she referred to Victor this way, the guard would be more sympathetic to her cause.

"Name?" he said brusquely, annoyed at her persistence.

"Durnovo, Count Victor Romanovich Durnovo."

His eyes narrowed, and he looked at her as if to say, "You don't look like a Countess to me," for Irena had dressed very simply in a plain walking dress of navy-blue silk.

When he returned some twenty minutes later, he wore a surprisingly sympathetic expression. "He'll be in the last group to leave the yard," the man said gently, and with none of the superciliousness he'd shown earlier. "I'm sorry, Countess, but—"

"Yes . . . well, thank you so much for your trouble, sir. And please take this as a . . . yes," she stammered as she pressed the two one-ruble notes into his hand.

Irena returned to the main gates just as they were opening and the prisoners were about to be led outside. All around her the crowd pressed forward, and as people wept for their loved ones, armed guards shoved them back, ready to use their rifles at the slightest provocation.

Then the first group of prisoners was led outside. These were the men sentenced to hard labor, easily recognizable by their half-shaved heads and the yellow, diamond-shaped pieces of cloth sewn onto the backs of their gray prison garb. Each convict wore fetters riveted to his ankles, so that the air vibrated with the clattering of chains. Behind them marched the penal colonists condemned to permanent exile in Siberia, wearing the same gray trousers and threadbare gray over-coats, but with chains attached to their wrists instead of their ankles. The third group consisted of those who were being deported without imprisonment or hard labor. Women followed after them, and like the men, were also divided into three groups, the largest comprising those who were simply being banished, and could at least hope to return to their families at the expiration of their sentences.

Irena had never seen such a horrible sight, nor had she even known such things existed. The prisoners could barely open their eyes, they were so unaccustomed to sunlight, and presented a uniformly grim and dismal picture as they lined up quietly in rows of four abreast. At last came the politicals, looking very different from the other deportees, for they were allowed to wear their own clothing. As they emerged from the yard, Irena made her way toward them, trying to catch a glimpse of Victor Durnovo.

It was only when the prisoners began to move, that Irena was able to approach the group of politicals. No sooner did she recognize Count Durnovo than a white-shirted soldier ordered her to stand back, as it was against regulations to fraternize with the prisoners.

By greasing the guard's hand with "palm oil," Irena was able to walk alongside Durnovo, who stared straight ahead and pretended not to notice her. Only when she spoke his name did he turn his head in her direction, looking at her with great sadness, and nodding as if he knew exactly why she was here.

Irena explained the nature of her errand, forced to raise her voice above the terrifying clanking of chains. Victor listened in silence, and when at last he spoke there was a sharp edge to his voice.

"I've been exiled for five years, Irena Petrovna, and when and if I return, I have no intention of forgetting what they've done to me. I won't put aside my beliefs, even if it means another arrest, and another term of imprisonment, and another five years of exile. And it'll go on and on like that as long as I have the strength. If I told Masha to wait, I'd be condemning her to the worst possible kind of life."

"But she's willing to wait, Victor Romanovich. Not just willing, she's determined."

"But not as determined as I. Don't you see, I can offer her nothing but unhappiness. Tell her I won't look for her when I return, that I'll make no effort to see her again."

"If only she'd believe that," Irena replied. "But she won't. I know her too well. When she gets better, as I pray she will, she'll go after you."

"Oh God, why did I ever return?" Victor cried. "Why did I fall in love with her when I had no right to fall in love with anyone? But you must make her believe I don't want to see her again. I tried to convince her, but I knew it didn't do any good." He grasped Irena's hand tightly in his. "I don't want her following me, and I don't want her waiting. Tell her I'm dead, that I died in prison. Yes, because that's the only thing she'll believe. Don't you see, I can only be responsible for my own life."

"It will break her spirit," Irena said.

Durnovo shook his head. "The grief she'll feel will pass. But if you go back and tell her that I don't want to see her again, she'll refuse to believe me. You mustn't let her spend her life in mourning, or hoping for the impossible. But tell her I died in prison, and in time she'll find herself again, and go on with the business of living. Do this for me, Irena. Do this for your sister, whom I love even more dearly than my freedom. She mustn't waste her life waiting for a man who won't change, who'll return and do exactly what he's done before."

Irena nodded, wiping aside the tears that had begun to trickle down her cheeks. "It will break her heart," she said again.

"No," the young Count insisted, "her heart will mend, and she'll soon find someone else who's worthy of her love."

Eleven

When Masha returned to Petrovka several weeks later, the harvest was all but over, and the empty fields, yet to be sown with winter grain, looked as stubbly and half-shorn as the heads of convicts. There was a desolate quality to the landscape, a stillness in the air broken only by occasional birdsong, or the chatter of cicadas.

Everyone soon learned of Victor's death, how the young Count had succumbed to cholera, and how the prison authorities had buried him in an unmarked grave. Masha took to her room, insisting that she would be fine, and that even Professor Ostroumov had suggested a period of rest before she undertook the trip to Samara. Everyone walked around as if on tiptoe, and the silence of the manor merged with the sultry and languid silence of these long, hot summer days, so that were a stranger to drive up to the house, he would surely think the estate was deserted.

Irena came to see her sister late one afternoon and stayed for dinner, surprised when her father took her aside and suggested they ride out to the birch wood at the northeastern corner of his property. The racing droshky rattled along a narrow road overgrown with pale-pink dodder and gray-green pigweed. The barren fields stretched on and on, and the dying golden light was so calm and peaceful that Irena imagined life would always be like this, changing only with the seasons.

Her father wasn't in a very talkative mood, though she knew him well enough to realize there was something on his mind. But as they neared the wood and he spurred his trotter on as if the forest were beckoning them to enter into its cool embrace, he finally turned to her and spoke.

"It's yours." He waved his hand in the air, indicating everything around them. "All of it. You're the only one who loves the land as I do." He looked at her for a long, solemn moment, then spoke so tenderly she might have been a little girl again. "Can't you hear it breathing, Irusha dear?"

Irena listened to the silky rustle of the birches, and the murmur of leaves like the patter of light rain. The wood closed in around them, and now a cuckoo laughed, and now a crossbill twittered loudly from the top of a nearby stand of pine. The strong, dank smell of mushrooms permeated the air, and the young birch trees looked as if they were made of silver, glowing softly in the dusk. Yes, she could hear the forest breathing, calling out to her too, so that she understood exactly what her father had meant.

Peter Semyonovich stopped the droshky in the middle of the wood, quickly descended, and went around to the other side to help Irena down.

"All these good mushrooms going to waste," he said as he picked a fat birch mushroom whose chocolate cap disappeared into his mouth, for these were best when eaten fresh. "I'll have to send Anninka out to pick them. We'll salt some down, make a nice tasty soup, and pickle the rest. So what do you think, Irusha?"

"I think it's unfair, Father. I thought you were going to divide the estate among all of us."

"And see it disappear through their fingers? There'd be nothing left of Petrovka by the time they got finished. No," he insisted, "my way is the best. If your mother survives me, Petrovka will be placed in a trust, to be administered by you. Then, when she's gone, everything will be yours. But you might as well know that the trust and the will are so written that if you attempt to parcel out the land under some misguided sense of loyalty to your brother and sisters, it will all go to Varvara, down to the last sod."

Was it spite that had made him write the will this way? Or was it merely that he couldn't bear to think of Petrovka depleted by so much as a single blade of grass? Standing there with the shadows of leaves falling across his face so that one cheek was dark, the other light, her father stared unblinkingly into her eyes, forcing Irena to accept what he had said.

"There will always be a Petrovka," he announced. "One day it will belong to your children, and their children after them. If you care for the land as I have, you'll never want for anything, Irena." Having said all that he'd intended to, he helped her back into the droshky, then started for home.

The letter was written on thick gray stock with deckled edges, covered in a precise and somewhat crabbed hand. The close script filled an entire page, so that it seemed to Henriette as if the Count had been reluctant to use the second sheet, where there were a few concluding remarks and a boldly inscribed *Count D. F. Ivanov*, painstakingly ringed by an ornamental scrawl.

A vain and frugal man, she decided. But economy was certainly no vice, not after the training she'd received in her father's house. With this in mind, she didn't hesitate to fold the second sheet in half, and with her paper knife slit the page in two. The blank and unused half she placed with a similar pile in the top drawer of her dressing table, then turned her attention back to the letter.

Having already read it three times, Henriette was certain she'd be able to quote lengthy passages, if ever she was called upon to do so. But even more important was her determination to make sense of everything Count Ivanov had written, the terms of their contract, the responsibilities he would place upon her. As governess of his two young children, he'd made it quite plain that she would be required to spend nearly all her time with them, and would only be allowed the day off every other Sunday. She would, of course, be provided with her own room, though he wanted it made perfectly clear—"so there will be no misunderstandings, *mademoiselle*"—that she'd take her meals with the children, who dined an hour earlier than he. The position paid forty rubles a month, and if she were ill—"though I trust you are of a hardy constitution, and do not suffer the usual female complaints"—the sum of one ruble, thirty-four kopecks would be deducted daily. If she found these terms suitable, he expected to receive word from her as promptly as possible, as he wished for her to assume her duties no later than the fifteenth of the following month.

About to read the letter all over again, Henriette heard someone out in the hall, and hurriedly stuffed the letter into the nearest drawer. A moment later the bedroom door flew open without even the courtesy of a knock.

Auntie V. smiled coyly, and her downy mustache glistened over her drooping upper lip. "Why aren't you ready, my dear?"

"For what?"

"Surely you haven't forgotten?" her aunt said with surprise. "General Tishin should be arriving any minute. You said that as soon as Masha came home, you'd give him your answer. Well, his impatience is now at a fever pitch, my child. So don't just stand there like a ninny. Put on something a little less dowdy, Henriette, and prepare yourself for your charming beau."

"And don't wear gray," Henriette said, half to herself.

"What was that?"

"I said, 'And don't be grim.'" She forced herself to smile.

"Grim?" exclaimed Auntie V. "On a day like this you should be anything but. Oh Henriette, Henriette, I shall cry with joy when the two of you are united in holy matrimony. Yes, cry with tears of pure joy, my child, that you've finally made a life for yourself."

Smiling as agreeably as she could, Henriette took her aunt by the elbow and steered her to the door. "Shall I wear red, do you think?" she said with a straight face.

"Red?" said Varvara, wrinkling up her forehead. "No, wear the blue. It's definitely more suitable. And don't take too long, *ma chère.* You know how rude it is to keep a prospective husband waiting."

Henriette closed the door behind her, then turned and faced the mirror. It's no use blaming the looking glass if your face is crooked, she thought. With this in mind, she began to change her clothes, determined to make herself look as hideous as possible.

"After all," she whispered, "that shouldn't take too much effort, should it?"

Peter Semyonovich was seated behind his writing table, going over his accounts. "Come in, Varvara, and close the door behind you."

Auntie V., about to enter her brother's study and recalling how she hadn't been in this room in more than thirty years, stood uncertainly by the door, seeing her past come face to face with her present.

"This was Father's room, wasn't it?" she said. "It's still the same. Hardly anything has changed."

The walls were covered with dark-blue paper, and on one

wall hung an assortment of rusty weapons—flintlocks, whips, sabers, and short saw-edged swords—mounted on a Persian carpet. There were several cupboards full of moldy books that smelled oddly of old chocolate, and a large leather-covered divan her brother probably used more often than his bed. On his writing table sat an inkwell in the shape of a pug dog, as well as two wooden-shafted penholders, wipers, and several sheets of blue paper such as sugar loaves are wrapped in. The coarse linen curtains were drawn so that the only light came from a bronze and glass lamp.

Varvara seated herself on the divan. "You wished to see me? We don't have much time, you know. General Tishin should be arriving shortly."

"And not a day too soon," her brother replied. He put away his work, then leaned back in his chair and cracked his knuckles, eying her with a thoughtful expression. "I would like you to accompany Masha, first to Samara for the kumiss cure, and then to Yalta, for they all say the weather there is a great boon to consumptives. I will, of course, provide you with whatever funds are required. But it would mean traveling for several months. Think of it as a holiday, if you must. I understand one needn't have consumption to take the cure. It might do wonders for your chronic dyspepsia, Varya."

"My dyspepsia hasn't troubled me of late, glory be to God," she replied.

But what did trouble her was the situation at Red Hill. If she failed to establish herself in the General's household from the very start, there was no telling what might happen. Were she to return three months after the wedding, she might find everything radically altered, and General Tishin no longer sympathetic to the plans they'd already made. That, of course, was something she didn't want to risk, not when her funds were at such a low ebb, and with no hope of improvement in the future.

Perhaps now was finally the time to be completely honest with her brother. "I've been thinking of leaving Moscow," she began. "General Tishin has been kind enough to invite me to stay at Red Hill. To help Henriette in running the household, you understand."

"Oh, you're a sly one, all right. Why, I wouldn't have thought of that myself, Varya. But do go on."

"Quite frankly, brother dear, were I to go off with Masha for several months, Henriette might not speak very kindly of me in my absence. But if you could assure me—"

"Of a roof over your head, you might consider chaperoning Masha."

She nodded.

"Well, I suppose the house is certainly large enough. We do get on each other's nerves, however."

"I shall try to be as pleasant as possible, Petya dear."

"And I shall continue to be my old rambunctious self," her brother laughed. "But if that's your wish, Varya, you have my word. You needn't worry about finding yourself destitute."

She got up and left the room. After all, there was no reason to be thankful, not when she was doing him as much of a favor as he was doing her.

Once again, they were all seated in the drawing room— Auntie V., Sophia Mikhailovna, Peter Semyonovich, and of course that extraordinary personage, Ardallion Hippolytovich Tishin. Knowing she could no longer delay the inevitable, Henriette made her entrance, dressed all in icy-blue, and with her frizzy hair so disarranged it looked like a bird's nest minus the twigs and feathers. A liberal coating of face powder lent a ghastly white pallor to her cheeks, accentuating her sharp, bony features, and making her look more like a corpse than a coquette.

"What have you done to yourself?" her aunt whispered, hurriedly taking her aside. "Rub that horrid stuff off this instant!"

Determined not to let Auntie V. get the better of her, for today she was going to savor her freedom, no matter how terrible the consequences might prove to be, Henriette called out to her suitor. "Do you like the way I look, *mon cher Général?*" She lumbered toward him in a thoroughly ungainly way, taking great pains to appear awkward.

No sooner had the General kissed her hand than her father cleared his throat and came to his feet. Reminding her of the promise she had made, and of the General's desire to make her his wife, he again asked for her decision.

Ignoring her mother's excited twittering, and the tiresome yelping of Laska, Henriette turned to the General and asked to have a few words with him in private.

"I've never heard of such a thing!" exclaimed her aunt, who was wearing the same malodorous black taffeta gown she'd worn for Vera's wedding. "Why, it's just not proper . . . unless, of course, I remain to chaperone."

"No, I'm afraid that wouldn't do," she replied. "Isn't that so, *mon Général?*" Taking things one step farther, she proceeded to chuck the General under his triple chin. The result was that Tishin's smooth-shaven cheeks turned a brilliant shade of crimson, and his sleepy blue eyes took on an alert and wide-awake expression.

"My heart will give out with joy!" cried Madame Petrova. She was seated across the room, and couldn't possibly have realized what her daughter was up to. "What a glorious day for us, Petrushka dear, to see these two young people billing and cooing . . . what a nuptial celebration we shall make for them. And though surely it shall take one year, one solid year off my life—for such things always do, you know—it will nevertheless be well worth the sacrifice. But come, my dear." Extending her slim, girlish hand, Madame Petrova waited for her husband to help her to her feet. "We must give them a moment to themselves. Surely they want to get down on their knees and thank God for having brought them together."

And so Henriette had her way, her aunt's sharp little eyes gazing at her disapprovingly as she reluctantly left the drawing room. No sooner had they gone, when she came swiftly to her feet, for the General reeked of Verona Violette, and the heavy floral scent was making her quite nauseous.

"Thank goodness you didn't come in with something nasty on your shoe," she began, reminding him of past unpleasantries, and thus setting the mood for the scene she was about to enact.

Ardallion Hippolytovich's rapturous expression began to fade, and he fidgeted uncomfortably, arranging and rearranging the numerous little trinkets that hung from his watch chain.

"Let us get down to the business at hand, General."

"Which concerns *your* lovely hand, if I may be so bold," he replied, is self-satisfied laughter ending abruptly when he saw th she wasn't the least bit amused.

"You want my hand, yes," she said severely. "So you wish to marry me, do you?"

The General came to his feet, no doubt made uncomfortable by the way she was standing over him. "Very much so, Henriette Petrovna."

"Why? Do you love me?"

"Why, of course, certainly," he replied, and began to go on in his usual florid and loquacious fashion.

Henriette cut him off with a curt, "Would you still love me if I were to have my own bedroom, a key to which would be provided for my use and my use only?"

The General blushed even more furiously than earlier. "I would never think of forcing myself upon you, *mademoiselle*. That would be abhorrent. After all, I'm a gentleman. But I would also be your husband, and if you'd permit me—"

"I won't permit you anything," she announced. "I want my own room and my own key. In addition, I understand that my hand is worth the tidy sum of five thousand rubles."

"Yes, but—"

"Yes but nothing," she interrupted. She was enjoying every moment of this one-sided exchange, and had no intention of backing down, or allowing the General to comment until she was finished. "My own bedroom, but with only one key to unlock its door, and the dowry, which I expect you to hand over to me *before* the ceremony, and not after. Do these conditions meet with your approval, General Tishin?"

"But Krasnaya Gorka is in need of—"

"I'm not interested in Red Hill, not the slightest bit," she said in her coldest and most calculating tone. "Do you agree to what I've proposed?"

"No, I do not!" exclaimed the General.

"Excellent," she said calmly. "Then there's no further reason for you to press your suit. Those are my terms." She was about to call her parents back when she felt the General's pudgy hand descend on her shoulder.

"But surely you realize how unfair this is. I'm not a wealthy man, Henriette Petrovna."

"Am I to marry someone who can't even provide for me?" she said shrilly.

The poor General looked on the verge of tears. "I'm far from indigent, *mademoiselle*. Life will be very lovely for us at Red Hill, very lovely indeed. But I only meant to say that the dowry would be used for refurnishing the house, so as to make your new home as pleasant and tasteful as possible. But, if you insist, I suppose that as a gentleman I have no choice but to accept your terms."

"What?" she whispered, unable to believe what she'd heard.

The General repeated himself, then reached for her hand, bringing it to his lips. "And now for a little kiss, my dearest, to seal the bargain."

Before she could pull free, he had his hands around her waist, his thick, fleshy lips just inches from her mouth. Staring at his turnip-shaped nose, and seeing the lecherous gleam in his eyes, Henriette wriggled free of his hideous embrace. Having never expected the General to agree to her terms, she was terrified of what might happen, and decided she had no choice but to be as cruel and unfeeling as circumstances dictated.

"One other thing," she said, "so there'll be no misunderstandings."

"Kiss me first, dearest Henriette. You've kept your Ardalosha waiting much too long, you naughty girl."

"I find you repulsive, General Tishin."

"I beg your pardon?"

"Repulsive. Loathsome. Disgusting," she enumerated. "My bedroom would be closed to you at all times. Our marriage will never be consummated, is that clear?"

The glazed and lovesick expression on the General's face was instantly transformed into an angry grimace. "I've never heard of such a thing."

"You hear it now. Yes or no?"

"Absolutely not, Madame. I'm not a eunuch, and I'm deeply offended that you think so little of my gentlemanly charms."

"Dear General," she said patiently, "you're neither a gentleman nor charming." Leaving the General standing there with his mouth hanging open, she called her parents back into the drawing room.

Laska bounded in ahead of all the others, snapping at her heels, and narrowly avoiding being kicked in the head when she lashed out with her shoe.

"Shall we call the priest and pledge the troth?" Sophia Mikhailovna asked excitedly.

"General Tishin has asked me to tell you that he's very sorry, but ill health prevents him from asking for my hand," announced Henriette.

"What?" gasped Auntie V., who appeared to be so infuriated by this unexpected turn of events that she seemed on the verge of throwing herself at her niece, much the same way Laska had done. "But the General is in the prime of his life, the very prime."

"Not anymore, I'm afraid," Henriette said. Supremely composed, and absolutely delighted by the way she'd handled things, she smiled at each of them and sailed gracefully from the drawing room.

La Belle Henriette, she thought as she hurried up to her room. Worshiping glances following my every step.

Not five minutes later the entire household was thrown into an uproar. Having locked herself in her room, Henriette listened with one ear pressed to the jamb. She heard the sound of angry voices, doors slamming right and left, and the General's carriage clattering down the lime alley. Then came a piercing shriek, followed by Laska's frightened barking.

"Water! Bring water, Anninka, water and smelling salts!" she heard her aunt cry out.

She unlocked the door and stuck her head out, the better to hear what was going on.

"*Mes entrailles, mes pauvres entrailles!*" her mother was moaning at the top of her voice. "The shame of it, the horror! *Ô cruelle fille! Tu as déchiré mon âme, complètement!* Cruel

196

daughter, you have lacerated my inmost being! My entrails, *mes pauvres entrailles èventrées!*"

"Water, bring more water!" shouted her father as he bounded up the stairs. He paused at the top of the landing, and seeing her standing by the door, he began to shake his fist at her. "Your mother has fainted, you stupid fool!"

A moment later Auntie V. darted into view. "Murderess! Scoundrel!" she cried, shaking her fist the same way her brother was doing. "Why, you ought to be tied to your bed, kept on bread and water—"

"Locked in a dark room," added her father.

"You're a wicked, ungrateful girl," her aunt went on. "Your poor mother's health is seriously impaired. She may never recover, and all because of you, you trollop!"

"He told us exactly what you said," her father informed her.

"Fainted dead away and she stands there grinning like a brazen hussy. May her evil tongue go dry, may her black heart burst—"

Henriette slammed the door, locking it securely.

"Mes entrailles! Mes pauvres entrailles!"

Her father began to pound on the door. "Come out this instant, Henriette!"

"No, I won't."

"Mes entrailles . . ."

"I'm ruined, ruined forever," groaned her aunt. "Why, even a harlot wouldn't say such things. Shake the soul out of her, Petya. You're a beast, Henriette! God won't grant you happiness, do you hear!"

"Unlock the door or I'll break it down!" threatened her father.

"Surely you must have a spare key, Petya," said her aunt.

"Of course I do. They're downstairs in my study. You'll find them hanging on a ring behind the door."

Auntie V. hurried down the stairs, and in her absence, Sophia Mikhailovna once again began to moan. "The devil himself planted you inside me!" she sobbed as she staggered down the hall to her room. "You should have rotted away in my womb for what you've done!"

"Now, now Sonyushka, it'll be all right," said Peter Semyonovich.

"All right!" Madame Petrova shrieked at the top of her voice. "How can it be all right when I've lost five years . . . no, not five . . . ten, yes, ten years of my life because of what she's done? I'm getting into bed and I won't come out, not ever again. I shall die because of you, Henriette!"

A key scraped in the lock and Henriette shrank back, terrified now that she was about to come face to face with her father. The door was thrown open with such force it was nearly torn off its hinges, and Peter Semyonovich stormed into the bedroom. Raising his hand, he slapped her across the face, not once, but three times in swift, merciless succession.

"That's for your impertinence," he shouted. "And for your stupidity and pigheadedness. Your one chance to make a life for yourself and what do you do, you insult your suitor in the filthiest and most degrading way imaginable."

Henriette refused to give him the satisfaction of shedding even a single tear. "I'm leaving, anyway," she announced.

"To a convent, that's where!" cried Auntie V. "Where they'll teach you obedience and the fear of God, to have done such a monstrous thing to your family."

"Shut up!" screamed Henriette.

"What did you say?"

"Shut your ugly little mouth, and keep it shut, you mean, spiteful old woman!"

"Don't you dare talk to my sister that way," warned her father.

"Then hit me again," she said defiantly, turning her head

to the side and presenting him with her cheek. "Because I'm leaving, just as I said."

"Are you now?" he said with a sneer.

"That's right. I'm going to Petersburg. I've accepted a position as governess."

Auntie V. looked at her in utter amazement. "No wonder she said such scandalous things. Why, the impudent slut, she never intended to marry him, not from the beginning."

"No daughter of mine is going to take up a position like a common serf. I'm a member of the nobility," her father reminded her. "I have my name to uphold, my reputation. A girl from a fine home, working for a living—why, it's absurd."

"But not as absurd as trying to make her marry against her will."

It was Masha, but before her sister could say anything else, her father ordered her back to her room, telling her it was none of her concern.

"I'll cut you off," he threatened, even as Masha stood there in the hall, trying to reason with him. "I warn you, Henriette, I'll leave you penniless."

"I'm twenty-four years old," she replied. "And if I have to make my own way in the world, then that's just what I'll do."

"I'll tie you to your bed, do you hear?" shouted her father, looking enraged that she'd dare to disobey him.

"No, I don't hear, Father," she replied, never once raising her voice, and so outwardly calm and unmoved by the exchange that her father was even more infuriated than he might otherwise have been.

Glaring at her with his little round gray eyes, Peter Semyonovich snatched the key off her dressing table, then slammed the door behind him. Henriette heard the key turn in the lock.

"That's where you'll stay," her father told her from behind

the door. "And if it means keeping you locked up for the next ten years, so be it."

They came to her in the darkness. Spirits, vaguely seen creatures composed of tattered shadows. Henriette pulled the bedcovers over her chin, peering at them with a mixture of awe and fright. At the foot of the bed a monk lifted the skirts of his greasy black cassock, displaying his grizzly thighs and pendulous sex.

Henriette slammed her eyes shut. "Go away," she whispered. "Leave me in peace because God will protect me. Go away, do you hear?"

The monk had no intention of departing. He capered about the bed, his goatish breath causing her to feel faint and dizzy.

"I did nothing. Why must you torment me so?"

"The torment hasn't even begun," replied the monk. "Wait until you arrive in Petersburg, *ma chère.*"

"Petersburg? What about it?"

"Don't be a fool, Henriette Petrovna," said this creature of her nightmares. He jabbed a bony finger under her chin, forcing her to look into his leering yellow eyes. "What do you see?" he demanded.

The visions danced before her, the colors thin and attenuated, unraveling like yarn. She saw a door opening, a servant in livery beckoning her inside. She saw two small, fragile-looking children curtsying before her, while behind them stood a tall, arrogant man with coldly menacing eyes.

"Go away, leave me in peace," she pleaded. She turned her eyes in the direction of the ikon stand, where the blood-red glimmer of the altar lamp illuminated the faces of the Mother of God and her beautiful, blond-haired Son.

"They won't help you," said the monk, "for the gates of heaven are closed forever. The Antichrist resides in Petersburg. Hurry to his side and you will be lost, Henriette

Petrovna. Disobey your father and the kingdom of heaven will never be yours."

"Go away, you spiteful creature. Go away and leave me in peace because God loves me, and His Son loves me, and the Blessed Virgin loves me, too."

With a rapacious grin, the monk raised his trailing skirts and beat a frenzied tattoo with his cloven hoofs, making her bed shake and causing the ikons to rattle about on their stand.

Henriette knew it was a dream. But when she pressed her lids tightly together, the drooling figure of the monk remained before her eyes, dancing obscenely at the foot of the bed.

"Watch me," he whispered, "so that you'll know exactly what awaits you, Henriette Petrovna!"

The door to her room flew open. A loud report echoed in her ears. She saw a stricken figure lying alone in the middle of a snow-covered field, surrounded by the dark ghosts of century-old pines.

"Who is it?"

"Another's happiness," replied the monk. "But look again."

There was a woman standing in the doorway, staring at Henriette with sharp and accusing gray eyes. She raised her hand, revealing the bloodied stigmata in the center of her palm.

"Drink of my chalice!" the woman shrieked in a terrifying voice.

"God be merciful!" groaned Henriette as the woman rushed toward her. "It's me, it's me!" she began to wail, even as she heard someone pounding on the door.

"Henriette! Wake up, wake up, Henriette! It was a dream! Damn him with his locked doors. A dream!"

Henriette opened her eyes, and looked around in confusion. Her skin was wet and clammy beneath her nightdress, the bedcovers in a tangle at her feet.

"Henriette, wake up!" cried Anninka from the other side of the door.

"I'm . . . I'm all right now," she called out. "It was a nightmare, Anninka. Find the key."

"He's hidden it, the wretch. Are you sure you'll be all right?"

"Yes, just a bad dream," she said again.

"I'll sleep out here in the hall, just in case," the old woman replied.

Just in case of what? she wondered. She gazed at the ikon shrine that rose like a black upright coffin in the corner of her room, seeking not only comfort, but also refuge and protection from the Evil One.

"Jesus Christ, my beloved, help me," she whispered fervently. "Teach me, and enter within me so that I may be purified of all these horrible thoughts."

A radiant light filled the room, so that for a moment she was blinded and had to look away. No sooner did it begin to fade than she felt His presence, then saw Him lying beside her as if He'd been there for hours. His beautiful silken hair was spread over the pillows in a golden halo, His skin smooth and milky-white, and the lance wound in His side just a narrow, puckered scar, scarcely visible. As He gazed at her with His sad and merciful eyes, she heard Him speak.

"I shall hold you, and make you safe," He whispered. "My love will warm you, Henriette, and we will be as one."

Yes, as one, forever safe, she thought as He drew her toward him and held her in His strong, young arms. Her body trembled voluptuously at His touch, and when He slipped His hands beneath her nightdress she closed her eyes and smiled dreamily. "Oh yes, yes, make me beautiful with your love," she told Him. Locked in His embrace, nothing could happen to her, and she drifted back to sleep, no longer tormented by nightmares or agonizing visions of her own damnation.

Peter Semyonovich kept Henriette locked in her room for three whole days, giving Anninka the key only to bring in food and empty the chamber pot. When, at the end of this period of time, he came to her and demanded an apology, Henriette refused to give in, and wouldn't yield to his threats and angry words.

Her father looked at her uneasily. "So you want to be a barren old maid, do you? Well, think again, Henriette. Think good and hard." And he closed the door and locked it.

Henriette was no longer frightened of him, however. Three days of solitude had been like a retreat, and she felt great peace of mind and certainty of purpose. That he would disinherit her no longer seemed a problem, not when she had the love and support of her sisters. Irena had come just the other day, arguing bitterly with her father, and was forced to speak to Henriette from out in the hall, for Peter Semyonovich wouldn't give her the key. She'd slipped a packet of rubles under the door so that her sister would have enough money for the train ticket to Petersburg and for whatever other expenses she might have before she started to receive her monthly salary.

Now, after nearly ten days of being kept a prisoner, Henriette was packed and ready to leave. Anninka had cleverly made an impression of the key in wax, and Gregor had driven to Mtsensk to have a duplicate prepared. As Henriette listened to the clock ticking in the hall, she trembled with both fear and excitement, now that she was about to embark on the first adventure of her life.

It was after midnight when the key turned slowly in the lock. Gregor put his finger to his lips, warning her to be as silent as possible. If Peter Semyonovich discovered what they were up to, not only would Henriette suffer the consequences, but he too would be in a great deal of trouble.

Gregor picked up some of her bags and started down the hall. Henriette didn't follow him, not immediately. She stood in the doorway, staring at her little room, now stripped of all the things she cared about. Her ikons were packed securely in one of her suitcases, but the three-tiered stand remained, its shelves sadly empty, and the wax-stained strip of carpet laid down before it still bearing the worn imprint of her knees.

Moonlight filtered through the curtains, making everything look as pale and ghostly as a vision in a dream. Or a nightmare, she thought, though she'd slept surprisingly well these last few nights. The letter to Count Ivanov had already been mailed, thanks to Gregor again, and so her arrival in the capital wouldn't be unexpected. For a moment she was afraid to move, as if taking one step beyond the threshold would instantly sever her from her past, and she'd no longer have any ties to the pasty-faced little girl whose room this had always been for as long as she could remember.

La Belle Henriette makes her adieus, she thought to herself.

At the last moment she put down her bags and rolled up the strip of carpet on which she made her obeisances. Then, with the narrow runner snug under one arm and a bag in each hand, she turned away without shedding so much as a single tear, and hurried down the stairs.

The next morning, upon learning what had transpired while he slept, Peter Semyonovich loudly proclaimed Henriette's death. Gathering his servants together, he warned them that from this day forth they were never again to utter his daughter's name. Then, in accordance with custom, he went from room to room, making sure every mirror was veiled. Even as a boy he'd been taught that in a house where there has been a death, a man who sees his reflection in a mirror must himself die soon after.

204

Twelve

SANKT PIETER BURKH. SANKT-PETERBURG. ST. PETERSBURG. PETERSBURG. "PITER." It had been called the most abstract and premeditated city in the world, the Venice of the North, dreaming of infinite glory and boundless power. Others spoke of it as an act of violence, a monument to the iron will of its founder. Built on swampland at the mouth of the Neva River at a cost of some two hundred thousand lives, the city spread across nineteen islands, furrowed by canals, linked by bridges, and always presenting its glittering front to the sea.

Taken by droshky from the Nikolayevsky Station after twenty-three harrowing hours in a bleak third-class compartment, Henriette cowered in her seat, clutching her wax-stained carpet as the little dark-blue droshky hurtled down the Nevsky Prospect. Bounding recklessly from the stone to the wooden roadbed, the *isvostchik* drove as if he were racing every other carriage that crowded the wide, straight avenue. Fashionable shops rose up on either side, yet there were few pedestrians about, and the broad thoroughfare looked deserted. Petersburgers didn't relish the hot, muggy weather, and those who could afford it summered in the country or on the outlying islands.

Shop signs danced before her eyes—a horn of plenty over a grocery store, golden bunches of grapes for a wine merchant, coats and trousers, boots even too large for Peter the Great, immense wedges of cheese, and sausages as thick as tree trunks. In swift succession they flew past the Liteiny Prospect and the Fontanka Canal, the Anichkov Palace, the Imperial Public Library, and then the long, white façade of the Gostiny Dvor, Petersburg's famous vaulted arcade of shops.

Henriette wanted to tug on the cord attached to the cabby's elbow, and have him stop again and again, but his shaggy little horse snorted and hurried on, dragging at the shafts. The hot summer air fanned her cheeks, and she held onto the edge of her seat as the *isvostchik* turned left at the Moika Canal and drove past silent rows of palatial residences painted in pale, restrained colors, austere and classical, and all testifying to the immense wealth of their occupants.

They were now in the Admiralteiskaya, the Admiralty Quarter between the Neva and the Moika, one of the most fashionable sections of the city. Henriette leaned forward and began to look anxiously about, as if she'd lost something, but couldn't quite remember what it was. In a few minutes they would be arriving at the English Embankment, where Count Ivanov maintained a residence she imagined would be just as lavish and imposing as all these others.

The pace of the driver's horse grew less frenetic, even stately and dignified as it trotted along. The *duga,* a wooden arch that looked like an enormous horseshoe and held the horse's collar to the shafts, swung sedately back and forth to the ringing beat of iron-shod hoofs striking the pavement.

When they turned right at the English Quay Henriette was

able to catch her first glimpse of the Neva, gently lapping against the pink granite parapets of the embankment. Facing the somber, blue-green waters of the river were more palaces and private residences, many with columned façades and balconies jutting over the sidewalk.

The driver tugged on the reins and came to a jarring stop before a town house. Decorated with frescoes and other Italianate ornaments, it was painted in the same pale and faded-looking yellow as every other building along the quay.

"*Angliskaya Naberezhnaya*," grunted the cabby. Having already received his fare, the *isvostchik* dumped her baggage onto the sidewalk and drove off.

Henriette stared at the town house and then at the turbid waters of the Neva that it faced. The oppressive summer air weighed heavily upon her, and she felt like giving up before she'd even started. Instead, she piled her bags under the columned portico that let out onto the quiet and deserted-looking street, with its unbroken façade and row of spindly shade trees. Finally there was nothing left to do but ring the bell.

She was admiring the bronze door handle, which was fashioned in the shape of a bird's claw clutching a glittering chunk of crystal, when the front door swung open. Standing before her was a lackey in gray livery with gold braid, a man of rather indeterminate age, with crooked teeth and a pronounced stoop. As he bent forward, he peered at her inquisitively.

"The laundress?" he asked.

Henriette stiffened. "Certainly not. I'm Mademoiselle Petrova, the new governess."

"Oh yes, the governess. Right this way." The footman held the door open, but made no move to help her with her bags.

Henriette, however, was determined to start things off on the right foot. After all, the Petrovs were a noble family, and even though she was now in someone's employ, there was no reason to consider herself any less well-born than when she lived at Petrovka. So she left her baggage under the portico, motioning to the motley collection of traveling cases with an imperious wave of her hand.

The lackey frowned, then stepped outside and took charge of her belongings. When he returned, it was only to pile everything at her feet, reacting with particular distaste to the rolled-up carpet. Without once taking his eyes off her, he ceremoniously flicked imaginary dust off his white-gloved fingertips.

"Polina Filippovna will be down to see you shortly," he announced.

She was about to ask who this Polina Filippovna was, when the lackey walked right by her and on into the front hall, where he turned a corner and disappeared from sight. Henriette remained behind in the stuffy little vestibule. Beyond the entryway stretched the marble-floored hall, lit by an enormous crystal chandelier. A wide staircase carpeted in cerise velvet faced the front door, a staircase such as *La Belle Henriette* might use to good advantage, its curving banister well suited to the requirements of a dramatic entrance.

It was along these wide red steps that a woman now descended. Dressed in black bombazine that rustled so loudly it made Henriette think of a belled cat, this newcomer appeared to be in her mid-fifties, with a long, thin neck, and the large, bulging eyes of a carp.

"Mademoiselle Petrova?" the woman asked, speaking with the rolling *r*'s of a Petersburg aristocrat. "I am Polina Filippovna, the Count's housekeeper." She extended her hand, her skinny white fingers sticking out from her black silk mitt.

Henriette found this arrangement rather extraordinary, having never seen such a fingerless glove. She must have stared too hard, for Polina Filippovna jerked her hand back as if it had been scalded.

"If you'll follow me, *mademoiselle*, I'll show you to your room. The Count has already left for the Ministry. He's not expected back for several hours."

"Shall I leave my bags here?" she asked.

"Surely you don't expect *me* to carry them, do you?" Before Henriette could answer, the woman turned abruptly away and started up the stairs.

Grabbing her wax-stained carpet, Henriette ran after her. She had no time to look around or get her bearings, for the housekeeper fairly raced up the stairs, not stopping until she reached the third floor.

"Yours," said the housekeeper, pointing to a door at the end of the dimly lit hallway. Again she turned abruptly away, so that Henriette sensed this was probably a habit of hers that would take some getting used to.

Promising herself that at their next meeting she wouldn't allow herself to be easily intimidated, having had quite enough of that from Auntie V., Henriette opened the door at the end of the corridor.

Before her was a room not much larger than a cubicle, with a high, narrow bed in an iron frame, a chiffonier with a cracked mirror, a washstand such as one found in cheap hotels, a plain wooden table, and a single chair. The bare floor was painted a muddy reddish-brown, and made the room look even tinier than it was. Dingy white curtains hung limply before the tall windows, of which there were only two, so narrow they scarcely allowed any light to enter. Dusty yellow wallpaper completed the wretched décor, peeling where it met the low ceiling, and cracked and spotted throughout.

Thinking of what she'd left behind, the sunny warmth of Anninka's kitchen, her own pleasant little bedroom, her brother's laughter, her sisters' love, Henriette felt like turning back, yet knew she could do nothing of the kind. So she took a deep breath, swallowed her tears, and went downstairs to get her bags.

Seeing her struggling with her traveling cases, the footman she'd met at the door grudgingly offered his services. His name was Foma Osipovich, and he turned out to be a decent enough fellow once she put aside her airs and refrained from talking down to him.

"Oh, she's a difficult customer, all right, that Filippovna. Stay on her good side if you can, miss, and you'll be all right, for the master believes everything she says, calls her his second set of eyes, he does." The footman smiled with his crooked teeth. "Nice little room you got," he remarked as he put her bags down on the bed.

"Nice?"

"I sleep in the hall, miss, as far from the stove as Siberia, if you ask me. Well, I'd best get downstairs. That Filippovna wants me by the door at every hour of the day and night. You'd think she was expecting the Tsar himself, the way she fusses about it so."

After unpacking her things and setting out her ikons, Henriette looked around and saw there was little improvement. The room still reminded her of a cell, and it would take considerably more than a few fancy pillowslips or a bright quilted counterpane to make it livable. Then, changing her clothes and praying that her situation wasn't as bleak as it appeared, she went downstairs to await the arrival of Count Ivanov.

But when she reached the second floor she paused on the landing, having heard the murmur of voices, and then a child's high-pitched and exuberant laugh. A door was ajar on her right, and unable to resist this opportunity to meet her charges, she knocked briskly and stepped inside.

She found herself in the children's nursery, where two little round faces turned curiously in her direction. Standing before them was a young man in his early twenties, with a face that might have been painted by an ikonographer. Pale and expressive, with a neatly trimmed, spade-shaped beard, and straight blond hair the color of corn silk, it was a face she was certain she'd seen before, though for the moment she couldn't remember where.

"Good afternoon," she said, putting on her best smile and introducing herself.

"A pleasure, a great pleasure," said the children's tutor. "Julian Andreyevich Golovin at your service, *mademoiselle*. We've awaited your arrival with bated breath and keen anticipation," whereupon he swooped down and kissed her hand, causing the children to laugh and even applaud his gallantry.

Henriette was immediately taken with Golovin's easygoing charm. Perhaps they'd become good friends, and she continued to smile, as she didn't often do, while the tutor introduced her to six-year-old Tanya and eight-year-old Misha.

"Enchantée de faire votre connaissance, mademoiselle," said the little girl with a charming curtsy.

Her brother said the same, though he spoke with an undercurrent of sullenness, eying her somewhat suspiciously as he returned to his chair.

"I'll let you get back to your lessons," she said as Julian Andreyevich showed her to the door. "I'm sure we're all going to get along splendidly, aren't we?"

As she descended the wide, carpeted stairs, she could still see the tutor's smiling eyes and lovely blond hair. A friend, she thought, won't that be nice to have a new friend, an ally. Perhaps even—Henriette smiled, and wondered if there was anything that could be done about her red nose and frizzy hair.

Having been on the road with her aunt for several days,

Masha was already worn out from traveling. The journey to Samara covered a distance of some nine hundred versts (six hundred miles by English reckoning), and could only be accomplished by the necessary evil known as "posting." This was a system supposedly designed to aid the traveler, but more often than not meant endless delays and bone-jarring discomfort.

Armed with a road passport that entitled them to horses, carriage, and driver, they'd already learned that the fee they'd paid for this document meant very little now that they were actually on their way. Every twenty or thirty versts they'd stop at one of the decrepit little post stations maintained by the imperial post organization, where they'd order fresh horses for the next stage. This meant unpacking and reloading their baggage every two hours or so, but the majority of the time they were told there weren't any horses to be had, and they'd have to wait.

"For how long?" Auntie V. would inquire.

The postmaster, as the proprietor of these ramshackle hovels was called, would invariably shrug and turn away without a word of explanation, having grown fat and complacent on the misery of travelers and a healthy diet of "palm oil." Pressed for a more specific answer, the stationmaster would mutter how it wasn't his fault, that according to government regulations he was bound to keep a certain number of horses in reserve for Crown couriers, high officials, and imperial mail postilions. He'd point these out if Auntie V. was insistent, then sit back and wait for his palm to be liberally greased.

Then they would have to load everything back into the tarantass, a springless vehicle that resembled an enormous baby buggy. Sitting on a pile of hay in what amounted to little more than a wicker basket on wheels, there was nothing to cushion them from the unending jolts and bumps.

By the fourth day out, Masha was reduced to silence, and lay in the bottom of the tarantass while Auntie V. leaned next to her, shouting loud orders and muttering profanities at the driver. It seemed to Masha that Samara was as far away as America, and that it was her fate to travel this way throughout eternity, never to reach her destination. What made it worse was her frame of mind, for she no longer cared if she took the cure, or did anything else to help herself. To be healthy meant very little, not when she felt she'd been denied her one chance for happiness.

Dead and buried in an unmarked grave, she thought, as if Russia itself had decided to forget that Victor Romanovich Durnovo had ever existed.

"Why is he stopping now, the drunken fool?" Auntie V. sat up and peered over the edge of the tarantass, just as the three-horse team turned off the road and into the dusty courtyard of yet another dismal posthouse.

Soon they found themselves arguing bitterly with the postmaster, who swore there wasn't a single horse to be had, not even the team he usually kept in reserve. Auntie V. refused to believe him, and insisted on a tour of the stables, just to make certain the man wasn't lying.

When she returned her shoes were covered with dung, and her exasperated expression made it plain that for once the stationmaster hadn't been telling a falsehood.

"What about the horses we've been using?" asked Varvara, motioning to the team that had carried them along the bumpy post road for the last two and a half hours.

The postmaster shook his head, pleading with her to believe him when he said they were already requisitioned.

"But what are we to do?" said Auntie V.

The official rolled his eyes heavenward, muttering that such was God's will, and that perhaps by tomorrow morning he might be able to find them a team.

"Might?" shrieked her aunt. "Not might, my good man. No, that won't do at all. This is a very sick girl you see before you. She's on her way to Dr. Postnikov's Kumiss Establishment. If we tarry here much longer her health will be in your hands, my good man."

"I can't help the *tarrying,*" replied the stationmaster, who motioned to the post station, and suggested they find room for themselves inside.

Masha, carrying as much as she could, went up the sagging steps that led into the travelers' common room. Several rough benches ringed the walls, which at one time had been white-washed but now appeared to be covered with grease. Two fellow travelers lay asleep at the opposite end of the room, snoring loudly and rolling their shoulders about each time a bedbug began its dinner. Masha spread her bedding across one of the benches. Giving everything a liberal sprinkling of Persian insecticide, she lay down, resting her head against her leather traveling pillow. Flies swarmed everywhere, and on the nearby window ledge sat a glass fly catcher filled with cider, but not a single fly.

She saw no washstand, though when Varvara came in she brought with her a towel soaked in water, so Masha could at least wipe some of the grime off her face. Then they made tea, a boiling samovar just about the only thing one could always count on finding in a post station. Rather than tempt fate by making a meal of posthouse provisions, notoriously vile and liable to upset even the most cast-iron stomach, they dined on white bread and tinned meat, the same as they'd had yesterday, and the same as the day before that.

The next morning Masha awoke no more refreshed than when she'd gone to sleep, though at least the flies had vanished, as well as their two neighbors. Auntie V. noticed their absence as well and flew into a rage, pounding on the flimsy door that led into the postmaster's living quarters. As soon as the official poked his sleepy head outside, she demanded to know how he could have sent two men on their way while leaving behind two poor, defenseless women.

"And one of them so sick that if you jabbed her with a pitchfork you probably wouldn't even draw blood," she insisted.

But for all her colorful imagery, the stationmaster was unmoved by her tirade. But maybe this afternoon, he promised, or perhaps this evening, he might be able to find them horses. If not, he could state categorically and on his word of honor that by the following day they'd certainly be on their way again.

Masha spent the remainder of the morning sipping tea and sitting out in the sun. Auntie V. sat next to her, stiffly erect in a hard-backed chair. Her eyes were focused on the road, and each time she saw something approach she'd jump anxiously to her feet. But invariably the cloud of dust that rolled down the post road brought with it a peasant cart, or an old-fashioned britska such as the poorer clergy still used, or a bailiff sitting high in a racing droshky, but still not a single government tarantass.

By late afternoon even Masha had begun to despair of ever reaching their destination. Taking pity on them, the stationmaster's wife brought out a plate of sausages, but the moment Masha took a taste, it was as if she'd sunk her teeth into a rat's tail smeared with tar.

"There's something!" Auntie V. cried out.

Although the carriage drove into the courtyard, it proved to be a privately owned vehicle. Masha went back inside and lay down on the bench, eying the roaches that crawled across the ceiling. But then the door flew open and Auntie V. rushed into the common room, ordering her to pack.

"A savior!" she exclaimed in a delighted voice. "God has been watching over us. We're saved, Maria Petrovna, and all because our patience has been justly rewarded. Oh, that beast of a postmaster to keep us here like prisoners. But now we're off, straight through to Samara." She rushed about the room and grabbed up their things, loading her arms with bundles and odd pieces of baggage.

Masha sat up, looking at her in confusion.

"Don't just sit there, niece. We don't want to keep him waiting. He's an important personage, a government courier, an officer."

"Who?" she asked.

Her aunt clapped an astonished hand to her mouth. "My goodness! I didn't even ask his name."

But not ten minutes later, as Masha sat comfortably in the calash that hardly swayed on its supple springs, she had ample opportunity to meet their benefactor. Captain Stepan Danchenko was an officer in the Guards, and looked quite handsome in his white linen tunic and matching trousers. He was an aide-de-camp, and in this capacity was on his way to Samara to deliver some important documents to the Governor of the province. "And when your charming aunt told me of your dilemma, my heart went out to you."

Masha smiled and expressed her gratitude, lowering her eyes and coughing into the handkerchief she kept in readiness, clutched between her fingers. "You must excuse our appearance, Captain. I fear we've been on the road far too long."

"There's nothing to excuse, *mademoiselle*," replied the officer with a gracious smile, one that somehow didn't go along with the inquisitive look in his eyes. These were his most striking feature, Masha having never known anyone with eyes of this particular color. Hazel was the closest approximation of their shade, though they actually verged on chestnut. Lucent and inquiring, they gave the Captain's face a kind of boyish curiosity that wasn't at all unappealing.

By the time darkness had fallen, Masha had learned a great deal about their host—or at least all those superficial details strangers are apt to share with one another. Several years older than she, Danchenko had grown up in Petersburg, the only son of a General who'd died shortly after his birth. His mother still lived in the capital, and it was her greatest wish that her son follow in the footsteps of his father. And so, when he came of age, he was enrolled in one of the military academies in St. Petersburg.

"And you, my dear Maria Petrovna," for by now they'd dispensed with the bulk of formality, "what awaits you in Samara, may I ask?"

Masha didn't want to talk about her illness, and told him simply that she was going to take the kumiss cure.

"But she'll be fine," chimed in Auntie V., sounding as if she were well on her way to arranging another match. "It's very minor, indeed it is, Stepan Alexeyevich. One of those Chinese bronchial things we've been hearing so much about. Isn't that so, Masha dear?"

Masha smiled patiently. But when she looked up, she noticed how something very sad and touching had come into the Captain's eyes. It wasn't pity for her, but rather an expression of empathy and concern. But though she began to eye him attentively in the darkness, and even joined in the conversation, a shadow soon crept across her thoughts, until the memory of her beloved Victor made her feel guilty for enjoying herself. Once again she grew silent, withdrawing like a night-blooming flower, whose petals draw shut at the first touch of light.

Vera was back at Petrovka, and for the first time since her wedding she was genuinely happy. For one, the steward's house that she and Simon had taken over was a great improvement over horrid Golovlovo. For another, whenever she asked Simon for money he would dip into his pockets and extract a lovely wad of bills, peeling off tens and twenties with a kind of reckless abandon. She bought herself an entire wardrobe of new clothes, and promenaded along the lime alley, twirling a pink sunshade and looking anxiously about for admirers.

But most of all she looked for Simon, waiting for him to return from his duties. If anything, marriage had made her even greedier, not only for material things, but also for the one form of pleasure that only Simon could provide. Not even Matriona, who had become her confidante, knew of Vera's feelings, the way she would tremble when Simon came into a room, or how she would lie there in bed until her patience was rewarded by the sound of his heavy footfalls on the stairs.

The door would open and he'd fill the threshold, eying her with a lewd smile that only excited her all the more. If she was good, he would allow her to undress him, and she would make a game of it until he was so aroused he couldn't control himself. That was the part she liked best of all, when he mounted her like a stallion and she pretended to resist.

"Whinny for me, Vera," he would say, and she'd peel her lips back, giggling and doing everything he asked.

If such behavior was sinful, then Vera willingly accepted the fact that she was doomed. But even if the fires of hell awaited her, she still could not stop herself, nor did she even make the effort to try.

Dr. Postnikov's Kumiss Establishment was the oldest of its kind in Russia, and was situated in a beautifully landscaped park that extended to the very brink of the Volga. Numerous brightly painted cottages were scattered among the groves of pine and oak. It was in one of these that Masha and her aunt had taken up residence.

Now, after nearly two weeks, there could be little doubt

that the kumiss was definitely of great value. A healthy color had returned to Masha's cheeks, and she'd gained nearly ten pounds. Each day she consumed some ten bottles of the nourishing tonic, a white liquid with a heady, sour flavor that always made her throat tingle. Kumiss, or milk wine, as it was sometimes called, was prepared right on the grounds of the hotel, where mares grazed on the rich plume grass of the steppe. Tatars were employed to milk the mares and make the kumiss, which was produced by an elaborate process of fermentation.

Even Auntie V. took the cure, though she claimed a great antipathy toward its taste, and insisted it made her feel unpleasantly tipsy. Yet her chronic dyspepsia, of which she'd suffered for so long, hadn't once flared up in the two weeks they'd spent here.

Although the heat was on occasion excessive, Masha took as many outings as her strength permitted. Armed with an umbrella to protect her from the sun, she set out almost daily, carrying a basket in which ten bottles of kumiss rattled about, as well as the nourishing lunch prepared for her by the staff. These day-long walks gave her much time for thought and reflection, and as her health slowly revived, so too did her spirits.

With a determined and self-reliant stride she would head out across the steppe, breathing deeply, and challenging the tubercular processes, as if willpower alone could rid her of the disease. Though she still carried the burden of her grief, it was gradually replaced by anger. There were times when alone on the steppe she would find herself actually shouting, railing at the men whom she felt were responsible for the young Count's murder. Turgenev, Belinsky, Kalinovich the *ispravnik*, all passed before the eyes of her imagination, and each she held accountable for Victor's tragic death.

One afternoon she discovered much to her chagrin that she

had an audience. He was a deeply tanned and gray-haired old man—a peasant, judging from his appearance, for he wore a coarse gray linen overblouse and matching trousers, with plaited bark sandals on his feet. When he proposed that they set out together, as he too was armed with a basketful of kumiss, she couldn't bring herself to tell him that she preferred to be alone.

"Who were you shouting at?" he asked when they resumed their walk. He spoke with a faint lisp, yet his voice—his entire demeanor, in fact—seemed to generate an aura of peace and well-being. "But you needn't tell me if you don't wish," he went on, "for I don't mean to pry."

Masha surprised herself, and as they headed across the steppe, breathing deeply of the dry, motionless air, she found herself telling him all about Count Durnovo.

"You would murder them all, wouldn't you?" said the moujik, his sharp, grayish eyes peering at her intently.

"Why shouldn't they suffer as he suffered?"

"Because it would be wrong," the old man said simply. "Don't you see, child, that if a man harms you, who are you to set yourself up to judge him, whether he's right or wrong? We can't use violence against each other, not even to oppose violence."

Masha sensed that she was in the presence of a *starets*, a wise man, who by prayer and meditation had come to understand many of life's great mysteries. Yet she was still unable to agree with him.

"There was no meaning to my friend's death, no purpose," she said. "Had he died for a cause, or a belief, then perhaps I wouldn't feel such anger. But he died merely that other men might fill their pockets from his misery, and that's unforgivable."

"Nothing is unforgivable," replied the *starets*, "except

perhaps to waste one's life. If you persist in carrying this anger about, in the end it will kill you as surely as an assassin's bullet. But if you learn to subdue your passions, and gain the upper hand of your pride, which is your first duty to yourself, then I promise you all the rest will come easy enough."

Masha smiled sadly. The old man made it sound so simple, as if he'd given her a formula with which she could structure the remainder of her life.

A light trap, drawn by a horse in English harness, now drew abreast of them. "Lev Nikolayevich!" the driver called out. "We'd best be leaving if we're to get there before dark."

"Isn't it always this way?" the *starets* told her with a laugh that was as gentle and tender as his smile. "We begin to get to some truth about ourselves, only to discover we're either too early or too late, or we're supposed to be somewhere and we're not. But permit me to tell you one more thing, child. Don't respond to dark deeds with dark deeds of your own, for they'll only cause you even greater sorrow. And as for the others, Turgenev in particular, you needn't waste your time being angry with him. I know him well. The man is completely indifferent to questions of morality."

"You know him?" she said with surprise.

The old man nodded. "I've been to Spasskoye on numerous occasions." He took her hand in his and held it for a moment, so that she couldn't help but wonder if he could heal her with his touch.

When he was seated in the carriage, Masha having declined his invitation of a ride back to the kumiss establishment, she told him what a deep impression their conversation had made on her, and how she would try very hard to take his advice.

"Where are you from?" he asked.

Masha told him, and the old man nodded as if he knew the

area well.

"Come and visit me when you can," he said. "Yasnaya Polyana is only a few hours from your home." As her mouth dropped open in astonishment, for she knew of only one man who could claim such an address, Count Lev Nikolayevich Tolstoy waved his hand and drove off.

Thirteen

Wrapped in the dismal yellow fog of autumn, Petersburg had turned dank and sullen. The early golden autumn had vanished with the last leaves falling from the trees of the Summer Garden, and an icy drizzle descended for days on end. The gray, slimy sky gave no promise of relief. When the rains stopped, the winds came, and for weeks now Henriette had listened to them blowing in from the sea. The Neva howled angrily below her narrow window, whipping the granite parapets of the embankment. When she looked out she could see nothing but a thick, nacreous fog, lit by the faint glow of Vasilyevsky Island on the opposite side of the river.

Drawing her shawl more closely over her shoulders, she sank down onto her little wax-stained carpet, but even the cheery glow of the ikon lamp failed to dispel her gloom. She had lived in this horrid garret for several months now, and not once had she heard a kind word from her employer. Dmitri Fyodorovich Ivanov was as vain and arrogant as she'd imagined, and the hint of frugality revealed in his letter ran much deeper than that. He was as penurious as her father, and took great delight in being able to save even a single kopeck. If she broke a cup, it was deducted from her wages. If Misha tore his trousers, as had happened when he'd caught them on a nail during one of their outings, she was held responsible, and the money to mend them was subtracted from her salary. But that seemed the least of it. She could survive the few missing kopecks, but she didn't know how much longer she could survive the loneliness, or that foul-tempered shrew of a housekeeper.

Only Julian Andreyevich made life bearable. With his smiling eyes and beautiful corn-silk-colored hair, he gave her reason to hope that soon she'd grow accustomed to her new surroundings, and learn to take the snubs and reproaches in her stride.

Yes, she thought as she rested her knees on her thread-bare carpet, one day it would all change, and she'd become Madame Golovina, Julian's proud and loving wife. If only I had the patience to wait that long, she thought, for Julian was so circumspect, always observing all the proprieties. They had ample opportunity to be alone, but even when no one else was around he never made advances, or took her hand in his, warming it with his touch. If the Blessed Mother's Son always came to her, why couldn't Julian do the same? He was the image of her Redeemer, which was why she thought she'd seen him before, the first time they met. So why couldn't he take her in his arms as gentle Jesus did, telling her his love would make her beautiful?

Tired of pretending to be meek and subservient, Henriette came resolutely to her feet. Now that Irena had moved here with her husband, it wouldn't be so terrible if she lost her job. I'll tell the Count I can't continue living like this, she said to herself. I'm a woman from a noble family, and expect to be treated as such. The audacity, to stuff me away in this wretched little room, so cold I might as well be sleeping out in the hall with poor Foma, as far from the stove as Siberia.

She heard a tentative knock, and looked curiously in the direction of the door.

"It's Julian Andreyevich," she heard the tutor say.

Don't run, she told herself.

Yet it couldn't be helped. She flew across the room, her fingers clawing at the doorknob. In the dim light of the hall he seemed all aglow, like the Redeemer in a crown of thorns.

"I don't mean to disturb you," the young man began.

She suddenly noticed he was in evening dress, a sparkling white waistcoat and shirtfront, and a tailcoat that smelled of benzine, as if he'd only just cleaned it himself. Henriette guessed that his clothes came from a first-rate tailor, though not very recently.

"And don't you look elegant," she commented, when a strangely familiar voice whispered in her ear, telling her to throw her arms around him before he got away. After all, said the voice, buzzing in her ear like a gnat, if you can give yourself to the Son of God, why not give yourself to someone made in His image?

But the tutor spoke up before she could say anything. He'd intended to take his sister to the ballet this evening, but he'd just received word that she'd taken ill.

"Nothing serious, I hope."

"No, not really," he replied, and hesitantly asked if she'd care to go in his sister's place.

She thought his shyness extremely charming, and equally attractive was the way he shifted his weight from one cracked patent-leather shoe to the other. But though she was sorely tempted to accept his invitation, she knew she wasn't supposed to leave the children.

Julian grinned mischievously, and told her that everything was already taken care of. Foma had agreed to stand watch outside the nursery. As for the Count and Filippovna, both were out for the evening, and weren't expected back until late.

"I'll need a few minutes to change," she said.

"I'll wait for you downstairs," and he hurried from the room as Henriette stood by the door and thought that a few minutes wouldn't do very much good at all.

But when she came downstairs some ten minutes later, attired in the steel-gray gown she'd worn for Vera's wedding, Henriette felt that her appearance was more than acceptable, and nothing to be ashamed of. Yet when they arrived at the Maryinsky Theater in time for the eight-o'clock curtain, she began to have her doubts.

For one, the old soldier at the entrance, whose job it was to take their wraps and galoshes, actually turned his back on them the moment they stepped inside. Julian had to tap him on the shoulder to get his attention, and even then the attendant wore a smug and condescending expression as he grudgingly took their coats.

Julian tried to make light of the snub, taking her arm and leading her upstairs. Henriette, who'd never been to the Maryinsky, let alone the ballet, gawked at everything she saw. But the higher they rose, the more self-conscious she became. When they reached the third balcony she was out of breath, and the beautiful dark-blue velvet carpet of the lower floors was now replaced by narrow threadbare runners, not unlike the one on which she knelt to say her prayers.

No one came forth to show them to their seats in the gallery. So Julian led the way, referring to their tickets, while Henriette eyed the motley crowd that filled the balcony. The people here were mostly clerks and students, overdressed women of the merchant classes munching chocolates from beribboned boxes, their boorish husbands and runny-nosed children, all of whom bore no resemblance to the cream of society occupying the first three tiers of boxes and the huge parterre of stalls.

As the orchestra tuned up, Henriette leaned over the balcony railing, though this in itself was considered highly unseemly, particularly for a young woman who belonged to the gentry. Down below was the world she longed to be a part of, a world that dazzled the eye with the glitter of diamonds and precious gems. The auditorium was ablaze with light, cascading from the enormous cut-crystal chandelier that lit up the entire theater. Everything was either cream-colored or nattier blue, with many gilt bas-reliefs, all done in a fanciful rococo style.

The scents of chypre, ilang-ilang, and frangipani drifted up to her. Far below she glimpsed dashing young officers of the Guards in full dress, elaborately coiffured women in elegant gowns, and attendants in long white stockings and red and gold livery decorated with black imperial eagles, racing up and down the aisles as they showed people to their seats. Although the four royal boxes near the stage were empty, there were numerous court dignitaries in scarlet uniforms, and members of the diplomatic corps in evening dress.

"I'm sorry I couldn't get us better seats," Julian told her when she finally sat down. "But they call the gallery 'paradise,' if it's any consolation."

It wasn't, but Henriette pretended to smile, even as she felt her stomach twisting into knots. "You mustn't apologize," she said, knowing those were the words that were expected. "We're poor, isn't that so? Just a poor tutor and a lowly governess, trying to impress each other with our courtly, society manners, when the truth is we're just as common as everyone else."

She motioned angrily to the tradespeople who thronged the gallery, this misplaced "paradise" that was so high up she felt as if she were being forced to sit with her head just inches from the ceiling. But then she realized what a fool she was making of herself, and that it wasn't Julian's fault this was all he could afford. So she stared at her lap, and the steel-gray folds of what she now decided was a most hideous dress, with such a feeling of bitterness and betrayal she could scarcely catch her breath.

Julian was about to say something when the orchestra struck up the first bars of the national anthem. The entire auditorium rose to its feet, silent and respectful as the broad, sweeping melody of "God Save the Tsar" rang through the hall. Then the lights dimmed and the heavy blue velvet curtain rose on a rather pedestrian backdrop of a lake and a fountain, and a few pale, stunted-looking trees.

Abruptly, Henriette came to her feet. Whispering to Julian that she had to get some air, she was feeling a little faint, she rushed outside. But in the foyer the air was just as close. An attendant eyed her crossly as she hurried past him and took the stairs as quickly as she could, not stopping until she reached the brightly lit corridor on the first floor. Here she paused, clutching the banister, and trying to overcome the terrible knot of tension and anxiety that had taken control of both her stomach and her reason.

Back home she was considered a young woman with impeccable credentials, daughter of one of the wealthiest landowners in the province. But here in Petersburg she was just another girl in the gallery, no closer to what she wanted than when she left Petrovka.

It was a terrifying realization, for it implied that she had sunk to a level of mediocrity from which there could be no escape. But as her stomach knotted even tighter, the outer doors blew open, bringing with them not only a gust of cold air, but also a group of fashionably dressed young men who were laughing very loudly as they tossed their furs to the two footmen who waited to receive them.

The corridor, lit with chandeliers and gas jets, illuminated their fresh, rosy faces. As a boxkeeper stepped forward to lead them to their seats, Henriette turned quickly away, lest Gregor notice her standing by the stairs.

The boxkeeper addressed her brother as "Your Excellency," and seemed to know Gregor quite well. Thumping one of his companions on the back, and looking just like the snob she'd always thought him in his new and elegantly cut suit of evening clothes, Gregor followed his friends into the darkened theater.

Henriette slunk back upstairs. She was consumed with jealousy, hating Gregor for the apparent ease with which he was already moving in society, but hating herself even more that she couldn't be a part of it.

At the Old Donon, near the Nikolayevsky Bridge and almost within sight of Henriette's garret window, Gregor and his friends had retired to a private dining room. Bored with the ballet, highly critical of the pompous scenery, the conventional costumes, the fact that no one danced to the music, and that there was no conception of the ballet as a unified whole, all had combined to make them hiss and create quite a stir at the Maryinsky. After cries of "Bring on the flying turkey" and "Let's have more of the cow on the ice," they were respectfully but firmly requested to leave. Even the venerable Director of the Imperial Theaters came down from his box, eying them disapprovingly as they were escorted up the aisle.

Now, surrounded by icy platters of delicious little Black Sea oysters, and numerous bottles of Veuve Clicquot, Gregor sat back with a look of great satisfaction. Waiters in spotless white cravats and gloves bustled about the table, and the distant strains of the restaurant's huge orchestrion, a mechanical organ capable of duplicating nearly every imaginable instrument, could be heard from behind the dining room doors.

Seated at the long table were six of his companions, members of that select fraternity of *jeunesse dorée*, the gilded youth he had often dreamed of befriending. That he'd already borrowed heavily to keep up with them was something he decided not to think about. That one of them had guessed his predilections was also something Gregor tried to put out of his mind. To live for the moment—this exact instant, in fact—was all that seemed to matter. So what if he'd already spent his next two months' allowance? So what that he always found a ready excuse when his friends proposed a visit to "that certain house," recently opened by a French procuress? His companions liked him for him, and not for what he did or didn't do behind his bedroom door.

"To the piano, Grisha, to the piano!" they now began to shout, banging on the tabletop with their knives and forks.

Even then a piano was being wheeled into the dining room. Wondering if it was indecorous to sing for one's supper, for somehow that was what this all came down to, Gregor pushed his chair back and came to his feet.

After playing several gypsy tunes he'd taught himself in recent weeks, his friends called on him to play one of his own compositions. That it was the only piece he'd written didn't seem to bother them. When the last note rang out and he turned to them with a smile, they pounded on the table, demanding he improvise another. The head waiter had just arrived with the bill, and as Gregor came up with a tune that delightfully enough blended with the faint strains of the orchestrion, he managed to get off without having to dip into his all but empty wallet.

Later that evening, bundled up in an expensive bearskin coat and a sable cap, both of which he was yet to pay for, Gregor rode home with his friend Naryshkin, the same friend who'd already found him out. The Naryshkins had been part of the Russian court since the time of Peter the Great, for it was Natalia Naryshkina who was Peter's mother. Although only distantly related, Konstanin—or "Kostya," as his friends called him—was nevertheless extremely wealthy in his own right. He was tall, dapper, and witty, with an unusually big head that was crowned with a shock of the brightest red hair Gregor had ever seen.

It was Kostya who'd introduced Gregor to his circle of friends, and who seemed to have decided that Grisha would be his protégé. Kostya was the first person to expose him to the opera and the ballet, to teach him the rudiments of art appreciation, to get him to return to his music. And it was also Kostya to whom he owed a great deal of money, and to whom he now turned for advice.

"You need a patron, Grisha," said the red-haired Naryshkin as they sat together in a small open carriage. "And I think I have just the answer. Have you ever heard of Prince Meshchersky?"

Gregor groaned and slouched down in his seat, burying his face in the collar of his fur while white frosty buildings passed in seemingly endless succession, an occasional porter standing half asleep at the door. Meshchersky was an archconservative and a reactionary, highly influential in court circles. His weekly magazine, *The Citizen*, enjoyed government protection, and at one time even Dostoyevsky had been one of its editors.

"They call him the Prince of Sodom, he's so corrupt. What makes you think he'd be interested in me?" Gregor asked.

"Am I suggesting you embrace his views? On the contrary. Embrace him, my dear boy, embrace him," Kostya replied with a laugh.

"You don't mean—?"

"Oh, but I do, Grisha. But if one is careful, one needn't

have to worry about such things. After all, platonism can be carried to extremes, *n'est-ce pas?*"

The *isvostchik* pulled up before the address they'd given him, a three-story building on Simeonovskaya Street, in the Liteinaya Quarter, an aristocratic neighborhood where Gregor had been lucky to find an affordable flat. He could see a light burning in his upstairs window, and knew that Kolya was waiting up for him.

"So you propose I become the Prince of Sodom's plaything, is that it?" he said.

"You needn't make it sound so repulsive, Grisha. After all, affairs between men are taken rather for granted these days, especially among members of society . . . although one must, of course, observe a certain amount of discretion."

"And he'll pay me?" Gregor asked.

"What a thing to suggest," laughed Naryshkin, his big head bobbing up and down. "'Pay me' sounds so déclassé. We're talking about spending money, Grisha, an allowance, bills paid, expenses met. Why, there could be no end to it— providing you play your cards right."

Gregor stepped down from the carriage. The air was cold and dry, smelling faintly of snow. His breath condensed in a cloud before his face, and when he glanced at the cabby's little nag, he saw that the horse's flanks were coated with a crust of ice. As it gnawed at its bit, the frozen perspiration began to break apart, falling in pieces onto the cobblestones.

Naryshkin eyed him inquisitively. "Well? Shall I arrange it for you?"

"Will it be as simple as all that?"

"When one is in the market for expensive pleasures, as Prince Meshchersky always is, arranging them is the simplest thing in the world," and with a nod at the *isvostchik*, the droshky rattled down the street, the shaggy little horse breaking wind at every jolt.

*   *   *

Returning from the ballet, where she'd found herself confronting the discrepancy between her dreams of what life ought to be, and grim reality, further unpleasantness awaited Henriette at home. Although she and Julian took the rear entrance reserved for tradesmen, they'd barely stepped inside when the dark specter of Polina Filippovna, the Count's housekeeper, reared up before them. Her bombazine rustling imperiously, and her large, bulging eyes staring at them as if they weren't even worthy of contempt, the woman stretched her long, thin neck much like a cobra about to strike.

"So you took advantage of *our* good nature, did you?" Filippovna began. "So you chose to disobey the rules of *our* household, did you? The moment *our* backs were turned, what happens? This one," and she pointed a finger at Henriette, "just leaves her babies behind with no further thought to their safety and well-being than a bird that shoves its fledglings from its nest. And this one," motioning to Julian Andreyevich, "encourages such duplicity, and thus becomes a partner to the basest of acts. How dare you leave *our* babies alone and uncared for, Mademoiselle Petrova?"

"I shall discuss that with the Count, and not the likes of you," Henriette replied.

The housekeeper opened her mouth in astonishment, and her eyebrows all but disappeared beneath her dainty white cap, no one having ever spoken to her this way before. "Indeed you shall," Filippovna said when she found her voice. "He's waiting in his study," and with another rustle of bombazine, the woman turned abruptly away.

Julian went in first, and though she stood by the door, Henriette was unable to hear what was discussed. A few minutes later the tutor backed out of the room, and now it was her turn to step inside.

Seated at his desk, the Count eyed her over the rim of his

pince-nez. Directly behind him hung a large portrait of his late wife, a severe-looking woman who seemed to gaze down at her with a look of disapproval.

"Do you have an explanation for your behavior?" the Count asked, staring at her so relentlessly she couldn't help but turn her eyes away, looking blankly at the shelves of leather-bound books.

"It's true, I had no right to leave the children. But I certainly didn't abandon them, or expose them to danger."

"That is merely your opinion, *mademoiselle*."

The Count left his desk to pour himself a cognac, taking no more notice of her than if she were a dog curled up at his feet. He was a man in his early forties, with a determined and athletic stride. Extremely well groomed and fit-looking, as vain men invariably are, with black, close-cropped hair that had begun to gray at the temples, Count Ivanov gave the impression of being in full control not only of his own life, but also of the lives of everyone around him.

"Tell me, Mademoiselle Petrova," he went on. "Do you find Golovin attractive?"

The coldly menacing look in the Count's eyes was still very much in evidence. But now she saw there was something else there as well, an expression of mockery the meaning of which was still not clear to her.

"Julian Andreyevich is a very nice young man. He's been very kind to me, especially when—" She paused, wondering if honesty were indeed the best policy.

"You were saying?"

"I'm not happy with my situation, Dmitri Fyodorovich."

"I didn't think you were," he said evenly. "After all, you're a girl from a good family. And then, to suffer such discourtesies as I no doubt have heaped upon your shoulders." He began to cluck his tongue sarcastically. "I suppose you view young Golovin as the answer to your prayers."

"That isn't true," she replied. "But I have prayed for a word of kindness, and a proper room, and the sense of being part of your household, and not a stranger. Yet as hard as I've tried to please you and do my job, despite whatever might have happened this evening, it doesn't seem to do any good."

"Strong words, *mademoiselle*."

"When one is forced to live no better than a serf, perhaps strong words are justified."

She expected him to fly into a rage. Instead, he eyed her curiously, then gradually began to smile. "I enjoy your spirit, Henriette. It's refreshing to come upon someone who's not afraid to speak her mind. I can assure you that in the future, your situation will be much improved. In fact, I can safely say your days of serfdom will now be a thing of the past." The Count laughed expansively, as if he were enjoying a private joke. "Why, I had no idea I had such a lady in my midst. But now that you've made it clear that you're as much a part of the gentry as I, well, I shall have to treat you accordingly, won't I?"

Was he mocking her, or did he actually mean what he said? Henriette wasn't certain, but found herself edging slowly toward the door. By now the Count was standing so close to her she could smell his English toilet water, and the hint of cognac on his breath.

"Won't you join me in a brandy?" the Count proposed, his fingers suddenly tightening around her waist.

Less surprised than she might have been a few minutes before, Henriette gently pried his hand away, then shook her head.

"Pity." Count Ivanov pulled her close, and as he began to kiss her, his arms encircled her waist and held her fast.

La Belle Henriette, she thought, tasting not cognac on his lips, but wealth and privilege. Worshiping glances ... Ah, there you are, *ma Comtesse*. Everyone's been waiting for you all evening. I've promised them *La Belle Henriette,* the Countess Ivanova, and now I've delivered her into their anxious hands. . . .

Henriette slipped free of the Count's hard and grasping embrace. "How nice to know I'm now part of the family," she said with a laugh. Then, playing the coquette for all she was worth, she sailed out of the library, feeling very gay and reckless, and just as calculating as her employer.

Arriving in Petersburg the day after Christmas, Masha was met at the station by her sister Irena. The kumiss cure, coupled with Masha's long stay in Yalta, had seen her condition take a remarkable turn for the better. Even Professor Ostroumov, with whom she'd consulted before traveling up to the capital, was greatly encouraged by the progress she'd made. Although there was still some evidence of tuberculosis, the extent of the disease appeared to have markedly diminished, and he had every reason to believe it might one day vanish altogether.

As she and her sister drove down the Nevsky in an elegant public sledge, Masha breathed deeply, savoring the coldness and the bright winter light. Irena had been corresponding with her regularly, and so Masha knew of the position Nikolai had taken, of the apartment her sister was living in, and of the difficulties Irena had experienced adjusting to her new life in the capital.

"Niki's doing very well," Irena said as the *likatch* raced down the broad, snow-covered Nevsky, dozens of other sleighs and troikas vying for room along the boulevard. "He's already been given a promotion, they think so highly of him. You'll meet the Minister himself this evening. We've been invited to a ball at his home, the first of the season." Irena reached over and gave her an exuberant hug, her gentle brown eyes sparkling as brightly as the snow-covered streets and the lofty expanse of clear, steel-blue sky.

At last they pulled up before a large town house on the Mokhovaya, not far from the Liteiny Prospect, and just a short ride to Gregor's apartment. The *dvornik* hurried over to help them, carrying Masha's bags up to the second floor. Katya met them in the vestibule, and soon Masha was warming herself near the massive white porcelain stove in the parlor, sipping a cup of tea, and enjoying her delightful surroundings.

"I just can't get over how wonderful you look," Irena kept saying. "Do you have any plans, now that you're feeling better?"

Masha told Irena that she wanted to start all over again, to put aside the memories of these last unhappy months, and look out on her future with renewed hope and confidence.

That evening she had ample opportunity to begin. At the ball given by the Minister of Public Instruction, she once again found herself in the company of her "savior," as Auntie V. had so breathlessly described young Captain Danchenko.

As the orchestra struck up the first strains of the waltz, he led her across the crowded ballroom. Then, taking her in his arms, he proceeded to waltz her around the room, her pale-lilac gown billowing about her ankles and showing her off her graceful little dancing slippers. But though there were dozens of people whirling along with them, Masha was only vaguely aware of their presence. The fairy-tale surroundings of the Minister's palatial residence, and the strong young hand at her waist, made her wonder if she were dreaming.

The Captain was several inches over six feet, and towered over her in a pleasantly protective way. But it was the young officer's eyes that once again made the greatest impression on her. As he spoke they reflected a wide range of emotions, at once tender and confiding, solicitous and compassionate.

"I've thought of you a great deal," Stepan Alexeyevich

whispered in her ear. "I even went to see you in Samara, but you'd already left."

"And I was certain you found me very uninteresting," she said with a generous smile. "After all, I hardly said two words all the time we traveled together."

"But your eyes carried on an entire conversation, Maria Petrovna. They're quite remarkable, you know."

Masha, flattered by his compliments, was nevertheless embarrassed, and laughed to conceal her self-consciousness. The Captain danced so gracefully she felt suspended, her feet not even touching the floor. A second waltz followed the first, and she could hardly remember when the music stopped and he asked her for the pleasure of another dance.

Afterward, she felt out of breath, and begged to sit out the quadrille. But even then the handsome young officer didn't leave her side. Instead, he brought her a glass of sweet champagne, and sat next to her, asking how long she intended to stay in Petersburg.

"I'm not certain." She laughed with something of the girlish enthusiasm she thought she'd lost months before. "I've no plans at all, and I rather like it that way."

"And the cure? Was it beneficial?"

Masha nodded, and immediately changed the subject, though it was Captain Danchenko who ended up doing most of the talking, his sparkling hazel eyes embracing her just as his arms had done when they'd danced.

"You are a quiet one, aren't you?" he said, inviting her to join him in a mazurka, for which she promptly rose to her feet. "You're filled with secrets, but I won't ask you to reveal any of them—not right away, of course. But be on your guard, because one day—"

Masha raised her eyes, and looked up at the Captain as if she'd never seen him before. Gripping his arm more tightly and giving the sleeve of his tunic a little squeeze, she saw in his handsome face all the promises she'd made to herself, and that vision of happiness and fulfillment she was so eager, even desperate, to achieve.

"May I have the honor of calling on you tomorrow?" Captain Danchenko asked when the evening's festivities drew to a close.

Eager to spend more time with him and discover who he really was, Masha nodded her head.

"Perhaps we might make a day of it, do you think?" Danchenko added with a broad and exuberant grin, as if the two of them were well on their way to sharing each other's secrets. "Or am I being too—"

"Of course you're being too forward, Captain," she said with a laugh. "But I won't tell anyone, if you won't."

"I want to tell everyone," he whispered. "You're so lovely, you amaze me," speaking with such earnestness it made her giddy. "Tomorrow then," and seizing her hand, he pressed it to his lips.

On New Year's Day, Vera wasn't awakened by church bells, or gay shouts, or Simon presenting her with a gift. Anninka didn't arrive with a tray of festive breakfast dishes to usher in the year in style. Instead, Vera turned over in bed and listened to something thumping, the sound very dreamlike, vague, and unclear. As she leaned back against the pillows, the sound became rhythmic, and gradually there reached her ears a low murmur of voices.

Snow crunched softly beneath her window. She sat up, cursing Matriona for not lighting the stove, for the room was very cold. Despite the icy floorboards, Vera slipped out of bed and hurried to the window. She drew the curtain aside and peered out. A moment later she was back in bed, shaking Simon and trying to awaken him. Even then she heard Matriona pounding on the bedroom door.

"May the Heavenly Empress protect us!" the housekeeper cackled. "Lord have mercy! What are we to do? They'll burn us out of house and home!"

Simon opened his eyes and looked at her in confusion. "What's all the noise about?" he complained.

Vera rushed to the door, opened it a crack, and told Matriona to get her father and bring him back with her.

"Simon Ivanovich!" came the cry from down in the courtyard. "Simon Ivanovich Belinsky!"

Vera, not knowing what to do first, finally began to throw on her clothes.

"Who the hell is that, waking us up so early?" Simon sprang out of bed, and when he looked out he saw some thirty peasants assembled in the courtyard. Many of them were armed with torches, spirals of smoke drifting up toward the bedroom window.

"Belinsky!" they continued to shout. "Come on down and show yourself!"

"What do they want?" Vera asked.

"Damned if I know." All the same, he pulled on a pair of pants over his nightshirt.

"Belinsky!"

The black smoke blew against the double window, darkening the panes. Vera saw everything going up in flames, all their lovely new furniture, and her wardrobe of fashionable clothes. She wondered if she should start to pack, but when she saw Simon shove a pistol under his belt, she decided she'd be better off naked and happily married than a well-dressed widow. So she followed after him as he went down the stairs, grabbing his sheepskin off the coatrack before he stepped outside. Vera hovered behind him, eying the sullen crowd of moujiks who stood in the yard.

"What are you doing here, waking me up on New Year's morning?" Belinsky shouted.

"We want our money," said one of the men, whose tangled beard was covered with icicles.

The cold was so intense it cut across Vera's cheeks and made her eyes tear. She hopped from one foot to the other, while she looked over Simon's shoulder and wondered what was keeping her father.

Addressing Belinsky with none of the customary deference reserved for the gentry, the peasant with the tangled beard accused him of embezzling the money the villagers had already contributed for taxes.

"I don't know what you're talking about," Belinsky replied. "Besides, it's not my concern but your headman's. That's what you elected him for, isn't it?"

Now, the men parted ranks to reveal their sniveling and terrified *starosta*, the elder whose duty it was to collect the taxes imposed on the village. He still wore the bronze medallion that was his badge of office, and from the look that come over Simon's face, Vera could tell that he and the *starosta* were well acquainted with each other.

"Tell them, Your Excellency, or they'll kill me as surely as winter follows fall," pleaded the old man, his voice quivering like the strings of a balalaika as he crouched on his hands and knees, thrown into the snow every time he made a move to get to his feet.

"What is he talking about, Simon?" Vera found this all very upsetting to watch, and wished that everyone would just go away and leave them alone.

"The money," the elder kept groaning. "The money for the taxes."

"I don't know what the old fool's talking about."

"You're a liar, Belinsky," said the spokesman for the group. He stepped forward, torch in hand, motioning to the mob of villagers who filled the courtyard. In a level though angry voice, he instructed them to set fire to the house, to unleash the red cock in retaliation for the money the steward had stolen from them.

Vera started to tell them what a mistake they were making. Simon wasn't a thief. Besides, he'd just sold Golovlovo, and so he had more money than he knew what to do with.

"Make room, you blockheads! Out of my way!" came a voice from the rear of the crowd. Peter Semyonovich stepped forward, and everyone moved aside to let him pass.

"Father!" Vera cried out excitedly. She ran down the porch steps, throwing her arms around her father's neck, and holding onto him as if she were drowning. "They want to burn us down, all our beautiful things. And for no reason, Father, no reason at all."

"Stop whimpering, Vera," he said crossly, disentangling himself from her embrace. "Now what's this I hear about embezzlement?"

Everyone started talking at once, and it wasn't until Petrov began to roar that the moujiks fell silent, allowing their spokesman to explain their grievances.

"Well, who's lying, Belinsky?" asked her father.

"On my life, Your Excellency," squeaked the *starosta*. "We split the money, two thirds for him and one third for me. And now I'll pay for it with my hide. But I only did it because he said he'd make me leave the village, that he'd have his friend the *ispravnik* banish me to Siberia. And me so old they'll probably bury me before spring, if they don't kill me first."

"He's lying, the old man's lying!" she began to shout. Simon didn't need their money. He had plenty of his own, a big roll of bills he dug out of his pocket whenever she asked for any. But where had they come from, to begin with?

"Well?" her father said again. "Did you steal the money, Belinsky, or didn't you?"

"Senya didn't steal anything," she cried out. "They're making this all up because he works them hard so you'll get your money's worth. He always thinks of you, *Papochka*, you and Petrovka both."

"How much did it amount to, Simon?" her father went on.

"Nine hundred," whimpered the elder, "and me so old I can't even get down before the ikons without feeling my bones breaking up. Six hundred for him and three hundred for me."

"Have you spent it all?" Petrov asked his son-in-law.

But though Vera hoped her husband would start to speak in his own defense, Simon held his tongue.

"And you?" Petrov said, addressing the elder.

"I have all of it still, Your Excellency, down to the last kopeck. It was only banishment I feared, for as they say, I already have one foot in the grave and smell of incense."

Promising to make up the difference, Peter Semyonovich ordered the villagers to disperse. "You may do with this old fool what you wish," he said, motioning to the *starosta*. "Though if he's as old as he claims, it might not be worth your trouble, for sooner or later God deprives a bad-tempered bull of his horns. But as for my son-in-law, that's my concern, is that clear?"

"Yes, Your Excellency. But of course, *barin*," replied the villagers, one after the other.

"*Batushka*, little father Peter Semyonovich," said their spokesman, "we are your children, and you are our father. If this is what you wish, then with the grace of God it will be done."

Vera ran back into the house, horribly ashamed of what had happened. She felt that her father had been cruel and unjust, taking the peasants on their word and choosing to ignore anything Simon might have said in response.

"You are to pack and leave immediately," her father told Simon when they both came in from outside. "Unless, of course, you prefer to be murdered in your bed. Even though they call me *batushka* to my face, they'll call me a lot of other things once they're back home again. You see, Vera," he went on, "too good a life drives even a dog mad. There you were, dressed in all your finery, puffed up like a bubble in the water, completely blind to what was happening. And now it's too late, daughter. He gave you what you wanted, didn't he? Unfortunately, it all came from other people's pockets. Have Matriona bring your things back to the house. Your room is where it's always been. As for me, I'm going back to bed."

"But I can't," she whimpered.

"Don't be a fool, Vera. They'll come back tonight and murder him in his bed, just like they murdered your grandfather."

"But I can't leave him, *Papochka*. He's my husband. Even if he stole that money, and I don't believe he did, he did it all for me, anyway, and so I'm as much at fault as he."

"Do as your father says, Vera," Simon now told her.

"Is that what you really want?" she asked. She gazed at her husband, tall and handsome, with his lovely dimples when he smiled, and his big bearlike hands that so easily wrapped her in their embrace. "Do you want to just go away and leave me, forget our marriage vows, all the promises we made to each other?" She reached up and put her hands on his shoulders, fixing her eyes on the stubble on his cheeks, and the square and forceful-looking line of his jaw.

"Tell her not to be a fool, Belinsky," her father spoke up. "You can't provide for her, you never could. She's better off staying here where she belongs. Perhaps in a year or two you might come back, if things quiet down."

"A year or two?" Vera whispered. "I can't wait that long. Will you take me with you, Simon? We can make a new start, with no mistakes, and I'll be good and I won't ask for so many things, I swear."

"Go upstairs and pack," Belinsky said.

"Pack for where?"

"You're my wife, aren't you? As soon as you get your things together, we'll be off."

"Fools, I raised a gaggle of fools!" her father said angrily. "You'll soon go hungry, Vera, and then you'll be sorry for not listening to me."

Vera decided not to answer, for what use were harsh words now that she was going away? When she returned to her bedroom she paused for a moment before the mirror. Her chin was just as pointy as it always was, her hair just as golden. But as she stepped closer and peered more intently at her reflection, she noticed several lines around the corners of her eyes, lines that had never been there before, and that no matter how hard she rubbed, refused to disappear.

Fourteen

The two weeks Masha spent in Petersburg were as much a
tonic as the countless bottles of milk wine she drank in
Samara. Each day, Stepan Danchenko came to call on her. He
would drive up in his elegant sledge and, seeing to it that she
was bundled up against the cold, take her out on "expeditions," as Anninka used to do when Masha was little. They
shopped at Fabergé, had tea with his mother, and visited a
group of Samoyeds camped out in the middle of the frozen
Neva. On another afternoon they went to one of Petersburg's famed ice hills, a high wooden chute paved with blocks
of ice, over which water was poured to form a smooth and
glassy surface. Here they climbed a flight of stairs that led to a
platform at the top of the steep incline, then got into a tobog-
gan and coasted down at a dizzying speed. Masha, kneeling
behind Stepan with her hands on his shoulders, felt the icy
winds rushing past her, and leaned so close to him that she
could smell the brilliantine on his hair and the eau de cologne
with which he'd dabbed his cheeks.

These joyous days came to an abrupt end when Stepan's

regiment was ordered on maneuvers and he had to say good-
bye. There were so many things she wanted to tell him that
last afternoon they spent together, but when he called on her
at Irena's, Masha found herself so tongue-tied she could
hardly put two words together.

"I've never thought myself shy," Stepan said. "But now I
just can't seem to tell you how I feel. Would it be forward of
me if I asked for an invitation to Petrovka?"

"Oh, I'd like that very much, Stepan. It's so beautiful
there this time of year, and I could show you the countryside,
and the little school where I teach."

"Then it's settled," he said. "As soon as I can get away, I
promise I'll come down to see you. I just hope I won't have to
wait very long. Why, I'm already impatient, and you haven't
even left. But you know why, don't you?"

Masha looked down at her lap, afraid to ask.

"I love you. I love you more than I ever dreamed I could
love anyone."

Gazing at him as he sat next to her, holding both her hands
in his, Masha again saw in his bright and inquiring eyes the
reflection of her own happiness. For a moment it was terrifying, and she wondered if it would all fall apart as it had once
before.

Trust him, she thought, and that way you'll learn to trust
yourself.

Back home at Petrovka even her father noticed the change
in her, and commented favorably. But it was with her mother
that she found herself sharing this great outpouring of joy.
Sophia Mikhailovna's imaginary ailments had finally caught
up to her, and remembering how harshly she had spoken to
her mother when she was ill, Masha tried to make it up to her
by spending as much time with her as she could.

In her frilled cambric peignoir, and with a little lace cap
perched atop her frizzy curls, Sophia Mikhailovna was not the

youthful figure she had been just a few months before. Her tiny wrinkled face was lost in the plump folds of her many pillows, while directly above her a gilded Cupid hung on a thread, suspended beneath the heavy brocade canopy of her enormous bier-like bed. This charming statuette had been hanging here ever since Masha could remember, though now the gilt was cracked and faded, and Cupid flew on just a single wing, the other having broken off so long ago Masha couldn't recall it any other way. But of late, Cupid's dart had lost its sting. The arrow he held in his chubby little hand, and that unhappily seemed to be pointed directly at her mother's heart, was missing its tip, so that only the shaft remained.

"It was Henriette who did it," Madame Petrova declared. "Yes, I ring and I ring and no one comes. It's true, Henriette took away my last years. Don't you remember that horrible day? And then to leave like that, without even saying good-bye. Your father made me cover the mirror of my dressing table, he's so stubborn. But he always was, you know. Even as a young man he'd set his mind on something and there'd be no convincing him otherwise."

"Were you very much in love?" Masha asked.

Madame Petrova turned her head to the side, gazing at the toy garden of dried grasses and straw flowers she'd arranged in the space between the double windows.

"And where is Laska, do you suppose? She never comes to stay with me anymore. Perhaps it's the smell of all this dreadful medicine." Her eyes motioned to the collection of bottles and vials crowding the circular cabinet near her bed.

"Shall I go find her for you?"

"No, she'll come when she's hungry. But open that drawer there, my dear." Her mother pointed to her dressing table, directing Masha to look for a small morocco case. "Now open it," she said after Masha had found it under a pile of letters.

Inside the case was a miniature of a young man, dressed in

the typical fashion of the forties, with a high wing collar, a green surtout, and an extravagant cravat. The portrait was so lifelike it had undoubtedly been copied from a daguerreotype.

"His name was Gabriel, a very unlikely name for a Russian, is it not? Gabriel Antonovich," her mother said with a sigh. "A wonderful story, just like one of those sentimental novels by Paul de Kock. He was very poor. Gentry, but they'd lost all their money years before. I loved him dearly, and would have married him had my father not intervened."

"Whatever happened to him, *maman?*"

Madame Petrova's lashes fluttered anxiously, weighed down by the two large tears that welled up in her eyes. "He died so young, just like little Paul in Mr. Dickens' book. But what's the use, when you can't bring back the past? I married your father. I lost my health. There you have it. The story of my life." She began to laugh shrilly, beating her hands against the bedcovers.

Masha tried to quiet her, but it did little good.

"No one understands me to this day," her mother continued. "I was sick, I tell you. After Gregor was born the milk rushed to my brain, and I was mortally ill for many years. But everyone snickered behind my back and said I was strong and healthy, and all I had to do was climb out of bed and I'd be fine. But I wasn't well, Masha. And as you see now, I'm not well to this day."

Madame Petrova reached out, clutching Masha's hand so that the veins stood out prominently from her wrist to her fingers.

"Do you think Henriette will come for the funeral? Will she get down on her knees beside my coffin and pray for me?"

"There isn't going to be any funeral, *maman*, not for years and years. You're going to get better, you know you are."

Her mother raised her eyes, staring at the chipped and

faded Cupid that swung lazily above her head. "He tyrannized me," she said with surprising strength. "From the very first night we spent together, your father made me kneel before him like a serf and promise to obey him. He told me I was frail, and I believed him. He thought me a fool, and I believed that, too. Do you know something?" Her mother fixed her with a frightened glance, determined to bare her innermost secrets now that she was certain she was dying. "He knew Gabriel Antonovich, and it was he who warned my parents about what we were planning. And then they forced me to marry him. Oh yes, they forced me, Masha. He was rich, you see, and every year he got richer. So you wonder why I became an invalid? Isn't it easier to worry about ailments of the body than ailments of the soul? But put away Gabriel's portrait, my dear, and promise you'll destroy it when I'm gone, for what good would it do any of us if your father should think ill of me? Now, where could my little Laska have gone to, do you suppose?" her mother asked, her thoughts wandering. "Here, *mon ange*, here, come to *maman*. She has a treat for you, *ma petite*."

The little spaniel bounded into the room, smelled the iodine and surgical spirits, and darted out again, where she sat in the hall and began to whine. Louder and louder grew her cries until they began to resemble laughter.

"See how they all abandon me?" said her mother. "Call the priest, Masha, and let me receive the Holy Sacrament."

"Mother, don't say that. You're going to be fine."

"Call the priest so I can make confession, because I never loved him. I only thought I did."

"Who are you talking about, *maman?* Gabriel Antonovich?"

"Peter Semyonovich," her mother whispered, and drifted off to sleep as Laska laughed in the hallway, and the faded Cupid swung overhead, its tipless arrow ready to fly.

*   *   *

In that unhappy spring of 1882, Vera found herself moving for the third time in as many months. Seated on top of a pile of bedding, and surrounded by various pieces of upturned furniture, Vera stared straight ahead, afraid of what she'd see if she let her eyes wander. And when she did, it was even worse than she expected, with row after row of squalid tenements, dismal factories, and filthy basement *traktiri* stretching before her like a pathway leading to hell.

A moujik in a greasy sheepskin coat drove the *rospousky*, a crudely constructed cart designed for hauling goods. Crouched among the bales and bundles, the driver spoke in the most endearing terms to his dray horse, whose disheveled mane hung so low it almost brushed the ground.

"Ah yes, Your Honor," said the driver in his drawling Moscow accent, "the rooks are back, I see. Spring is sure to stay for a while, though it might still snow. Now, what do you mean by that, turning without permission? It's Malaya Gruzinskaya Street where we make our turn, and not before, my precious beauty."

They drove up Bolshaya Presnenskaya, into the grim heart of Moscow's cheerless western district, the workers' quarter known as the Presnia. The unpaved streets were ankle-deep in mud and offal, and the sickening stench of sewage filled the air, causing Vera's eyes to smart.

Simon sat at the back of the cart, his legs dangling over the side. "Cheer up, Verochka," he called out. "The Zoological Gardens aren't very far from here. We can always share our peanuts with the elephants."

Vera clenched her hands until her nails dug into her palms. She hated him, but hated herself even more for not being able to live without him. Each day was now more wretched than the next, for luck seemed to have deserted him. What of the money from the sale of Golovlovo? Gone, that's what, spent in gambling dens and houses of ill repute. What of the money from Jerichovo? Vanished too, and the tax money as well, so that now they were down to less than fifty rubles. Fifty rubles! They might be able to live on that for a month, maybe two. But not longer. As for their belongings, each day something else was either sold or pawned, so that all that remained was the bed, a table, a few chairs, a chest of drawers.

The rumble of heavy machinery reached her ears. Overhead the sky was black with the continuous outpouring of smoke. They were passing rows of barracks now, gray, dejected-looking buildings where factory workers were housed in dormitories, two workers often occupying the same bed. Work at all the big factories never stopped, and when someone on day shift slept, someone else on night shift toiled until dawn.

When the drayman turned into Gruzinskaya the street narrowed, and what little light remained was soon swallowed up by high stone walls covered with graffiti. The walls enclosed a furniture factory on one side, a textile mill on the other. At regular intervals wicket gates came into view like those of a prison, guarded by men on horseback.

The *rospousky* sloshed through the muddy snow, stopping before an old three-story stone house in an alley just off Malaya Gruzinskaya. In one of the ground-floor windows she noticed a miniature red coffin, a sign that a coffin maker had his shop here.

"Perfect," she said as she climbed down from the cart. "When I drop dead, you won't have to look very far, will you?"

The house was painted a dirty yellow color, and again she thought how ironic it was, since "yellow house" was what everyone called an insane asylum. Thankful that he hadn't sold her rubber boots, Vera stepped gingerly through the slush and made her way to the lodging house.

"It's not a *suite de luxe,*" Simon told her, "but at least it's a roof over our heads." He left her standing before the tenement, which couldn't even boast a proper front door. Instead, a gloomy archway led into a dark, garbage-strewn courtyard.

Surely this was all some ghastly mistake, she thought. How could the promise of her life have been wiped out so completely, with hardly a trace of it left to remind her of what it used to be? It's because of my godless ways, that's why, godless because every time I look at him something terrible happens, and I can't control myself.

Yet Vera knew this was all she had left, just those moments of pleasure when the sordidness of her surroundings would dissolve, and she'd see nothing but Simon and feel nothing but lust and physical release.

As Simon helped the drayman unload their belongings, Vera crept back into the archway of the tenement, where her husband had cajoled the landlady into letting them a room without having to pay a month's rent in advance. He probably threw her down on the bed, gave her a taste of what he has to offer, she thought. Dear Mother of God, why didn't I listen to Irena? Why did I ever let him touch me in the summerhouse, caressing my breasts and calling me his little dove? Yes, his little pigeon. And I liked it, even then. Yes, even before he took me in his arms I liked it and wanted all of it, and couldn't wait until we got back to Golovlovo, that he'd show me what it was all about. Scum, Vera, that's all you are. Why didn't I tell him I'd never be his wife, that he was forbidden to ever set foot in my father's house, that we all knew what he was like, and that he was beneath me?

Shouldering a trunk filled with household effects, Simon led the driver of the *rospousky* into the courtyard. Vera grabbed two cases and followed after them. In the far corner of the unpaved yard, a dark and narrow staircase led up to the second and third floors. As in all old houses, the staircase was of stone, and wound around a thick stone column, the surface of which bore traces of more graffiti, some even filthier than what she'd already seen. The steps were wet and slippery, strewn with cucumber peels and cabbage leaves. At the top of the landing they came out onto a gallery that ran around the entire second story and overlooked the yard.

Simon, pointing out the privy, for there were several grimy doors, each looking exactly like the next, led them halfway around the gallery. When he found the door he was looking for, he pushed it open with his boot.

"Too bad the landlady isn't here with bread and salt," he said. He set the trunk down on the floor, and hurried out again, lest someone down in the street make off with the few things they still possessed. The drayman, leaving behind the table he'd been balancing on top of his head, followed after him. Vera remained outside in the open passageway, where an icy draft whipped the mud-stained hem of her dress, making it flap heavily against her ankles.

When at last she went into the flat, she had to bite down on her knuckles, because otherwise she knew she would have begun to howl like an animal in pain. Littered with old newspapers and illustrated magazines, greasy rags, even several bones so clean they'd probably been picked by rats, the room was perhaps a dozen paces long, with two square windows, each consisting of four tiny greenish panes. There was a large stove, the tiles of which had long since disappeared, and a water faucet that stuck out from the wall like a crooked finger. A corner of the room was screened off for the bed, the makeshift partition just a ragged sheet draped over a length of rope.

"You can't expect me to live here," she said when Simon and the drayman returned with another load.

"Fine," Simon said in an even tone of voice. "Don't," and was gone just as quickly. But soon he returned with the last of their pitiful belongings, closing the door behind him and leaning against it as he tried to catch his breath.

"I won't live here," she said again, stamping her foot against the dirt-encrusted floorboards.

"Then write your father for money."

"I already have."

"And?"

"He refused to send any."

Oh, if she could only throw something, or hit someone, or punish the people responsible for her unhappiness. But who were they, after all? Just the two of us, she thought, for there's no one else to blame.

"You can always go home," Simon told her. "We still have enough for a ticket."

And prove to that little bully he was right? No, she wouldn't give her father the satisfaction, even if it meant living in a room that wasn't fit for animals.

"Why haven't you found a job at least?" she asked. "All you do is waste the money. First you gambled, then you drank, then you gambled some more, did other things too I don't even want to talk about. Why did you ask me to leave with you if you don't even care about me?"

"But I do care, Vera. You're my little dove, remember?"

"Your little dove is beginning to look like something the cat dragged in. I don't even own a mirror to brush my hair. I don't own anything. And I hate this life and I'd rather be dead and you're so mean and lazy I hate you too. I do, I hate you, I hate all of you!"

She rushed across the room and began to pound her fists against his chest. Simon just stood there, making no effort to stop her, as if waiting for the tantrum to run its course.

"I was young and pretty," she cried, dropping her hands limply to her sides. It took too much energy to be angry, and energy was just another of the many things she didn't have.

"Look at me. Look at what you've made me become. I'm your whore, that's all I am, Simon Belinsky's little whore. The Colonel's mistress, that's what!"

Simon grabbed hold of her then, and as she tried to twist free he began to rub against her, back and forth until she finally quieted down. "There," he said, kissing the top of her head, "now isn't that better, my sparrow?"

She pulled free of his loathsome embrace, then sat down in the scratched and rickety chair that was all that remained of their handsome five-piece suite.

"I'll be back before dark," Simon said at the door.

"Where are you going?"

"To find a job."

"A likely story," she said, laughing sarcastically.

And all because of my godless ways, Vera thought again. I'll have to write Father another letter, only this time I'll beg if I have to, and tell him what a terrible time we're having, and that if he has any love for me at all, to please send some money. And Irena, and Gregor, too. Yes, I'll write all of them. Surely they won't deny me, not their Verochka whom they all loved so dearly. Or did they? Maybe they're glad this has happened to me. Maybe they think I'm getting what I deserve.

"Why so glum, dearie?" came a voice from the door. "All you had to do was say 'Nina Pavlovna,' and I would've been right here. But now that I am, you can call me Saltychikha, for it's Nina Pavlovna Saltykova, but Saltychikha is what I answer to."

Leaning against the doorway was a slovenly dressed woman with a large nose, tiny, shortsighted eyes, and a greedy mouth. Her greasy brown hair was plaited in a rat's tail, and as she poked her head inside, Vera could see the rings of dirt around her neck.

"So here I am," the woman said, stepping into the room before Vera could extend an invitation. "And not a moment

too soon, judging from those tears in your eyes, dearie. I'm
the landlady, so if you have any problems, you know who not
to call." Saltychikha laughed. "My, you are a little thing,
aren't you? And so young, too. What happened, dearie, he get
you into trouble?"

"Certainly not," said Vera. "Just minor setbacks, that's all.
He went out to look for a job, and he'll come back and everything will turn out fine."

"Sure, I don't doubt it for a second, dearie. After all, he
looks like a gentleman. No reason a refined type like that
can't find himself some work. Good-looking too, if you don't
mind my saying." The landlady eyed the pile of boxes and
packing cases. "So you're here for a while, are you? Well, it
seems to me the first order of business is getting your stove
lit. You're trembling something awful, dearie, and if you
don't mind my saying, you don't look too good, either."

It was true, she wasn't feeling very well at all. Everything
had begun to spin around in slow, dizzying circles, and as
Saltychikha went about lighting the stove, Vera clutched both
arms of the rickety chair and waited for the room to right
itself.

"Can I get you a nice cup of tea, dearie? I'm not charging,
if that's what you're worried about."

Vera nodded, then swallowed hard, hoping she wouldn't be
sick.

"You had something to eat today, didn't you?"

"Yes, but it's not that." Despite the presence of this odious
woman with her prying eyes and slobbering mouth, Vera
couldn't help herself, and began to cry.

The landlady, having finally managed to get a fire going,
patted her on the shoulder. "There now, it can't be that bad.
And you so young and attractive, too."

"Do you really think so?" She didn't know what had
become of her handkerchief, and so she dried her eyes with

257

her hands.

"Why, you're a lovely little thing. Very delicate, and quite the lady. A girl from a fine home, no doubt. Then why stay here, if you don't mind my asking? Won't they take you back?"

"Yes, but I don't want to go home. He can't go back with me and I won't leave him."

"He's a handsome devil, I grant you. But love's an ugly business, dearie," replied the landlady, stroking Vera's hair with her greasy fingers. "I've had my share, and I can tell you from someone who knows, there's not a man out there who's worth the fuss and bother." Saltychikha started to the door, only to stop and glance back. "Sure you don't need a doctor or something? You really don't look too good."

"It's all right, I've been dizzy before. It always goes away if I sit long enough."

"You mean to say—"

"I'm going to have a baby." Vera looked down at her lap, filled with shame and self-disgust, that her selfishness had gotten her to such a horrible place.

"Baby?" said the landlady. "Does he know?"

She shook her head.

"Sooner or later he's got to find out."

"Then it'll be later," Vera said. "And not until it shows."

PETERSBURG, APRIL 17, 1882

My dearest Masha,

It was so good to get your last letter, though my initial reaction was one of considerable trepidation, as I was certain you'd write that *maman's* condition had worsened. But thank goodness her health hasn't deteriorated. This must be a great trial for you, especially now that you're only just getting back on your feet. But if you need your Irusha, you mustn't hesitate to ask me to come.

I was so pleased to hear of all the letters you've received from Captain Danchenko. He sounds like a very able young man, and Niki tells me the Danchenkos are a fine old family, well thought of here in the capital.

There's so much news to write about, I hardly know where to begin. Just the other day I paid a call on Henriette, who'd gotten permission from Count Ivanov to have me in for tea. I'm very worried about her, Masha. She seems to have taken it into her head that the Count is in love with her. I asked her if he'd actually said as much, and she told me that even though he hadn't come out with those very words, she knew that was what he was feeling. I sensed something was wrong, but I was afraid to ask too many questions because she had the strangest look in her eyes. They were all shiny, and she talked in such a loud voice I thought the entire household would hear. And if that weren't enough, she insisted that the tutor, this very decent young man named Golovin, was in love with her, too.

I told her she was working too hard, just like Niki I said, and that perhaps she needed a little rest, a trip somewhere. "Why should I leave now," she asked, "when both of them dote on me as if I were a princess?" I didn't know what to say. But it only got worse. This Golovin of whom she'd talked came in to have tea with us—at Henriette's insistence, I might add. Why, she actually suggested he take her to my house for dinner. The poor young man got very flustered, and spoke of his sister, whom he said had been ailing. Then he rushed out, saying he had to get back to the children, as it was time for their lessons. I asked Henriette if she'd met this sister of his, for something about it struck me as rather odd. "No," she said, "but he talks about her all the time. They're very close, just like we are."

After that I just changed the subject, because you know how Henriette is, if you start to disagree with her she can get very insulting, as I understand happened with General Tishin. Do write her, Masha, and see what you can find out. Perhaps it'll be easier for her to express her feelings in a letter, as opposed to an actual visit.

I did hear from Vera though, and while I begged her to come and stay with us since she won't go back to Petrovka, she refuses to leave him. She says he's working, but when I suggested that I might come down to Moscow for a visit, she wrote back with all sorts of excuses, so I know things aren't the way she makes them out to be. Is there anything we can do for her, Masha? She's such a child, and though she's been spoiled all her life, I know in her heart she's a good person, and deeply regrets the mistakes she's made in the past. I suggested she write to Father, and try to make it up to him. I suppose you know more about that than I, as I haven't heard from her since.

As for Grisha, to round out news of the family, we're all very proud of him. He's writing delightful little articles and feuilletons for Prince Meshchersky's magazine. Although Niki insists it's a vile publication, at least Grisha's articles are apolitical. He wrote a fascinating review of that new opera by Rimsky-Korsakov, and even though all the other critics came down very hard on it, he praised it to the skies. Where he's learned so much about music, and now art, which is his new interest, is quite beyond me. I'm afraid we don't see very much of each other, however, as he's been keeping himself very busy.

So there you have it, all the news from Petersburg and environs. Spring is here to stay, I trust, and at Petrovka they're probably ready to start planting. Niki asks to be remembered, and praises the work you've done with the children these last few months. It's his belief that we must do everything we can to educate the peasantry, and prepare them for the new Russia of tomorrow. Only God knows what that will be like, but I don't tell Niki that, because when it comes to politics he's already considered a bit "too" liberal by his fellow workers at the Ministry.

Kiss Anninka, Father, and *maman*, and tell them that I love them dearly. I think of you all the time, Masha, and let us never forget that we're sisters. As long as your health continues to improve, I know that everything will be all right, and you'll find what you're looking for, no matter what it might be.

The Lord be with you.

Your Irusha

Two days after St. George's Day on the twenty-third of April, Masha gave a party for the children of Petrovka, hoping to induce them to continue their schooling when the work in the fields was done. Not only did all the children turn out, but most of the village as well, so that the strains of music from the balalaikas and accordions could be heard all the way back to the manor house.

When she arrived home after the festivities the new groom came at a run, splashing through the mud.

"A visitor, *mam'selle*," he burst out, taking great pride in the fact that he knew a word or two of French.

"He came," Anninka said excitedly the moment she stepped inside the kitchen. "He's waiting in the drawing room. Pretend it's a surprise."

"Who is it, Gregor?"

"A surprise," Anninka said again, her pink cameo brooch bobbing up and down as she clasped Masha's hands, tugging on them as if they were a bellpull. "My lips are sealed."

Forgetting that her boots were muddy, Masha hurried to the drawing room. The instant she saw him she stopped short and just stood there with a smile, feeling herself tingle all over.

"Oh Stepan, what a wonderful surprise!" she cried out.

Captain Danchenko bounded to his feet and, disregarding all the rules of propriety, took her in his arms and held her so tightly that she felt weak. When he finally stepped back he continued to hold onto her hands, gazing at her with a rapturous expression and grinning so broadly that his entire face seemed to glow.

"I've missed you terribly," he kept saying. "I wanted to come earlier—months ago, in fact—but it was just impossible to get away. But now that I'm here, I don't intend to leave without you."

Now that he'd finally told her what she wanted to hear, Masha was overwhelmed. She looked around for a chair, feeling her legs about to give out beneath her.

"I don't think I understand," she said, even though she did. "It's all happening so quickly, Stepan."

"Quickly?" he exclaimed. "Why, it's been months, Masha, months and months. I love you and I want to marry you. Look at me," and he began to laugh. "I'm not here ten minutes and I'm already proposing. But you don't have to give me an answer, not until you're ready. But if you say no, I'll camp out in the yard, and won't go away until you change your mind."

He towered over her, and as he put his arms around her slender waist, brushing the top of her head with his cheek, Masha felt so wonderfully safe and protected that she would have been content to have him hold her like this for the rest of her life. What a marvelous thing it was to be in love, to know it as surely as she knew her name, to think of all the happiness that was theirs, and would continue to be theirs, long after this moment had passed.

Her mother's bell began to ring, then stopped abruptly.

She eased free of Stepan's embrace, gazing up at him as if seeing him for the first time. He was so full of life it dazzled her, his youthful exuberance like a bright light shining in her eyes. Yes, there could be no doubt how much he loved her. In the months that they'd corresponded his letters had grown increasingly affectionate, intimate too, and she'd come to feel she understood him, knowing exactly what kind of man he was. He wasn't Victor, but she realized it was foolish to spend her life looking for a substitute or a replacement for what she'd once had. She had found someone else who would love her as she loved him, and that alone seemed important.

Again she heard the tinkle of her mother's bell.

"My mother," she explained. "I'll be down in a few minutes."

"No one answers," Sophia Mikhailovna complained as Masha entered the sickroom. "And where is Henriette when I need her most? She always answered my bell, and now she never comes anymore. And where's Laska? I need a little water, I think. I can't swallow. Oh, it's so cold," she said, shivering. "Will winter never end? And Varya, has she returned from Red Hill?"

"She's expected back tomorrow, *maman*." Masha poured a glass of water, then helped her mother sit up in bed, holding the glass to her lips.

Laska stood guard out in the hall, whining softly, and

looking into the bedroom with her doleful brown eyes.

"We're all getting old, Laska too," murmured her mother as she sank down against the pillows, while overhead the chipped and faded Cupid spun on its slender thread. "Whose carriage was that? Has Henriette come back to apologize?"

"Captain Danchenko," she explained, having already told her mother about Stepan. "*Maman*, he's asked me to marry him. I have your blessing, don't I?"

"Durnovo, did you say?" Madame Petrova's large, child-like eyes filled with confusion. "And Laska, has she been fed? My little precious looks so skinny it breaks my heart."

"She's been fed, *maman*," Masha said patiently, and repeated what she'd said a moment before. "He's come all the way from Petersburg just to ask me to be his wife. He wants me to go back with him."

"And leave me all alone with no one to answer the bell?" her mother said in alarm. "Oh Masha, how could you desert me? And where is Henriette? She promised to come to see me, didn't she? Wasn't there a letter in yesterday's mail? Oh, I don't feel well at all. Have you destroyed the picture for me, the one in the morocco case? Oh Gabriel, I'll be with you soon, my beloved."

"Mother, you're going to get well. How can you not when there's to be another wedding soon?"

"I don't have the strength," whispered her mother. "Varya will have to help."

"But I need you, *maman*, you must believe that. That's why you're going to get well. We all need you here. Petrovka's just not been the same these last few months."

Madame Petrova shook her head. "Call the priest," she said.

"To pledge the troth? Yes, I'll do it right away. May I bring him upstairs to meet you, *maman*? He'd so like that."

Sophia Mikhailovna stared at her in bewilderment. "Who? Gabriel Antonovich? He's dead, Masha, just like all of us. Oh yes, call the priest, and burn the picture before your father finds it. If he finds out what I've done he'll never forgive me, and carry his anger to the grave. Yes, what a wicked girl I am, to have deceived him all these years, closing my eyes when he kissed me, and seeing only poor sweet Gabriel in his place."

Masha quietly left the room, but before she was halfway down the stairs she heard the familiar sound of her mother's bell, and then Laska's excited and high-pitched barking. Masha hurried back to the bedroom. The little spaniel had jumped up onto the bed, and was now snarling angrily, snapping at the faded Cupid Madame Petrova clutched to her breast. Somehow her mother had managed to reach up and tear it down, so that the chubby amoretto was now nestled in her arms.

"*Maman?*" she cried out. "*Maman,* are you all right?"

Sophia Mikhailovna could no longer answer. But death had been very kind. Her eyes were closed, and a faint smile, gentle, timid, and as childlike as always, was spread across her lips. Her face looked very smooth and white, and the wrinkles that had formerly gathered across her cheeks and forehead were nowhere to be seen.

"There now, Laska, there now, *ma petite,*" Masha whispered as the spaniel continued to snarl from the foot of the bed, baring all her considerable teeth, and bristling in a kind of impotent rage that she couldn't rouse her mistress. Masha reached out to stroke the little dog that had been her mother's dearest companion, only to feel Laska's jaws snapping shut around her wrist. Masha screamed and jerked her hand back as Laska bolted from the room, yelping as she ran down the hall.

The little King Charles spaniel was never seen again.

Anninka said she'd gone off somewhere to die, for her heart was broken. The day before the funeral Masha hid the portrait of Gabriel Antonovich among the dense folds of white ribbed velvet that lined her mother's coffin. After a suitable period of mourning she was married, and went off to Petersburg with her husband, still bearing the marks of Laska's teeth upon her wrist.

Book Two

1885 = 86

One

In the summer of 1885 Count Ivanov had, as usual, removed his household to the largest of his estates. Located in the Ukrainian province of Ekaterinoslav, Ivanovka was a working farm of some fifteen thousand acres, with a handsome manor house situated at the confluence of two streams, the Shurov and the Solenenkoi. Henriette's bedroom windows looked out on the orchards that stretched across the bottomland where the two sluggish little streams came together. For the past three summers she'd been very happy here. But now, at the age of twenty-eight, she felt she could no longer make excuses to herself, and that it was time to put aside discretion and make a stand, no matter how painful that option might prove to be.

She was now the Count's housekeeper, another governess having been hired to take her place. Polina Filippovna had resigned her position more than two years before, claiming she couldn't work in a home where licentiousness and a lack of decorum were the rule rather than the exception. Having taken over her duties, Henriette found it very pleasurable to give orders and relegate menial jobs to the large staff of domestics over whom she now had complete jurisdiction.

The Count had left Ivanovka a few days before, called back to Petersburg on important government business. Although she'd hoped his feelings for her would deepen in time, Dmitri Fyodorovich rarely if ever allowed himself to behave as he had the night she returned from the ballet. He was respectful, even thoughtful of her, but invariably kept his distance. As a result, she could only count on one hand the number of times he'd kissed her, and held her in his arms. Thus she'd increasingly turned her attention to Julian Andreyevich Golovin, who was still employed by the Count as tutor.

If only he would hold her close, she was certain Julian would discover what a rare and marvelous creature she was. After all, *La Belle Henriette* wasn't profligate with her affection. So why didn't Julian appreciate her many virtues, and respond as she'd so often prayed he would? It was a question she'd avoided these past four years, knowing that if the answer didn't turn out in her favor, she wouldn't be able to cope with her disappointment.

But now she could wait no longer. All too often the devil himself would visit her at night, flashing lightning across her ikon stand. Then she would moan voluptuously and thrash about in her bed, feeling the presence of the snake of Eden rippling tantalizingly between her legs. Only when she crossed herself would the serpent slither away, and the gray goat that was the devil draw back in alarm. Yes, her Redeemer never failed to materialize when she begged Him to intercede, and save her from the Tempter that rippled its long, thick coils at the foot of her bed. How wonderful it was to know that she, above all others, could claim Him as her secret lover. Not only did He lie next to her, holding her in His safe and comforting embrace, but also of late He would ease the bedcovers down, then help her strip off her nightdress so that she would be as naked as Eve before the snake taught her to revile the word of God.

On one such evening she'd awakened with the pillows tangled between her legs. Fearing that she'd been raped by the demons who frequently came to taunt her, she hurried from her bed, tiptoeing down the hall to knock softly on Julian's door. Only then had he held her close, telling her she had nothing to fear, and that it was just a dream and nothing more. But even though she'd stepped into his room, gazing longingly at the crumpled sheets of his bed, the tutor had escorted her back down the hall to her room, patting her on the shoulder as her brother might have done.

Today she was determined that all that would change. She had to know what his feelings were, and why he'd deceived her for four years, and might very well continue to deceive her for another four, unless she put a stop to it, once and for all.

"I don't know what you're talking about, Henriette," the tutor insisted when she managed to get him alone, several days after the Count had departed by rail for the capital.

She had found him lazing along the bank of one of the streams, lying beneath a willow, his wide-brimmed straw hat covering his eyes.

"I'm talking about us," she went on, annoyed at the way he feigned ignorance, gazing at her with his innocent blue eyes. "How much longer do you intend to make me wait?"

With these words, Julian sat bolt upright, looking at her in confusion. "What in the world is this all about, Henriette? Has something happened that I don't know about?"

"The something that's happened," she said, "is that I'm tired of waiting, and being led on, and deceived."

Julian came to his feet, and the face she'd always found so pale and expressive wasn't nearly as attractive as it once was. "I've never deceived you, Henriette. I've always held you in the greatest esteem, and respected you at all times. How have I led you on?"

Henriette swallowed hard so that she made a loud gulping sound, just as her sister Vera used to do whenever someone gave her a dressing down. "I gave up countless opportunities because of you," she said hysterically. "You told me you'd marry me—not in those very same words, of course, but words to that effect. And now look what you've done. Here I am, four years later, and not once have you set a date, or taken my hand in yours, or even kissed me."

"Henriette Petrovna, you don't know what you're saying," Julian replied.

"Will you marry me or won't you?" she shouted.

"Henriette, stop this!" he cried out. "You know I've never thought of you that way. We were friends, or so I hoped. But now that you've brought it up, you might as well know that next week I plan to leave Ivanovka. I've resigned my position here. Suffice it to say that your behavior this afternoon has only convinced me that I'm doing the right thing."

"God will punish you for deceiving me, Julian Andreyevich! Oh yes He will, and don't look at me like that because I know what I'm saying. I speak to Him, and hear His voice, and feel His arms around me. So you're just running away from me, are you? I suppose you'll go right to the arms of your sister, won't you?"

"You know she's not my sister. You knew that long ago, and yet you persisted in deluding yourself. I'm not in love with you, Henriette. I never have been. I never will be. So why make a fool of yourself like this?"

She struck him across the face. "That's for your lies," she said, remembering then what her father had done, how he'd slapped her the day she insulted General Tishin. "But I'm not a cruel person, and so I forgive you, Julian. I'll give you one more chance to make it up to me. Your sister's turned your head against me, that's all it is."

"I have no sister. And you've never met my fiancée."

"But the ballet?" she said, looking at him in bewilderment. "And then when my sister came to tea—"

"I lied, and later explained myself, because I didn't want to hurt your feelings. But that was nearly four years ago, and we've both changed since then. And there's nothing between us but the Count's purse strings." He turned away, and began to follow the dusty path that led back to the manor house.

"You've ruined me!" Henriette cried after him. "You tricked me, Julian!"

He did lie to me, didn't he? Or was I the one who did the deceiving? I can't remember. I can't remember any of it.

She sank down onto the scorched yellow grass, feeling the heat of midday descending like a shower of brimstone. Henriette knew she wasn't well, but didn't know how she could be cured. It wasn't her flesh but her spirit that was ailing, and as she lay there on the grass a voice she'd heard before spoke without moving its lips.

"See what you've done, Henriette? You knew all along, didn't you? You just wanted to end it so you could turn your attentions back to the Count. So calm yourself, my child, that you'll be ready to receive him, and take him into you, and be as one, forever locked in his embrace."

Slowly she came to her feet. She felt very sad, for somehow it seemed much easier to be dishonest to herself, to dream of what might be, rather than accept the reality of what was. But accept it she did. After all, someday she would be *La Belle Henriette*. Then, in a state of utter ecstasy, *toute transportée*, she'd share her visions with her admirers, and prove to the world the remarkable nature of her gifts.

Vera crouched on the floor alongside the little girl's narrow bed, two cracked boards set on sawhorses, and covered with a skimpy mattress stuffed with bast. Several knitted blankets were wrapped around the child's painfully thin body. Even though the stove had been lit that morning, it no longer retained much heat, and an icy draft blew in from under the door. Vera had tried stuffing rags across the threshold, but it didn't seem to do any good. Shivering, she drew her shawl around her shoulders, and gazed at the child who provided her with the only happiness in her life.

Pauline was three years old, and though she had the pale and prematurely haggard look of a child raised in the Presnia, there was something about her features that gave every indication that in time, and in other circumstances, she might very well turn into a great beauty. She had her mother's limpid, almond-shaped blue eyes, but her hair was like her father's, an extravagant profusion of lustrous black curls that spilled down along the sides of her face, hanging in loose, glossy ringlets around her little neck. She even had Simon's cleft chin, and when she smiled, dimples appeared in her cheeks, and her white teeth shone brightly when she laughed.

"There now, my little princess," whispered Vera, her knees against the cold, splintery floor. "This is all just temporary, and it's bound to change. After all, you're my princess, my precious little darling. And someday you won't even remember this. It'll be like a dream."

"Is Papa coming home soon?" the child asked.

"Yes, very soon. He works very hard for us. But you must try to get some sleep." Vera bent over and kissed the little girl on the forehead.

Pauline closed her eyes, and her breathing soon became deep and regular. For a long time Vera remained where she was, crouched on the floor until the backs of her legs began to ache and she came reluctantly to her feet.

For more than three years now they had rented this wretched little room from Saltychikha, living in the old dirty-yellow stone house off the Malaya Gruzinskaya. Beyond the moldy greenish windowpanes, an endless winding sheet of snow wrapped itself around the Presnia, beating against the glass, and making the panes rattle as if someone were trying to get inside. As she listened to the wind, now howling monotonously, now moaning almost drowsily, Vera thought of Petrovka, its snug rooms and roaring fires, everything bright and cheerful, with thick feather quilts to snuggle under, and delicious things to eat.

Although Irena continued to send her money every month, Vera had long since given up trying to keep it from Simon. No matter where she hid the packet of bills, he always managed to find them, spending some on drink and the rest on Pauline, for it was only through the child the he was able to express his love. He was employed at a tobacco factory, where he stood on his feet thirteen to fourteen hours a day, chopping tobacco and breathing in the caustic dust and nicotine fumes. Every evening when he returned home he could barely keep his eyes open, they were so red and inflamed. For this he received seventeen rubles a month, and had so little energy at the end of the day that it wasn't unusual for him to fall asleep while sitting in his chair, eating the meager supper Vera was able to provide.

Yet she still found him incredibly handsome. Even though he rarely had a kind word for her, and even though they rarely made love, Vera would still look at him and recall how it used to be, when he'd given her everything she wanted, and her body had trembled at his touch. But now that all seemed behind them. She'd long since given up gazing into mirrors, or wondering if her chin was still pointy, her skin smooth and unblemished, her hair a dazzling shade of gold.

When Simon returned that evening, stamping around in the gallery outside their door in order to get the snow off his boots, he seemed in a particularly unhappy mood. He now sported a full beard of dense, wiry black hair, and his hands had grown calloused and yellow from handling tobacco.

As soon as he came into the room he went over to Pauline's bed, watching his daughter for a moment before he peeled off his old sheepskin coat and sank into a chair.

"How do you expect me to eat this swill?" he said when Vera set his supper before him, a plate of salted cucumbers, a hunk of black bread, and a bowl of cabbage soup. "I'm sick of it, the same old slop day after day."

"Simon, please, you'll wake Pauline."

"And I'm sick of her having to live like this, too."

Pauline awakened, and called out to him.

Simon took her in his arms and began to carry her around the room, much to the little girl's delight. "And how's my princess?" he said, grinning mischievously at the child. "Getting more beautiful by the day, just like your mother used to be."

Vera looked down at her lap, contemplating the ragged edges of her broken fingernails, and the pale-blue tracery of veins that stood out along her thin, weathered hands.

I was young, pretty, she thought. But God punished me. But then He gave me Pauline, so the past doesn't matter anymore.

"But now it's time to go back to sleep, princess," she heard Simon say as he put the child to bed, arranging a chair near Pauline's head so she wouldn't fall out in the middle of the night.

"I love you, Papa."

"I love you too, princess." He kissed her good night, and when he turned away Vera saw how he clenched his hands, so that beneath his grimy flannel shirt the muscles tensed. He sat dejectedly at the table chewing on a crust of bread. "I want you to leave," he suddenly announced. "I don't want her here. My father was gentry. So is yours. She's so pale and sickly looking I can't bear it. I want her to be strong, so she'll learn how to cope with life, how to get what she deserves. I don't want her living here in the Presnia where there isn't even enough air to breathe."

Vera watched the shadows flickering across the walls, the kerosene lamp smoking and guttering, in need of fuel.

We don't even have that, she thought.

She sighed loudly, then stood behind Simon's chair, draping her arms over his shoulders. He needed a bath, but so did she. She picked a nit from his hair, rubbed it between her fingers, then wiped her hands on the greasy apron that was tied around her waist.

"You have to go back," he insisted. "It's no use pretending things'll get better, because they won't."

"Back to Petrovka?" She laughed bitterly. "Why should he bother to take us in? The little bully hasn't changed. He doesn't even answer my letters—when we have the money to mail them."

"When he sees his granddaughter he'll change his tune."

"I could've gone back three years ago, Senya, but I didn't. I'm no good without you. I love you too much."

"This is what you love, Vera," and he pointed between his legs. "That's what they all used to love," he said, half to himself.

"Don't you love me anymore, Senya?" she heard herself ask.

"There's no love in the Presnia, Vera. Do you call this love?" He swept his hand about the room. For all her efforts, it was still a dingy little cubicle, twelve paces long, twelve paces wide. "I'll make out. My luck's bound to change one of these days. And when it does, I'll send for you and we'll start all over again."

"Why can't you start over, too?" she said, keeping her voice down lest she awaken Pauline. "It's been more than three years, Simon. Surely they've forgotten what happened."

"And work for your father? I'd rather stay at the tobacco factory. I've made friends there, powerful friends. They know where I come from, and that I'm a gentleman." He wolfed down what was left of his supper, then put on his sheepskin and started to the door, telling her he had a meeting to go to.

"What kind of meeting?"

Simon lowered his voice. "We're going to strike. We're men, Vera, and we can't keep living like this. Christ, even before the serfs were liberated they lived better than we do now."

"But strikes are illegal. They'll arrest you, Simon, and throw you into jail."

"You and Pauline will be long gone by then. There's money enough for a ticket. Three rubles ninety, I already checked. I want you to do as I say. I won't have my child living here anymore."

"But what about me, Senya?"

"Anninka will fatten you up again, my dearest, and you'll soon put this out of your pretty little head. Besides, I'm not giving you a choice, Vera. If you don't take Pauline to your father's, I'll take her there myself."

The dim light of a lantern quivered overhead, briefly illuminating the raggedly dressed bodies huddled together along the wooden bench. Each time the lantern moved, swinging wildly when the train rounded a curve, it shed its uncertain light on yet another passenger, picking each traveler out of the darkness. The drab, foul-smelling third-class carriage had a central corridor, with rows of benches on either side. Vera stared out the window and watched the sparks from the engine rushing past like a swarm of angry bees, lighting up the darkness with brilliant little flashes of fire. Thick, milky-white flakes of snow beat against the double window, which nevertheless didn't keep in the heat, for drafts of raw wintry air kept brushing against her cheeks. She looked down at Pauline, who clung to her even as she slept, the child's eyelids fluttering as she dreamed of warm feather beds and a full stomach.

One of her fellow passengers kept throwing logs into the iron stove at the end of the corridor, so that even though the compartment was drafty, it was also insufferably close. When the train slowed for yet another of its innumerable stops, lingering at each and every station, Vera came to her feet, making sure that Pauline was comfortable before she went out to get some air.

The little girl's pale, translucent eyelids flew open with a start. "Where are you going, Mama?"

"I'll be right outside, princess."

"Will we be there soon?"

"Yes, my sweet, very soon. Go back to sleep now."

As soon as the train came to a stop, Vera stepped down onto the platform. The uncleared snow reached halfway to her knees, but the air was crisp and tingly, alive with a fragrant, resinous scent. Up ahead, the lights of the first-class buffet shone brightly. Through the windows of the station restaurant she could see Tatar waiters rushing about, their coattails flying out behind them. Vera couldn't help but think this was how she used to live, traveling first-class, being able to afford whatever she wanted.

"You just ate," she heard a woman exclaim. "Why, it's a disgrace. All you do is eat and fall asleep, Ardalosha. And there isn't time."

"Just a taste of sturgeon, Varvarushka," came a man's plaintive and almost childlike reply.

"Absolutely not. We'll be home soon enough, and then you can stuff yourself to your heart's content. Now go back inside before you catch your death. And what's that you have in your hand? How many times do I have to tell you never to eat sausages in public?"

For a moment Vera stood stock-still, trying to collect herself. Then she raised her hand, her voice cracking in fear as she called out to her aunt.

"Auntie V.!" she cried, first faintly, and then as loud as she could when her aunt didn't hear her, having already started back to the first-class carriage at the front of the train. Vera rushed down the snow-covered platform, shouting at the top of her voice. "Aunt Varvara! It's me, it's Vera!"

Her aunt stopped just short of the steps leading up to the carriage. "May I help you?" she said, gazing at her inquisitively, and with a searching expression that made it clear she had no idea who Vera was.

"It's me, Vera, your niece," she said. She started to embrace her aunt, but Varvara Semyonovna took a nervous step back.

"Vera? No, it couldn't possibly."

"But it is, it's me. I have my little girl with me, too. Auntie V." She motioned in the direction of the third-class carriage at the opposite end of the platform.

"But where are you going? And what's happened to you, Vera?"

"I was going back to Petrovka but I'm so afraid, Auntie V. What if he won't take me in again?"

"Varvarushka, why are you standing out in the cold? I've just heard the most amusing story, and I want to tell it to you before I forget." General Tishin, whom Vera recalled having met at her wedding, looked down at them as he stood on the top of the steps, his sleepy blue eyes fixed curiously on Vera.

"Go back inside," Varvara said testily. "Can't you see we have trouble on our hands? Oh, you poor thing," she went on, turning back to Vera and reaching somewhat hesitantly for her niece's hands, for Vera's gloves weren't very clean. "What an extraordinary thing to happen. But you can't go back looking like this. Oh no, you'll have to come with us. We're on our way to Red Hill. My new home, you know. Oh yes, the General and I have been enjoying marital bliss for nearly two years now, ever since that blessed day when— Well, enough of my happiness, for we must now see to yours. Oh Vera, Vera." She drew her arms around her niece and held her close, sniffling loudly, even moved to several tears.

Vera too began to cry, having never expected such kindness from her aunt.

"We'll take care of you, child, don't you worry. Married life has taught me a few things, let me tell you. Now you just get your little girl and hurry back. There's room in our compartment, more than enough. To think, a Petrov traveling third-class. Why, it's an absolute disgrace."

Vera rushed down the platform, while her aunt remained behind, clucking her tongue, and calling out to her husband to make room in their compartment, for thanks to her quick thinking, they'd just averted a terrible calamity.

Varvara took charge of things, and the following morning she wouldn't let Vera and Pauline leave the dining table until they'd literally stuffed themselves. The little girl had never seen so much food at one time, nor had she ever eaten until she was unable to take another mouthful. Gazing at the "raven-haired little minx," those being the words Varvara used to describe her grandniece, the woman continually clucked her tongue in both pity and astonishment.

"What grace, what mien," she proclaimed to the entire household, who rushed back and forth between the dining room and kitchen, heaping Vera and Pauline's plates with one tasty dish after another. "She's precious, Vera. A precious ebony-haired angel."

"How can I ever thank you, Auntie?"

"There's no need for thanks, Vera. You're blood, are you not? I've learned that family isn't something one can stuff away in a drawer—much as it sometimes seems the best thing to do. Your father's a hard man, we all know that. But you needn't worry that he'll turn you away. I know how to deal with my brother. He'll snap to or else I'll make quite a scene." Varvara laughed to herself. "And as I'm sure you know, I'm quite good at scenes, Vera dear, oh yes indeed."

Vera hadn't been pampered like this in years, and for the next few days all she seemed to do was eat and sleep. In a short period of time, the circles beneath her eyes began to fade, and as she sat before the dressing-table mirror in the charming room her aunt had given her, she couldn't help but marvel at the change in her appearance. Yes, her chin was still a trifle pointy, and no doubt so it would always remain. But her hair no longer looked as lackluster as straw, and the lines around the corners of her eyes and mouth spoke not of great trials and suffering, but of character and poise, lending what she imagined was a certain dignified maturity to her otherwise youthful features. Of course there was still the unfinished business of her father, and when it came time for her and Pauline to make the trip to Petrovka, all Vera's fears resurfaced.

Bundled up in furs and lap robes in General Tishin's handsome mahogany sleigh, they set off for Petrovka on one of those sparkling winter days when all one can see is an endless expanse of white, broken here and there by an occasional stand of trees reaching toward the blue and cloudless sky.

Pauline had never seen the country, and now she gazed every which way at once, her blue eyes wide with excitement. A fresh, rosy glow suffused her cheeks, making her look even more beautiful than ever. Auntie V. couldn't stop marveling, and was continually hugging the little girl, and popping sweets into her mouth, having brought along an ample supply of fruit drops, caramels, and tasty peppermint cakes.

When Petrovka came into view Vera felt her heartbeat quicken, and she could hardly believe her eyes. It wasn't the magic kingdom she'd so often portrayed to Pauline, but there was still a sturdiness about the estate that fueled her determination to make it up to her father and start a new life for herself and her child. Once she wrote Simon and told him how wonderful things were, she was certain he'd come back to her, and there they'd be, safe in their bed in the steward's house, living just as they used to.

It was Anninka, stooped and aged but still amazingly spry, who came out to see who the visitors were. When she laid eyes on them she let out a cry that could be heard in three provinces.

"Father God!" she shouted as she rushed through the snow. "Our darling's come home! Heavenly Empress, you've answered my prayers. And who might this little angel be?" she asked as the coachman helped Pauline down from the sleigh.

"Pauline, ma'am," the child said shyly.

"Well, you come right inside, Pauline, because Anninka is going to make you a nice cup of chocolate." She turned to Vera, and an uneasy expression came into her eyes. "Verochka, you poor child, how I've prayed for this day. Every time you wrote I begged him to answer, but no, he's so stubborn."

Anninka led them back into the house, and no sooner did they enter the kitchen when the door leading into the dining room flew open and the little bulldog stepped inside, picking solemnly at his teeth with a quill toothpick.

Vera gave Pauline a gentle nudge, having already rehearsed her daughter so that the child knew exactly what was expected of her.

Pauline stepped forward, curtsying like a perfect lady. "Good afternoon, Grandfather."

"Good afternoon to you. What's your name, child?"

"Pauline Simonovna, Grandfather. Mama says you're the only grandfather I have."

"Your mama must say a lot of things, child. Afternoon, Varya," and her father turned away without once acknowledging her.

The door swung shut behind him, her father's strutting steps throbbing in her ears. "It's useless," she whispered. "He hates me, and he always will."

"Nonsense," said Varvara, who didn't seem the least bit put off by her brother's brusque reaction. "Now take off your coat and follow me, my dear. Pauline can stay here with Anninka."

Off they went, trooping through the warm, snug rooms of the house, where even the cracks in the wallpaper and the faded upholstery seemed welcome, and strains of music whispered in Vera's ears as she glanced into the empty ballroom. When they reached her father's study, Auntie V. didn't even bother to knock, but just pushed the door open and marched inside.

Seated behind his desk of old Karelian birch, her father glared at her as if she were an intruder. "You're too late for the funeral," he said angrily.

"I didn't have the money, Father. It cost four rubles," Vera replied, speaking very softly, and making no effort to stop herself from trembling. "It takes Simon an entire week to earn that much money."

"Then for your mother's sake you should have walked here."

"Can't you see she's suffered enough, Petya? Leave the child alone and stop thinking of yourself," Auntie V. said shrilly. "They were more dead than alive when God put me in their path. Don't you think our poor Sonyushka is looking down from heaven right this very moment, her heart breaking all over again to see you treating your daughter this way?"

"And what of *my* heart, and *my* feelings?" he shouted.

"*Papochka*, you must forgive me, if only for Pauline's sake." Vera dropped down onto her knees as if she were doing penance. "We've lived from day to day, hour to hour. Your granddaughter's gone to bed hungry all her life. See what I'm wearing? That's all I have, just rags. But I've worked hard, Father. I've tried to make a home for my husband and my child. How can you send us back? She'll die there. Forget about me, Papa. But Pauline is your grandchild. Send me away, but don't send her."

"So I've been proven right, have I?" Peter Semyonovich said smugly, and his little round gray eyes were bright with victory. "Didn't I tell you not to go off with him? Didn't I warn you, Vera?"

"Stop browbeating her, Petya," scolded her aunt.

"You keep out of this, Varya. You've done your good deed and now you can rest easy. And don't kneel there, Vera. You're not a serf. Get up and come to your father."

Vera was afraid he'd beat her, but nevertheless did as he asked. He had aged, but the little bulldog looked very much the same, just a few more wrinkles and a little less hair, his clothes hanging a bit more loosely on his otherwise bulky frame.

"Beg my forgiveness," he said.

Vera quickly recited the humbling words her father wanted to hear.

Peter Semyonovich eyed her with something less than satisfaction. Then, speaking in a harsh, fulminating voice, he said, "If your mother hadn't been taken from me, I wouldn't hesitate to tell you to go back to that thief you made the mistake of marrying. But my poor Sonyushka's dead, and I have no one. Therefore, against my better judgment, and only because of the child—for there's no reason the girl should suffer because of her mother's stupidity—you may stay. If you expect nothing from me you won't be disappointed."

Vera nodded silently.

"I will expect something from you, however. Anninka's all alone now, what with that toothless old Matriona having gone off to God knows where. So in return for a roof over your head, and food in your belly, you're to help her and make yourself useful. I won't have you pretending you're the mistress around here. Petrovka's *barinya* is dead and buried. No one else can take your poor mother's place."

"Yes, Father," she whispered, gulping loudly. "I'm not afraid of work."

"That, my dear, remains to be seen."

Two

Nikolai Volsky had just turned thirty-six, and though he still made a point of concealing his ambitions behind a pleasant and agreeable smile, he was in fact a man who had gained a reputation for making his opinions known, speaking out on issues that the majority of his colleagues preferred to ignore.

Having successfully switched ministries a year before, he was now head of the factory inspectorate, established a few years earlier and placed under the direction of the Minister of Finance. Charged with the task of enforcing several new laws designed to improve the lot of Russia's working class, the inspectorate was given broad though somewhat nebulous powers. While the government insisted it wanted its labor legislation upheld, it said so in a whisper, rarely if ever following up on the extensive reports of its inspectors. Nevertheless, Volsky threw himself into his work with his customary sense of responsibility, determined to see the labor laws enacted to the letter.

But wherever he went he met with resistance. Inspectors

were directed to visit factories and mills without notifying the owners beforehand, who more often than not refused them entry to the plants. Even the workers were unhappy with the new laws, and during the previous autumn, a series of strikes and disorders had spread through the empire, causing great hardship for both workers and management.

Yet despite all these obstacles, Volsky was persistent. He refused to be discouraged, just as he'd refused to be discouraged when, in the last three years, Irena had twice become pregnant, and had twice been unable to carry to term. Now she was pregnant a third time, and whenever he looked at her he felt afraid to breathe, lest something terrible happen. Only with the greatest of reluctance had he left her, as his work required him to spend a week in Moscow. Here he went from one factory to another, assisting the Moscow district in preparing its annual report.

Led on a tour of the workers' dormitory attached to the Trumpeter Tobacco Factory, Volsky was utterly appalled by what he saw. A musty, putrid stench of sweat and excrement filled the rooms. Whatever windows there were, and there were few that he could see, were either boarded up or nailed shut, so that not a breath of fresh air could be had. There were rows of bare plank beds crammed one against the other and stacked like logs, the highest less than two feet below the soot-blackened ceiling.

Everywhere Volsky looked he saw children, naked infants crawling over the muddy floors, little boys and girls with pale, pinched faces sitting quietly on the narrow beds and staring vacantly into space. Trumpeter didn't provide separate cubicles for married workers and their families. Thus, everyone lived on the most primitive level imaginable, with absolutely no privacy whatsoever.

When Volsky saw two people having intercourse, with only a rag of a blanket shielding them from the eyes of the curious, he looked away, sick at heart that nothing was being done to help these people improve their lives. The owner's representative, a slight, balding man with moist, beady eyes, began to snicker as he eyed the unfortunate couple.

"Things like this happen all the time. Why, it's just like at the zoo," the man said with an oily laugh. "Women even give birth right out in the open, in front of everyone. Most of these people are peasants. Modesty's something they've never been taught."

Nor the kindness of the likes of you, Volsky thought angrily. But he kept this to himself, announcing instead that he was ready to be shown around the school.

"What school?"

In a calm, dispassionate, and altogether bureaucratic tone of voice, Volsky informed him that according to the law of June 12, 1884, a special factory school had to be established by the employer for the instruction of minors who hadn't received an elementary education.

The slight, balding man began to stammer. But Trumpeter's owner wasn't at all at a loss for words. "Now see here, Mr. Volsky. You just can't go around ordering us to do this, that, and the other thing. We permit these children to work for us out of pity. If not, most of them would be out on the streets, starving to death."

"I asked about the school," Volsky said patiently. "You employ juveniles. There's no public school nearby. Therefore, you're required to establish a school of your own."

"I'm not required to do anything of the kind, Mr. Volsky," the owner insisted with a clickety-click of his singularly white false teeth. "However, I'm a reasonable man, as you can see," whereupon Trumpeter's red-faced owner shoved a bulging envelope across his desk, nodding with his chin and inviting Volsky to examine its contents.

The manila envelope was filled with enough "palm oil" to

grease both his arms, clear up to his elbows.

Volsky tossed the money aside. "I intend to see that you're prosecuted to the full extent of the law. It's small, selfish men like yourself who'll be the ruination of the empire, not these so-called revolutionaries we hear so much talk about."

Before he could come to his feet, the factory owner stopped him with a loud and insinuating voice. "I wouldn't threaten me if I were you, Mr. Volsky," the man warned. "I believe your chief is Mr. Ermakov, head of the Department of Trade and Manufacture."

"What of it?"

"He happens to be my wife's brother." With a final click of his teeth, the owner asked his beady-eyed assistant to show "Mr. Inspector" to the door.

As it happened, Volsky had passed within ten feet of his brother-in-law, when earlier that day he'd inspected the tobacco factory. Neither had seen the other, but after Simon finished his shift late that evening, he was approached by several of the men with whom he worked. It had been snowing all day, and now the temperature had dropped considerably. All he could think of was hurrying home and trying to get warm.

"An inspector came by today. We heard he wasn't too happy with what he saw."

"They can inspect every day for the next year and it won't change anything," Simon replied in a whisper. They were right outside Trumpeter's gates, and he didn't want anyone to overhear the conversation.

"That's why there's going to be another meeting tonight," said one of the men who worked with him in the chopping room. "We're almost ready to get things moving, Simon Ivanovich. Can we count on you to be there?"

He nodded, and set off at a run through the dark, narrow

streets, the freezing snow stinging his face, and the icy slush penetrating the thin soles of his worn leather boots. He passed other men just like himself, the fortunate ones who didn't have to live in the workers' barracks, and could afford squalid little rooms of their own. Heavy carts rumbled by, sending sheets of muddy snow splashing against the buildings that flanked the alleyways. When he reached the Malaya Gruzinskaya, he turned into the alley and was soon climbing the narrow steps that led to the second floor of the old stone house.

"If you don't mind my saying," said a voice from the top of the stairs, "you look like you could use a drink, dearie."

It was Saltychikha, his landlady, the one person he hadn't wanted to meet. Already two months behind in his rent, Simon was afraid she was going to ask him either to pay up or find himself another place to live.

As soon as he stepped inside the woman's room, the finest in the lodging house since it was located a goodly distance from the foul-smelling privy, he went right to the stove, peeling off his gloves and warming himself by the grate. The landlady brought him a jelly jar filled with vodka, and as the white, hot liquor settled in his stomach, Simon slowly began to recover from the cold.

The landlady's room was just as dirty as his, though it was considerably larger, and not nearly as drafty. Overhead, an oil lamp hung on a rusty chain, scattering smoky light across the kitchen table. At the far end of the room stood a cast-iron bedstead, half hidden behind a curtained partition.

"Now you sit yourself down, and let Saltychikha take care of you. I've a nice hot bowl of soup all ready, Simon Ivanovich, and more vodka, too."

Simon wasn't certain what all this was leading up to, but he wasn't about to start objecting. The soup and the vodka made him feel very good indeed, and when Nina Pavlovna joined

291

him at the table, unplaiting her rat's tail and shaking out her greasy brown hair, he began to figure out what she wanted from him.

"If you're worried about the—"

"Now, now, dearie," Saltychikha interrupted. She reached over and laid her hand on his arm, giving it an affectionate squeeze. "Have I said anything about the rent? I know you're good for it, Simon Ivanovich. Besides, there's no reason we can't strike a bargain, now, is there?"

The woman was a pig, but with his eyes closed, what did it matter? So he leaned forward, staring at Saltychikha and asking what kind of bargain she was talking about.

"All kinds," the landlady said with a grin. "But let's not talk of business, not just yet."

"Fine with me." He pushed his chair back, and as he came to his feet he was already unbuttoning his shirt.

Saltychikha laughed nervously. "My, you don't waste any time, dearie, do you?"

"Life's too short, Nina Pavlovna. But that's about the only thing that is."

He was barely out of his clothes when the woman drew the curtain across the bed, then slipped beneath the covers.

When it was over she shared a cigarette with him, keeping one hand on his privates, as if she weren't quite willing to give them up. "I have a friend," she said, "who'd be very interested in meeting a man like you. He'd like to know what's going on at Trumpeter, if you follow my meaning."

Belinsky eyed her suspiciously. "Nothing's going on there, except a lot of backbreaking work."

"Come now, dearie, this friend of mine is willing to pay for the information you can give him. And what he pays is a lot more than you're making now."

"Who does he work for?"

"Let's just say he knows the right people. But if you don't

want to meet him—"

"I didn't say that."

"I can set up a meeting for you tomorrow night, if that's all right."

"And he'll pay?"

"For the right information, he'll probably give you more than enough for the two months' back rent you owe me. But seeing as how you're a gentleman, Simon Ivanovich, and a man of considerable talent," and she toyed with him under the grimy bedcovers, "I'm not even going to ask you for it. After all, dearie, one good turn deserves another."

The landlady climbed on top of him, and not even bothering to put out her cigarette, she set to work getting her money's worth.

The ninth of January was Stepan Danchenko's name day, the day sacred to St. Stephen, the first Christian martyr. To celebrate, name days being much more important than birthdays, Masha decided to give a party in her husband's honor.

For the past year and a half, Stepan, now a Lieutenant Colonel, had been posted at the Selistchev Barracks, some three hundreds versts from the capital. The camp was located at Grusino, the estate that had once been the property of Count Araksheyev, a notorious martinet who was Alexander I's closest confidant and adviser. It was built along the banks of the Volkhov River, and for miles around there were vast birch and pine forests, and dozens of charming lakes and ponds.

Masha had been very happy here, though of late she'd become a figure of considerable controversy. Not content to sit at home, she'd established a school in one of the nearby villages, just as she'd done at Petrovka. But the authorities weren't pleased with her interest in popular education. First the Marshal of the Nobility for the district tried to persuade her to put aside her plans, saying that they weren't becoming to a daughter of the gentry. Then a school inspector came to see her, and said that she'd best allow the village elders to decide how they wanted their children educated. "The village elders have given me carte blanche," she replied, and refused to hear anything more about it.

It didn't end there, however. Now it was being said that Masha was spreading dangerous ideas among the common people, advocating methods that were contrary to government policy. She was accused of pursuing a dangerous course that could only result in hardship and ultimate tragedy for both herself and her husband.

Masha took all this gossip with a grain of salt. There was nothing politically suspect about teaching children to read and write and do simple sums. If the government wasn't providing primary education for the peasants, that was their fault, not hers. She said as much at Stepan's name-day party, her outspoken views providing her detractors with fresh ammunition, and her admirers with further cause to hold her in high esteem. Of the latter, none were more vocal then Eugene Borisovich Trigony, a Captain under Stepan's command.

A graduate of His Imperial Majesty's Corps of Pages, the most exclusive military academy in all of Russia, Trigony was a handsome young man from an aristocratic family, with a reputation for marksmanship and womanizing. He was a few inches shorter than Stepan, with wavy blond hair and a tiny pug nose more suited to the face of a child than a grown man. But it was this very button of a nose that lent to his features a look of boyish good humor, and which he would periodically tap with the tip of his finger whenever he engaged in conversation.

On this particular winter's evening he'd already had a bit too much to drink. As a result, he began to argue rather heatedly with one of his fellow officers, declaiming in an authoritative voice that if Madame Danchenko believed in the virtues of popular education, that was certainly recommendation enough.

"But you see," Trigony said, speaking so loudly that many of the guests turned to look at him, "even if we educate these people, we're still left with the job of civilizing them. A moujik can be taught to count from one to ten, but how in the world can you convince him not to waltz when they play a mazurka?"

Laughing, Captain Trigony looked around at the guests, no doubt hoping they found his remarks as amusing as he did. Several of the officers' wives tittered politely, though it wasn't because Trigony had been particularly witty, but merely because he was considered such a rake.

Although Trigony had often made a point of speaking out in her behalf, this evening his behavior gave Masha reason to believe his motives for befriending her were not altogether altruistic. He'd now succeeded in cornering her, and thrusting out his chest like a pouter pigeon, the Captain proclaimed his allegiance to her cause in no uncertain terms.

"I'm very pleased that you support my work," she said. "It's most gratifying, Captain Trigony." She tried to step past him, when he reached out and laid his gloved hand on her arm. Now she was certain his character wasn't nearly as spotless as his uniform.

"One has need of protectors, Madame Danchenko. And yet you've never said, 'Now, see here, Eugene, why don't you give a few hours of your time and come to teach my little urchins?' I would, you know, if only because you asked."

"If you'll excuse me, Captain." Again she tried to slip past him. Again he reached out and held her fast.

"I've only had one vodka too many," Trigony insisted. "But tell me: How did you ever land someone as innocent as

Stepan Alexeyevich? After all, you must admit that while he's a jolly good sport and a charming fellow, he's still quite a boy."

"You're drunk, Captain, and you're the one who's beginning to sound like a schoolboy," she replied, making no effort to conceal her annoyance.

"Wouldn't it be to your advantage to be a little more friendly, Madame Danchenko?" the officer asked, tapping his nose with the tip of his finger. "After all, scandal must be checked whenever possible."

"There is nothing scandalous about my work. You're behaving quite rudely, Captain. If this is how you engage in innocent banter and flirtation, your methods are sorely lacking in charm and good taste."

Trigony's mouth dropped open, though a moment later he recovered his composure and leaned forward to whisper in Masha's ear. What he said couldn't be repeated in polite society. But Masha refrained from slapping him across the face, for if she did, she knew Stepan would demand an explanation. And once he found out what Trigony had told her, he'd probably try to murder the man, right then and there.

Count Ivanov received on Tuesday evenings, and among the guests who frequented his at-homes was the Countess Ignatieva, a woman whose reputation rested solely on her preoccupation with the occult. Tireless in her devotion to what she called "the magic world of spirits," the Countess would sit herself down in a chair and not waste a moment sharing her latest revelations and mystical experiences. Three times a week she held what was already being called a "black salon," where her friends would assemble to talk of spiritualism and the supernatural, read the tarot, and hold séances.

Henriette had often heard her employer speak of the

Countess with something less than respect, even going so far as to suggest that the only reason he liked having her around was because her mania for the occult kept his parties quite lively. Tonight, however, Henriette could tell that things weren't going as the Count might have wished. As she finished her supper in the kitchen, hardly a sound could be heard from the drawing room, where more than a dozen guests were assembled.

"If you ask me," whispered Foma Osipovich as he returned with an empty tray, "the master's downright bored, Henriette Petrovna. They're all sitting in there looking more dead than alive."

Ever since Julian had left, Henriette had done everything she could to rekindle Count Ivanov's romantic interest. But for all her efforts, the Count remained decidedly lukewarm. Not about to give up, especially when she had no one else, Henriette continued to press the issue whenever she could. Thus she was very pleased when Foma hurried back from the drawing room with the news that her presence was "most graciously requested."

"Ah, there she is," said the Count when Henriette entered the drawing room, and he immediately ordered Foma to pour her a glass of wine. "I don't believe you've had the pleasure of meeting my guests."

Count Ivanov went the round of introductions, which included several civilian Generals, white-haired and waxen-faced, three or four clerics in their black vestments, with long, untrimmed beards and equally long hair, as well as several fashionably dressed women, each looking more severe and unfriendly than the next. Among these, the Count singled out the Countess Ignatieva for special favor. As he introduced her he went on at great length, telling Henriette of the woman's interest in mysticism and the occult.

"Seeing as how you've taught yourself to read the tarot,

Henriette, and have on occasion revealed a rather uncanny gift for that sort of thing, the Countess wondered if you might be inclined to conduct a séance for us."

Henriette looked nervously at the Countess, who peered at her from behind her tortoise-shell lorgnette. She was a buxom woman in her late thirties, with a red, blotchy face and elaborately curled hair that was so black it had to be dyed. Although she wasn't particularly attractive, there was something wistful in her expression, an ingenuousness that Henriette found quite charming.

"Countess," she said, "I really wouldn't know where to begin. I've taught myself to read the cards, but I don't place great faith in them, I'm afraid. I have had visions, though."

No sooner had she uttered these words when everyone leaned forward in unison, fixing her with one curious glance after another. The Count pulled up a chair, and before she knew it she was the center of attention, a position she found so pleasing that she hardly thought twice about what she was saying.

"Extraordinary," whispered the Countess after Henriette told them of the gray goat, and the serpent of Eden.

"Amazing," said one of the Generals when she described her encounter with the cloven-hoofed monk who'd capered at the foot of her bed.

And when she alluded to being visited by the Redeemer, everyone gasped with sheer delight, for nothing could have thrilled them more than to have "discovered" a gifted new spiritualist in their midst.

"And right under our very noses, too," declared the Countess. "Shame on you, Dmitri Fyodorovich, to have kept Mademoiselle Petrova a secret all this time." The Countess' face turned even redder. Now she was truly excited, and couldn't wait for the séance to begin.

Foma brought in a card table and arranged the chairs, while

the Countess explained to Henriette what would be required of her. A few minutes later, as the guests seated themselves around the table, Henriette prayed that her imagination wouldn't fail her, that her performance would be so convincing no one would ever suspect it was all a charade.

Foma put out the lights and shut the door, plunging the drawing room into darkness. The guests joined hands, and after a few additional instructions and words of encouragement from the Countess, there was absolute silence.

Determined to give them the best possible séance they'd ever experienced, Henriette closed her eyes and began to count. She didn't want anything to happen too quickly, and so two or three minutes went by before she brought her knee up against the table, rapping three times in quick succession. One of the ladies squealed excitedly, and the Countess, who was seated on her right, squeezed Henriette's hand reassuringly.

"*Je te dirai des cieux tous les profonds mystères,*" Henriette began, trying to speak in a husky, low-pitched voice that bore little resemblance to her own. "I shall tell you all the profound mysteries of heaven. But wait . . . who's that? Filippovna! Are you dead?"

"Who's Filippovna?" someone whispered.

"Shh," came the reply.

"What do you want?" Henriette said in a terror-stricken voice. "It wasn't my fault you left. I swear, I didn't do anything to harm you. Where are you now, Filippovna?" Henriette hadn't had so much fun in years, and as she smiled to herself she suddenly let out with a gasp that made the guests tremble with fear, certain she'd already made contact with someone from the other side.

A light began to shine in her eyes. She blinked, but it wouldn't go away. A delicious warmth was beginning to flow through her body, and as she looked straight ahead, not certain where the light was coming from, Henriette had the distinct impression there was actually something there. It hovered before her, a foot or two above the table. Gradually she made out a face, one that glowed so brightly it seemed to be painted with phosphorus.

"What is it?" she heard the Countess whisper, speaking to her as if from a great distance.

"A face," she said.

There were gasps and muttering all around, but Henriette could no longer understand what was being said. She saw before her a man whose eyes were like pinpricks of fire, with long, stringy hair, a thin and scraggly beard, and a strange bald patch with a kind of scar above his forehead.

"His acts proceed from God," she whispered, both terrified and fascinated by what she saw.

Henriette knew she wasn't asleep, and yet here she was experiencing a vision that was more unsettling than any she'd had in her dreams. The man was talking to her, but his lips didn't move. She felt him caressing her, though he had no arms that she could see.

"If you do not sin, you cannot repent," she said, repeating what he'd told her.

Then a terrible smell filled the room, strong and penetrating. Where was it coming from? She didn't know, but it made her very dizzy, as if it were sucking up the oxygen and making it impossible to breathe. Something touched her leg. She screamed and threw herself back, more surprised than frightened. A moment later she found herself on the floor, looking up at a circle of anxious faces.

The Countess passed some lavender smelling salts under her nose. Henriette coughed and tried to sit up.

"You poor child," said the woman. "You gave us quite a fright." She turned to the Count, who had a rather cynical expression on his face, as if he didn't believe Henriette had seen anything at all. "We'll need a vinegar-soaked cloth. And a glass of strong spirits is very useful at times like these."

Soon she was stretched out on a sofa, while everyone bustled about, trying to be useful.

"It's never happened like that before. That smell, in particular."

"What smell?" said one of the Generals.

"It was like a goat, only worse, like an animal penned in a cage. I could hardly breathe."

"How fantastic!" exclaimed the General. "Though I'm afraid I didn't smell it myself. But those things happen, you know. Oh yes, I've heard of such cases before."

"You must let Mademoiselle Petrova rest now," said the Countess, who continued to hover over Henriette, seeing to it that she was comfortable.

The Count glanced at Henriette with undisguised annoyance. "I'm sure Petrova will be fine," he said crossly.

"Yes, but you must bring her with you next week," the Countess made him promise. "If this is what happened the first time, there's no telling what delightful miracles are in store for us once she's had a little more practice. Isn't that so, dear?"

Henriette looked up at the woman's round, purplish-red face. "Oh yes," she said, "with a little more practice, and your friendship and support, Countess, I'm quite certain most anything can happen."

Volsky paced the drawing room, anxiously twirling the tips of his mustache. In honor of the occasion he'd waxed it with *pommade hongroise,* and now his fingertips were greasy as he kept twisting each daggerlike point, unable to stop his hands from shaking. Down the hall there was a continual opening and closing of doors, hurrying footsteps moving between the kitchen and the bedroom. Occasionally he heard Irena, sobbing softly and then loudly; then she would be silent for a moment, and then there would be another frightening outburst.

Fathers have gone through this for thousands of years, Volsky thought. So why does it feel as if I'm the only one who's ever experienced it before? But as long as she's all right, the rest doesn't matter.

He looked in the direction of the ikon stand, where a lamp burned brightly, scattering its light over the dim, kindly face of the Virgin. Volsky wasn't a religious man, but now he crossed the room and knelt before the Mother of God, clasping his hands together.

"I know I have my faults," he told whoever was listening. "I know I'm ambitious and have little patience with other men. But I mean well. So if you can see it in your heart to make it easier for us, to spare my beloved, that's all that matters."

From the bedroom he heard another series of agonizing cries. Then the door flew open and Katya rushed outside.

"What is it?" he shouted.

"Soon, soon," said the maid, flushed and distracted as she ran off to get more water.

What do they need all this water for? he wondered. But she's strong. Yes, Irusha is strong and nothing will happen to her.

From behind the bedroom door there now came a horrible symphony of groans and wild, animal-like cries, muttered warnings, mysterious creaking sounds, and then a long, drawn-out sigh such as the dying must make before they give up the ghost. Volsky rushed across the drawing room, stumbling and tripping though there wasn't anything entangling his feet.

"It can't be! It mustn't!" he began to shout, when the bedroom door was flung open.

There was the doctor, red-faced and sweating profusely. For just an instant, no more than a heartbeat, Volsky stared at him with unconcealed rage, certain the man was a fraud and a charlatan, a quack of the basest sort.

"My wife," Volsky said. Then he rushed into the bedroom, where the midwife who'd assisted the doctor was busying herself by the foot of the bed.

"Niki?"

Thank God, thank God, to know that she was alive, that she hadn't deserted him when he needed her most!

Remembering what she'd made him promise, Volsky tripped again as he lighted the two candles that he and Irena had held during their wedding ceremony.

And the shirt, he thought, looking everywhere but at the bed. He was yet to hear another kind of cry, and was afraid to ask if things were as they should be.

"Yes, the shirt," Irena said weakly.

Oh God, he thought, please make it right for us.

He put down the two lit candles, found the shirt he'd worn the night before, flung it over his arm, once again lost his balance, righted himself, grabbed the candles, burned his hand with dripping wax, and rushed to the bed.

Now what? he thought.

But then he knew. Nestled in her arms was a tiny wrinkled face, red and pinched, squalling now and flailing at the air with two determined little fists.

"Thank God," he said aloud.

Volsky set the candles down on the bedside cabinet, then ever so gently wrapped the infant in his shirt. Like the nuptial tapers, this too was part of an ancient Russian custom. His father had done the same for him, and Irena's father for her, on back, generation before generation, to those ancient nomadic tribes that were his forebears, who had swaddled their newborn in animal skins, warming them against the cold, lashing winds of the steppes.

"What is it? I mean— Oh Irusha, I love you so, my angel." Tears dripped down his cheeks, and he laughed and did a little dance, he was so overcome with joy.

"A boy," she whispered.

"A son? Oh my goodness, how wonderful. A son! A son!" he cried out with delight, and the little red wizened thing in his arms twisted about with amazing strength. "A boy, a big, healthy, strapping boy. Andrei, say hello to Papa. Say hello now. Oh Irusha my precious angel, never was one man so happy in all his life."

Three

That summer, after endless delays, the committee of workers of which Simon was a member finally set a date for the strike. Though they'd hoped Trumpeter's owner would willingly agree to their demands, he'd repeatedly refused to meet with them, claiming he had no time for rabble-rousers, and little sympathy with revolutionaries. The evening before the scheduled strike, a meeting was held in what was considered a safe house, for strikes were illegal, and those who engaged in such activities were subject to prosecution by the authorities.

But the men were not there an hour when the door burst open and a detachment of police and gendarmes took everyone into custody. Grossly outnumbered, the workers offered little resistance, and a short while later they were all riding in the back of a police wagon, rattling over the cobblestones in the direction of Butyrky Prison. Several policemen, or *gorodvoi*, stood guard inside the wagon, the green piping on their uniforms glowing faintly in the dark. They warned the strike leaders not to communicate with each other, and so

Belinsky remained silent as he sat on the floor of the wagon, resting his head against his knees.

Soon he found himself thrown into a damp, narrow cell, perhaps nine feet long by five feet wide, the ceiling so low it nearly brushed against the top of his head. It wasn't the kind of place he cared to grow accustomed to, and when he sat down on the pallet, a swarm of roaches and bedbugs came out of hiding, crawling over his arms and legs.

He was still trying to brush them off when the judas opened wide, and an eye filled the narrow chink of the spy hole. Simon remained where he was as the door was unlocked. A "blue archangel," as the gendarmes were nicknamed, stood in the threshold, his sky-blue tunic far too bright and cheery for the likes of Butyrky.

"Simon Ivanovich Belinsky?"

He nodded.

"This way." The gendarme motioned him to step into the corridor. "You're to do exactly as you're told. If not—" The officer glanced down at the Colt's revolver he wore on his hip.

The gendarme led him through a maze of stinking corridors, dimly lit, with wet and slimy stone walls. Finally the officer paused before a heavy oak door like that of his cell. But when it was unlocked, it opened onto an inner courtyard, where a carriage stood waiting, its windows draped with black cloth.

The gendarme pushed him forward, while a policeman descended from the carriage and held the door open for him. As soon as Simon climbed inside, the policeman joined him, and for the next thirty minutes or so the cab swayed and rocked as it carried him to his unknown destination. The policeman sat across from him, and though Belinsky tried to engage him in conversation, the *gorodvoi* refused to say anything, and contented himself with picking his nose, then wiping what he found on the edge of his seat.

When at last Simon heard the driver rein in the horses, he leaned forward with a certain anticipation, curious to know where he'd been taken. He saw very little, however. No sooner was he ushered from the carriage than he was led into a brick building so nondescript it might have been located anywhere in Moscow.

There were people everywhere, with gas jets brightly illuminating the neatly painted hallways, and an air of efficiency such as one might expect in a well-run shop.

"He'll see you now," said the policeman, who showed him into an office as lacking in character as the exterior of the building.

The door closed behind him, and the man who was seated at the desk at the end of the room motioned him to step forward and pull up a chair. "Sergei Zubatov," he said.

"Simon Belinsky."

"Cigarette?"

"Thanks."

"I believe this is yours." Zubatov handed him a plain white envelope. "It's all there, though you can count it if you like."

"That won't be necessary," he said as he pocketed the money. "If you can't trust the Okhrana, then who can you trust?"

"Me," said Zubatov with a laugh. He was a man of medium height, with chestnut hair and eyes of an indeterminate color, as he wore tinted spectacles. His hair was brushed smoothly back, and with his small, neat beard he looked like a typical intellectual, someone who'd be quite at home lecturing at the university.

Saltychikha had always spoken very highly of Zubatov, though this of course was the first time Simon had met him. Ever since he'd agreed to provide the secret police with information, Simon had had to conduct his affairs with the utmost discretion, knowing his life would be worth very little if any of the men on the strike committee discovered what he was up to. Even the police who'd arrested him earlier that evening hadn't known he was working for the Okhrana, which was why he'd been taken to Butyrky along with everyone else. But once the men were put into separate cells, they had no way of knowing that Belinsky had been released, or that he'd been driven to the secret headquarters of the Moscow branch of the Okhrana.

Although only a section head in the organization, Zubatov's responsibilities were far-reaching. It was his job actively to recruit new agents, to which end he'd had Simon brought to his office.

"What I'm proposing," Zubatov said, "is a job in our Investigations Department. The position pays fifty rubles a month to start, with a bonus at New Year's."

After what he'd been living on since moving to Moscow, fifty rubles seemed like an enormous amount of money. "And what exactly would I be doing?"

"Okhrana means 'protection.' You'll be protecting the empire, and serving your Tsar. We're not interested in repression here, merely prevention."

"Of what?"

"Criminal activities, particularly those of a political nature."

"Revolutionaries, in other words."

"Wrong. Terrorists. It's our sworn duty, our sacred obligation if you must, to defend the empire against those who seek to destroy it. As a member of our organization, you'll be trained and provided with whatever skills you need to do your job."

"And when would I be able to start?" Simon asked.

"You already have," Zubatov said with a smile, and he put out his cigarette as vigorously as he defended the principles of autocracy.

*   *   *

Masha had sent the children home, and was just closing up the school when she heard the sound of hoofbeats, and the muffled tramping of feet. Were there maneuvers going on nearby? she wondered. Curious, she glanced out the window, only to see a cordon of soldiers taking up their positions around the schoolhouse. A moment later she was out in the yard, demanding to know what was going on.

"Orders, ma'am," one of the soldiers spoke up.

"From whom?"

"Captain Trigony, ma'am, and the district *ispravnik*."

"I can explain everything, Madame Danchenko," came a familiar voice as Trigony dismounted. Leaving his horse in the care of an orderly, he crossed the schoolyard and suggested they talk about it inside. "I'm afraid we're going to have to search the premises," the Captain told her after she reluctantly led him into the school.

Masha bristled. After enduring Trigony's rudeness, his sly remarks, and lingering glances, she'd now reached the limits of her patience. But when she started to object, he told her of the *ispravnik's* determination to search the school for subversive literature, as rumor had it that she'd been teaching the children sedition.

Outraged by his accusations, Masha glared at him and said, "I've been teaching the children their ABC's. I leave sedition to the likes of you."

"Now, now, Maria Petrovna, there's no reason to get excited," replied the Captain, grinning as if this were all a lark, and he couldn't understand why she wasn't smiling as broadly as he. "But I'd certainly hate to see your school ransacked, or even put to the torch."

"You're acting without my husband's authority, Captain. I believe that's more than sufficient grounds for a court-martial."

"True," replied Trigony, still with his grin. "But by the time you got to your husband, and by the time you came back, there might not be a schoolhouse left, my dear Masha."

"I am not your dear Masha. I've put up with you for months now. I don't intend to any longer."

Trigony continued to smile. "How odd, though, that you've never once told your husband. Are you afraid of what might happen if he tried to satisfy his wounded honor?"

"You're even more despicable than I imagined."

"Be that as it may, I'm now giving you a choice," Trigony said. "I believe Stepan is leaving for Petersburg tomorrow on some regimental business. Do you agree to receive me when he's gone?"

"But why are you doing this?" she pleaded, trying to reason with him even though she suspected it would do little good. "You'll ruin your career, all your hopes for the future. And for what, a moment of passion? I'm in love with my husband, Captain. I have no interest in you whatsoever."

The Captain gave out with a funny little laugh. "That remains to be seen. Well, yes or no? The *ispravnik's* waiting outside, and he's even more impatient than I am."

Masha glanced wearily about the schoolroom, seeing all her hard work going up in flames. The villagers had built the school only with the greatest of reluctance, as they weren't being paid for their labor. If it burned to the ground, it would take months to convince them to rebuild. But if she denied Trigony what he wanted, that was precisely what would happen.

"You don't care that I find you repulsive?"

"It's not me you find repulsive, Masha, it's only my persistence. I find you extraordinarily attractive. Once you get to know me better—"

"Don't even suggest such a thing, because it won't happen. I will receive you, however, just this once."

The Captain bowed from the waist, clicking his heels smartly together. "Remember," he warned, "if Stepan finds out about this, there's only one way it can be settled."

"There will be no duel, Captain, not this week and not ever."

"A wise decision, Madame Danchenko. After all, I'm considered the finest shot in the regiment, if I do say so myself."

It had been nearly a year since Vera had left Moscow, and nearly a year since she'd heard from Simon. Early on, a few letters arrived, each written in her husband's unexpectedly meticulous hand. But for months now there hadn't been anything for her in the postboy's satchel, not a single word to give her reason to belive they might soon be reunited.

How painful it was to hear Pauline ask after her father, to have to lie to the child, telling her that Papa was working very hard, and that as soon as he could, he'd come to visit them. "This is your home now," she told the little girl. "And isn't it nicer than where we used to live?"

"Yes, but I want my Papa."

At night, Vera wanted her *papochka*, too. Lying in bed she could feel Simon's absence so acutely that at times she was actually in pain, and she would curl up in an angry ball, pressing her knees to her chest, slamming her eyes shut, and praying for him to return. Now, with the first rime turning the burdocks to silver, and sending the thrushes fleeing from the orchard that was carpeted with fragile golden leaves, she asked her father for permission to go to Moscow to find her husband.

"I thought you would have learned your lesson by now," he told her. "Haven't months of silence been answer enough? If he were a proper father, a proper husband, do you think for one moment he would have treated the two of you like this? The man is a scoundrel. The only loyalty he has is to himself."

"But I love him," she said.

"You love him like a mare loves a stallion," Peter Semyonovich said angrily. "But when you leave his bed, what's left for you, Vera? Just a memory of pleasure, and nothing else to sustain you."

Perhaps he was right. But she had no shame, and felt no embarrassment. She was also a guest in his home, not free to argue with him as she once had, lest she endanger the welfare of her child.

"Just let me look for him," she pleaded. "Let me try to find out what's happened to him."

"Nothing's happened to him that hasn't happened before. He's gotten himself into trouble, no doubt. But if you want to go, I won't stop you."

Why was he being so understanding? Vera was afraid to ask, not wanting anything to interfere with her plans and hopes. Yet when she mounted the stairs that led to the second floor of the old dirty-yellow house off the Malaya Gruzinskaya, all these hopes seemed to crumble like the stones beneath her feet. Even if she found him here, she knew she could never go back to the life she'd once led.

A sharp, cutting wind blew down the length of the rickety second-floor gallery. Although Vera had been gone almost a year, the stench was still the same, and nothing had changed. When she knocked on the door of the room where they had lived, she realized too late that Simon was probably still at work, and that she'd come all this way for nothing. She should have gone looking for him at the tobacco factory.

"Looking for someone, dearie?" a familiar voice called out from the end of the open corridor.

Yes, nothing had changed, least of all Saltychikha.

"I'm looking for Mr. Belinsky," she said.

"Simon Ivanovich? You won't find him here, dearie."
The landlady stepped into the gallery, making ropes of her

skinny white arms as she shivered and rubbed them against each other. "Don't I know you?" she said, peering at Vera with her tiny, shortsighted eyes.

Vera let down the fur hood of her cloak, shaking out her hair.

Saltychikha smiled broadly, and beckoned Vera to step inside her room. "My word," the landlady exclaimed, as if they were long-lost friends. "Why, I hardly recognized you, dearie. And how's your little girl? Growing more beautiful by the day, isn't she? But come in out of the cold. The samovar's bubbling and you'll soon warm your bones with a nice cup of tea. Oh dearie, you do look lovely. Life's been good to you, I see."

Saltychikha ushered her to a chair as if she were a queen, and the rush-bottom seat her throne.

"I'm looking for my husband," Vera said as the landlady set down a cup of tea and a cracked plate with several yellow lumps of sugar.

"He's gone, has been for a couple of months now. Just up and left, didn't even say good-bye, and me so nice to him, too. Owed me rent, he did. Never see that money again."

"But he must have left a letter for me, or a forwarding address. Something," she asked hopefully.

Saltychikha shook her head. "Didn't leave anything, 'less of course there's a couple of little bastards wandering around looking for their daddy."

Vera rushed to her feet. The idea of putting her lips to one of the woman's cups was abhorrent, and she couldn't leave fast enough.

"So he's deserted you, has he? Well, I'm not surprised. A man like that, eager to make something of his life, 'specially with his talents. No wonder you miss him so."

The woman's obscene laughter followed her down the stairs, then out onto the grim alleyway with its incessant rumble of carts and wagons. In the ground-floor window a miniature red coffin was propped against the moldy glass, just as it was the day she'd first arrived here.

It could have been mine, she thought, and hurried toward the Malaya Gruzinskaya to see if she could find an *isvostchik* to take her to the tobacco factory. But when she found her way to Trumpeter's offices, it was only to discover that Simon was no longer in their employ.

"Picked up by the police, I believe," one of he clerks told her. "Planning a strike, if memory serves me. You might want to check with them, miss, just to make sure."

The police had no information for her, and the following morning, when she went to the Address Bureau on Znamensky Lane, it took all morning to discover there was no listing for a Simon Ivanovich Belinsky. Even though he'd registered with the police when they'd first moved to Moscow, and his internal passport had been stamped by the authorities, that information now seemed to have vanished, as if someone had purposely torn out the sheet on which was inscribed all the particulars of her husband's life.

"But what if he's left Moscow?" she asked.

"We'd know about it," said the overworked clerk who had patiently searched through the stacks of big wire files.

"Is there anything you can suggest?"

The clerk shook his head. "It would appear that this gentleman you're seeking no longer exists. But then, some people want to disappear, miss, if you know what I mean."

Vera knew exactly, and left for Petrovka that very same day.

How happy Masha had been these last four years, how confident she was about her future. She'd married Stepan almost on an impulse, only to discover how true her instincts were, for there was never a moment when she regretted what she'd done. But now a force for evil had entered her life, and she was faced with the terrifying prospect of seeing her happiness shattered as it had been once before.

On the eve of his departure, she begged Stepan to take her with him to Petersburg. Afraid to tell him what had happened earlier that day, when Captain Trigony had presented her with his ultimatum, she had decided that if she wasn't home to receive him, Trigony might accept her absence as proof of her unwillingness to yield to his demands.

"But you told me yourself—just a few days ago, in fact— that you couldn't get away because of school."

"Yes, but that was before—" She broke off, trying to pretend as if nothing were the matter.

"Now what's this all about, my love?" Stepan asked.

"Nothing," she said hurriedly. "I just wanted to see Irena and the baby, that's all. And maybe Gregor if he has the time, and Henriette."

"If you're so adamant about going, then fine," he said. "As long as you don't think it'll tire you."

"No, it won't, I'm sure of it. And it'll be good for me to get away. Yes, I'll have the maid pack my things. Thank you, Stepan, thank you, my darling."

"Just because we're going to Petersburg?" he said with a laugh.

"No. Just because you're you."

But when they returned, they returned to ashes.

A deputation from the village arrived at their door, and even before a word was spoken, Masha knew exactly what had happened.

"A fire, *matushka,* with flames everywhere and none of us able to stop them. We worked hard, but it happened so quickly and we were all asleep in our beds when we heard the church bells ringing."

"I'm so sorry, Masha," she heard Stepan say. "But you can

conduct lessons here. We'll clear out the drawing room, and when spring comes we'll rebuild."

"There are no books or anything, *matushka.*"

"Then we'll get more books, and more pencils, and slates and chalk and whatever else we need," she said, raising her voice, and trembling with rage that Captain Trigony had succeeded in destroying everything she'd managed to accomplish.

"But who's to say it won't happen again?" said the headman.

"What do you mean?" Stepan asked.

There was an uneasy shuffling of feet, and each time the peasants moved, their felt boots left damp imprints on the parquetry.

"The *ispravnik* said it was the army, Your Excellency," replied the *starosta.*

"The army?" exclaimed Stepan. "But that's ridiculous. Why would the army want to burn down your school?"

The headman shrugged, as if to say it wasn't his place to question the powers that be.

"Well then, I'll just have to speak to the *ispravnik,* and find out for myself."

Stepan ordered his horse to be saddled, and before Masha could start to explain, or even begin to figure out what she might say, he rode off.

When he returned a short while later, his face was twisted with rage. Afraid to ask what had happened, she kept jabbering away until Stepan finally cut her short.

"You don't seem to understand, do you?" he said. "The *ispravnik* claims he received orders from Trigony. And do you know what Trigony claims? He had the audacity to tell me you deceived him. What did he mean by that, Masha?"

"I don't know," she insisted. When she tried to leave, Stepan grabbed her and held her fast.

"What did he mean?" her husband said again. "We've always been truthful to each other, Masha. There hasn't been any basis to these rumors, has there?"

"No, of course not. How can you even say such a thing? I can't even bear to look at the man."

"Then what was he talking about?"

"He . . . that is . . . no, I won't tell you, I won't," she said defiantly. "I love you too much, and I won't say anything. The man is out to destroy us, don't you see? First the school and now you. He won't be satisfied until he has what he wants, Stepan."

"And what does he want, Masha?"

"Your position, that's what," she shouted, hoping that in the heat of the moment he'd believe her.

But Stepan was no fool, and as he looked down at her he shook his head sadly. "What does he want, Masha?"

"He wants our happiness," she whispered, "and you mustn't let him have it, Stepan. No matter what, you mustn't let your pride interfere with your reason. We'll go away if we have to, but I won't . . . no, I lost one love. I won't lose another." But even as she began to cry, and even as she tried to hold him back, Stepan had already started to the door, determined to find out what this was all about.

When Lieutenant Colonel Danchenko returned, he wasn't the same man who'd left an hour before. The lucent and inquiring expression in his hazel eyes had completely vanished, and in its place he faced his wife with a grim and unfamiliar stare. The youthful enthusiasm that revealed itself when he smiled was absent as well, and his lips were set in a fiercely resolute and unwavering frown, so that his features appeared to have been recast in stone.

"We meet tomorrow morning," he said as he started upstairs to the bedroom. "Our seconds are already attending

317

to the details. Trigony must be taught what it is to be both an officer and a gentleman. What I don't understand is why you permitted it to go on as long as you did. Am I not your husband, Masha? Don't I have the right to defend your honor?"

"What good is honor if I lose you?" she said, hurrying after him.

"I'm sorry, but the challenge has been accepted—gleefully, too, I might add—and I don't wish to discuss it further."

Masha thought of the girl she had once been, and the woman she had become. She cared nothing for honor, nor would it matter if everyone thought less of her husband for refusing to demand satisfaction of Trigony. She would willingly leave Russia if necessary, so long as her husband didn't have to face the Captain over the barrel of a pistol. But though she begged Stepan to reconsider, though she got down on her knees and wept, what she was asking of him went against everything he'd been taught, and everything he'd come to believe.

"How can you even consider facing a man like that?" she said in desperation. "To meet him in a duel is just a way of indulging him, and playing into his hand. You should be holding him up to ridicule, not taking him seriously."

In response, Stepan took her in his arms, pressing his lips to the top of her head. "There now, my darling," he whispered. "This is the way it will always be. You don't have anything to fear, Masha, not when honor and decency are on my side."

"It's not honor, it's stubbornness!" she cried, twisting free. "Stubbornness and pride." She remembered then what Count Tolstoy had said, and repeated his words, that to gain the upper hand of pride was the first duty one had to oneself.

"Then I'm less of a man than Count Tolstoy," replied Stepan. "But I won't be less of a man to myself."

*   *   *

The first light of dawn broke over the horizon, wan and uncertain. Half asleep in a chair in the drawing room, Masha roused herself and shivered. The yardman hadn't fired up the stoves yet, and the house was cold and uninviting. Stepan was stretched out on a sofa, still dressed in his uniform.

Perhaps if he overslept, the whole thing would be called off, and they could get on with their lives, uninterrupted. But even before she reached the foot of the stairs, intending to go up and change, she heard him yawn, the sofa creaking loudly as he came to his feet.

The yardman came in with a load of wood. Seeing them standing there in the drawing room, each facing the other and not saying a word, he started to retrace his steps.

"Do what you have to, Fedya."

"Yes, Your Excellency," whispered the porter, who hurried over to the stove with a fearful glance in Masha's direction.

"I won't permit you to go through with this," she announced, as calmly as she could.

She heard footsteps on the front porch, and then the door swung open to reveal two young officers, one tall and one short, but each dressed in identical uniforms of close-fitting white tunics ornamented with gold braid, and gray cloth greatcoats draped over their shoulders.

"Lieutenant Grinevich!" she cried out, addressing the shorter of the two men. "How can you allow this to happen? Stepan is your friend. Can't you put a stop to it?"

Grinevich lowered his eyes, too embarrassed to respond.

"I'm ready, gentlemen," said Stepan, holding himself stiffly erect as he buttoned his tunic. "How much time do we have?"

Grinevich consulted his watch, a rather cumbersome affair he had difficulty removing from his pocket. "Twenty-five minutes, sir."

"Then we'd best be off if we're to reach the pine wood." Stepan turned his eyes to his wife, so that his seconds realized he wanted to be alone with her. The two young men, looking flustered and very much like little boys dressed up for a costume ball, hurried outside. Fedya too went off to the kitchen to complete his chores, so that once again they faced each other with silence, as much consumed by their anguish as they were by their love.

"Why can't we go away?" she asked. "You can resign your commission and we can live at Petrovka."

Stepan shook his head. "I'll be back before you know it," he said softly. "We spent nearly all night talking this over, Masha. Let's not say any more about it. Kiss me and give me your blessing, and then we'll get down and pray together."

They knelt before the corner ikons, but Masha could only look at her husband, gazing at him so that his features would be forever imprinted upon her memory. At last he straightened up, then helped her to her feet. She reached out and brushed a speck of dirt off the gold braid of his high, stiff collar.

"There," she said with forced and unnatural gaiety, "you're as fit a duelist as any man in the regiment. And when you return we'll breakfast together, and perhaps plan a trip for the spring. Would you like to go to Italy, do you think? If you'll play Vronsky, I'll be Anna Karenina, and between the two of us we'll shock the world." But though she struggled to laugh, all she could give him were her tears, and without another word she rushed upstairs.

Trigony and his seconds arrived a few minutes after Stepan reached the pine wood, which was located several versts from the Selistchev Barracks. Freshly shaven and smelling of scent, the Captain appeared to be in a cocky and ebullient mood, smiling broadly as he jumped down from the sledge and approached his adversary with a bold and determined stride.

"Sorry to keep you waiting, old sport," said the Captain, speaking very loudly, and in a somewhat affected tone of voice. "I believe you know my seconds." He motioned to the officers who'd accompanied him.

"Let's get on with it, shall we," Stepan said impatiently.

The short and portly Grinevich now stepped between them. "Gentlemen," he said, "let's put an end to this horrible misunderstanding before it's too late. Why sacrifice the honor of the regiment by blackening its name with a duel, when we all know that our beloved Tsar has expressly forbidden such things, under penalty of exile? So instead of facing each other with animosity, why not try to reach an amicable solution?"

"This man has insulted my wife," replied Stepan, unable to bring himself to utter Trigony's name. "However, if he resigns his commission and leaves the regiment, I shall consider such action sufficient cause for retracting my challenge."

"Surely that's not unreasonable," said one of Trigony's seconds.

"No one asked for your opinion," Trigony said angrily, a muscle twitching above his right eye, and giving the unfortunate impression that he was winking. He tapped his pug nose with the tip of his index finger, then shook his head. "I have no intention of resigning, not today and not tomorrow."

"As you wish," Stepan solemnly replied. "The pistols," he said, turning to Lieutenant Banin, the taller of his two seconds.

Banin produced a palm-wood case lined with red velvet, inside of which lay a pair of pistols inlaid with mother-of-pearl. Stepan waited until Trigony had chosen one, then took the remaining pistol for himself. An anxious silence fell over the group, and Stepan could hear the jackdaws in the trees, scolding them for their stupidity. But it was too late to change anything. Now, one of the seconds drew his saber and scratched two marks in the snow, counting off ten paces from each line. These would be the barriers, beyond which neither could advance.

Stepan heard the seconds repeat the conditions of the duel, as he stepped behind the barrier at his end, gazing around at the tall and somber pines that ringed the clearing, and then at the gray sky that promised snow.

Was it stubbornness and pride, as Masha had so bitterly claimed? Was he doing this merely because he wasn't man enough to retract his challenge? Or was it the very opposite, that failure to go through with the duel was tantamount to cowardice, both in his eyes as well as in the eyes of anyone who cared to pass judgment?

"Each of you must stop at the barrier," someone was saying in an uncertain voice, "though you may fire at any time before, so long as the signal's been given. The fight will last until one or both of you is *hors de combat*—that is to say, no longer able to defend yourself. Is everything understood, gentlemen?"

He saw then that it was round little Grinevich, such a jolly fellow, and now nearly reduced to tears. Stepan longed to embrace both him and Banin. He wanted to draw them aside and tell them how much their friendship meant, but somehow couldn't even bring himself to raise his voice.

Banin now crossed the barriers. "You're the only one who can put a stop to this, Stepan," he said with great sadness, his eyes moist with unshed tears.

"It's too late. Remember everything I've told you. All the necessary documents are in my study. I leave it to you and Grinevich to inform my wife if—"

"Don't even suggest such a thing, Stepan. We'll soon be joking about it, and that pig will have finally been put in his place."

They embraced, kissing each other three times. Grinevich did the same, his rosy cheeks damp with tears as he shuddered and tried to wrap his arms around his friend.

"There now," Stepan said in much the same tone of voice he'd used earlier when speaking to his wife, "it'll be over soon enough, my friends. Take your places now, and remember that we're officers."

"You will please wait for my signal," someone called out in a hesitant voice.

His pistol cocked, Stepan looked across the barrier, where Trigony faced him with the same snide and arrogant expression he'd no doubt used when trying to have his way with Masha. Yet as contemptible as the Captain was, as devoid of character and human decency, Stepan no longer despised the man. Realizing that, he thought, How odd, how very odd that even now I can't hate him, much as he'd like me to. I won't shoot to kill. I'll wound him, and make him pay dearly with his shame that I was able to get the better of him and still come away with my dignity and my pride. Yes, that's the best solution. Let him lie in bed a couple of weeks and repent. Then he'll resign and we'll be rid of him.

Stepan was so satisfied with his plan of action that he found himself smiling, even as the signal was being given, and one of the seconds shouted, "Forward!"

How soft the snow felt beneath his feet. How light and graceful was the pistol in his hand, like a bird nestling in his palm, not even struggling to escape.

"Murderer!" he heard someone scream.

Startled, he perked his eyes away from Trigony, just in time to see Masha descend from a sledge and rush toward the barrier. Even then a shot rang out, and though Stepan also squeezed the trigger and felt the pistol buck and jump and quiver with life, he knew his shot had gone wild, missing its mark.

Well, we'll just have to try again, he thought, when he found himself looking down at the snow, and couldn't understand why it was so difficult to raise his eyes. What's this? There was a red flower blooming across the front of his tunic. How could such a thing have happened? But I didn't even feel it, he thought, so amazed that he didn't realize he was kneeling in the snow, unable to stay on his feet. I must lie down, he decided. Yes, that'll make it easier. But I didn't even feel it. I heard the shot, yet felt nothing. How odd, and I missed him, too. Well, we must try again, that's all.

Stepan kept saying these things to himself not because he believed them, but simply because he was afraid to think of anything else. One look at the red blossom hideously discoloring his snow-white tunic and he knew it would unfurl its petals and there'd be no end to the blood. So he tried to regain his balance and struggle to his feet, only to give up when his legs refused to cooperate, lying there in the snow as if they didn't even belong to him.

But there she was, kneeling beside him, so that tears fell against his cheeks.

What good is honor to such a futile end? Stepan wanted to say, begging her to forgive him for his sin of pride. There was nothing romantic about dying, for when it came time to breathe one's last, all men were the same. But it was difficult to speak, and though his lips moved, he couldn't find the strength to make himself heard.

Masha leaned very close, pressing her ear to his lips.

"What shall I do?" he whispered, feeling a terrible icy chill slowly taking hold of him. "Where . . ."

"Tell me," she said. "I'm here, Stepan. I'll be here always."

". . . without you . . . shall I go?"

"No," she cried, "don't go, not yet," and she began to rock

back and forth, cradling his head in her arms as if he were an infant she was putting to sleep. "There's so much to say, Stepan, so much we haven't told each other. Oh my darling, don't you see, I'm here now and everything will be all right."

Stepan closed his eyes then. He was very cold and tired, and needed to rest.

Book Three

1891 = 94

One

Early in February of 1891, when Gregor Petrov, Petersburg's noted arts critic, had turned a very boyish and
youthful-looking twenty-eight, he arranged an exhibit of Russian watercolors that was held at the Industrial Art Museum.
This undistinguished pseudo-baroque building was located on
the Bolshaya Morskaya, or Great Sea Street, an avenue of
luxury shops, fashionable restaurants, and first-class hotels.
Flocks of pigeons circled above the heads of the elegant
strollers who promenaded here each afternoon between the
hours of two and four. The birds were well fed, provided with
winter rations from the grain warehouses along the nearby
Ekaterininsky Canal, where ten years earlier a bomb had
exploded at the feet of Alexander II.

It was the slain monarch's son, Tsar Alexander III, who
complained of the pigeons that winter. It was his belief that
they were defacing the capital's numerous monuments, and
costing the government untold sums to clean up their drop-
pings. Accordingly, a ukase was issued expressly forbidding
anyone to feed them, and soon their numbers began to
decline.

The Tsar commented about this when he attended the

exhibit Gregor had organized, and scarcely paid any attention to the watercolors that had been so lovingly mounted in the museum's ground-floor hall.

"Yes," Alexander III would say periodically as he paused for a moment before each of the pictures, "they're filthy birds. Why, I wouldn't even expect our peasants to make a meal of them, though I understand the French eat pigeon pie. No accounting for tastes, is there?"

"No, Your Majesty."

The Tsar grunted in response, and continued to shuffle along in a thoroughly ungainly manner, one that didn't seem at all suitable for the Emperor and Autocrat of all the Russias. He was an enormous bear of a man, six feet four inches tall, and though nearly every drop of blood in his veins was German, he reminded Gregor of a typical Russian peasant— stubborn, phlegmatic, and taciturn.

Now, reaching the end of the hall, the Emperor stopped abruptly and looked down at Gregor from his rather considerable height. "Interesting," he said, "though not my taste."

"'Interesting, though not my taste,'" Gregor repeated that evening, imitating the Tsar's rolling basso, and then coming to his feet to lurch comically across the dining room as he insisted Alexander himself had walked earlier in the day.

"But tell everyone what you asked him," said Princess Denisheva, a handsome woman in her early thirties who was giving the dinner in Gregor's honor.

"Yes, do," urged Prince Orlovsky, who was sitting directly across from him, and listening attentively.

"Now I'm embarrassed," Gregor said, playing the little boy, and waiting until there was a general uproar, and the twenty or so people at the table began to stamp their feet, pleading with him to go on. "Well," he said at last, pausing to look at each of the guests in turn, for after all, he was the guest of honor and didn't want to slight anyone, especially someone whose friendship might someday prove valuable. "He was about to turn away, and the crowd had parted ranks, when—and don't ask me what possessed me, because I can't even remember myself—I reached up and tapped him on the shoulder. 'Yes?' said the Emperor, turning to face me. 'Your Majesty, I wonder if you wouldn't think it impertinent of me, but is it true you can bend an iron poker over your knee, and tear a pack of cards in half?'"

"Grisha, you're impossible," said the Princess, her merry laughter like the tinkle of bells.

"But what did he say?" asked the guests.

"'Mr. Petrov,'" said Gregor, still imitating the Tsar's deep, booming voice, "'not only can I tear a pack of cards in two, but I can also crush a silver ruble between my fingers.' And do you know what? He did just that. Here, I can prove it."

Gregor teached inside his waistcoat pocket and removed the ruble in question, one that was folded as neatly as a sheet of paper, and which he tossed to Prince Orlovsky, who hadn't been able to stop looking at him all evening."

"A souvenir, *mon Prince,*" he said with a grin.

"You did well, Gregor," Princess Denisheva told him when the party had broken up and the guests had departed. "Wasn't I correct in assuming you'd find him attractive? You've been alone too long. That's your problem."

Gregor toyed with the stem of his wineglass, then set it down and folded his small, well-shaped hands in his lap. He'd been in Petersburg ten years now, and though he'd certainly grown older, he wasn't much wiser, still looking for someone to care about, and still struggling to meet his expenses. Although his reputation as a music critic was more or less secure, and there was no end to the articles and reviews that flowed from his pen, he was still dissatisfied. His liaison with Prince Meshchersky a thing of the past, he'd already been forced to borrow several thousand rubles from the Princess.

But unless he found a position that paid a respectable salary, or again found a patron to support him, he'd never be able to pay off the promissory note when it came due.

"Orlovsky was greatly taken with you," the Princess remarked after listening to his silence for several minutes.

Gregor made a face.

"Don't you find him attractive, Grisha?"

"Very much so."

"Then what's bothering you?"

"The same things that have always botherd me: money, fame, true love." He laughed bitterly and changed the subject, tired of talking about himself and playing the *enfant terrible* when he didn't even know where the next ruble was coming from. "The exhibit went quite well, even if the public hated the pictures. Well, as the Tsar said, there's no accounting for taste. Thank you for a lovely evening, Larisa. Once again you've shamed me with your generosity."

Larisa Antonovna, who in the last year had become one of his closest friends, laughed in her charming and guileless way. Gently brushing her fingers across his wavy, light-brown hair, she told him he looked adorable when he pouted.

"Orlovsky wants to see you again," she said.

"And is he willing to support me?"

"Don't be mercenary, Grisha. It's unattractive."

"I'm afraid I have no choice."

The Princess stood with him on the steps of the carriage porch while he waited for Kolya to bring his sledge around. "Shall I arrange a meeting?" she asked.

Meshchersky, Orlovsky . . . what did it matter? You could look for love all your life, and probably wouldn't even recognize it when it stared you in the face.

"Do you love me, Larisa?" he asked with surprising earnestness.

For a moment the Princess was taken aback. "Of course I

do," she said hurriedly. "Like a brother."

"Then if you think Orlovsky and I . . . whatever you think is fine. Kolya, I'll sit up front with you, my boy," he called out, and climbing into the sledge he pressed his leg against Kolya's and wondered if it wouldn't be better to stay at home more, and be content with what he had.

When they reached Simeonovskaya Street, where Gregor had lived ever since arriving in Petersburg, Kolya turned to him and said, "I'm getting married, Gregor Petrovich."

"You're getting what?"

"Married."

"Wonderful, just wonderful. Exactly what I needed to hear." He climbed down from the sledge and hurried upstairs, not wanting Kolya to see him when he started to cry.

Wrapped in an elegant black velvet *shuba*, a long cloak lined with curled Tibetan goat, and with an otter toque sitting atop her unruly collection of frizzy curls, Henriette was perfectly content, or as perfectly content as someone of her disposition could be. She shared a bearskin lap warmer with her companion, Countess Ignatieva, whose friendship and patronage had been a great source of comfort to her these past five years.

Ever since Count Ivanov's soirée, Henriette and the Countess had been all but inseparable. This afternoon they sat together in the grandstand that had been erected adjacent to the Palace Embankment, and almost directly across from the dreaded Fortress of St. Peter and St. Paul. Every fifteen minutes the bells in the Fortress Cathedral chimed "Lord Save Me," and at noon a cannon shot was fired by which Petersburg set its clocks, and every workman in the city left off for the midday meal.

The Neva's green waters were hidden under three feet of ice, over which a racetrack was marked off. The ice races were an annual event in the capital, open to anyone who wished to participate. They were extremely popular with the public, who never failed to turn out in large numbers whenever they were held.

The fourth and final race of the afternoon would begin shortly, but Henriette watched what was going on with only one 'eye, too busy listening to Countess Ignatieva. The woman's face was redder than usual, owing to the sub-zero temperature and the stiff winds that blew toward them from the opposite bank of the river.

"All I'm saying, *ma chère,* is that it's time you made a clean break, once and for all. It's not proper, Henriette. How can we tell people you're a housekeeper and expect them to deal with you as an equal?"

"I quite agree with you," replied Henriette. "But you know my situation. I'm all alone, with only you to protect me. Were I to leave the Count's service, I'd have no means of supporting myself."

The Countess eyed her from behind her tortoise-shell lorgnette, which quivered on its thin black ribbon and made her eyes look smaller than they actually were. "You've been saying that for years, you silly girl. But as of today I've decided I no longer want to hear you make the same excuses. I'd like you to come and stay with me and Alexander Pavlovich," she said, referring to her husband. "You'll be my companion, my *paid* companion," she stressed. "No one need know, of course. You're my dearest friend, and what business arrangements we might have are strictly our concern and no one else's. And who, may I ask, is that?"

The Countess motioned to the area of the course closest to the tribune, where an elegant sledge had taken its position alongside a primitive troika, such as one rarely saw in the city. It was a rustic peasant vehicle harnessed to a trio of skinny little horses, as hairy as bears and covered with icicles.

Henriette eyed the moujik who gripped the reins, oblivious to the jeering of the crowd.

"Now, where are my opera glasses, do you suppose?" said the Countess, whose absent-mindedness was well known among those who frequented her "black salon."

"Why, if they were a snake they would have bit me." The Countess held the glasses in one hand the lorgnette in the other, moving each back and forth until she managed to get them into focus. "Why, it's Colonel Trigony, of the Chevalier Guards!" the Countess exclaimed after peering down at the track.

"Colonel who?" said Henriette.

"Trigony. Oh, he's a dear man, quite a rake. Alexander Pavlovich knows him well. He's the Emperor's cousin . . . several times removed, of course, but you know what they say. Blood is blood, however tenuous the link. He's only been back in Petersburg a short while. He was banished to his estates, right about the time you had that extraordinary vision of my future, when I was walking toward paradise, and all the saints had turned out to greet me. And there was a woman holding my hand, and guiding me along, and that woman was you."

Henriette smiled to herself that the Countess still believed what she'd told her years before, that they were destined to remain inseparable, both in this life and the next.

"But now he's back in society," the Countess went on, "and looks none the worse for what he's been through, does he?"

Henriette nodded, for even from a distance she could see how handsome the officer was.

"They say he killed a man," whispered the Countess.

"My sister's husband," she replied.

As the Countess' mouth dropped open, the signal was given and the race began. Some half a dozen different teams started to careen down the ice, but it was Colonel Trigony and the peasant who drove alongside him who claimed the public's attention. By the time they were halfway down the backstretch they'd left the other vehicles behind, each driver standing up in his seat and gripping the reins as tightly as he could. As both troikas rounded the curve they were neck and neck, and the crowd was on its feet, now cheering for the moujik, now shouting for the Colonel, delighted that they were being given such an exciting show.

Their manes matted with frozen sweat, Trigony's Orloff trotters plunged gamely forward, the Colonel striking at them with his whip again and again. As Henriette shared the glasses with the Countess, she found herself praying for the peasant's victory. But though the moujik put up a brave fight, the Colonel's heavier purebred team managed to nose him out at the finish line.

"Disgusting little creature," said the Countess as she came to her feet. "Those horses of his looked as if they hadn't been fed in weeks. Why they allow that kind of participant is beyond me. But come, *ma chère,* you'll want to get back. And you won't forget what I've asked, will you?"

Henriette, eying Trigony for a moment as he proudly displayed his trophy, looked back at the Countess and nodded. "I'll give him notice just as soon as possible."

"Make it sooner than that, my dear, because the longer you wait, the more impatient I'll become. Tomorrow I intend to call in the decorators. I thought I'd do your room in gray. Such a refined, restful color, don't you agree?"

"Yes," said Henriette, smiling patiently, "I've always been partial to gray."

The little bulldog was nearly seventy, and complained of gout and indigestion, shortness of breath, and an irregular heartbeat. In the last few years he'd become increasingly dependent upon his steward, whom he relied upon as he often wished he might have relied on his son. Rodion Sorokin, or Rodya, as he was called, had been born at Krasnaya Gorka, where his father was headman of the village. General Tishin had taken a great liking to the boy and had personally supervised his education. Having graduated from one of the local technical schools, Rodya had returned to Red Hill to repay the General's kindness. But he and Varvara, the *Gheneralsha,* did not get along very well, and frequently found themselves at odds. It was General Tishin who suggested he work at Petrovka, and within a few years Rodya had not only earned Peter Semyonovich's trust and respect, but also the position of steward.

Rodya was a big, strapping fellow of thirty-three, with a powerful build and a boyish, very Russian face. He'd never married, though there were no end to the offers, as he was considered quite good-looking, and with excellent prospects for the future. "I'll marry when I get the master's affairs in order," he would say, because of late Petrov seemed to have lost his touch, and Petrovka wasn't nearly as profitable as it once was.

It was for this reason that Peter Semyonovich had decided to sell off some of his holdings, and had accepted an offer for the birch wood at the northeastern corner of the estate.

"I just don't understand it," he told the steward one winter's afternoon when the white hills resembled sugar loaves, wrapped in a thick, powdery mantle of snow. "I bought that birch wood when I was your age, younger even."

"I'm afraid we have no choice, sir," replied Rodya, who began to crack his knuckles, having acquired the habit from his master. "This past harvest was way below expectation. And they're offering you a very fair price."

"Still, it's like cutting off some part of myself. But if that's how it has to be, see to it the papers are drawn up."

There was a knock on the door, and then a little girl with serious blue eyes and an extravagant profusion of curly black hair poked her head inside the study. Pauline was nine years old, a quiet and obedient child who was particularly partial to her grandfather, with whom she shared a special rapport. Each doted on the other, and today Peter Semyonovich had promised to take her on an outing, a team of horses already harnessed to a sleigh and waiting in the courtyard.

"You little minx, I bet you think I'd forgotten," Petrov said with a laugh. "But I haven't, princess. Just a few more minutes, and then we'll be off."

Pleased that he'd remembered, the little girl ran off to the kitchen where Granny Anninka gave her a bag of sweets to take along for the ride. By the time Pauline was bundled up in her fur-trimmed pelisse, with thick white gaiters on her legs, white rubber galoshes, and a snug quilted hood that matched her cloak, Grandfather was ready and so they went outside and climbed into the sledge.

"Watch out for the wolves," laughed Granny, no one having seen a wolf in these parts in more than ten years.

"And don't drive too fast, Father," Vera cautioned. "And if you get too cold, princess, mind you tell Granddad to take you home."

Pauline nodded, and snuggled up against him, delighted that she and her grandfather would have the afternoon all to themselves.

"Where are you taking her?" Vera asked.

"The birch wood," replied Peter Semyonovich. With a flick of the reins the high-spirited team surged forward, the runners gliding smoothly across the snow.

When they were no longer in sight, and Anninka had gone back inside, Vera hurried across the yard and down the path that had been cleared to the steward's house, where years before she'd lived with her husband. There was no one else around, which was just as well, as tongues were likely to wag if someone saw what she was up to.

Once she reached the steward's house, she paused to lock the door behind her, then ran up the stairs to the bedroom. Without breaking stride, she flung the door open and skidded to a halt.

Rodya was lying in bed with a cigarette dangling between his lips. "No one saw you, did they?"

"And if they did, who cares? What is he going to do, lock me in my room?"

She'd been a prisoner here long enough, and now she intended to make up for lost time. The steward might not be as handsome as Simon, but he was young and strong and eager to please. Besides, she'd already decided he was better than nothing, and since he had her father's ear, he was definitely someone worth cultivating. So Vera hurriedly undressed and was soon lying in bed, safe in the crook of his arm.

"Did you find out anything about the will?" she asked as Rodya put out his cigarette, then pulled her over on top of him.

"Later."

"No, tell me now."

Rodya smiled dreamily, easing her up so he could see her more clearly. "I did what you said," he told her, having suggested to her father that since his health wasn't what it used to be, it might be a good time to review his will, just to make sure he was satisfied with its provisions.

"And?"

"He told me it was none of my business."

Certain he was leaving everything to Irena, she scowled with annoyance. "The least you can do is find out where he hides it," she told him. "He'll drop dead and then we'll all be out of luck." Again she scowled, then smiled despite herself when Rodya began to trace circles around her breasts, tickling her with the tips of his fingers.

"Why worry about it? Your husband sends you money."

"In a plain envelope with no return address. Besides, I've saved all that money for Pauline. I want to send her to a proper boarding school, and see that she has all the advantages. She's not going to suffer the way I have, either from a bad marriage or an empty pocketbook."

"But what about you?" asked the steward.

Vera closed her eyes, then arched her back and stretched like a cat. "I'm satisfied . . . for the time being." As if to prove the point, she reached down between his thick-set thighs and guided him into place, crying out for just a moment when he entered her, and then giving herself up to pleasure.

"Thirty years," Grandfather was saying as the shaggy Kirghiz ponies trotted through the snow. "I bought that wood before your mother was born, and now someone else will have it all to himself. The best mushrooms in the district, princess. And berries! My word, there were so many different kinds I can't even begin to name them all."

"Then why must you sell it, Granddad?"

"Because," and he sighed, flicking the leather reins so that one of the ponies, Turk, who was her very favorite, glanced back to see if anything was wrong. "I just have to, princess."

Snow began to fall—thick, wet flakes that melted the moment they touched her cheeks. Granny had knit her a woolen scarf, and now Pauline pulled it up around her mouth and nose. It was even colder than when they'd left, and she didn't want her nose to fall off, as Granny had warned would happen if she didn't dress warmly. Granny said a lot of things, though, and sometimes Pauline wondered how true they all were. For instance, whenever the old *nyanya* lost a tooth (and by now she had hardly any left at all), she made sure that she saved it, and even had a special little box to put them in.

"Everything must be together," Granny Anninka had said. When Pauline asked her why, the housekeeper laughed and said that the teeth had to be put in her coffin and buried with her, so that when her soul went to heaven she wouldn't have to waste any time crawling around searching for her bones. Granny also said you must never have three lit candles in the same room, because that was the symbol of death, and considered very unlucky. Once, when her mother had done just that, Granny ran right over and blew out the third candle, she got so upset. And if anyone mentioned the devil, why, that was even worse, because Granny would cross herself in a panic, and then she'd say very loudly, looking all around in case the Evil One was listening, "Don't mention him ever again, for if you call him up like that he'll start to walk around the house and there'll be no getting rid of him." Then she'd sprinkle the rooms with holy water that she kept on hand in a big bottle on a shelf in the kitchen, saying that now it was safe, and that she'd scared him away, sending him back where he belonged.

Grandfather leaned over and kissed her forehead. "See what happens?" he said. "I'm getting old and so I'm losing my land just like I'm losing my hair. Can't be helped, I guess."

Lilac-colored hoarfrost was sprinkled like salt over the boughs of the trees. The snow continued to fall, soft and cushiony, and so light that when she blew across her arm it scattered like dandelion fluff, swirling and tumbling through the air.

"Can you see it now?" Her grandfather pointed with his leather-covered mitten, while directly ahead the birch wood seemed to swallow up the road, marked here and there by stakes, some of which were already hidden beneath the fresh fall of snow. "What a wonderful wood it is, princess. So cool during the summer you'd want to stay there forever. And so dark during winter you can't wait to get away."

Pauline shivered, clutching her grandfather more tightly. Granny had told her terrible tales of the nasty creatures who lived in the forest, and she was frightened by the thought that they might soon meet up with them. The worst one was Baba-Yaga, a hideous old witch with a hooked nose and sharp iron teeth. She moved around in a mortar, with a pestle in one hand to club the unwary, and a broom in the other to sweep away the signs of her passage through the snow. Meeting her in the woods was horrible enough, but what if they stumbled onto her house? Again Pauline trembled, remembering that Granny had said the witch lived in a hut mounted on chicken's feet, so she could take it anywhere she wanted. But when she stayed put, she built a fence around her house that was made of the bones of the children she'd stolen and gobbled up, feeding their fingers to the evil black cat who lived in her yard.

But if they were lucky enough not to cross Baba-Yaga's path, who was to say they wouldn't find themselves having to deal with a *leshi?* They were mean, spiteful creatures even if they didn't eat you, with blue skin and big protruding eyes. They danced around on their cloven hoofs, leading people astray in the forest and then leaving them there to starve. Granny said that if you ever met up with one, the best thing to do was put your left boot on your right foot and wear your coat back to front, because this confused the wood sprite and made him leave you in peace.

Grandfather drew in the reins, and the ponies shook all over, hidden for a moment beneath a cloud of powdery snow. "Well, here we are," he said. "No sense climbing down, is there? Snow's too deep. But we'll come back in the spring—if they don't cut this all down first. It's beautiful then, when the trees are first starting to bud, and the birds are back."

Pauline thought she heard someone whistling from deep in the wood. It must have been a *leshi*, because they tricked people by imitating the sounds of birds and animals. There it was again, a shrill and mocking sound, first behind her and then up ahead.

"Let's go back, Granddad."

"Cold?"

She leaned forward, whispering just in case a sprite was around, or awful old Baba-Yaga herself. But after Pauline told him what Granny had said, her grandfather laughed and made her promise not to believe all of Anninka's stories.

"Besides," he said, "you're with me, so you mustn't worry about anything." He guided the ponies around, who seemed grateful that he was leading them back in the direction of home.

It was getting colder by the minute, and the snow began to sting her cheeks like bits of icy metal. Pauline sat back, just as glad as Turk and Coco, now that they were leaving the wood behind them.

"Is this the road, do you think?" Grandfather asked, almost as if he were talking to himself. "No, here it is. Step lively, my boys!" he called to the ponies. "Mind you, don't fall into a drift. Why look, princess, it's already up to their knees. Now you snuggle up to your granddad and don't you worry what Granny said."

Grandfather put his arm around her and Pauline smiled and leaned against him, pulling the bearskin lap robe all the way up to her chin. All she could see was snow and more snow, descending like a lacy white curtain.

They went over a bump in the road and she heard her grandfather cry out, as if he'd left his stomach behind. Then he slumped over, so that she was pinned to the edge of the seat. She wanted to laugh because he was acting so silly, but he was too heavy and it began to hurt, and so she tried to push him away.

"Come on now, Granddad, I can't even move you're squashing me so."

Peter Semyonovich didn't answer. Pauline tried to get him to sit up, managing to free the hand that was trapped beneath him. But though she shoved with all her might, and still continued to scold him for pretending to be asleep, her grandfather remained where he was.

In the distance Pauline heard the *leshi* whistling and clapping his hands, as if he were very pleased with what was happening. She shook her grandfather as hard as she could. Just then the reins slipped from his fingers, and as she reached out to grab them they disappeared through the woolen net that was attached to the dashboard of the sleigh.

Coco, the less well behaved of the two ponies, suddenly bolted forward, dragging Turk and the sledge along with him.

"Grandfather!" she cried out. Though the snow was up to their hocks, the ponies were hurrying on as if they were as much afraid of Baba-Yaga as she was. It hurt her so the way he leaned against her that she pushed and pushed until she finally got him to sit upright. But instead of opening his eyes and ending the game, Peter Semyonovich toppled over against the opposite end of the seat, one arm hanging down limply and dragging through the snow. It was only then that Pauline realized he wasn't playing a game or trying to fool her.

"Granddad!" she cried again, shaking him with both hands. But nothing she could say or do would get him to wake up. Was this what happened when you got old, or had he just fallen into a deep, deep sleep? Pauline didn't know, but as she leaned forward to try to pick up the reins, Turk stumbled and lost his footing. Tangled in the traces, the pony whinnied helplessly while the sledge teetered and rocked back and forth, first on one runner and then the other.

Clutching her grandfather and trying to maintain her balance, Pauline shouted at the horses, trying to get them to stop. But they were oblivious to her cries, and were now heading directly for a tree instead of staying on the road. At the last moment they swerved, Coco turning to the right as Turk veered to the left. The front of the sleigh hit the tree with a loud and frightening crunch, sending Pauline tumbling head over heels into the snow.

For several minutes she just lay there, aching all over. Finally she roused herself and managed to get to her feet.

"Grandfather?" she called out, certain he'd awakened by now. "Are you all right?"

In response, Turk snorted loudly, pawing at the snow with his half-buried feet. When she made it back to the sledge she found her grandfather hanging halfway out of the seat, and though she tried to push him back he was much too heavy for her and she couldn't budge him. She looked about in every direction, trying to remember where the road was, unable to see anything but tree after tree, the forest stretching away into the distance.

You mustn't be afraid, she kept telling herself. There aren't any Baba-Yagas, or wood sprites, or wolves, either. Those are just stories grown-ups tell to frighten you, but they're not true.

"Is anyone there?" she shouted. "Can anyone hear me?"

Cupping her mittened hands to her mouth, she howled *Ulyulyu* the way Grandfather did when he went hunting. The sounds echoed through the woods, deep and booming, and causing the ponies to nervously prick up their ears and switch their knotted tails.

Something tinkled in the distance, low and mournful.

"*Ulyulyu!* Help, someone help us! *Ulyulyu!*"

"*Ulyulyulyu!*" came the echo, and then the tinkling again,

louder than before.

"Here, over here!" Pauline shouted at the top of her voice. If only she knew where the road was, but the trees were so close together there was no way to tell.

"*Ulyulyu! Ulyulyu!* Is anyone there?"

"Oh yes, here, this way, over here!" she yelled. She reached up to the top of the *duga*, striking the little bells that hung down from the shaft-bow, making them ring out loudly, over and over again.

There was something moving between the trees, and then she heard bells tinkling as she had earlier. A team of horses came into view, and as the troika plunged through the snow, its big hunting bell rang out loudly, while the two smaller bells alongside it tinkled in tune, so that a reassuring melody echoed through the forest.

"Easy there, easy," she heard a man say. Then a second voice joined in, this one sounding as if being in charge of things was second nature, and ordered the driver of the team to rein in his horses.

They drew up alongside the sledge where Grandfather still hung halfway out of the seat. Pauline hurriedly explained what had happened, more concerned about her granddad than anything else.

Of the two men, the one with the bossy voice did most of the talking, and when he and the driver carried Peter Semyonovich to the sledge and set him down, he ordered the *yamshchik* to harness Turk and Coco to the back of the sleigh, making room for her next to her grandfather. Peter Semyonovich's eyes were still closed, but she could tell he was breathing because every now and again he made a little whistling sound and his lips, blue with cold, fluttered ever so gently.

When they were all settled in the sledge, and the driver had taken his place, the passenger introduced himself. He was a little girl's grandfather too, he said, and was on his way to visit his daughter at Golovlovo, where she and her family had recently taken up residence.

Pauline had heard of Golovlovo, but since she didn't know where the road was, she had no idea how to direct the men to Petrovka. The *yamshchik*, however, a surly character who kept slapping his leather mittens together and complaining of the cold, said he knew how to get there and immediately set off, following a path that didn't look like a road, though Pauline was certain he knew more about this than she did.

Sure enough, before too long she recognized where she was, glancing nervously at her granddad and hoping he would soon be himself again. By the time they reached home Peter Semyonovich had begun to stir. The man who was on his way to visit his daughter told her to run on inside and tell them what had happened, while he and the driver carried her grandfather into the house. Pauline did as she was told, shouting as she ran across the courtyard, so that Granny hurried outside without even taking the time to put on her coat.

Pauline could barely get the words out when Anninka raised her voice in alarm, shouting for Rodya to come quick, there was trouble. Within just a few minutes not only Rodya, but also Vera, and Aunt Masha too, had all come running to see what was wrong. Pauline tried to follow them when they carried Grandfather upstairs to his room, but her mother shooed her away, telling her to stay in the kitchen and not get underfoot. Pauline thought this was terribly unfair, especially since she was with Granddad when he took sick. But Mother was very firm, and so Pauline decided not to argue, sitting all by herself in the kitchen and wondering if somehow she'd end up getting blamed for what had happened.

A stroke, declared the eminent physician from Mtsensk,

and went away shaking his head, as if to say there was nothing more to be done. Vera, however, had other things on her mind, and her father's condition seemed the least of it. A letter had arrived several days after Peter Semyonovich had been carried upstairs to his room, a letter that at first made her feel faint, then restful, then infuriated. After an absence of six years, Simon had written to say he planned to be in Mtsensk on business, and could he possibly stop at Petrovka to pay her a call? But since there was no return address, she had no way to reach him, and though she composed the letter of rejection over and over again in her mind, there was no reason to put her feelings down on paper. She told no one about this, however. Even though rage was the one emotion that dominated her thoughts, she also knew she would be lying to herself if she insisted she didn't want to see him.

It was Pauline, who had just come upstairs after having spent the morning playing in the root cellar, who first heard the horses snorting in the yard. When she poked her head out, a man she'd never seen before was striding purposely toward the front door, walking like someone who knew exactly where he was going.

Maybe it was another doctor, and so she hurriedly opened the door to greet him, only to hear her mother telling her to go upstairs, she had lessons to attend to. For a moment, though, Pauline had the strangest feeling that the man knew who she was. But Mother was yelling now, and so Pauline frowned and turned away.

"Straight to your room, young lady," Vera said in her sharpest tone of voice.

"But there's a visitor."

"Just do as you're told, Pauline. I'm in no mood for arguments."

"But who is he, Mother?"

"Someone—it's not important, believe me."

Vera waited until her daughter had gone upstairs before she acknowledged the man, who was certainly no stranger. Wondering if he'd find her as attractive as he once did, she held herself very stiff and erect and beckoned him inside. But despite all the promises she had made to herself, just to look at him made her want to fall into his arms.

Yes, it was the same Colonel, all right. Older, of course, for he was thirty-eight or thereabouts, but with the same square and forceful-looking jaw, the same black-black hair, the same cleft chin, and big, bearlike hands.

"How well you look," she remarked, lacing her fingers together so that she didn't strike him when he came near. "And prosperous, too."

"You received my letter?" Simon asked, speaking in that deep, rolling voice that had thrilled her in the summerhouse, and that had continued to thrill her long after they were apart.

Vera nodded, then turned and led him into the drawing room. "Surely you don't think I'm ready to pack my bags and go off with you, do you? It's been six years, Simon. Six years," she said, raising her voice though she didn't want him to see how upset she was.

"I haven't come to take you with me, Vera."

Enraged at his arrogance, she raised her hand to slap him, stopping herself only at the very last moment. "Then why did you decide to come here?"

"I thought I explained that in my letter. I wanted to see you and Pauline."

"Well now that you've seen us, you can go. I despise you," she said bitterly. "I always will."

Simon responded with a smile, and dimples just like Pauline's appeared in his blue, smooth-shaven cheeks.

She tried to hit him, but before she could slam her angry little fists against his chest, he captured her hands and then her mouth, crushing her against him so that she was nearly overcome by the rage of her desire. For a moment all her resolve melted. But though she felt this agonizing need for him that six years of longing had only intensified, her anger was much the stronger of the two, and she finally managed to pull free.

"I suppose you thought I'd fall at your feet, pay homage to the Colonel. I'm afraid not. But she didn't recognize you, did she?"

Simon shook his head.

"That's fine, because I don't want her to know. You'll do that one thing for me, won't you?"

"If you insist."

"I insist. I'd also like you to leave, and as soon as possible."

"But you've kept my money all these years, haven't you, Vera?"

She smiled scornfully, hating that part of herself that still wanted him, and would have flown into his arms, coupling with him on the floor like an animal.

"You're still slime," she said, "just like you always were, that you'd even think I'd touch that money. It's all there, every ruble, and it's all for Pauline. Pauline!" she shouted, shrill and vindictive.

Light footsteps descended the stairs. Vera swallowed hard, tried to collect herself, and nervously touched her hair with the tips of her fingers.

"I thought I told you to stay upstairs," she said when Pauline came into the drawing room.

"There wasn't anything for me to do." The child looked curiously at Simon, as if waiting to be introduced.

Belinsky smiled, but said nothing.

"Your grandfather asked me to go over some business arrangements with Mr.—"

"Saltykova," he said.

"But now he has to be on his way."

"Actually, Madame, if you'd permit me to spend the night, I'd be much obliged. I wouldn't be able to reach Mtsensk before nightfall, and the weather doesn't look very promising."

There was no getting around it, and so she told Simon he could stay at the steward's house, instructing him to ask the housekeeper for whatever bedding he required.

"Come, princess," she said to Pauline, reaching out and taking her hand, "we'll go upstairs and see how your grandfather is getting along."

Oh, but he was handsome, so devilishly handsome. Vera shuddered to herself and started up the stairs.

Masha and Vera sat beside their father's bed, where Peter Semyonovich lay stretched out like a corpse, the bedcovers barely stirring with each faint, shallow breath. His skin was a dull waxy shade, and lank strands of thin gray hair framed his face. His hands, once so powerful, now hung limply by his sides, the short, stubby fingers curled up in half fists, as if he were readying himself to do battle, beating death at its game.

"Do you think he's going to die?"

"You say it with so little feeling, Vera."

"What did he ever do for me? Took me in and made me work like a serf, that's what. If it weren't for Pauline, he would've turned me away without thinking twice about it. Isn't that so, *Papochka*? Yes," said Vera, answering herself, "the old bull's horn isn't so hard anymore, is it?"

Vera's words came as no surprise. Each of them shared a common ground of bitterness, each feeling as if life had denied them what was rightfully theirs. It was, Masha had often thought, as simple as that, because all it took was a single bullet to snuff out not only a life, but also all her hopes and dreams for the future.

But now she had no time to think of herself. Though she and Vera had never been very close, she recognized all the symptoms of her sister's pain, and now reached out to grasp her hand, holding it firmly in her own.

"You know then, don't you?" said Vera.

"Yes, I saw him outside."

"He wrote that he wanted to come, but—" Vera shrugged, her narrow shoulders shuddering convulsively.

"And Pauline, does she know?"

"No."

How sad and tired she looked, Masha thought, but with something spiteful lurking around the corners of her eyes, and giving her features a hard, embittered cast.

"And she's not going to know, either," Vera continued, raising her voice and totally ignoring the fact that she was sitting by her father's bed. "I won't share him with her. I won't even give him the pleasure of knowing her. That'll be his punishment. After all, you know something of revenge, don't you? Yes, you of all people should know exactly what I'm talking about."

Masha eyed her lap, feeling a familiar uneasiness stealing over her. "I don't know what you mean," she murmured.

Vera looked at her with contempt, as if to say she was nobody's fool, and that she'd learned her lessons, and learned them well. "Come now," she taunted. Her chin looked even more pointed than usual. "You must be living just for the day when you'll get back at him for murdering Stepan."

"I don't want to talk about it, Vera."

"And why not? You don't fool me in the least. You're no saint. You've walked around here for the last four years as if someone died and we haven't gotten around to burying him yet."

"How can you be so cruel?"

"It's not cruelty," Vera insisted. "It's time you stopped pretending, Masha, just as it's time I stopped pretending, too. Because if you don't, you'll never make peace with yourself."

"When I'm strong enough," she finally said, "and lonely enough, God will grant me my revenge. On that you have my word."

Vera wasn't certain why she sat up that night, long after everyone had retired. The doctor had paid another call that afternoon, pronouncing Peter Semyonovich's condition "grave but stable," and offering little hope for improvement, saying he could linger like this for months on end, or he could go tomorrow if that was God's plan.

And what if he dies and the will hasn't been changed? Vera wondered. Oh, the little bully, to have ruined my life like this, ignoring my princess, pretending he loves her, and then leaving her without a kopeck.

Of course, she still didn't know that for certain. But with Rodya's help she might be able to find the will, and if the provisions weren't to her liking, surely something could be done about it. She hadn't told the steward that Mr. "Saltykova" was her husband, and didn't intend to now that she'd decided to seek a divorce. Simon need never know about that either, because if she could prove desertion she might be able to win her suit. Then, with a divorce decree, the way would be open for Rodya to marry her.

Yes, I deserve another chance, she thought. He loves me. He's fond of Pauline, and he's done a good job for Father. I'm young, and I'm still pretty. I deserve something, don't I, some happiness at least.

In the cold, dark places of her mind she saw it all very clearly. Yet she waited here as if tempting fate, surprised that he was taking so long. But soon her diligence was rewarded.

First she heard the back door swing open, followed by the whoosh of the wind and then the hinges squeaking as he closed the door behind him. Next came footsteps across the brick floor. Then the door leading into the dining room was thrown open, and in the darkness she could see his silhouette, filling the threshold.

"Here!" she wanted to cry out. Instead, she remained where she was, curled up on the sofa, a blanket wrapped around her feet. The stoves were still giving off heat, though it was growing colder by the moment. How she needed to be warmed, and told she was beautiful, and reminded of all the promises they had once made to each other.

He passed through the dining room, walking very carefully, as if watching where he put his feet.

Vera shivered, and eyed him silently. The flame of the lamp alongside her flickered brightly, sending its sharp amber rays rushing across the room. Illuminated in its glow, his eyes looked as yellow as a cat's.

"I thought you might be waiting up," Simon said as he came into the drawing room.

Even when he spoke softly his voice excited her. How she hated him for the way he'd treated her, and yet how desperately she wanted him. But this would be the last time. Although she might be weak, she wasn't a fool, and would never again permit herself the luxury of letting her passion get the better of her common sense.

"I hope when I get up tomorrow you'll be gone," she told him as she unwrapped the blanket and sat up, both feet on the floor.

"You needn't worry, Vera." He joined her on the sofa, and without another word he had her in his arms, his big, bear-like hands caressing her cheeks, cupping her face as he gazed into her eyes. Then he put one hand on her breast and the other on the small of her back, holding her this way as his tongue explored the recesses of her mouth before sliding down along the length of her slender neck.

Shivering with six years of longing, and needing this moment of valedictory pleasure before she could find the courage to send him away, Vera reached down, groping shamelessly between his legs.

Brazen hussy, she thought. Vile slut. You deserve the Presnia again. But if he were there to share it with you—

He began to say things to her, words she'd not heard since Pauline was an infant, wonderfully, wickedly obscene words that made her tremble almost as much as his hard, calculating touch.

"Where can we go?" Simon whispered, licking the rim of her ear with his raspy tongue. "Upstairs, my little dove?"

"No, they'd hear. Father's study." She took his big, bearish hand in hers, seeing it disappear in his grasp as she led him to his feet. But before she took a step, Simon pulled his hand free, then pushed her down until she was kneeling before him.

"Remember what you did in the summerhouse?" he whispered, thrilling her with his deep and mysterious voice. "Remember how you got down on your knees like this, and what you did afterward?"

How could she possibly forget? She saw it all, remembering the summerhouse and the shadows of cobwebs and the damp, spooky half light. She recalled how he'd made her kneel before him in homage and adoration, showing her how to do justice to the Colonel with her lips and her tongue and her slim young fingers. Now she unbuttoned his trousers for him, rubbing her lips back and forth against the rigid length of his enormous sex, shivering and despising herself, yet unable to do anything but what he asked.

"See how the Colonel adores you, Vera. See how eager he is? He's missed you, my little sparrow, and now he wants to

355

make up for lost time." Simon flung himself against her, thrusting eagerly with his hips, and pressing his hands to the back of her head so she couldn't free herself.

Only when the two of them heard footsteps on the stairs did he release her, turning away quickly to button his pants. Vera rushed to her feet, trying to compose herself.

Filth, slime, whore, she kept saying, the words twisting around her heart like a noose. God will punish you for sure. Next time it'll be the devil, and then you'll choke to death for your sins.

"Mother, are you all right?" Pauline called out.

"Yes, dear," she said, trying to speak in a normal tone of voice. She glanced anxiously at Simon, who was now seated on the couch, both hands folded over his lap.

Pauline came into the drawing room, her black curly hair falling abundantly about her shoulders, and her charming little figure white and luminous in a long muslin nightdress. But when she cast a glance at Mr. "Saltykova," the inquisitive expression in her eyes at once turned hard and brittle.

"Why is he still here?" the child said, stamping her foot as her mother often did. "I thought he was going to go away and leave us alone. I know who he really is, but I don't care anymore. He hasn't been a father to me before, so why should he start acting like one now?"

Vera looked at her sharply, praying the child hadn't been standing there on the stairs, witnessing the scene in the drawing room.

"I heard you and Aunt Masha talking," Pauline explained. "I didn't mean to listen in, really I didn't, but you were talking so loud I just couldn't help it."

Simon came to his feet, looking at her with such gentleness and concern that his features were transfigured. "You were only a baby, Pauline. How can you possibly remember how terrible it was when we lived in Moscow?"

"I can't remember much of it, it's true," Pauline said. "But I can't remember you at all. Now you come back out of nowhere and you're making my mother unhappy. It would've been better if you never saw us again."

Simon bent down before her, reaching out to put his hands around her waist. But Pauline stepped nimbly back, refusing to let him touch her. "But I love you, Pauline, I always have. I've sent your mother money for you all along. There were very good reasons why I didn't come back."

"What reasons?" she demanded.

Simon's voice broke. "I can't tell you that, even now."

"Then I won't believe you, I won't!" She tossed her head defiantly, and her lustrous curls flew back and forth like the wings of a great dark bird. "You're a mean, hateful man, that's what you are! You don't love me and you never have. Why don't you go away and leave us alone. We were fine before you came here making trouble."

"But I love you," he said again.

"You don't know anything about love, Mr. Saltykova, Mr. Simon Belinsky Saltykova." Before either Vera or Simon could say anything else, Pauline turned away and rushed upstairs.

Simon straightened up and looked at her helplessly, as if to say he'd tried.

But no, Vera realized, he'd hardly tried at all, and even seemed relieved now that it had finally come out, and his child, his flesh and blood, had told him she never wanted to see him again.

"Come," he said, reaching out for her hand, "we'll talk about this in the study."

Vera shook her head. "I don't want to be with you anymore, Simon. My child needs me. Good night." She started for the stairs, but stopped when he called out to her.

"At least give me a chance to explain."

"The day I left Gruzinskaya Street, you told me it was only the Colonel I loved, not you. I didn't believe you at the time. But you were right, Simon. That's just what it was." She left him standing in the drawing room and continued up the stairs. It was the princess who mattered now, and nothing and nobody else.

Two

Kneeling on that same threadbare strip of carpet she had
dragged with her from Petrovka ten years before, Henriette
posed the one question whose answer the Redeemer had yet
denied her. "What shall I tell him?" she whispered. "If I
leave here, then I can never hope to be his wife. But if I stay I
might lose the Countess' friendship, and then I'd be worse off
than when I started."

She pressed her forehead to the floor, feeling the blood
rush to her temples. If only He could tell her what to do,
she'd follow His advice without a moment's hesitation.

Yes, she thought, He knows the secrets of my soul as no
one ever will. He knows that a fraud I can be, and knows
when I'm telling the truth. When He lies next to me He has
the power to make me whole again, and comfort me, and make
me beautiful. Beautiful! But perhaps it's a curse, as Vera has
found out. Besides, *La Belle Henriette* has other gifts, other
talents, such as the Countess has already discovered for
herself.

"Why haven't You come to me?" she whispered, gazing
feverishly at the ikons. "Are You angry with me, too, for
what I've done? But You know how long I waited for You,

and when You didn't come I became afraid. You know I needed someone, my dear sweet gentle Jesus. You know I prayed for You, and begged for an answer. But You didn't come and I was frightened."

So she had become the Count's mistress. She was thirty-four years old and tired of thinking of herself as a withered and bloodless old maid, incapable of love, frigid and unresponsive to a man's touch. Thus, for the past two years, ever since the Count had knocked on her door, slipping silently into her bed without a word of explanation, she had managed to evade the Countess' pleas to come to live with her, never revealing the actual reasons why she was reluctant to leave Count Ivanov's employ. But now she could no longer make excuses, especially since she knew Dmitri Fyodorovich had no intention of marrying her, as she had once foolishly believed.

Having finally made up her mind to return the keys to his stores, to give up her position as prime minister of his household, and accept the Countess' offer of patronage and a newly decorated steel-gray room, Henriette went downstairs to tender her resignation.

"Resignation?" the Count said in a disbelieving tone. "Don't be absurd, Henriette. This is your home, *ma chère*. One just doesn't leave one's home on a whim."

"I think I've fulfilled my obligations here as best I can. It's time to move on, and the Countess has asked me to come and stay with her."

"In what capacity?"

"As her companion."

"As her resident clairvoyant, you mean," Count Ivanov said with an unfriendly laugh.

Why couldn't she handle him as she'd handled General Tishin? All it would take was a starchy manner, a sarcastic phrase or two, a pose to fully match his arrogance. Yet she was incapable of pretending she was his better, and perhaps, she reasoned, that was why he'd never asked her to be his wife, nor ever called her his "lover."

The Count stuffed his pince-nez into his jacket pocket, rubbing the fiery-red indentations along the bridge of his nose where the eyeglass guards had rested. "So Countess Ignatieva is taking you in, the absent-minded fool. I suppose she intends to take you out into society, too. You, a former governess, a housekeeper."

"The Petrovs are gentry," she reminded him. "You certainly didn't think them ill bred when you slipped into my bed."

"Do spare me your class distinctions, Henriette. The only reason I slipped into your bed was because it was the most accommodating one in the household."

How she would have liked to pull him up from his chair and shake him, telling him that the only reason she ever allowed him to touch her was simply because she wanted to be the Countess Ivanova, and not because she found him so irresistible that she lost her head. But perhaps one day he might again prove a useful person to know, and so she bit down on her lower lip, stifling her outrage.

"But I know what you're after, Henriette," the Count resumed, leaning far back in his chair so that his gold watch chain stretched tautly across his waistcoat, reminding her of a noose she would have liked to see strung around his neck. "The Countess is merely a stepping-stone. Afterward you'll find yourself a Grand Duchess, become her confidante and spiritual adviser. Where will it end, do you suppose? The Empress, no doubt. You'd like that, wouldn't you, to be granted the rights and privileges of being received at court? But what are you, after all? A rather homely girl from the provinces—hardly a girl, actually—desperate to be told she's beautiful."

Henriette smiled and smiled until it felt as if her lips were cracking, and the mask of her cordiality would shatter and fall to the floor. "Thank you, Dmitri Fyodorovich. Your kindness and generosity will never be forgotten. In fact, it is my most heartfelt wish that you spend the rest of your life in the company of people just like yourself. Won't that be pleasant? I think it will." She started from the study, but not before she heard him applauding.

Then his voice rang out with a chillingly sarcastic, *"Touché, ma petite bête, touché!"*

Unable to come up with a suitable rejoinder, she held her tongue and didn't look back.

In Peter Semyonovich's study, behind the Persian wall carpet on which was mounted a variety of rusty weapons, a loose panel was discovered. When Vera and Rodya pried it free, they finally found what they had been looking for for months on end.

The old man's will, tied up with string and stuffed into the narrow space behind the wall, proved to be exactly the document Vera had imagined. One glance and she knew all her fears were justified, and that her father intended to leave the entire estate to her sister Irena. There wasn't a single mention of any of his other children, nor a provision for his granddaughter, for whom he'd so often professed such love and devotion.

"No wonder he's half paralyzed," Vera said after mulling over the contents of the will. "God is punishing him for his selfishness. But I won't let him get away with it." She flung down the document, so angry she didn't know what to do first. "Who's been taking care of him since he got sick? Me, that's who."

"And Anninka and your sister, too," Rodya volunteered. He proceeded to crack his knuckles, pausing only when she shot him an aggravated glance. "But you got the money for the birch wood, didn't you?"

"How many times must I tell you never to mention that?" she hissed.

Rodya's ingenuous brown eyes, so placid and good-natured, opened wide. "But it's true," he said. "We forged his name to the papers, remember, because that was the day he had the stroke."

Vera sunk into her father's lumpy leather-covered divan. "Sometimes I think I intend to marry a fool," she said caustically. "The money is for Pauline, and I don't want to hear any more about it."

"But what about the money from the mill?" asked the steward. That too had recently been sold, Rodya having forged his master's signature on another set of documents.

"We need to eat, don't we? If we waited for him to recover his wits we'd all end up starving to death."

She turned her attention back to the will, while Rodya remained seated in a nearby chair, yawning contentedly and patting himself on the stomach. Vera glanced at him out of the corner of her eye.

"Do me a favor, Rodion, and stop sitting there like a nitwit."

"But I was only waiting for you to decide what to do, Verochka."

"I've decided. We're going to write a new will, that's what. After all, justice is on our side, isn't it? Irena hasn't even been here since he took sick. So why should she be left the entire estate when it's only fair that Pauline and I get our rightful share. We'll draft a *coddlesill*, that's what. Yes, a *coddlesill*."

"A what?" said the steward, yawning again.

"A *coddlesill*, isn't that what they're called? Something that you add to the last sheet, making changes. There's a lawyer in

Mtsensk who'll do anything for a fee. We'll drive out to see him tomorrow, tell him our poor father is *in extremis,* and needs some legal advice. Yes, and no one'll be the wiser. Now put the papers back where you found them," she said, waving her hand in the direction of the wall hanging.

Rodya sighed and came to his feet.

God, she thought, I'm giving up being married to a fox to marry a rooster, he acts so dumb half the time.

But perhaps she was underestimating him. After all, lots of people said Sorokin was clever, and that behind his easygoing manner was a man who knew exactly what he wanted out of life, exactly how to go about it, too. If that were true, then maybe it wouldn't turn out to be such a bad marriage. And if it weren't true, that was also just as well, because it would be very nice to control the purse strings for a change, and get whatever she wanted whenever she wanted it.

"Yes," she said, watching him as he returned the will to its hiding place, pounding the loose panel back into position with the side of his hand, "we'll drive into Mtsensk first thing tomorrow. And afterward . . . afterward we won't have to worry about silly little wills, not ever again."

Some four hundred versts southwest of Moscow, along one of the innumerable little rivers that fed into the Dnieper, Gregor was agilely manning a long, narrow skiff hollowed out of a poplar. At the tiller sat his friend Larisa Antonovna, Princess Denisheva, with whom he'd spent the last two weeks in a state of blissful anticipation.

"Do sit down, Grisha, before you lose your balance," the Princess kept crying out as the light, sharp-prowed boat rocked back and forth.

Gregor dropped down into a sitting position. He wore a cream-colored tussah suit and a stylish straw hat tied with a muslin scarf that fell along his neck as a protection from the sun, the rays of which had already given him a nasty burn. Having left his shoes on the bank, his trousers were rolled up along his calves, and now and again he'd reach down to swat a fly.

That summer the Princess had invited him down to Talashkino, her husband's magnificent estate near Smolensk. It was an area of densely wooded hills and narrow, fertile valleys. Fields of yellowing rye, thickly dotted with corn-flowers, rippled invitingly with each stray breath of wind. Here at Talashkino, Gregor and the Princess were laying plans for an exhibit of historical Russian portraits, a major undertaking for which he'd already begun compiling lists of possible selections. But it wasn't portraiture that was on his mind this afternoon, but rather the imminent arrival of Prince Orlovsky.

Gregor thought of the happiness he'd enjoyed these last few months, and wondered if he hadn't finally met someone with whom he cared to spend the rest of his life. Yet it frightened him each time he thought of it, and made him all the more apprehensive about the Prince's arrival.

Larisa Antonovna, so slim and fetching in her pale-beige dress, apparently knew what he was thinking. "Is it love, do you suppose?" she called out letting her hand trail through the clear blue-green water. "I've always thought you capable of a great romance, Grisha, truly I have."

"Abélard and Héloïse, or Damon and Pythias?"

"Both, in their fashion."

"Such a diplomatic Larisa," he said with a grin.

Gregor stowed the oars, and letting the gentle current take them where it would, he turned to face her and the great manor house of Talashkino that rose up behind her like a vision out of a fairy story. Flanked by dark clusters of oak and birch, an alley of tall fir trees formed a beautiful cool avenue leading to the columned portico.

"Is it really love, Grisha?" the Princess asked again while he picked up the oars and sculled quickly, easing the skiff away from the bank.

"I've never been able to decide what love is."

"Unfair," she laughed.

"It certainly is," he replied. "But I feel a great warmth for him, and a tremendous amount of affection. In fact, I'm so content that sometimes it's even a little boring. Only you mustn't ever tell the Prince that." Then, turning his head to the side, he scanned the riverbank, hoping to catch sight of a droshky, and the tall, slim figure of Prince Orlovsky.

They'd met exactly five months before, and had been intimate five months less four days. Vladimir Danilovich—Volodya, as he was known to his friends—had the sleek elegance of an English racehorse, and even parted his hair *à l'anglaise*. He was a softspoken man in his mid-thirties, seemingly incapable of raising his voice, yet quite adept at getting people to do what he wanted.

"Isn't that him?" Larisa cried out excitedly. She let go of the tiller and rose swiftly to her feet.

"No, don't!" Gregor shouted, her sudden movement having set the skiff rocking dangerously. "Get down, get down!" he yelled, unable to stop laughing as the boat tipped this way and that, and Larisa, clutching her straw hat with one hand, and the side of the skiff with the other, tried desperately to maintain her balance.

"Hello there!" a cultured and well-modulated voice called out to them.

But it was too late. The skiff suddenly rolled over like a dog performing a trick, and she and Gregor were unceremoniously tossed into the water. A moment later Gregor came up sputtering, his muslin scarf completely covering his face so that he looked out through a veil of soaking wet gauze.

The Princess' straw hat floated past him. He snagged it,

then treaded water, trying to pull the scarf out of his eyes as he looked around for his friend.

"Here!" she cried out. She was hanging onto the upside-down skiff, which now resembled the poplar trunk it once was, more than the boat it had eventually become.

Trying not to laugh so that he wouldn't swallow water, Gregor swam toward her, while on the bank the Prince began to rib them good-naturedly. By the time they maneuvered the overturned skiff to the shore and their feet touched bottom, Prince Orlovsky was already wading into the water to lend them a hand. Gregor threw himself down on the grass, alternately laughing and choking so hard he couldn't catch his breath. Sprinkling water over his face, and blaming him for the mishap, Larisa sat down beside him, her thin silk dress clinging tightly to her body.

The Princess' maid and old *nyanya* came running, certain she'd come close to drowning. Larisa waved them away, saying that she was fine, and sent them back to the house for refreshments.

Meanwhile, Gregor cast shy glances at Volodya, who now crouched before him, looking remarkably fresh and rested despite his long journey. Gregor wanted to reach out and embrace him, but though Larisa knew nearly everything there was to know about their affair, there were still certain proprieties that had to be maintained. Besides, Volodya was never demonstrative in public, believing that one's personal life should never be put on display, thus affording people the opportunity to gossip. Nevertheless, the Prince suddenly reached out and grasped his hand, holding it a moment before letting go.

"Have you recovered?" asked Vladimir Danilovich. "Because if you have, I bring momentous news from Petersburg."

"That's quite a big word," said Larisa.

"But one that suits the occasion," remarked the Prince, "for you're looking at none other than the new Director of the Imperial Theaters."

It was an unprecedented appointment for someone as young as he, as the position was much envied, and afforded its recipient impeccable social credentials. The Director had constant access to the Emperor, an honor that not even Ministers could obtain, unless through special application to the Minister of the Court. As a court rank, the Director could visit with the Tsar whenever he was present in his box at any of the imperial theaters. Such close personal contact with the court had long been Gregor's dream, and now he looked eagerly at Volodya, hoping the Prince intended to include him in his plans.

"But what of our Grisha here?" asked Larisa. She was always looking out for him, and never missed an opportunity to speak highly of him with those in a position of power.

"A charming fellow, to be sure," said Prince Orlovsky with a straight face. "Though with a certain predilection for gaudy headwear. But I thought that if he'd get rid of this ridiculous hat of his," motioning to the straw boater with the multi-colored scarf, "I wouldn't hesitate to attach him to my staff."

Gregor, jumping to his feet, picked up the stiff sennit and sent it sailing out across the water, where it landed with a splash and immediately started downstream, the long muslin pugree trailing behind like the tail of a kite.

"How does Functionary for Special Missions sound?" asked the Prince.

Like the power behind the throne, Gregor gleefully thought. He let out a whoop, and grabbing Larisa by one hand and Volodya by the other, he danced around, certain his fortune was made, and that after ten years of struggling to find a niche for himself, he was finally on the verge of success. With his help, and the help of his many artistic friends, the imperial theaters would now embark on a new golden age. And if he had his way, Russian opera and ballet would never be the same.

In their apartment on the Mokhovaya, Katya, the Volskys' maid, rushed about from room to room, seeing to it that every stick of furniture was covered in brown linen sheets. Long cardboard boxes the shape of coffins were lined up along the bedroom floor, filled with winter clothes over which camphor and pepper had been generously sprinkled. Numerous traveling cases of canvas-covered wood with brass clamps and fancy corner bumpers, and a variety of leather valises, some shaped like well-stuffed sausages and others like oversized pots, stood ready in the front hall.

Tomorrow Irena was leaving for Petrovka in the company of her two sons, five-year-old Andrei and his brother Sergei, who'd celebrated his first name day just a few weeks before. Nikolai would be staying on for several days before joining them, but when he returned late that afternoon he didn't look like a man who was anxiously awaiting the start of his summer holiday.

Instead, Volsky appeared both dejected and greatly disturbed, and was chewing nervously on the long hairs of his mustache as he came into the bedroom to greet his wife. His downcast, Asiatic eyes only added to his look of despair, and as he kissed her on the cheek he did so with little feeling.

"I had a meeting with Count Ivanov today," Volsky said, reminding her of the Count's position at the Ministry, and the fact that he was directly accountable to him. "I was asked to resign, and not make a fuss."

"But why?" Irena held herself very stiffly, not wanting Niki to see how she had begun to tremble.

"Because I was a fool, that's why," Volsky said angrily. "Because for months now I've been telling them that unless they do something about the plight of the workers, it's going to blow up in their faces. And do you know how they responded? They asked me to resign, and implied I was a troublemaker, and that the inspectorate would be better off without me."

"Then you must take your case even higher, to the Tsar, if necessary."

Volsky laughed, and it wasn't the laugh of a man who thought lightly of his future. "I said as much," he replied, "and the Count told me how naïve I was. The Tsar doesn't grant audiences just because someone asks for one. And he hardly reads anything either, unless it's been screened beforehand. Do you know who does that? Pobedonostsev, Procurator of the Holy Synod, the man they call 'the Tsar's eye.' And as far as he's concerned, there's no such thing as a Russian working class. That's what I'm up against."

"Did you resign as he requested?"

Volsky nodded wearily. "But that doesn't change anything, Irusha. The people are starving, and they say this year's harvest is only going to be worse than the last. They'll rise up for sure if something isn't done to help them. And will I have had the last laugh? Who knows, we might all be dead by then."

The door was flung open with the force of a little hurricane, and five-year-old Andrei rushed inside. He threw himself into his father's arms, crying out, "Papa, Papa, why didn't you come and say hello to us? Did you bring me a surprise like you said you would?" The little boy snuggled up against him as Volsky lifted his son into his arms.

"Reach in there," Volsky said, motioning to his breast pocket.

"What is it?" Andrei asked, tossing his beautiful little head while he eyed the pocket in question.

"If I told you it wouldn't be a surprise."

The little boy's hand darted into the coat pocket, and a moment later he proudly displayed the bottle imp he found, listening attentively as his father explained how it worked. Inside the small glass tube a pale-blue figurine of a man with a long red tongue and a monkeylike tail floated in the colorless liquid. When the rubber stopper over the mouth of the tube was pinched and pulled, the little imp danced.

"It's made in America," Volsky told his son. "See how it does tricks?"

"What's America?"

Volsky tried to laugh. "It's too far away to explain," and watched his son rush back to the nursery to show his little brother his new toy. Then Volsky sighed and looked back at his wife.

"Gregor has friends in high places," Irena reminded him. "There are other ministries, Niki, other positions you'd find challenging."

"Who'd hire a troublemaker?"

"You mustn't say such things. I have great confidence in your abilities. Something good will come of this, I'm certain."

"How can you stand there so calmly?" he said, raising his voice in exasperation. "Why don't you ever get angry, or throw things, or storm about?"

"Because what would it solve, Niki? I love you because you're willing to put your future in jeopardy in defense of your principles."

"If I can't put bread on the table, what good are principles? They don't stop you from going hungry, Irena."

"We're never going to go hungry, Niki."

"If we stay in Petersburg we might."

"If it comes to that, and I don't think it will, then we can always move to Petrovka."

Volsky shot her an angry glance and went into his dressing room to change.

*　　　*　　　*

Two years had passed since Irena had last been at Petrovka. But even in that relatively short period of time there had been a great number of changes. The outbuildings were all gray and in disrepair, with loose, rotting boards nailed haphazardly in place. The veranda at the back of the house had suffered in much the same way, the railing that enclosed it lacking half its balusters. She had to warn Andrei not to play there, lest he fall over the side and land in the nettles that had taken over much of the garden.

But it was the change in her father that affected her most of all. When she went upstairs to see him, she found herself confronting only half a man. Peter Semyonovich's entire left side was paralyzed, including that part of his face. As a result, one little round gray eye was all but hidden beneath a puffy, drooping yellow lid. His stubbly cheek sagged like soft clay, and the left side of his mouth hung down so that a steady trickle of saliva dribbled over his chin, forming a puddle across the towel that rested between his neck and shoulder. But if his left side no longer seemed part of him, his right side was still very much his own. The moment Irena came into the room her father raised his one good hand, waving his fingers by way of greeting.

Irena knelt beside him, kissing his hand.

"Irusha," he said, speaking with surprising clarity, "why did you take so long to come? All winter I waited for you, all spring. But I won't be angry, not now. Nothing pleasant about a sick old fool, is there? Besides, I have business for you."

His head began to shake uncontrollably, so that she had to reach out to stop the tremors.

"Important business," he said. "You understand?"

"Yes, Father."

"Good," and he nodded as she tried to dry his mouth with the damp towel. "Did you go to your mother's grave yet?"

"I will, I promise."

"Better that she doesn't have to see me like this. They don't leave me alone, all of them. Always fussing. I don't want anyone around when I'm like this. Let them remember me when I was strong. You understand?"

Irena nodded.

"Good. Now you bring me my will that's in the study," and he told her where she could find it. "We'll read it together, and then make changes. I want my grandchildren to remember me when I'm gone. And the berries I like. Bring those, too. Anninka will know."

It made her feel very old to see him like this. The last time she'd been here he was still the robust little man of her childhood, filled with boundless energy, watching over the estate, and seeing to it that everything ran smoothly. Now that he was dying so too was Petrovka. Only the familiar scent of lime blossoms that Anninka set out on the windowsills, and that lay there all winter, was a link to the past, reminding Irena of how things used to be, and might never be again. But no, she couldn't allow that to happen. The land was still rich, black, and fertile. Petrovka would once again flourish, for to let it simply wither and die was like killing off a part of herself, something she'd never permit.

"Well?" said her sister Vera when she came down the stairs. "What tales is he telling today? And have you ever seen anything so disgusting as the way that man drools? I have to change that didy around his neck every hour or so, it gets so wet."

No, Irena wouldn't get into an argument, saving her breath for more important things. "He wants to see his will," she announced. She started past the ballroom when Vera rushed after her, clutching at her shoulder and forcing her to stop.

"What does he want the will for?" Vera asked, alarm in her voice.

"He wants to leave Pauline some money."

Before her sister could stop her Irena entered the study, which was dim and dusty and smelled faintly of stale tobacco and old chocolate. She threw open the curtains, and bright summer sunlight spilled eagerly into the room, fading the dark-blue wallpaper and scattering dust motes into every corner. After undoing the iron bolts to open the windows and air out the room, Irena paused before her father's desk, where the inkwell in the shape of a pug dog reminded her of Laska. Then she lifted the edge of the heavy wall carpet, trying to locate the panel her father had described. When she couldn't see where it was she asked Vera to give her a hand.

Vera pursed her lips together. Her cheeks looked pinched, and the sharp point of her chin dominated her face. "Why should I?" she snapped. "He never intended to leave me anything, so why should I even lift a finger to help?"

"One would think that at your age, Vera, you'd have finally learned to stop acting like a child."

"So high-handed," Vera said scornfully, and she put her hand on her hip and stamped her foot. "Suddenly you come home and we're all supposed to bow before her majesty, our oldest sister."

"What in God's name has gotten into you?" she shouted. "I arrive and you don't even have the courtesy to welcome me. I ask for your help and you insult me. But when you were hungry, did your sister Irena ever forget you? Well, did I?"

Vera nervously played with the ruffled front of her shirt-waist. "That was years ago. It's over now."

"Let's hope so. And let's hope you learn a little kindness, too."

Without Vera's help Irena found the loose panel and soon located the will. But when she untied the string and smoothed the papers out on top of her father's writing table, it didn't take long to realize the document had been tampered with.

The last sheet amounted to an about-face, the codicil attached to the will leaving virtually the entire estate to Vera and her daughter. Having been told of the provisions of the will years before, Irena knew something was very wrong. Surely this wasn't her father's signature along the bottom of the page, nor did the wording of the codicil bear any resemblance to the rest of the document.

She heard Vera swallowing hard, and when Irena looked up her sister was already slinking to the door. "Are you going to explain what this is about, or shall I go upstairs and ask Father?"

"Explain what?" But Vera's expression was so shamelessly transparent that it was all Irena could do not to rush across the room and slap her.

"Are you so selfish, Vera, is that it? Is your heart so bitter you think only of yourself?"

Vera shook out the full balloonlike sleeves of her blouse, admiring the shirtwaist, and looking quite pleased with herself. "I think of my princess," she said calmly. "That's all that matters."

Vera turned away, but had barely stepped outside when Irena caught up to her. Grabbing her by the wrist, Irena spun her around.

"I've never raised a hand to you, not even when we were little. But in just another minute I'm going to lose my patience."

Vera eyed her scornfully, though her lower lip had begun to tremble. "I'm not your baby sister. You can't hit me. Who do you think you are, anyway? The *barinya's* dead, in case you haven't been told."

Irena, clutching both of Vera's hands, began to shake her back and forth until she heard her sister's teeth rattling and her bones making popping sounds just like when her father cracked his knuckles.

"Stop it, stop it!" Vera kept crying, her yellow curls flying this way and that, and her shouts causing Anninka to hurry as fast as she could from the kitchen.

"Dearies, dearies," the old woman begged, "you mustn't act like this when he's upstairs trying to get his rest. Think of your poor mother, if nothing else. She's watching from heaven and shaking her head, to see her two girls squabbling like cats on a fence."

Irena let go of her sister and stood panting, still so angry she could barely see straight. "Anninka, please, go back to the kitchen. Everything is fine, I promise. I just want to talk to her alone."

"You were my own precious babies," the housekeeper reminded them. "We went on expeditions and—"

"Oh, do be quiet for a change, you old busybody!" Vera said shrilly.

At once the old woman seemed to crumble, and her wrinkled face visibly deflated. With a mournful sigh, she turned and shuffled back to the kitchen, her battered goatskin shoes slapping hollowly against the floor.

"I only wanted to protect Pauline," Vera suddenly cried out. Although she threw herself against Irena and began to weep, Irena's hands remained by her sides, for she couldn't find it in herself to comfort her sister. "He wasn't going to leave her anything and she's all I have and she has no father and . . ."

Irena pushed her aside, watching Vera rub the tears from her eyes. "You're nearly thirty years old, and yet you haven't learned a thing, have you? Petrovka is ours, Vera. It's our birthright, our future, too. Did you think I'd be so selfish as to exclude you from sharing it with me?"

"But that's what the will says," whimpered Vera.

Irena explained why it was written this way, so that Petrovka wouldn't be broken up, parceled out in so many little pieces, and brought to ruin as a result. "Calling you a child doesn't excuse things anymore, Vera, because you're not a child. You're a grown woman, an adult, for God's sake."

"Who cares about silly old wills, anyway? When I'm dying in my bed you won't come to see me, so what's the difference?" Vera replied, gulping loudly again as if she couldn't swallow. "Besides, you're the one who always got everything because he liked you the best. And what did I ever get? Nothing, that's what!"

There wasn't anything else Irena could say. She felt as old and tired as her father, and as she climbed the stairs to bring him his will, she thought she could hear her mother's bell ringing faintly and forlornly, and then Laska chiming in with a petulant and lonely little bark.

When they found him he looked surprised, astonished that such a thing could have happened to him. His little round gray eyes were opened wide, even the left eye, which he hadn't been able to open for months now. He sat there in his chair, staring with amazement at what lay ahead. Rodya had carried him downstairs just an hour before, Peter Semyonovich having complained that he was tired of lying in bed, and wanted to sit out in the sun. And there he sat, thinking thoughts no one would ever know until, astonished that it was his time, he'd opened his eyes as wide as he could, even raising one hand, which now rested against his sunken chest. It was as if he'd tried to ward away the uncertain promise of the hereafter, for what value was anything that couldn't be measured in the palm of one's hand, or in that all-encompassing glance that took in acre upon acre of solid fertile earth, upon which all fortunes ultimately rest?

"How light he felt in my arms," Rodya had marveled. "It was like carrying a little puppy, he hardly weighed anything at all."

"Oh, but he was a fighter, he was. He wouldn't give up," said Anninka, dabbing at her eyes with a towel. "If only he'd made it up with Henriette. But no, they were both too stubborn to realize how much they needed each other."

"On the contrary," said Gregor, who'd arrived at Petrovka just a few days before. "He didn't need her at all. If he did, he wouldn't have treated her like an outcast, covering the mirrors, and telling everyone she was dead. Believe me, she's very much alive, and quite happy with herself, too."

A group of women from the village went upstairs to wash and lay out the body. They didn't see Pauline, crouched in a corner, hiding behind a chair.

How could such a thing have happened to her granddad? It was unfair, terribly and cruelly unfair that they'd made him go away, so that nothing she could do would ever make him wake up. She couldn't see for the tears, and oh how she hated them for touching his clothes and moving his arms and legs as if he were a doll, just a make-believe person. When she began to scream, the bedroom door flew open and her mother rushed inside, gathering her up in her arms even as she kicked and scratched and tried to pull free.

"Leave him alone! Leave him alone!" she kept shrieking until Aunt Masha too came running, and then Aunt Irena and Granny, and even her little cousin who'd been told to stay downstairs. They were all pressing around her and she couldn't breathe. "Granddad," she said, "it's Pauline, it's your princess, your little minx. Don't you remember?"

"He's dead," said Aunt Masha. "He's with the angels."

"He doesn't look dead," said Cousin Andrei, peering over the top of Grandfather's bed.

Aunt Irena took her son by the hand and led him from the room. Then Aunt Masha went away, and even the hideous old women who'd tried to take off his clothes. Only Mama remained, kneeling before her and holding her against her soft, warm breast.

"He loved you more than anyone," Mama whispered. "And when you grow up, he left a present for you, so you wouldn't ever forget him."

"I wouldn't ever forget him anyway," said Pauline, as her mother brushed away her tears. "Only now we don't have anyone, do we? We're all alone again."

"But soon you'll have a new papa," said her mother, stroking her hair and kissing her again and again. "And then we'll be a family, just like when you were little."

"I don't remember when I was little. I don't want to remember. Only Granddad understood."

Pauline eased free of her mother's embrace, then tiptoed to the bed as if she were afraid of awakening him.

"Good night, *dedushka*," she whispered.

But when she leaned over to kiss him on the forehead, he was so cold, so very cold and still, that a horrifying shadow like Baba-Yaga rose up before her. With a wail of terror, Pauline ran from the room, straight down the stairs, and then along the path to the summerhouse, where it was cool and dark and safe, and no one would ever think of looking for her until she was ready to come back.

Three

In September everyone returned from the country to shake the camphor off their winter clothes and get down to the serious business of making it through another year. But when Volsky returned from Petrovka with his wife and children, he felt like a man left stranded on a desert island, not unlike the character of Robinson Crusoe, whose adventure had so delighted him as a boy. When the clock in his room struck seven he climbed dutifully out of bed and went through all the motions of readying himself for the start of another day, only to realize he had no place to go. He had no office, no position, and no prospects for the future. So he took to walking, and for several weeks he wandered about the city, turning corners he'd never thought to turn before, visiting monuments and museums merely because he had nothing better to do with his time. To have no occupation, to face his fortieth birthday with nothing ahead but more walks and more museums, terrified him as nothing else had before.

Against his better judgment he finally agreed to pay a call on his brother-in-law. It wasn't that he had anything against Gregor. On the contrary, he found his wife's brother an amusing if somewhat irresponsible fellow, perennially in debt and with concerns that had little in common with his own. The world of art and music, theater and the ballet, held relatively little interest for Volsky. What good was culture when the vast majority of Russians could neither read nor write, and millions of his countrymen went to bed hungry each night? But he knew it wasn't his place to criticize, having learned all too painfully that voicing one's opinions was a most dangerous occupation, and that the wise man kept silent.

So on this particularly blustery and unpleasant fall afternoon, with the gilded dome of the Church of St. Simon and St. Anna visible in the distance, Volsky headed toward Simeonovskaya Street and his brother-in-law's apartment. Even before Volsky reached the third floor he could hear Gregor, who was alternately shouting and laughing while several other voices joined in as counterpoint. Then a woman's laughter, as light and frivolous as a child's, rang out loudly, making itself heard above the uproar.

The door to the flat was ajar. Volsky knocked and let himself in. The first person he saw was Kolya, and a moment later his wife, a boyish little woman with hardly any breasts at all. She was struggling under the weight of a tray filled with cups and saucers and plates of biscuits, while her husband had both arms around the gleaming copper samovar, holding it as lovingly as if it were a child. As soon as Kolya caught sight of him he burst into a smile. After rushing into the dining room with the samovar, he rushed right back again and proceeded to vigorously shake Volsky's hand.

"Nikolai Alexandrovich," the former groom kept saying, "what a pleasure to see you. And how is Madame Volskaya, and your two boys? Gregor Petrovich talks about his nephews all the time."

"They're fine, Kolya, thank you."

Kolya motioned him into the dining room, whose French

doors were thrown open so he could see the confusion going on within. Clustered around the dining table were six or seven of Gregor's friends, including the woman whose high-pitched bell-like laughter Volsky had heard on his way up the stairs. Gregor immediately took him in hand, making him feel very much at home as he went the round of introductions.

"Irena told me you were working on the *Annual*."

"Not working, my dear fellow. Slaving away. Everything has to be ready by March, and as you can see," gesturing at the photographs and papers strewn across the table, "we've barely gotten started."

The *Theaters Annual* recorded all the performances of the five imperial theaters, providing lists of the various companies, and pictures of the principal dancers, singers, and actors. But Gregor was determined to change all this, for previous issues of the yearbook were so dull and uninspired that no one bothered to read them.

"We've been given a budget of just under twenty thousand to work with," Gregor explained, "though I suspect we'll need a bit more. Everything is getting frightfully expensive these days, as I'm sure you're aware."

"Why Grisha dear, you never told me your brother-in-law was so handsome." It was Princess Denisheva, whom Gregor hadn't as yet gotten around to introducing. She linked her slender arm through Gregor's, smiling inquisitively at Volsky.

"I have undying loyalty to my sister, that's why," Gregor replied. "Larisa Antonovna, my esteemed brother-in-law, Nikolai Alexandrovich Volsky."

The young woman smiled politely, and her shiny blue-green eyes took in his full measure.

"A pleasure," he said.

"Not when you get to know her," Gregor said with a laugh.

"You'll scare him away, Grisha. Shame on you," replied the Princess. She was so slim and girlish it was as if spring itself stood before him, and Volsky found himself smiling broadly.

But he hadn't arrived at his brother-in-law's to pay a social call, and soon they retired to the privacy of Gregor's study. Gregor sank into a comfortable-looking easy chair, its nicely worn condition making it apparent it was his favorite seat in the house. Volsky perched on the edge of the leather sofa, eying the pattern of the expensive Bukhara carpet beneath his feet.

"Irena's told me all about it, Niki, and I've already worked out a plan," Gregor began. "Princess Denisheva's husband is a millionaire, with a monopoly of all the passenger steamers that ply our rivers. Needless to say, he's on a first-name basis with the Minister of Ways of Communication. As you've probably been reading, their main interest these days is building that railway across Siberia. But of course the Ministry's responsible for all aspects of transportation. If that area of work interests you, it won't be any problem arranging an interview with the Prince. Impress him favorably, and I'm sure he can do something for you. I'd also tell him exactly what happened at the inspectorate, Niki. Denishev prides himself on being a member of the intelligentsia, and he's extremely interested in social causes. He'll certainly have much more respect for you if you're open about your beliefs."

Volsky pictured himself wrapped in a heavy bearskin coat, supervising work along the Great Siberian Railway. He smiled to himself, then came to his feet and shook his brother-in-law's hand, grateful for Gregor's help. But at the door, all thoughts of bearskin coats, howling winds and freezing temperatures, tigers and wolves, and desperate bands of escaped convicts—in short, everything one associated with Siberia—vanished when he looked down at the slender and graceful figure of the Princess.

"I'm sorry you're unable to stay, Mr. Volsky," remarked Larisa Antonovna, eying him so intently that he began to chew on the long hairs of his mustache.

"Perhaps another time," he finally blurted out. "I know how busy you must be."

"I shall make Grisha promise to bring you around. Artists can be very flighty, as I suppose you know. One often feels the need for a more settling influence."

The Princess held out her hand to be kissed. As Volsky touched his lips to her cool, satinlike skin, he wondered if something couldn't be done to make himself into a more dashing and romantic figure. Perhaps he should begin to wax his mustache again, and sport the bold, multicolored waistcoats such as Gregor always wore.

So instead of going directly home, he hailed a passing droshky and had the *isvostchik* take him to his tailor on Millionnaya Street, where he ordered a waistcoat in raspberry velvet, and another in a gray and brown check, several flowered-silk neckties, and a pair of imported gloves of yellow dogskin with broad black stripes. Afterward, he had his hair dressed at the Nevsky Prospect Gentlemen's Barbershop, then went next door to Quisisana, ate a plateful of tiny shrimp patties and spiced sausages, and walked home through the dusk feeling altogether like a man who'd reached a turning point in his life, only to successfully negotiate the obstacles that lay in his path.

But when he reached home and Irena met him at the door, Volsky couldn't help but feel a twinge of dissatisfaction. Attributing this to the spiced sausages, which perhaps weren't as fresh as they could have been, he kissed her perfunctorily and went off to his study, wondering if indigestion and infatuation weren't merely two sides of the same coin.

Moscow's Okhotny Ryad—"Hunters' Row"—was an outdoor market near Theater Square, where game and other foodstuffs were sold, and where, according to the popular saying, "Both priest and bug stand snug," for everyone came to Okhotny Ryad to haggle.

A motley crowd of housewives and vendors thronged the stalls, oblivious to the cold as they pinched the produce and hawked their wares. Itinerant tea sellers strolled about with leather racks slung around their necks, whole rows of glasses rattling loudly with each step they took. *"Sbiten!"* they would cry. "Fresh, hot *sbiten!*" One kopeck bought a glass of the tasty brew, a fragrant mixture of honey, laurel leaves, and sundry spices. While peasants squatted on the rubble pavement, surrounded by cages of cackling hens and honking geese, other vendors tramped through the marketplace, offering sausage rolls or meat patties served up on gaudy bluesprigged saucers and flooded with bouillon from a brass flask the vendors attached to their belts.

But Simon had been promised a considerably tastier dinner, and so he made his way through the crowd in the direction of Egorov's restaurant, as anonymous a place to meet as any Zubatov had thought of in the five years Belinsky had worked for him.

The headwaiter directed Simon upstairs, where he came out into a vestibule lined with furs. Leaving his padded greatcoat with its cheap German beaver collar, he went on into the next room, where a table was laid with *zakuski*, those delectable Russian hors d'oeuvres without which no meal was complete. Sampling a slice of reindeer tongue, a sweet pickle, and a few bites of fat smoked eel, he quickly downed a glass of vodka and continued on into the dining room.

Zubatov was already seated, a bottle of champagne perched within easy reach. Taking scant notice of the ikons in the corner, Simon crossed the crowded dining room and sat down opposite his chief. Zubatov immediately poured him a glass of the slightly sweet champagne, so cold that needles of ice were suspended in the bottle.

"I thought you deserved a fine dinner, Belinsky, and so I've taken the liberty of ordering for you. How does suckling pig with horseradish sound?"

"Excellent." But even if it hadn't, it would never have occurred to him to disagree with his chief, even on so minor an issue as the choice of a main course.

Zubatov smiled affably and, lighting a cigarette, he leaned back in his chair, eying Belinsky behind his tinted spectacles. "Have you heard of the Social Democratic Workmen's Party, the Social Democrats, as they're called?"

"Founded about two years ago, I believe, consisting of various splinter groups dedicated to socialism and the overthrow of our present form of government."

"What a pleasure to know a man who keeps abreast of current events," Zubatov replied with another agreeable smile. He waited until the headwaiter had covered their plates with slices of the savory and juicy pork. "I want you to infiltrate their ranks," Zubatov then told him.

"As an *agent provocateur?*"

"Don't use their terminology, Belinsky. I prefer to think of you as a *secret collaborator,* working on behalf of the Tsar."

Spearing a piece of meat and dipping it into the horseradish sauce, Zubatov proceeded to explain the two avenues that were open to them. One was actively to support the work of the factory inspectorate, even if there were those in the government who disagreed. Thus, as conditions improved for the workers, they would be less likely to be attracted to the revolutionaries. But it was his belief that they must also make every effort to create as much dissension and strife among the Social Democrats as they possibly could.

"In short, we undermine their conspiracies with conspiracies of our own," Simon replied, washing down his roast pork with another sip of champagne.

Zubatov nodded. "Your job will be first to provoke them to acts of terrorism, and then annihilate them before they have a chance to succeed."

"You never sanctioned murder before."

"Not murder, my dear Belinsky. Political assassination, something they've been practicing for more than ten years now, ever since that unspeakable incident on the Ekaterininsky Canal. All I'm asking is for you to help eradicate a cancer that threatens to infect every last one of us. The only efficient means of keeping abreast of their plans is for someone like you to become one of them. I believe you're just the man for the job. And now that we're going to have to provide you with an entirely new identity, we'll have to increase your two hundred rubles a month. I'd imagine three hundred should do for the time being. If you find that you need more, I'm sure we can work something out."

"And who's going to be my contact?" he asked.

"You won't have one, Belinsky. It's too risky. You're going to have to go into this on your own. We're particularly interested in a man named Durnovo. Have you heard of him?"

Simon shook his head, hoping his eyes wouldn't betray his emotions.

"He was in exile for several years, but from all accounts he recently managed to slip back into European Russia, where we've completely lost track of his whereabouts. From what I've been able to piece together, he's one of the prime movers in the party."

If he admitted that he was well acquainted with Victor Durnovo, he'd have no cover and no chance of getting the assignment, or the additional hundred rubles a month that went along with it. And so, practicing the same brand of deception he'd soon be called upon to use when he made contact with the revolutionaries, Simon repeated Durnovo's name aloud as if committing it to memory, then took the liberty of pouring himself another glass of champagne.

Irena read the long, rambling letter from Masha, half a dozen closely written sheets jammed into a faded, rose-colored envelope. "I'm not consumed by grief so much as by stoicism," she wrote, "because for a long time now, ever since that day, it's as if my heart had no more feeling than a peach pit. I gave up on crying, and sometimes I think I've even given up on all those other heartfelt emotions that go along with tears.

"Vera and I squabble endlessly. Now that the divorce decree has come through and she intends to go ahead with her plans to marry Sorokin, she came to me asking for a dowry, as if it were within my power to grant her whatever she wished. I reminded her that there's a famine beyond our gates, that we barely harvested enough grain to feed ourselves. She started to scream at me, saying I was giving everything away to the villagers, that I had no right using Father's money to set up a free kitchen and distribute clothing and firewood to the peasants. 'I want things, too!' she kept shouting, so that I finally rushed out of the room just to get her to stop."

Masha also wrote that it had become imperative to sell off some of the acreage, or they wouldn't have any money to run the household. She felt they had no choice and would see to it that they got the best possible terms.

Mulling over the details of the letter, and feeling guilty for leaving Masha to run the estate in her absence, Irena went into the nursery to say good-night to her boys.

"Isn't Papa coming in, too?" asked Andrei, who looked just like a cherub with his fat, rosy cheeks and tousled curls. "He said he would."

Irena leaned over her son's bed and kissed him on each cheek. Seriozha was already asleep in his crib, while the children's *nyanya* picked desultorily at her *broderie anglaise*. Making the sign of the cross over both her babies, and promising Andryushka that she'd send his papa in to kiss him good-night, Irena slipped out of the nursery and went directly to her husband's study, where she found Nikolai dressed and ready to go out.

"I'm expected at the Denishevs," he said in that same preoccupied tone of voice she'd noticed for the last several months, ever since he began working at the Communication Ministry. He twirled the tips of his waxed mustache, frowning as if he considered her presence an unwarranted intrusion. "They're at home this evening, and I promised to stop by. I'm sure it'll be the usual boring business discussion. But the Prince has done a great deal for me, so I mustn't let him think I'm unappreciative."

"Yes, of course. But I thought they received on Thursdays."

"It's been changed," Nikolai said hurriedly. "They find Tuesdays more convenient."

Irena straightened his white piqué tie, adjusted a pearl shirt stud, and stepped back to admire his elegant appearance, as it was only of late that he'd taken such an interest in his wardrobe.

"You needn't bother waiting up," he said at the door. "These affairs always run late. And the Minister himself might be there, in which case there's no telling when I'll be able to get away."

Irena gave him her cheek, then remembered that he hadn't gone into the nursery, as he'd done nearly every night since his sons were born.

"I'm sorry, dearest, but I'm terribly late as it is," he replied. "Besides, they're probably asleep by now." He let himself out, and without looking back started down the stairs.

Glad that she had her babies to look after, Irena hurried to their room, trying not to think about Niki and why he'd gone off without even asking her to join him.

Pauline was certain the only reason she was being sent away to school was because of the baby, that awful scrawny, squalling thing they said was her sister. So here she sat in the summerhouse, the shadows of the tangled, overgrown raspberries and the dark, murky green nettles making lovely patterns across her hands.

She wondered why they hated her so that they'd send her all the way to Moscow, a place she'd seen only in pictures but that she knew had to be as cold and heartless as her mother. They were just trying to get rid of her, that's what it was, just so they could spend all their time with the baby.

I bet they think it's my fault she's sick all the time. So they're sending me away so she'll get better.

Resolved never to come back, so that when her mother finally decided she missed her Pauline would be nowhere to be found, she came unhappily to her feet, tearing at the silky cobwebs that hung from the low, broken latticed ceiling. Wouldn't it be nice if she could wrap herself in them, and like the fairy tale of the princess who donned the cloak of invisibility, just disappear forever?

"Pauline!" she heard them crying. "Pauline, where are you, it's time to go!"

Maybe she could disappear right now, and like her real father, never be seen or heard from again. Sticking out her tongue, Pauline licked the cobwebs that hung down like pale, torn curtains, so finely spun she could see right through them. They tasted like dust, but melted in her mouth like sugar. Then she ripped down a spider web that had been there all last winter and then all last spring, with little balls of dead things hanging from it like ornaments on a Christmas tree. It was just as if the witch Baba-Yaga were touching her, she felt so slimy and unclean, like the time she'd gone swimming and a big black leech had stuck itself to her leg.

"Disappear," she said aloud, pressing the spider web all over her face, and shivering because it felt so creepy. "Make three wishes and disappear."

"Pauline, where are you?"

The voices were coming closer, Mother and Aunt Masha, who'd promised to take her all the way to Moscow, where they'd leave her and never come for her again.

The dusty threads clung to her eyes and nose, covering her hair like the net Granny always wore. "Wish one: I don't want to ever see them again because they don't love me. Wish two: I want to be with Granddad again. Wish three . . ."

"Pauline, what are you doing in there getting all dirty, you naughty girl?" Her mother clucked her tongue. "How could you be so inconsiderate when you know we're waiting?"

Sending Aunt Masha back to the house, because if they didn't hurry the train would leave without them, *maman* grabbed her by the hand and dragged her along, down the path through the still and golden orchard, where there was dew all day long on the sparse, yellowing grass. A flock of lapwings flew overhead, calling noisily now that they too were going away.

"What were you doing in there, princess?" asked her mother as she tried to wipe off the cobwebs.

"Thinking."

"About what?"

"About how you're sending me away just so you can be with Lizochka all the time."

Her mother stopped short and looked down at her, her nostrils opening and closing like the gills of a fish. "How could you even think such a thing?"

"I can think whatever I want. It's allowed."

"You take pleasure in hurting me, don't you? Haven't I

saved money for you all these years, just so you could have all the advantages?"

"You never told me what advantages were," Pauline said sullenly. "I looked it up in the dictionary once and it still didn't make sense."

Her mother let out with an exasperated sigh, grabbed her by the hand again, and hurried back to the house. Everyone was assembled in the courtyard, where all of Pauline's bags had already been loaded onto the carriage. Platon the coachman, a big, fat, merry old man who always smelled of vodka, was waiting alongside Grandfather's phaeton. He stood talking to the horses and rubbing their noses while everyone else gathered near the porch to wish her good-bye.

"Where's Granny?" she asked.

Before her mother could stop her, Pauline ran back into the house, heading straight for the kitchen. When she pushed the door open and stepped inside, she found Granny sitting at the table, taking deep breaths as if she too had been running.

"I came to say good-bye and tell you I love you," Pauline said.

The old housekeeper raised her grizzled head and smiled, showing her toothless gums. She slowly straightened up, shuffling across the kitchen as if she were too tired to lift her feet.

"Now you mustn't eat them all at once," Anninka urged, handing her a paper cone filled with mint gingerbreads, "'cause they're meant to last all the way to Moscow, my little darling. Now give Granny a kiss and then you'll be off."

"You'll be here when I come back, won't you?" she asked. "You won't go away like Granddad did?"

"Me, go away?" Anninka exclaimed with a laugh. "Not when I still have a few good years left, my precious. Granny'll be here come summer, you wait and see."

When Pauline came out of the house her mother was carrying Elizaveta in her arms, and the baby was crying just as she always did. "There, there," Vera kept saying to the infant, telling Pauline to step close and kiss her little sister good-bye.

"I don't want to," she said, loud enough so that everyone could hear, even Aunt Masha, whom she liked.

Her mother raised her one free hand as if she intended to hit her, only to change her mind and smile nervously. "Then say good-bye to your father, at least."

Rather than answer, she climbed into the carriage, clutching the paper cone Granny had given her, and wondered if the housekeeper would keep her promise and still be here when she returned.

"You be good now, you hear, little one," said her stepfather, yawning as he reached up to tousle her hair.

Pauline pulled away. She didn't want anyone to touch her, not now when they were sending her away just because she hated the baby.

"The little brat hates me," she heard Rodya say to her mother.

Then everyone, all the servants and their families and Granny too, and her mother and her stepfather, began to wave their hands, calling out "Christ be with you" and "God's angel keep you" and "May the Holy Mother care for you," until Aunt Masha joined her in the carriage and there was no excuse for Platon not to start.

Pauline sat very still as they drove off, looking down at the sticky cobwebs that still clung to the pleats of her sailor skirt, and hearing in the distance the peevish cries of her half sister. But when they passed the old yellow church where jackdaws cawed from high up in the cupola, and then the cemetery with its tin crosses painted to look like birch boughs and its fine stone monuments erected by the Petrovs, she put down the cone of gingerbreads and jumped to her feet.

Holding onto the edge of the seat so she wouldn't tumble out, Pauline raised her voice above the rattle of the carriage wheels. "I'll be good, really I will," she called out. "You'll see, Granddad, I'll be special, just like you always said."

Four

Although the *Theaters Annual* was considered a great artistic success, and even won the approval of the Tsar, it did little to enhance Gregor's reputation. For one, he'd exceeded the budget allocated him by some ten thousand rubles. For another, he'd provoked numerous officials, and was often forced to use Prince Orlovsky as a go-between. Gregor was charged with being overbearing and tactless, though by the autumn of 1893, accusations of a more scandalous nature had begun to circulate.

When Prince Orlovsky had appointed Gregor to the staff of the theater directorate, he'd done so at considerable risk to his own reputation. Now, a year later, he'd begun to have serious misgivings. These came out when he arrived at Gregor's apartment with a gaudily wrapped package he'd received earlier in the day. Inside, there was a pink powder puff and an anonymous note—"For you and Mademoiselle Petrova."

"Being talented and ambitious does have its disadvantages," the Prince said gently. "You've made many enemies,

Grisha. Nearly every day someone comes to me with one complaint or another. So I think for the time being it would be best if you put aside any thoughts of assisting me, and concentrated your efforts on the *Annual*."

"And what about us?" he asked.

The Prince's silence was answer enough.

"You've met someone, haven't you?"

"Grisha, don't be ridiculous. Of course I haven't met anyone. I haven't looked for anyone, either," Volodya replied in that cultured and well-modulated voice he used even when he was angry, for he wasn't the kind of man who ever allowed himself to lose his temper. "It's just that I have my position to think of, my reputation at court. I'm the Tsar's representative, and you know how imperative it is that scandal be avoided. I've given this a great deal of thought, and it's not something I find particularly pleasurable, I assure you."

Gregor, who'd been sitting in his favorite chair, now came to his feet. Leaning against his desk, he looked down at the Prince, as if that kind of insolent posture would give him a momentary advantage.

"So whatever we had is over, is that what you're trying to tell me?" he asked.

"And what did we have, may I ask?" replied the Prince. "You shared my bed one night a week, two at the most. In exchange I made sure . . . well," he broke off meekly, "that's not the important thing."

"What? That you gave me an allowance? I worked for it, didn't I? Editing the yearbook is an honorary appointment. I never received a salary, though God knows I deserved one."

The Prince, so sleek and elegant, gazed at him with something approaching sadness. "Grisha, you just don't understand the position you've put me in."

"You're a coward, Vladimir Danilovich, simply because you're letting rumor and innuendo get the better of you. You should have thrown that filthy thing away," motioning to the package the Prince had opened earlier, "and just dismissed it as a schoolboy prank."

"I'm not asking you to resign your position, Gregor. I'm merely suggesting you concentrate your efforts on the year-book and leave the running of the theaters to me. Don't you realize what's begun to happen? It's one thing to be a homosexual in the privacy of one's bedroom. But brought out into the open—flaunted, as it were—it could make things very unpleasant for both of us. People are talking, and what they're saying isn't at all complimentary."

"People have been talking about me for years. It's when they stop talking that it's time to get worried," he replied. "Besides, who are these *people*, may I ask, these nameless faces who have the audacity to tell us how to run our lives? If they knew that half the people involved in any one production were men of our persuasion, would they still flock to the theaters? Of course they would, because without men like us there'd be no Russian art of any value whatsoever."

"I didn't come here to listen to Gregor Petrov's homosexual proclamation."

"Then what did you come here for?" Gregor shouted.

The Prince came slowly to his feet, smoothing out the wrinkles in his trousers. "I came to say that we can still be friends."

"But not lovers?"

"I'm afraid we'd need a desert island for that."

After he'd shown Prince Orlovsky out Gregor returned to his study, where he slammed the door shut and flung himself into his favorite chair. So Petersburg was talking, was it? So the public was scandalized by his behavior, merely because he went to rehearsals and told Kchessinskaya, the Tsarevich's mistress, to try not to sneeze when she danced. So they thought him an upstart, did they? Well, perhaps they were right, because if you didn't fight for a place in society, no one would step aside to give you one.

He could understand all these things, and on a purely intellectual level even sympathize with them. But what he couldn't understand was the Prince's willingness to end a good relationship that had lasted almost three years. Was it simply because the public made no allowances for deviant behavior?

He stretched out on the leather sofa and closed his eyes.

If I were one of Dostoyevsky's characters, now would be the perfect time to suffer an attack of inflammation of the brain. I could lie here for weeks on end, feverish and delirious, while a steady stream of well-wishers came to pay their respects.

He imagined how they would all shake their heads sadly and point accusing fingers at Prince Orlovsky, who would remain in Gregor's favorite chair and never leave his side until the crisis passed and all was well again.

Instead of succumbing to a fictional illness, and all the histrionics that went along with it, Gregor went into his dressing room to change. Kostya Naryshkin would be calling for him within the hour, and he had no intention of canceling his engagement merely because he was suffering the shame of knowing he didn't have a broken heart.

Several weeks after Prince Orlovsky had come to see him, Gregor received a desperate call from his brother-in-law, who begged him to meet him at his office. Gregor took a cab to the Ministry, and when Volsky greeted him he knew there was trouble. Never before had he seen Niki so distraught, not to mention disheveled.

"I slept here last night," Volsky said, scratching nervously at the unshaven stubble on his cheeks. "And I suppose I'll have to sleep here tonight, as well."

Gregor screwed up his eyes in confusion and asked Volsky what he was talking about.

"You mean you haven't heard?"

"What?"

Volsky turned his eyes away, listening for a moment to the sounds that drifted up to his window. Whipped by the wind, the dark turbid waters of the Fontanka lashed high above the mooring rings, rattling the lanterns along the embankment. A chilly yellow mist swirled beyond the windowpanes, and when he turned back to face his brother-in-law, Volsky felt as grim and cheerless as the weather.

"It's all over between us," Volsky said. "It's ruined, destroyed. I've made a horrible mess of things, Grisha."

"You still haven't told me what you've done."

"I've behaved dishonorably, that's what. I've wounded the dearest woman in the world, the mother of my children. I've . . . oh Jesus," he broke off, shuddering violently as he pressed his head to his hands.

A moment later he felt Grisha's comforting hand on his shoulder, and after taking a deep, steadying breath, he told him what had happened. Irena had discovered that he'd been having an affair with Princess Denisheva and was now packing to leave for Petrovka, demanding a divorce in no uncertain terms.

For a minute or two Gregor didn't say anything. Then Volsky heard him laugh. "You and Larisa? Come now, surely you're not serious."

"Oh, but I am, I am," Volsky moaned. "You've got to help me, Grisha. Please, I beg of you. Speak to Irena before it's too late. If she leaves me I don't know what I'll do."

"You should've thought of that before . . . well, that's not my place to say. You'll have to break it off with Larisa, of course, and the sooner the better."

"I already have. I don't think it really bothered her, either.

She was probably getting bored with me. But don't you see, it was nothing, just an indiscretion that got out of hand, that's all it was. I never loved her. I didn't, Grisha, you must believe me. I never wanted to hurt your sister. Only now it's too late because she knows everything, and refuses to speak to me."

"How long did this *indiscretion* last?"

Ignoring the smug and somewhat condescending tone he heard in his brother-in-law's voice, Volsky admitted that it had gone on for more than a year. "Though we only saw each other once a week, twice at the most."

"Doesn't that sound familiar," Gregor said bitterly, not bothering to explain what he meant. "But how could you, Niki? Granted, she's a beautiful woman, and I could understand if it happened once. But to take a mistress—you, who's always professed to be a family man?"

"Don't criticize me, Grisha, please," he said, sobbing now. "You don't have to tell me what an idiot I am, because I already know that. Just talk to her. I'll do anything she asks, but I can't bear the thought of her leaving."

Irena heard the doorbell ring, then seven-year-old Andrei speaking tearfully. "Uncle Grisha, Uncle Grisha, they had had a terrible fight and *Mamochka* was crying and *Papochka* left and . . . and . . ." followed by her brother's soothing tones. "Come now, you're braver than that, old sport. Grown-ups do strange things sometimes, that's all it is. But everything'll be all right, Andryushka, I promise."

"How dare you stand there eavesdropping!" Irena shouted at Katya her maid, who'd been listening by the bedroom door. "Get on with your business and mind your manners. There are plenty of girls who'd like nothing better than to have your job, just remember that."

Katya flushed scarlet and mumbling an apology, returned to the packing of her mistress' clothes. Irena stormed about her bedroom, throwing open one drawer after another and hating herself for all the years she'd spent being the most calm and understanding of women, only to be taken advantage of in a way that left her defenseless, with no choice but to leave.

It wasn't that Nikolai had held another woman in his arms. But that he'd seen fit to lie to her, to deceive her at every turn, actually to take a mistress—and an aristocrat at that— was more than she could accept. Hadn't she been a perfect wife and mother, giving him the sons he'd always wanted? Hadn't they cared for each other, and hadn't they been friends as well as lovers? Then why had he gone out of his way to hurt her?

She said as much to her brother after he knocked timidly on the door and asked to be admitted. "So he's sent an emissary, has he? Well, you can tell him from me that he can send all the emissaries in the world and it still wouldn't do any good." She couldn't stop herself from trembling, and she slumped down at her dressing table, so depressed there didn't seem to be any reason to go on.

"He's terribly contrite, Irusha," her brother resumed. "He wept like a baby, I swear he did."

"Of course, because like a baby he'd like to have his way. Did he tell you that six months ago he promised never to see her again? No, I can see by your expression he said nothing of the kind." She described the scene they had had, after she'd followed him to an apartment the Princess maintained. "So don't think me rash, Gregor, because I'm not overreacting. I gave him his chance, and rather than break it off, he went back to her. What choice do I have? Surely you don't expect me to remain in the same house with him, do you?"

Gregor crossed the room and crouched before her. "He loves you, Irusha," her brother said softly.

Laughter caught in her throat. "Love? He doesn't even

401

know what the word means. He's risked everything, and for what? Is she that beautiful, or am I that unattractive?"

"Of course you're not. But men . . . losing his job and all, I'm sure he felt very vulnerable. But no matter what happened, Irena, you just can't turn your back on twelve years of marriage."

"Thirteen," she said, not about to lose count.

She stood up then, brushing her hands nervously across the skirt of her cashmere wrapper, and told him that maybe you had to be cruel to people to get any respect. Maybe that's what had taken her thirty-seven years to learn, that if you went out of your way to be nice, you'd always be taken advantage of.

"Will it make you any happier to go away?" asked her brother.

"No, not happier. But I see no reason to remain in Petersburg on my own. Andrei's tutor has expressed his willingness to accompany us. Petrovka will be a very nice change."

"Then there's no changing your mind?"

"None whatsoever," she said, very loudly and resolutely, so that if Nikolai were listening on the other side of the door he wouldn't have any trouble hearing her.

"Will you at least speak to him?"

She didn't know what to say, and so she looked all around at the half-opened drawers, and piles of clothes she still hadn't packed. So much needed to be attended to that she didn't know where to start.

"Allow him the opportunity to apologize," her brother said, still pleading Nikolai's case.

How sensible he's become all of a sudden, she thought. Now I'm the flighty one and Grisha's the man of the family. But Papa would be pleased, wouldn't he? Or perhaps he wouldn't even care. Yes, maybe that's what it's all about. Not caring. Nor permitting anyone to get too close, because if they do they'll only thrust in the knife.

Yet she nodded, agreeing to speak to her husband.

Gregor hurried from the room, and when the door opened again she found herself facing her contrite and woebegone spouse. For all his recent attention to sartorial splendor, there was nothing of the Petersburg swell about his appearance. Rather, Nikolai looked like a man who'd spent the night walking the streets.

"Lot of good your fancy waistcoats did you," she heard herself remark in a mean, spiteful voice that was as foreign to her as it must have been to him.

A single childish tear made its slow, mournful passage along the dark stubble of his cheek. "Please don't do this to me, Irusha," he begged, pleading in a voice that jumped from one octave to another.

"To *you!*" she shouted. "Don't do this to *you?* Why don't you think of what you've done to me and the children?"

"As God is my witness, I haven't stopped thinking of you, not for an instant."

"You never thought of me, Niki. You thought of yourself, and what a man you were, how you'd taken a mistress, just like a Grand Duke. Oh yes, I can see it all very clearly. The poor, downtrodden *chinovnik* suddenly blossoms into a man about town. Do you want to hear something funny? I'm almost inclined to feel sorry for you, that you've acted like such a fool."

He moved toward her, and with each hesitant step she drew back, not wanting to be near him, unable to tolerate his touch. When he reached for her hand she heard herself snarl like an animal caught in a trap.

Nikolai wept openly then, and sank down onto his knees, raising his hands imploringly, and embarrassing her with his obsequious display. This wasn't the man she'd married. The man she'd fallen in love with would never have been so

callow, nor would he ever have permitted himself to be
disloyal. And so even though he spoke at great length,
whimpering and rubbing at his runny nose and the tears that
continued to trickle down his unshaven cheeks, Irena wasn't
the slightest bit impressed.

When he told her he'd reform, that he'd learned his lesson
and would never again do anything to hurt her, she began to
laugh.

"How can you hate me so?" said Nikolai, a fresh wave of
tears welling up in his reddened eyes.

"It's very easy," Irena admitted sadly. "When you devote
your entire life to someone, when you bare your innermost
secrets to him, and have no defenses whatsoever because you
love him so, then you learn to trust him as much as you trust
yourself. But then when that person treats you like vermin,
someone to be used and lied to and deceived, then it's very
easy to hate."

Nikolai pulled himself upright, unable to look her in the
eye. "And the divorce?" he said, speaking in a whisper.

"I don't know yet. Perhaps six months or a year from now
I might feel differently. I don't think so, but I might."

"And after a year, Irusha, what then?"

"I don't know," she said again. "But right now I don't even
want to think about it."

Simon Belinsky was dead. In his place there arose Simon
Bazarov, a man who smiled good-naturedly when reminded
that he bore the same name as the ill-fated nihilist in
Turgenev's *Fathers and Children*. "An amusing coincidence, I
agree," he would say, grinning so that people were invariably
charmed by the youthful dimples that appeared in his cheeks,
"though I suspect Turgenev might have known a distant
relation of mine. Perhaps you've heard of him, Vasily
Bazarov? He was a close friend of several of the Decembrists,

and the only one of them who managed to avoid arrest. I believe he died in France, which is probably where Turgenev made his acquaintance. Quite a character, from all accounts."

Simon Bazarov was a character too, but one of such modesty and decency, such high principles and ethical standards, that he soon became a favorite of Moscow's Intellectual Aid Society, a group whose members were drawn from the most notable of the city's intelligentsia. These well-meaning men and women favored a constitutional monarchy and a parliamentary form of government modeled along British lines. They were far from dangerous, though the Okhrana thought otherwise. It was through this organization that Simon Bazarov first made his appearance, behaving very much the way a bona fide revolutionary might behave if he were anxious not to attract undue attention to himself. By involving himself in the society's activities, he gradually became known to those who had peripheral contact with the Social Democrats, the party that Zubatov wanted him to infiltrate.

To this end, he found a sympathetic associate in the person of Anna Abramovna. Small, dark, and intense, she was a young woman whose outspoken political views led him to believe she was much closer to the revolutionary leadership than she let on. For six months he played his part with all the conscientiousness of a dedicated thespian, never allowing her—or anyone else, for that matter—to see the man who actually lived beneath Bazarov's skin.

Utterly taken in by every aspect of his performance, Anna Abramovna not only agreed to take him to a clandestine meeting, but was also amenable to his suggestion that she move in with him. Thus, in a relatively short period of time, Simon not only took a mistress, but also established himself as someone who could be trusted, having done absolutely nothing to arouse anyone's suspicion.

The winter snows were melting, and everywhere one looked there were porters out on the streets, scattering yellow sand onto the footpaths and pavements. City workers cleared the snow with their flat wooden shovels, piling it up in great shapeless masses and then lighting bonfires to make it melt. The fires shone brightly through the darkness when Simon and Anna Abramovna took a streetcar to the brothel district near Trubnaya Square, where the meeting was to be held.

The bells of Moscow's countless churches sang out in the chill night air, the rattle of the horse-drawn tram adding its voice as it hurried through the streets. Sitting near the front platform, Simon calculated the moves he would make. He would say nothing unless called upon to speak, so that while declaring himself to be sympathetic to their cause, he'd in no way force his presence on the party's leaders.

"*Trubnaya Ploshchad!*" the driver called out.

Waiting until Anna got to her feet, for he didn't want to appear too eager, Simon followed after her, drawing his mangy beaver collar up around his neck and ears. The driver flicked the reins, and the white-hooded horses continued on their way.

Anna kept up a steady stream of conversation as she led him across the empty square, as it was only on Sunday mornings that the Trubnaya teemed with life. Then it was filled with peddlers, and nowhere else in Moscow could one find a better selection of household pets.

"You should see it then," she said. "They set up an arcade where the bird-catchers trade. From a distance you'd swear you were hearing a music box, the way the finches and nightingales love to sing."

Leaving the square behind them, they followed a succession of identical-looking alleys, each as tortuous as the next. But when they reached Grachovka Street, and Anna pointed out the house where the meeting was being held, Simon felt as if the wind were suddenly knocked out of him. Hurriedly stepping back into the shadows, he clutched his stomach and began to groan.

Anna's lively dark eyes opened wide, and judging from her expression one would have thought he'd been shot. "Senya, what's the matter?"

"I don't . . . it's . . ." He didn't say anything else, but doubled up as if he were in terrible pain. Yet even as he pretended to be ill, Simon kept his eyes riveted on the passerby he'd noticed a moment before. Only when the man disappeared into the same building Anna had just shown him, did he slowly straighten up.

"What's wrong?" she kept saying. "Senya, are you all right?"

"No, it's . . . terrible cramps," he told her, making it sound as if he could barely get the words out. "I don't think I can—"

Anna held onto his arm to steady him. "Come, we're taking you home," she said in that same authoritative voice she used at meetings.

Simon gritted his teeth. "That's . . . best," he managed to say. "It'll pass, but . . . oh Jesus, I'm in agony."

Anna Abramovna led him back the way they'd come, Simon clutching his stomach and taking care to pause every few feet as if he were in too much pain to keep up with her. Actually, he was in pain, though it was purely mental. He was trying to figure out what to do now that he'd finally laid eyes on Victor Durnovo, the one man who could expose him, and by so doing, ruin everything he'd spent the last six months trying to achieve.

"Doctors!" Vera exclaimed. "They know nothing, absolutely nothing at all."

A succession of medical experts and so-called specialists

came and went, each prescribing a different course of treatment. But Elizaveta continued to cry from morning till night, steadily losing weight though she hardly weighed anything at all. Bathed in bouillon, she cried for hours on end. Given linden-flower tea, and then a decoction of dried raspberries, she perspired profusely and sobbed until dawn. Anninka recommended melted sheep's fat in boiling milk, with a homemade tallow candle stirred up in the milk until only the wick was left. Elizaveta took one swallow and began to cry worse than before. More doctors came, several from as far away as Orel, and additional bottles of medicine made their appearance in the nursery, crowding against each other like a display of nostrums in a pharmacist's window.

"Colic," declared the midwife from the village, and suggested dosing the baby with laurel drops to get her to sleep.

Elizaveta slept soundly for several hours, but awoke crying, unable to keep her food down. Vera didn't know what to do, and walked back and forth across the nursery with Lizochka in her arms, crooning to the baby as she sobbed and churned at the air with her tiny little hands. Liza was so beautiful that to see her features all twisted up, and her sallow cheeks always wet with tears, tore at Vera's insides as nothing had before. She began to bargain with God, agreeing to any of His demands so long as her baby got well.

"She's so helpless, You must do something for her," Vera kept saying, so that when Irena came into the nursery she was surprised to find her sister alone.

"Let me have her for a while, and you try to get some sleep," said Irena.

"No, I don't want anyone to hold her. That's why she's so sick, because everyone's touching her and handling her and she doesn't know what to make of all these strange faces. There, there, Lizochka, my little duchess. There, Mama's here, and Mama'll stay."

"Vera, you're exhausted."

"Go away, just go away and leave us alone," Vera said angrily, pressing the swaddled infant to her breast and rocking the still and seemingly lifeless bundle until plaintive cries were heard and Elizaveta began to sob anew.

Vera didn't want any interference. She would stay here until summer if necessary, afraid that if she let the baby out of her sight for even an instant, something dreadful might happen and she'd only have herself to blame. So at night she remained in the nursery, ignoring Rodya's pleas to come to bed. She'd already discharged the nurse they had hired, refusing to give the woman the money that was due her, and even going so far as to accuse her of contaminating her child and bringing on the spells of colic.

Now Vera was alone, with only Lizochka to worry about. She sat in a chair, holding her daughter in her arms, and remembering what Anninka had said when she'd given birth to Elizaveta. "Not a mark on her," the old woman had announced after examining the baby. "Not a single mole or devil's mark upon which malice can fasten."

Then why was the baby so sick all the time? Was God punishing Vera, testing her faith? Was He angry at her for always thinking of herself, trying to change the provisions of her father's will, sending Pauline off to school?

"Eat," whispered Vera. "Please, Lizochka. You wouldn't take my milk or the nurse's milk, so try this."

She held the nursing bottle with the rubber nipple up against the baby's beautiful little lips. Lizochka opened her mouth, but after one or two feeble sucks she tried to push it away by shaking her head, and whatever goat's milk she'd managed to take only dribbled down her chin.

"You have to eat or else you'll never grow up. You can't stay a baby all your life. God knows I tried," and Vera laughed and laughed, hoping Lizochka would laugh too.

Instead, the baby began to squall and then to cough. Vera held her up against her chest, patting her gently on the back. The coughing only got worse and so she laid the infant down in her little reed cradle that was trimmed with real Valenciennes lace and lined with baby-blue satin, the very finest money could buy.

Such a pretty sight she was, if only she wouldn't cry. Vera got out the cherry laurel, carefully measuring five drops, and then adding a sixth for good measure. The baby swallowed the medicine without having to be coaxed, and soon she was sound asleep. Vera was gradually overcome by exhaustion as she watched over her, and, returning to the chair, she leaned back and closed her eyes.

When she awakened it was already dark outside, though the overhead lamp had been lit so that the nursery was suffused with a bright and cheery glow. How still it was, so quiet she could even hear a bird calling somewhere in the darkness. She went over to the cradle, smiling to see her baby sleeping so peacefully.

"You're Mama's precious little duchess," she whispered as she gently lifted Liza in her arms, then rocked her back and forth. "Someday you'll have everything, just like your sister Pauline. My two little princesses. Oh yes, you'll be a great beauty, and marry into a noble family. Wouldn't you like that, my darling?"

How still she was, so small and frail and still. Vera straightened the child's tiny, close-fitting cap that Anninka had embroidered with dainty sprigs of flowers.

"Oh, but you're cold," she said, clucking her tongue, and chiding herself for not having realized it until now. "Don't you worry, Mama will warm you. Yes, Mama will keep you nice and warm."

She sat down again, holding Lizochka on her lap, and gazing at her daughter's delicately modeled face, the skin as pale and translucent as the finest china. How quiet she was; why, she hardly made a sound, lying there fast asleep.

The nursery door opened softly and Rodya stepped inside. His fair hair lay in tousled curls across his large white forehead, and with a lusty yawn to proclaim he'd put in an honest day's work and now deserved a rest, he smiled and walked on tiptoes, not wanting to awaken the baby.

"How is she?" he asked, speaking in a whisper.

Vera looked up and smiled dreamily. How still it was. Yes, the silence was a lovely thing. It hadn't been this quiet in months, but now there wasn't a sound to be heard.

"Vera?"

"Shh," she whispered. "Shh."

"Vera, let me have the baby."

"What?"

"The baby. Let me hold the baby."

"No."

"Vera," he said, raising his voice.

"No, go away. You'll wake her. See how nicely she sleeps. Oh yes, my little duchess is very tired, aren't you, Lizochka? Oh yes, she's so tired, so sleepy. But Mama's here, isn't that so?" she said in a lilting voice, rocking the still little bundle she held tightly in her arms.

Rodya reached down to take it away from her and Vera drew her lips back, hissing like a cat.

"Just let me hold her for a moment. Please, she's my daughter too, Vera." Rodya bent down and put his fingers to the baby's lips, holding them there for a moment. Then he put his ear to her chest, listening to the silence.

Vera wondered what he was doing, and tried to push him away before Liza awoke and began to cry.

"Oh no," Rodya said in a voice Vera heard from far, far away, like a bird calling out on the steppe. "Oh God in heaven!" he cried out. "Vera, please, give her to me. You've got to."

"Go away, just go away and leave us alone. Isn't that so, duchess? Isn't that so, my little sweetheart?" and she continued to rock the baby in her arms, even as Rodya hurried from the nursery.

When he returned it was with Irena. Vera looked at them as if through a cloudy mirror, and didn't understand why they were here. Couldn't they see that her blessed little angel was fast asleep?

"Vera, you must give me the baby now," Irena said in a scarcely audible voice.

She looked up at her older sister and didn't understand.

"Give me the baby now," Irena said again.

"Why should I want to give you the baby?" she replied, her shrill cries breaking the stillness she'd found so pleasant and restful. "You can't take her away from me. She's asleep. She's fast asleep, my little duchess."

"Vera, my love," whispered Irena, dropping down onto her knees and reaching out for the baby with both hands. "Vera, look at me."

"No, I don't want to."

"Vera, the baby is dead," Irena said.

"Go away!" she shouted. "Just go away and leave us alone. Can't you see how happy we are? Can't you see how sweet she looks, just like one of God's little angels?" She began to sing, crooning softly.

Rodya reached down to take Lizochka away from her. She smashed her hand across his face, spitting at him and pushing herself back against the chair.

"Vera, I beg of you," her husband pleaded, his calm and placid brown eyes now filled with dread. "The baby is dead. We did everything we could for her."

"Dead? No, she's not dead. How can you even say such a thing? She's asleep, that's all, just fast asleep."

But then they took Lizochka away from her. She tried to stop them, but Rodya held her down in the chair while Irena gently but firmly pried her hands away from the baby.

"You're still young, Vera," said her sister. "You can have another."

Vera heard her, but only faintly. She clutched both arms of the chair and stared straight ahead, not at the ikons that faced her from across the room, but at something all dark and mysterious, as uncertain as fog. It was a shapeless creeping terror that grew and grew and grew until she began to scream, and couldn't stop herself, and didn't even want to try.

On Easter Eve, the villagers of Petrovka, and all of the Petrov family as well, made their way to the churchyard after the midnight service. In every hand a little taper burned, surrounded by a collar of brightly colored paper as protection against the wind. At the cemetery, eggs of painted porcelain were hung upon the arms of the crosses, that the dead wouldn't be excluded from Christian rejoicing. But for the Petrov sisters there was little cause for joy that year. Vera was inconsolable. She drifted into and out of reality like a boat tossed about at sea, and when she threw herself down on Liza's grave, clawing at the freshly dug mound of earth, her husband had to lift her up in his arms and carry her away.

"If only she'd have another child," said Irena, "she might be able to find herself again."

"How changed she is," Masha agreed. "When she acted like a spoiled little girl it was much better than seeing her like this. And I don't like seeing you this way, either."

Irena pretended not to hear, but gazed at her parents' graves, and the identical black marble crosses that were erected over each of them. There had been talk of a more substantial monument, an impressive stone tomb in which Sophia Mikhailovna and Peter Semyonovich would be permanently interred. But nothing had come of it, and so here they lay, with the delicate porcelain eggs glowing faintly in the light of the slender candle she held in her hand.

"They never did find Laska, did they?"

"What a strange thing to ask," said Masha.

Irena shrugged. "It just came into my head. I think she loved that little dog more than she loved us."

The boys had run on ahead, an elaborate supper awaiting them at home. Now, as Irena took the path that led back to Petrovka, she felt none of the pleasure and sense of inner peace she'd always experienced at Eastertime. Even the service, and the joyous songs of the choir, had failed to lift her spirits. When the men and boys had sung "Rejoice, O ye people!" she'd wanted to get down on her knees and weep that she had so little to be thankful for. But no, she had her sons, and they alone comforted her as nothing else could.

"It's been nearly six months, Irena," her sister reminded her. "Hasn't he suffered enough?"

"Have you suffered enough?" Irena said sharply. When Masha didn't answer, Irena went on. "He betrayed a sacred trust. Am I supposed to play the fool for the rest of my life, just turn the other cheek and allow him to continue whipping me?"

"Then divorce him," Masha blurted out. "But don't pretend you're making him suffer when you know you're making yourself suffer just as much."

White spring fog hung low to the ground, drifting across the barren fields, where little hillocks of half-frozen manure released their pungent, earthy scent. The air was alive with the promise of rebirth and the joyous remembrance of Christ's resurrection.

"But I don't want a divorce," Irena said when they reached the lime alley and the lights of Petrovka shone brightly through the darkness. "Don't you see, I still love him. I'm just not certain if he loves me."

With the smoke from her taper, Anninka had traced a faint yet recognizable cross above the door. She came out into the porch to greet them and exchange the traditional Easter kiss.

"Christ is risen!" the *nyanya* called out, a scent of vanilla clinging to her black alpaca dress.

"Yes, He is indeed," replied Irena, and pressing her lips to the old woman's cheek, Irena couldn't help but wonder where Niki was tonight, and if he missed her half as much as she missed him.

Reluctant to take any unnecessary risks, and certain the Okhrana's Moscow headquarters was being carefully watched, Simon sent a message to Zubatov's home, requesting a meeting with him. As they wandered through the recently constructed bazaar in the Red Square, ignoring the bearded merchants who shouted at them to come and admire their wares, Simon explained what had happened, telling Zubatov that he was convinced he'd met Durnovo while living in the Presnia, although he'd known him under a different name. But now that Durnovo had been pointed out to him— this being the story he'd concocted—he was afraid the man might recognize him and destroy his carefully assumed cover.

"How odd," said Zubatov, peering at him curiously from behind his tinted spectacles. "None of the reports I've read indicated anything of the sort. But I see your point, of course. Were he to recognize you, there'd be no way you could continue with the assignment."

"I've managed to find out where he lives," Simon went on. He followed Zubatov down a long, brightly lit corridor where hundreds of people were strolling, pausing at the numerous trading stalls that rented space in the huge sandstone building. "I suppose you'll have to decide what you want done with him."

"Alive, he might prove very useful, especially if we can get him to open up to us. Dead, he's just another body to dispose of. And when he's buried, we'll be burying all the information he could provide us with."

"Do you want me to be in on the operation?"

"No, I don't think it's necessary. Just tell me where we can find him, and we'll handle it from there."

Durnovo was living in the Khitrovka, the worst slum in all of Moscow, and one that made the Presnia seem cozy and hospitable by comparison. It was an area of crumbling stone houses spread over a vast square in the heart of the city near the Yauza River, where five-kopeck-a-night flophouses, gambling dens, brothels, and shabby *traktiri* catered to the very dregs of humanity. Here, tens of thousands scrabbled for a living, crowding the tortuous alleyways, where at every corner one might find ten- and eleven-year-old girls selling themselves for half a ruble. Beggars—many carrying babies rented out at twenty-five kopecks for the day—left here each morning to fan out across the city, the infants they had hired to arouse the sympathy of passersby usually dead by the time they returned at nightfall.

It was here that Victor Durnovo had found shelter. A man could lose himself in this wretched labyrinth of narrow foggy streets, easily eluding the authorities. That was precisely what Victor had in mind, for he had no intention of being sent back to Siberia, not after having spent nearly ten years there. He'd served out his initial sentence only to learn that the government had additional plans for him, plans that called for another five years of exile on the grounds that he was still "politically untrustworthy," and therefore a serious threat to the welfare of the empire.

Armed with false papers and an assumed name, he'd

managed to make his way back into European Russia, that area of the empire west of the Ural Mountains. He survived through the kindness of his political associates, as well as by working as a copyist, copying plays for fifty kopecks an act.

Despite all that he'd suffered, Durnovo was still a moderate, dedicated to the overthrow of autocracy but only through peaceful means. In this he wasn't alone, many of his fellow Social Democrats equally opposed the use of violence, believing that acts of terrorism only served to undermine the goals of the movement. Yet this moderate wing of the party was fast losing ground and, though Victor was always vocal in his beliefs, he knew that a time would come when men like him would be in the minority, and perhaps even considered politically suspect themselves by their former comrades.

As he headed home that evening, the noise of the Khitrov market surged forward like a tidal wave. He heard drunken shouts, cries for help, an endless wailing that was the dirge of poverty, from which there seemed no escape. Yet there must be an escape, he realized. Men could not continue to live like this forever. Human nature would surely rebel, if only there were someone to lead them into battle.

Climbing the stairs of the shelter where he rented space on a wooden shelf for six kopecks a night, Victor decided it was time to take chances again. There were limits to anonymity, for a man must retain something of his own identity if he was ever to survive. Perhaps he might be able to find work in the Presnia. Even Siberia hadn't been half as wretched as this, with the stink of urine following him up the stairs, and a roomful of wasted lives to greet him when he reached the landing.

Dozens of men pressed against each other like corpses in a mass grave. Ever so carefully he made his way to an empty spot at the end of the long, narrow room, trying not to step on the bodies that were curled up under their rags. One group slept directly on the floor, and those who had an extra kopeck to spend, on a sloping wooden platform a few feet higher.

But he'd barely crossed the room when a dozen or so of the inmates began to stir, rising up like specters in the light of the single oil lamp burning dimly overhead. Victor started to stretch out on his bunk when he suddenly realized the attention he was creating, the raggedly dressed men all staring at him intently.

Something was wrong. Despite their shabby clothes, they all looked like outsiders, too alert for men who were accustomed to drinking themselves into a stupor.

He edged back along the bunk, knowing the only exit was the way he had come. The men stepped closer, and no sooner did one of them utter his name than he knew they were *Okhranniki,* since no one else would have called him Durnovo. He wasted no time shoving aside the nearest slat, then threw himself into the opening, drawing the board shut behind him.

Here in the fetid darkness below the platform, men groaned and tossed about in their sleep, and the air was filled with the nauseating stench of vomit and excrement. He pulled himself along, crawling over the densely packed bodies that slept on the floor, while the "outside agents" of the Okhrana, disguised as residents of the district, shouted instructions to each other, their rapid footfalls echoing above his head.

A board was pulled aside a few yards away. Victor fell face down on one of the men who was trying to sleep and not the least bit interested in finding out what was happening. Things like this took place all the time, and a man could lie here dead for days on end, knifed in the back for the few kopecks he might have in his pocket, to be discovered only when the smell became unbearable.

Victor held his breath, pretending to sleep even as the man below him tried to push him aside. Only when the bunk board was shoved back in place did he continue to inch his way along, trying to make it to the door. But when he finally reached the end of the crawl space, he saw that his escape route was blocked, several of the agents standing by the stairs. Either he could wait here all night, and try to make his way to freedom in the morning, when the shelter dumped its human refuse back onto the streets, or he could try to charge past them and hope for the best. As he lay there on the floor, cheek by jowl to a man who snored so loudly Victor could hardly hear himself think, he decided that if he tried to slip away now he'd at least have the advantage of darkness to aid him in his escape.

He drew himself up into a crouch, when the loud, guttural snoring stopped abruptly, and something came down across the back of his head. As he slumped forward, he heard his neighbor shouting, "Here, the bastard's over here!" Then he didn't hear anything else, not until someone tapped him on the shoulder and said, "Welcome to Butyrky Prison."

For days now Andrei and his brother had been on tenterhooks, knowing that their father was finally coming home. What might happen was anybody's guess, though Sergei, who was nearly four and certain he was well on his way to becoming a man, had it all figured out.

"First, Papa will say, 'I love you, Mama.' Then Mama will smile and say, 'Papa, do you really mean that, really truly?' And Papa will play with his mustache and say that on his honor as a gentleman, he loves Mama as much as we do."

Andrei looked up at him from where he was playing on the floor of the empty ballroom, surrounded by a toy railroad station and a train that moved around on a little metal track. He decided that the cardboard figure of the man with the big brown suitcase was his father, and he took him off the train and set him down on the platform. Now where was the figure that would be Mother?

"Did you steal it, Seriozha? I bet you did." With a suspicious glance at his younger brother's bulging pockets, he grabbed Sergei by the shoulders and gave him a good shake, ordering the little boy to give it back.

"I won't. I want it. You can't make me," said Sergei in a whining voice, completely forgetting that just a few minutes before he'd announced he was as much a man as his brother. "Let me ring the station bell and then I'll give it to you, I promise."

"Baby," said Andrei, as if being younger was just about the most contemptible thing in the world. He was certain that other boys his age didn't have to suffer baby brothers the way he did, always having to drag Seriozha along with him wherever he went. Mother wouldn't even let him go swimming down by the river with the boys from the village, because Seriozha didn't know how to swim and started to whimper at the thought of being left home alone.

Yes, there was nothing more difficult than being eight years old. Why, that was twice as old as Seriozha. Then why wasn't he twice as tall? Sometimes even the simplest things didn't make sense, Andrei thought as he got down on his knees again, warning his brother not to ring the bell too hard or else he'd break it.

The French doors were opened wide, and sounds from the yard carried into the room. It was Sergei, trying to divert his brother's attention from the fact that he'd just broken off the tiny clapper of the bell despite all warnings to the contrary, who suddenly jumped to his feet and ran out onto the terrace. Standing at the very edge of the veranda, and ready to risk a jump into the nettles just to be the first one to reach his father's side, the little boy shouted at the top of his voice.

"He's here! He's here! Andryushka, come quick, it's Papa!"

Having given his brother fair warning, Sergei threw himself down the broken stairs, tripping over his feet in his haste to race across the dusty courtyard.

"Papa! Papa!" he kept crying, and if he had had a cap he would have waved it in the air, he felt so happy.

Volsky, descending from the carriage with the grim uncertainty of a man who didn't know what tomorrow might bring, suddenly let lose with a roar and charged the boys like a raging bull. Grabbing them up, one in each arm, he held them aloft and kissed them again and again, squeezing Seriozha so hard that the little boy finally wriggled free of his father's joyous embrace.

"Oh Papa, we missed you so. It's been years, years and years and years," said Seriozha, as tears tumbled down his rosy cheeks.

"It was months, nine months and a little more," said his older brother. "But it seemed like years, Papa, really it did."

Volsky kept looking from one to the other, so delighted he didn't know what to say. They both seemed to have grown so tall it was hard to recognize them. Had it really been only nine months? No, it had to have been longer than that, for they'd fairly sprung up like weeds.

"And your mama, how is she?" he asked. "Did she miss me, do you think?"

Sergei stared glumly at his feet and the shoes he'd scuffed even though his mother had made him promise to be careful. "I don't know, Papa. I hope so," he said, his voice squeaky now, as if it were much too difficult to talk of grown-up things.

"Welcome home, Niki."

Volsky looked up with a start, and his heart twisted so that he couldn't breathe. He held out his hands for her, grateful she didn't shame him in front of the boys by refusing this simple embrace. Clutching both her hands in his, he gazed at her as if he'd never seen her before.

The familiar scent of Irena's White Rose perfume drifted toward him like an unspoken invitation. He stepped closer, pleased to see how she didn't pull away.

"Your father and I have many things to talk about," Irena told her boys.

"They don't want us around," Andrei said knowledgeably, taking his little brother by the hand. He marched Sergei back to the house, where both of them went through the motions of play. Actually, they were holding their breath, terrified that something might go wrong and Papa would drive off without even being allowed to say good-bye.

For more than a week Volsky acted like a guest who wasn't certain if he'd overstayed his welcome. Having left his fancy waistcoats back in Petersburg, his *pommade* as well, he came downstairs for breakfast each morning with a look of woeful insecurity, as if the act of buttering his toast were fraught with danger. It was Masha who advised him to take things slowly, to woo back his wife with loving patience and kindness. With the boys in tow, they went on picnics and other "expeditions" Anninka saw fit to organize, and gradually he began to feel less self-conscious in Irena's presence, though no more confident about his chances than when he'd first arrived.

On one such afternoon they managed to slip away on their own, and drove out toward the birch wood Peter Semyonovich had been forced to sell just before his death. Volsky, casting surreptitious glances at his wife as she sat beside him, felt the thrill of doing something forbidden, something that made his skin break out in gooseflesh as he drove the little two-wheeled carriage down the rutted road. He wasn't quite sure what it was, but the way Irena sat so close to him, the lovely yellows of her dress, and the tendrils of hair that fell along the back of her beautiful white neck, all combined to make him tremble. He couldn't resist putting his arm around her waist, then drawing her gently toward him.

"Forgive a silly fool who loves you desperately," he said, the words coming not from his lips so much as from his soul. "I thought I needed excitement. I thought I was getting old and staid, Irusha, and it frightened me. I'm not saying that to make excuses, because nothing in the world can excuse what I've done. But if I've hurt you, and I know I have, think how terribly I've hurt myself, by wounding all that's dear to me."

Irene gazed at him silently, then turned her head away, the willful tendrils of rich brown hair at her nape fluttering as if caught by a breeze. But a moment later she pressed her hand to her mouth, and a look of horror came into her eyes.

The birch wood spread out before them, but it was no longer a wood, just a collection of stumps that stretched far into the distance, so barren and forlorn she couldn't help but feel uneasy.

"He was luckier than he thought," his wife said when she found her voice. "It would have killed him to see it like this, Niki. He loved it here as much as I did. And now—" She waved her hand weakly in the air. "Please, let's turn around. I want to remember it as it was, not what it's become."

A year before Volsky might have laughed at her, and called her hopelessly sentimental. But somehow he understood her feelings now. Oddly grateful for that knowledge, that awareness of what mattered to her, he turned the gig around and started back the way they'd come.

Irena looked once more at what remained of the birch wood, and though her eyes were dry he knew she was crying. He drew in the reins and paused in the middle of the road, the faint honeyed scent of a vanishing summer sprinkled like pollen on the wind. A crane cried sadly overhead, and the roadside lindens stood motionless in the heat of the afternoon. Then a greenfinch called from the weeds, singing of summer's promises and summer's end.

"I'll stay here with you if you'll let me," Volsky said. "I know what the land means to you now, and if that's what's important, I won't turn my back on it and pretend it doesn't exist. I'll stay if you want me to, Irena."

"No, I don't want you to stay," she said.

Volsky drew himself back, stunned by her rejection.

"No," she said, seeing the look of anguish that came into his eyes, "you don't understand. I can't make you love Petrovka. Your future isn't here, and you know that as well as I do. So next week we'll pack, and then we'll all go home together."

He was so grateful, he didn't know what to do first. Drawing her up in his arms, Volsky held her close, nuzzling her soft and fragrant hair. That such a treasure had now been confided to his care was something he swore he'd never forget.

"We'll grow old and happy together," he laughed. But then he turned serious, and still holding her gently in his embrace, he said, "You must remind me of this day, Irena. You mustn't ever let me forget. A man matures not by the amount of gray in his hair, or the wrinkles on his face, but by the weight of his responsibilities, and the commitments he makes to those he loves. And I do love you, Irena Petrovna, more than I've ever allowed myself to realize."

They drove home through the golden dusk of summer, and when the boys ran out into the yard to greet them, one look and they knew that all was well again, and that once more they were a family.

Book Four

1899 = 1903

One

When Henriette arrived at Petrovka in the spring of 1899, she had been gone nearly twenty years. The tall and bony girl who'd often lamented her red nose and frizzy hair had grown into a stiffly erect woman of forty-two, her posture as rigid and inflexible as her personality. *La Belle Henriette,* however, was still wrapped in the soft down of daydreams. Known to her circle simply as Countess Ignatieva's companion, she'd made her reputation among that set that found comfort in talk of the hereafter, spirit guides, and messages from the beyond. Young men didn't come to the Countess' house on the French Quay, begging to see their beloved Henriette, nor was her box at the theater filled with handsome admirers, jostling each other in their eagerness to kiss her hand. In truth, she was still very much the Henriette of old, yet to totally cast off those insecurities that had plagued her as a girl.

But now she would make a grand and dramatic entrance, a gesture of defiance to the little bully who'd forced her to leave home so many years before. "Drive around to the back," she called out, tugging at the cord attached to the driver's elbow. She could scarcely believe her eyes and looked around in confusion, astonished to see how shabby everything had become.

Surely I never lived here, she thought. Why, it's so small, and poor-looking.

The green iron-sheeted roof was red with rust, and several of the windows must have been broken, as they were now boarded up. Even the lime alley, which had always been beautifully maintained, was now overgrown with weeds. A number of trees had fallen, a wild growth of elders, monkshood, and nettles having sprung up around their broken and lifeless trunks. Only the old stone church, which came into view as the *isvostchik* drove into the rear courtyard, looked the same as it had years before, with the thatched roofs of the village clustered nearby.

And where was the tumultuous welcome she'd planned for herself? Why wasn't Anninka hurrying from the kitchen to greet her, calling out to Masha and Vera to come quick, their beloved sister was home at last, back in the bosom of her family? Instead, all she heard was the driver, talking to himself as he drew in the reins and the creaking droshky rolled to a stop.

"Petrovka it is," said the driver, jumping down from his seat to unload her baggage.

A few scrawny hens pecked miserably in the dust, squawking loudly as Henriette crossed the yard and opened the kitchen door, certain that everything would soon be as it should once she saw Anninka. But instead of finding her old *nyanya*, the kitchen was empty. Suddenly a bell rang out. She gave a little gasp and hurriedly set down her bags. It was as if she'd been gone just a few days, and *maman* was still upstairs, calling to her fretfully and ringing her bell.

Henriette walked through the dining room whose floor no longer gleamed, then slowly mounted the stairs that creaked noisily beneath her feet. Again she heard the tinkle of the bell.

"I'm coming, I'm coming, for goodness sake," she called out, recognizing in her loud and strident voice the Henriette of old, who used to mount these stairs ten and twenty times a day, completely at her mother's beck and call.

But *maman* was dead, and recalling how she hadn't come for the funeral, she trembled as the bell kept ringing. Who could it be? she wondered as she walked down the hall to her mother's room, then knocked softly and let herself in.

The curtains were drawn, and for a moment she couldn't see who it was that lay in her mother's bed. But then, as Henriette's eyes grew accustomed to the greatly diminished light, she made out a woman with coarse yellow hair and a sharp little chin.

"Vera, is that you?" Although she knew it was her sister, she couldn't think of anything else to say.

"Go away," came the weak and dispirited reply. "I don't want anyone to see me like this."

"It's Henriette. I've come home to see you," she said with forced gaiety as she came near and looked down at her younger sister, finding it difficult to believe this was the same spoiled little Verochka whose beauty she'd envied for so many years.

"Henriette? Henriette lives in Petersburg."

"Yes, but I've come home to see you," she repeated, though in truth that was hardly the case.

She pulled the curtains back, the better to see her sister, and perhaps even to take a perverse pleasure in what had happened to her.

So old, Henriette thought as light streamed into the room, scattering its rays across the faded French wallpaper, upon which cracked and peeling bouquets of roses sadly unfurled their withered petals.

"But you were so much younger," Vera said as Henriette sat down on the edge of her mother's enormous bierlike bed. "You can't be . . . but I was younger, too." Vera picked up the hand mirror that lay alongside her, examining her reflection in the waning afternoon light. With a terrified sob she flung the mirror down, and pressing both hands to her face, began to weep.

"Now why are you crying, Vera? Aren't you glad to see me? And why are you in bed? Haven't you been feeling well?"

Vera gulped loudly, making antlers of her fingers and then peering at Henriette from between the prongs. With a strangely disturbing giggle, Vera said, "You still have terrible hair, Henriette. I always had the nicest hair of all of us, didn't I? Oh, it was lovely, so soft and golden. Remember how pretty I looked at the wedding? Why, they said there wasn't a prettier bride in three provinces."

Vera's features suddenly crumbled from within, and a network of wrinkles spread across her cheeks and forehead. She pulled herself up until she was leaning against the pillows, staring at Henriette accusingly.

"You never liked me, did you?" Vera exclaimed. "That's why you came back, isn't it, just to gloat. And that's why they put me in *maman's* old room, to punish me for being bad."

"You mustn't say such things, Vera. I would never wish you harm, you know that."

"That's what they all say, but I don't believe them."

Henriette was about to reply when she heard someone coming up the stairs. She straightened up, patting Vera on the hand. When Henriette stepped into the hall, Masha cried out in surprise and rushed into her arms, embracing her so warmly that for a moment Henriette was overcome by her sister's affectionate welcome. But after they'd spoken to each other for several minutes, Henriette glanced in the direction of the bedroom, gesturing with her eyes.

Masha nodded, motioning Henriette to follow her downstairs.

"Why didn't you ever write and tell me?" she asked when Vera was out of earshot.

"Would it have mattered?" Masha replied, though she said this in such a neutral tone of voice that Henriette knew she wasn't trying to make her feel guilty. "Besides, she's not always . . . what I mean to say is, sometimes she knows exactly where she is and what's happened to her, why she's doing this to herself too, I suppose. Then she gets up, and for a few days you'd swear she was as sane as you and I. But she always slips back, as if she were reaching out for us, but can't quite manage to grasp our hands."

The doctors, Masha went on to explain, said there was no hope for her. Though they recommended committing her to an asylum, both she and Vera's husband refused to take their advice.

Masha led Henriette into the kitchen, saying that she must be hungry after her journey. A freckle-faced woman with pale, watery eyes was standing by the stove, stirring the contents of a pot with a wooden spoon.

"Where's Anninka?" said Henriette.

Masha sighed deeply, as if the years were too great a burden, and even she was tired of wearing black. "She left us two Christmases ago. She was over seventy, God rest her soul. But she always took care of us, even to the end. Why, she was up and about the day she died. Then she went to sleep that night and never woke up. This is Akulina, who used to help her." Masha smiled patiently at the woman by the stove. "Is the samovar boiling?"

"Yes, *barinya.*"

"We'll take tea in the drawing room."

Henriette followed her sister from the kitchen. She felt

431

very cold, and rubbed her hands against her arms.

Even Jesus grows old in my dreams, she thought. Oh Anninka, I did love you, truly I did. You were so good to me, and even though I may be selfish, I'll never forget you, I promise.

"She doesn't want Pauline to see her like this," Masha was saying, "and so during the holidays Pauline stays with Irena, and spends her summers with school friends."

Henriette, avoiding the lumpy blue sofa where she'd once sat alongside General Tishin, pulled up a rickety chair. A moment later, freckled Akulina brought in the samovar, which hissed and bubbled as she sat it down on a nearby table.

"I'll be in Moscow in a few months for her graduation," Masha continued. "Pauline wants to go to the university. You haven't seen her in some time, have you?"

"No, I haven't seen very much of anyone."

"She's grown into a lovely young woman. Considering what she's been through these last few years, I think the child has done remarkably well."

Masha seemed to Henriette to defy the act of growing old, looking very much as she had when they'd seen each other last, well over ten years ago. She went over to the table and poured the tea, and Akulina brought in a tray of cakes and Kiev preserves, a squat little pitcher of cream, and lemon cut in rounds.

Noticing a pile of magazines on the table alongside her, Henriette leafed through them until she found an issue of *Art for Art*, the illustrated journal her brother had edited for the last several years.

"Yes, we never fail to receive the latest number," remarked Masha. "Have you seen him lately?"

Henriette nodded and smiled with genuine affection. "His name is very often mentioned in the newspapers," she told Masha. "What with the magazine and the art exhibits he keeps organizing, you'd think he'd taken it on himself to teach Russia to appreciate its art."

"And is he as happy as you are?"

Was it sarcasm she heard in her sister's voice, or merely irony? "I'm sure you know as much about Grisha as I. He's different from other people, and despite what anyone might say, in my mind he's a very kind and loving man." That settled, she stirred her tea with a little gold spoon worn to maple-leaf thinness, so delicate she could feel it bending in her hand.

Masha told her of her work at school, and how several of the children she'd taught had gone on to become teachers themselves, returning to the district to help establish new schools of their own. Although Henriette listened attentively, she wasn't terribly interested, for what happened to the peasants seemed to have little bearing on her life.

"But I suppose you find our lives terribly dull and provincial," Masha said when Henriette let her go on like this for several minutes. "I imagine the Countess keeps you busy with balls and soirées and the like."

"A bit quieter than all that," she admitted. "We have our circle, our connections at court. Tell me," and here she paused until she was certain she had Masha's attention, "have you ever heard mention of Eugene Borisovich?"

Beneath Masha's long dark lashes her black eyes sparkled angrily. As she stared at Henriette, it was easy to see all her rage coming to the surface, rage that she'd managed to keep out of sight for years.

"Why would you even ask me that?" Masha demanded.

Henriette smiled to herself. How lovely to know that beneath Masha's placid façade was the sister she always remembered.

"You've isolated yourself here for how many years now?" Henriette asked. "Thirteen? And yet the moment I mention

Colonel Trigony—"

"Colonel?" said Masha with surprise.

"Oh yes, for as long as I've known him. He's aide-de-camp to Grand Duke Paul, the Tsar's uncle."

"Hasn't he come up in the world. And to think that when I knew him he was just a lowly captain . . . not to mention a murderer." Masha came abruptly to her feet, and when she went to pour herself another cup of tea, her hands shook so violently that the delicate Sèvres cup rattled against its saucer, threatening to shatter. "Do you and the Countess entertain him often?"

"Masha dear, how can you even think such a thing?" she said, speaking in French to emphasize her surprise. "We've met on occasion, it's true. But do you think me so unfeeling that I'd consent to sit at the same table with such a man?"

"Then why did you mention him, to begin with?"

"Curiosity. Nothing more."

"I don't believe you."

"Oh, but you must, Masha. I was just interested in seeing your reaction, that's all."

"Well, now that you've seen it, why don't we talk of . . . no," said Masha, changing her mind and glaring at Henriette with some of the stubbornness she'd inherited from her father. "I want to know more about him. In fact, I want to know as much as you can tell me. Has he ever married?"

Henriette gave out with a brittle laugh. "A man like that? Hardly likely, not when he's considered one of the most notorious rakes in the capital. Why do you ask?"

"Curiosity," replied Masha in the same ironic tone she'd used earlier.

"One would think that after thirteen years you'd have laid the issue to rest."

"On the contrary," replied Masha. "There isn't a day goes by that I don't wish him dead."

"My goodness," she exclaimed, secretly thrilled to hear her sister speak so passionately. "I certainly have opened a can of worms, haven't I?"

"Merely to live vicariously through my pain, no doubt. More tea, sister dear?"

"No, but I will have another cracknel."

From upstairs, Vera's bell began to ring. Before she knew what she was doing, Henriette put down her cup and jumped to her feet, only to realize that habits last a lifetime.

Henriette knew she was causing trouble, and yet she couldn't resist. What Masha had said about living vicariously was probably as accurate an appraisal of the situation as any she herself could have made. It seemed to her that Masha had hidden herself away for too many years. Surely someone as intelligent and attractive as she deserved more from life than just the gratification of being nursemaid to a lunatic, and schoolmarm to a bunch of ill-bred, runny-nosed brats.

Henriette thought of these things as she traveled east, Petrovka having been only a stopover on a considerably longer journey. Her ultimate destination was Verkhoture, a monastery located at the foot of the Ural Mountains, where she intended to seek guidance from a *starets*, a man of God whose miraculous powers were much talked about in Petersburg.

Of late, Henriette had grown increasingly dissatisfied with her life. That she had never married, and had never even had a suitor other than that ridiculous buffoon, General Tishin, was something that continually preyed upon her mind. If Masha seethed with rage over events of her past, Henriette burned with resentment, bitter for having been denied the great love she'd always dreamed of, the love that would be as pure and beautiful as that which the Redeemer had long ago taught her could be hers. Yet it wasn't hers, as Julian Andreyevich, Count Ivanov, and several others had already proven. No longer did she blame her looks for this indifference from the opposite sex. Rather, as she told the Countess, it was her soul that was ugly, and she needed to go away for a while to try to understand the person she had become.

Thus she'd embarked on what the Countess referred to as "a journey of spiritual rebirth," traveling east for three days to the Ural Mountains town of Ekaterinburg. She put up at the American Hotel and although she was greatly fatigued from her long trip, sleep didn't come easily, and she knew by the tangled rope she made of her bed sheets that the snake of Eden had visited her sometime during the night. Were it not for this she might have stayed another day or two, but now she made arrangements to travel north to Verkhoture, a two-day ordeal by tarantass. Yet for all the jolts and bumps she endured along the way, she wasn't unhappy, and even relished the bruises the trip was inflicting upon her. Like the heretical sect of flagellants known as the Khlysty, who whipped themselves into a frenzy in order to achieve communion with God, Henriette viewed the rigors of travel as proof of her devotion, the aches and pains she suffered adding the proper note of penance to her pilgrimage.

At Verkhoture, she found lodging at an inn, where a waiter—as inn servants were called—took her bags and led her upstairs to her room, sighing with each step he took, and looking back at her as if to say, "Yet another of God's fools has come to stay with us."

Rather than unpack, Henriette decided to go directly to the village church, where she'd heard there existed a reliquary in which the bones of St. Simeon the Just were preserved. These proved to be no more than several whitened splinters, not much larger than toothpicks, and in her estimation of dubious provenance. Yet she knelt before them nevertheless. Pressing her forehead to the floor, she tried to recall why she'd traveled all this way, so that she wouldn't lose sight of her goals.

It was getting on toward dusk when she left the church, pausing in the courtyard where a monk, wearing a round calotte and a belted cassock of thin black nankeen, was seated at a little table collecting alms. An ikon depicting St. Simeon of Verkhoture was set up beside him, next to a tray covered by a cloth on which a cross had been painstakingly embroidered, its arms concealed beneath a pile of kopecks. Henriette added several of her own to the collection, and as her coins clattered loudly the monk looked up and smiled.

"You wish to meet with Father Makary?" he said.

Henriette wasn't surprised. In a village of this size it was very easy to pick her out as a stranger. She nodded and told the monk she'd traveled all the way from Petersburg just to meet the *starets.*

"Be here tomorrow morning, my child. A guide will be waiting for you."

Early the next day, Henriette returned to the church, where a young novice waited to take her to the *starets,* who lived in a hut several versts from the monastery. Makary, she was told, was of gentle birth, and like many young men of his generation, had led a dissolute and profligate existence. One morning, explained the novice, Makary had awakened as if from a dream, but a dream of such frightening intensity he was certain the Lord had visited him as he slept. Casting off all his worldly possessions, he set off in search of spiritual redemption, for had Christ not said, "If thou wilt be perfect, go and sell all thou hast, and give to the poor, and thou shalt have treasure in heaven; and come and follow me." Yet the monster of lust pursued him, and for many years he mortified his flesh, scourging himself and wearing heavy chains beneath his clothing, the better to follow the path of righteousness. Gradually his fame spread, and pilgrims came from all over Russia to ask for the blessing of this wise and holy man. It was said that no one ever left the *starets* without feeling the power of the Lord behind his radiant and healing gaze.

At last they reached a clearing in the woods, where a desolate hut was framed against a backdrop of trees and rugged boulders. A group of pilgrims was squatting beside the entrance to the anchorite's humble dwelling, and at Henriette's approach they glanced back, eying her for a moment before returning to their prayers.

The novice told her to get down on her knees as well, to pray for guidance while he arranged for Father Makary to see her. Henriette did as she was told, wondering why she felt so skeptical. She'd come all this way, thousands of miles, but now that she was here it all seemed so pointless. How could a man she'd never met before give her the comfort she'd been denied all her life? How could some stranger, no matter how holy he might be, be able to look into her soul and see what it was that made her feel so sick at heart? Surely all it would take to cure her was a man's kind and loving touch, and she was certain she would be reborn. But no man had ever come forth to embrace her as Jesus often did, and at night she slept with a memory of unrequited passion, tormented by the hideous demons who came to her in the darkness, whispering unspeakable obscenities, and touching her with their cold and leprous hands.

Hearing the sound of angry voices, and recognizing one of them as her guide, Henriette looked up and saw him arguing with a man with long, stringy hair, and a broad, pockmarked nose. The novice pointed in her direction, and then the other man smiled and nodded his head. Even from a distance she was able to see the distinctive scar on his forehead, a kind of bald patch that was darker than the surrounding skin.

"Father Gregory will see to your needs," the young novice

informed her. "He didn't think Father Makary would be able to see you, but now it seems he's changed his mind."

Henriette glanced at the *starets'* disciple, wondering why the man looked so familiar. "How will I get back?" she asked.

"The path is easy to follow, but I will escort you back if that is your wish," replied Father Gregory, tilting his head slightly to the side as priests invariably do when they hear confession. "You are—?"

"Madame Petrova," she said, still unable to shake off the feeling that they'd met once before.

The man smiled, his thin, pale lips half hidden by his scraggly mustache. "Gregory Efimovich Novy," he said, bowing from the waist.

"Otherwise known as Gregory Rasputin," she heard the novice say as he turned away and started back to Verkhoture.

"A nickname, to be sure," replied Rasputin, scrutinizing her with his blue-gray eyes. They were small, bright, and very piercing, so much so that Henriette put her hand to her throat, as if she were standing naked before him. "You've come a great distance, haven't you?"

"Yes, from Petersburg," she murmured.

It was just at this moment that she realized where she'd seen him before. It was both terrifying and implausible, yet Father Gregory was the same man whose face had appeared before her the first time she'd conducted a séance at Count Ivanov's. It was the scar on his forehead that convinced her, and when he turned away and went back to the *starets'* hut, Henriette sank down onto her knees and closed her eyes, trying to make sense of what had happened.

How could it be possible? she kept asking herself. Surely it was just a coincidence, and nothing more. But even coincidences were part of the grand design. Rasputin had appeared to her in a vision. Now, many years later, he was once again making himself known. Did it not follow that the Redeemer who controlled her destiny had arranged for this to happen?

When the anchorite was ready to receive her, Rasputin took her by the hand, and led her into the dim and musty little hut. He remained by the door while she prostrated herself before the holy man, whose hands were bound in iron fetters, and whose clothing consisted of nothing more than a ragged loincloth, while around his waist he wore a girdle of thorns.

Finally she heard him speak. When she lifted herself off the earthen floor, she saw before her not a half-naked madman, as she'd cynically imagined, but someone whose eyes radiated great inner peace, and whose smile was the smile of gentle Jesus whenever He appeared before her. Henriette, pressing the *starets'* bony hands to her lips, kissed them passionately, so that the chains rattled loudly, momentarily drowning out the sound of the elder's voice.

"Tell me of your pain," said Makary, in a voice that was so faint it was as if he were speaking to her over a boundless space.

With an anxious glance in the direction of his disciple, she lowered her eyes again, as it was too difficult to face the *starets* without being intimidated by the Christlike aura that surrounded him. At first, she tripped over her words, but as he murmured encouragement, she spoke more rapidly, telling Father Makary of her loneliness, the visions she'd had ever since she was a girl, the hideous nightmares and vile acts to which she was constantly subjected.

"From my youth up the lusts of the flesh have tormented me. Lord Jesus Christ, do you condemn me therefor," recited Makary. "Now say that after me, my child."

"From my youth up the lusts of the flesh . . ."

Yes, it was true, for even the Only-Begotten had never been able to protect her from the serpent of Eden, whose thick, monstrous coils wound between her loins, slithering voluptuously across her body. Even then she could feel the presence of the gray goat, rearing up before her on its cloven hoofs, mocking her and wagging its rigid sex before her terrified eyes.

"From my youth up the lusts of the flesh have tormented me!" she cried out in a shrill and hysterical voice.

"Yes, but now God is watching over you, my child, and you must trust in His infinite wisdom. It is by repentance alone that you can win your salvation, and be assured your rightful place in heaven."

"But surely God doesn't love me if He sends these devils to constantly, torment me," she said, whimpering now, and afraid to open her eyes lest she catch sight of the goat taunting her and gesturing obscenely.

"He is testing your faith, my child. Come, we shall pray together."

But instead of praying, Henriette looked back at Father Gregory. His eyes, deep set beneath their bushy brows, watched her so intently that for a moment she was certain she couldn't move. These were the same glowing eyes she'd seen in her vision, and as a strange warmth spread over her body, Rasputin moved toward her, laying his hands on her head and then helping her slowly to her feet.

When she turned to face the *starets*, Makary seemed to be in a trance. As he rocked back and forth the irons around his wrists rattled feebly, signaling an end to her audience. Rasputin led her from the hut, where the bright morning light made her eyes tear, and the sight of the raggedly dressed pilgrims made her feel ashamed that poverty was one cross she no longer had to bear.

"You did well, Madame Petrova," said Rasputin. "Many women of your station in life come here to be amused, having nothing better to do with their time. But you impressed the holy father by your sincerity. Oh yes, your pain touched him deeply. But you must never lose hope. Surely you know the proverb, 'If you do not sin, you cannot repent.'"

Taking her by the hand, his skin rough and calloused against her own, Rasputin began to lead her through the forest. He moved as if he were crushing vermin beneath his feet, with great noisy strides and an ungainly bearlike gait. Suddenly he paused in the middle of the path, turning to face her so that she noticed how a yellow blotch disfigured one of his eyes.

"You came to Makary with your pain, and yet you're still in pain, isn't that so? Then you must remember what I've told you, that it is only by repentance that you can win your salvation."

She felt very dizzy, exhausted by all that she'd been through. But when she made a move to continue down the path, Rasputin reached out and grabbed her hand, holding her fast.

"Don't you see, when God places temptation in our way, as you yourself have admitted, then it's our duty to yield. Only those of us who debase ourselves through sin can thus repent in a way that is truly acceptable to the Lord."

Henriette didn't know what to say, and so she looked away. She was afraid of the man's eyes, and the way they seemed to see right through her. Not only did she feel naked, but also completely vulnerable and at his mercy. But then he reached out again and stroked her cheek with the side of his hand.

"You take liberties, Father Gregory," she said loudly. "Is that what Father Makary has taught you?"

"Such a sharp, scolding tongue," Rasputin said with a laugh. "I'm no 'Father,' I assure you, though there are many from my village who think otherwise. It's just that you're too beautiful to be so unhappy. Oh, you may laugh, but in my eyes you're one of God's children. We were all created in his image, were we not? Then how can any of us be ugly?"

"You're talking of spiritual beauty. There are those who think nothing of that."

"But spiritual beauty is beauty eternal," replied Rasputin. He put his hands on her shoulders, and his eyes radiated such conviction and strength of purpose that again she felt weak, and incapable of disagreeing with him. "Have you ever heard of the People of God, the Khylsty? They believe in the highest worship of the Lord, a mystical experience you must participate in to understand fully."

Henriette knew the Church considered the Khylsty heretics. But when she reminded Rasputin of this, he laughed and told her that half the monks at Verkhoture belonged to the sect.

"What the Church doesn't know is that the Khylsty are nearer to God than any of us. Come with me tonight to one of their meetings, that you may see these things for yourself. If not, the snake of Eden will torture you forever."

"How do you know about that?" she demanded. It was as if he were reading her thoughts, and she felt betrayed by her fears.

"The world is looking for a miracle," Rasputin said. "Even the Little Father, the *batushka* Tsar, seeks answers and cannot find them. Come with me tonight, so that when you return to Petersburg you may share these experiences with your friends. Have you met the *batushka* Tsar, Madame Petrova?" He looked at her eagerly, as if her connections at court were of great importance.

"No, but many of my friends have."

"That's good, yes, very good." He put his finger to his ear. "If the *batushka* listen, then Russia listens, too."

If this coarse and unwashed peasant had been sent to her by God, then surely she must do as he asked. And so Henriette agreed to attend the meeting of the Khlysty, knowing it would only give her something else to talk about when she

443

returned home.

Promptly at sundown, Rasputin arrived at the inn where she was staying. He was dressed in a shirt of coarse linen, his wide trousers tucked into heavy top boots. His tangled beard and long, flowing hair looked freshly washed, though he still smelled strongly of the barnyard. He had no carriage waiting, and so they set out on foot, passing the monastery of Verkhoture, whose tall spires and domes were surrounded by a massive stone wall that reminded her of a prison. When Rasputin started to lead her through the woods she hesitated, uncertain if she should follow.

"Do I frighten you, Madame Petrova?"

About to tell him of her vision, Henriette decided against saying more than she had to. Besides, if the *starets* thought highly of this man, who was she to disagree? So she followed after him, eventually reaching a tumbledown cottage whose moldy windows were covered with thick curtains, allowing only a faint glimmer of light to be discerned within.

Rasputin rapped on the door, then whistled loudly. No doubt this was a signal, for a moment later the door was unlocked. A man wearing a long white robe beckoned them inside, hurriedly bolting the door behind them. Henriette found herself the object of immediate curiosity. The men and women who were seated on the rough benches along the walls all turned their eyes in her direction, murmuring among themselves until Rasputin raised his hand, assuring them that though she was a stranger, she was still a friend.

He led her to an empty place on one of the benches, patting her hand with his long, coarse fingers, and smiling in a peculiarly seductive and comforting way. For the next thirty minutes or so, the congregation sang hymns, the verses of which Henriette had never heard in any church service she'd attended.

Although the singing began on a somber and mournful

note, the voices gradually became more jubilant. Proclaiming the advent of the Savior, and His appearance among His flock, first the men and then the women rose from their places, their ecstatic voices announcing their closeness to God. But when Henriette saw the congregation begin to strip off their clothes with no more thought to what whey were doing than a group of children at a swimming hole, she had no interest in remaining there any longer.

Rasputin caught her by the elbow as she started to her feet. "They're only putting on white robes," he explained, "the garment of the departed spirits and angels."

"I don't care what they're doing," she whispered angrily. "This is blasphemy, and I don't want to be a part of it."

"But we're all a part of it. By stepping over the threshold, you've willingly entered the ark of the righteous. To leave now would be a far greater sin."

It was too late to argue, the Khylsty having already donned their robes. As the white-robed man who'd greeted them at the door stood in the center of the room, the sound of exultant hymns once again filled the air. Two by two, members of the congregation began to leave the circle they had formed, dancing in time to the singing.

Rasputin, his voice low and close to her ear, whispered that the man around whom everyone was dancing had experienced what the Khlysty called "the miracle of the mysterious death." As a result of this mystical resurrection he could now foresee the future, perform miracles, and heal the sick.

"His acts proceed from God," said the *starets'* disciple, gesturing at the silent figure who stood in the middle of the room.

Suddenly everyone paused, and all movement came to a halt. The eyes of the congregation were turned heavenward, filled with such wonder that Henriette couldn't understand why she wasn't experiencing the same sense of awe and reverent mystery. The man who'd undergone the miracle of the mysterious death now began to speak. Although she listened attentively, she was unable to follow anything he said. Was it a foreign language, or was it merely gibberish? He alternately laughed and wept, his voice changing with each breath he took. The congregation huddled at his feet, crossing themselves and trembling with excitement.

Rasputin too seemed caught up in the Khylsty mystery. He rocked back and forth as Makary had done, clutching his knees with his long, bony fingers, and whispering the same maddening double-talk as the man around whom everyone had congregated.

"The Holy Ghost is among us!" someone cried out. He threw himself back from the circle of worshipers and began to roll about on the floor as if he were having a fit.

"Rebirth through sin," muttered Rasputin, seizing her around the waist and forcing her to stare into his eyes. "Now do you understand what I've been trying to tell you?"

As one after another of the Khylsty began to cry out, writhing on the floor and tearing at their robes as if they were on fire, Henriette felt Rasputin's hands on her breasts. She pushed him away and started to the door, only to feel someone grabbing hold of her ankle and pulling her down to the floor.

Henriette screamed at the top of her voice. But her shrill, terror-stricken cries only made the man who'd attacked her groan feverishly.

"Angels," he whispered as he began to tear at her clothes. "Angels and demons and . . ."

From across the room she saw Rasputin trying to make his way toward her. By now the entire congregation was caught up in the madness, ripping off their robes and copulating with wild, frenzied cries.

Henriette tried to wrestle free, but she was pinned to the

floor, a leering face hovering over her, just like the monk who'd danced at the foot of her bed.

"Oh God in heaven, gentle Jesus!" she screamed, when Rasputin managed to haul her to her feet. As she staggered outside she heard the bestial cries of these so-called People of God, and when she looked at Makary's disciple her glance was filled with scorn and unconcealed hostility.

"Monster!" she wanted to shout. "You're the gray goat and the serpent of Eden, you're the Tempter!"

But though she fully intended to say these things, to rail at him for what he'd subjected her to, she was again held captive by his gaze, and could do nothing but stumble back to the village.

"I mustn't leave you like this," Rasputin said when they reached the inn. "Please, let me come upstairs with you, that we may get down on our knees together and pray for divine guidance."

Although she didn't say anything and merely turned away, Rasputin followed after her, his great, lumbering footfalls echoing in her ears. He closed the door behind them, crossed the room, and knelt before the ikons.

"You've seen God in one guise, and tonight you've seen Him in another," Rasputin told her as she wearily got down beside him, facing the ikon of the Redeemer she had brought with her from Petersburg. "Yet it is only through sinful encounter that we can ever hope to attain redemption. Do not fear the snake of Eden, my child. The Lord has sent me to watch over you." He ran his hands over her tangle of frizzy curls, his voice deep and mysterious and filled with rapture.

Henriette trembled, and gazing up at gentle Jesus, she saw the scar the crown of thorns had left upon His forehead. Rasputin too wore such a scar. She had seen him years before, and now he was beside her, stroking her cheeks with the tips of his fingers, whispering of things she dared not share with anyone but the Redeemer. Who but the Only-Begotten Son could understand her terror of the gray goat who brazenly fondled her and made her writhe as helplessly as the Khlysty? But Rasputin understood, murmuring calm and encouraging words as his hands slid ever so lightly across her breasts.

"Do not fear the Tempter," he whispered. "The serpent slithers between your legs, licking you with his hot and fiery tongue. But he is not a man created in the image of our Lord." He kissed her eyes and then her lips, cupping her face in his coarse, horny palms, and forcing her to look into his eyes.

Was this why the Son of God had sent her all the way to Verkhoture? She had been alone for too long, and the thick, swollen coils of the serpent were cold and slimy against her flesh. Rasputin warmed her then, holding her fast in his eager embrace until tears spilled down her cheeks.

"God has sent you to me, hasn't He?" she asked, fixing her gaze on the pinpricks of light that shone from his eyes.

"Yes, *matushka*, God has sent me to find you, and to comfort you in your loneliness, that we may all be as one."

Henriette came slowly to her feet, drying her eyes with the back of her hand. "Then we must not disappoint him," she heard herself say.

She turned down the lamp so that the only source of light was the candle whose flame glowed brightly before the ikons. Each time it flickered, a shower of golden sparks illuminated the gaunt and ascetic face of the Son of God, who smiled with His sad, merciful eyes as Henriette took off her clothes and climbed into bed.

Two

The wan and prematurely haggard child of the Presnia had blossomed into a beautiful slender girl with curly blue-black hair and serious blue eyes. Pauline was sixteen years old, and the night before she was to graduate from St. Ekaterina's a ball was held. The hall was decorated with garlands of roses that made her want to weep, for she'd never seen anything half so lovely.

Although the ball wouldn't begin until seven, Pauline and her friend Julia had slipped into the hall, where they hid behind a pillar and watched the candles being lit in the five big chandeliers whose crystal pendants scattered the light from one end of the ballroom to the other. Julia, a plump and hopelessly romantic girl who had been Pauline's inseparable companion for nearly all of the six years they'd spent at the Institute, clasped her pudgy pink hands together and rolled her eyes up until only the whites showed.

"Oh, it's wonderful, isn't it?" she whispered in Russian, although it was expressly forbidden to speak anything but French. "I think I shall faint, Pauline, it's all so beautiful."

Then she rolled back her eyes and looked sadly at her friend. "I still think it's unfair. You've spent every summer with us for years now. Why must this year be any different from the others?"

Pauline promised to visit with her for a week or two, but it was so long since she'd seen her mother that she felt obligated to spend some time at Petrovka. Of all the girls at school, only Julia Andreyevna knew of her mother's illness, one of numerous secrets they'd shared over the years.

"But in September we'll be back in school together," Pauline reminded her. "Summer will go quickly, you'll see."

"I wouldn't even be going to that horrid university if it weren't for you," Julia replied. "I just want to fall in love and live happily ever after. Besides, why does a girl need to know so much, anyway? Men don't listen, Pauline, so why go through all the bother?"

There was no time to answer, for right then and there an all too familiar voice called out.

"And what do you think you're doing down here, *mesdemoiselles?*" It was Mademoiselle Grushina, the history teacher, known to the girls as the Crocodile, not only because of her vicious temper, but also because she seemed to have more teeth in her mouth than was humanly possible.

"Nothing," squeaked Julia, first in Russian and then in French.

Flushing the color of a poppy, she grabbed Pauline by the hand and ran from the ballroom, then up the wide, winding stairs to the dormitory on the second floor. Here Julia stopped, quite out of breath, no doubt due to all the bonbons she'd devoured over the last six years.

"Do you think she'll tell the headmistress?" asked Julia as she stood there on the landing, glancing nervously in the direction from which they'd come.

"And if she does?"

"Maybe we won't graduate." Julia looked at her hopefully. At that moment, the idea of growing up and leaving St. Ekaterina's was almost as terrifying as evoking Mademoiselle Grushina's displeasure.

"We'll graduate, Julia, never you fear." Then, putting her hand around her friend's ample waist, Pauline marched her into the dormitory, for it was time they got ready for the ball.

From the platform erected at the end of the hall, the head-mistress eyed the proceedings through her lorgnette. She was a tall and regal-looking woman with great masses of gray hair piled in elaborate curls upon the top of her head, and from a distance Pauline imagined the principal was wearing an exotic fur cap.

"It's a wig," whispered Julia Andreyevna, who was dressed like all the other girls, in a full woolen skirt and a thin batiste apron edged with lace.

This evening, their long green woolen frocks and shoulder capes were tucked away upstairs, and in the light of the dozens of candles that burned overhead, the girls bared their arms and whispered anxiously among themselves, casting furtive glances at the cadets who stood at attention on the opposite side of the ballroom.

These young men were members of the II Cadet Corps, and were joined by pupils of the Alexis Military School, all of whom were proud of their full-dress uniforms and faint waxed mustaches. The ball had opened with a polonaise, but now the first candles had burned out, and as new ones were lit the younger girls were sent upstairs to bed while preparations for the third quadrille got under way. This quadrille was considered the most special of all, as it signified love. As a result the girls were far more nervous now than at any time all evening, since the cadet who asked for this dance might very well be the person to change their lives forever. They were all quite serious about this, and even though Pauline said it was just a silly superstition, the girls were particularly careful about whom they allowed to sign their dance cards.

Julia now covered her flushed and perspiring face with the side of her hand, whispering that Pauline had an admirer.

From across the hall Pauline caught sight of the young man whose eyes were singling her out of the crowd. "He's looking at you, Julia, I can tell," she insisted.

Julia protested with a playful slap on the shoulder. "He's not, you silly. It's you he's interested in. Look how he's staring. Oh, it's shameless, just shocking," she decided. "Why, he looks like a frog, the way his eyes keep bugging out."

"Perhaps if I kissed him he'd turn into a prince."

Julia looked even more scandalized than before. "You're terrible," she said. "But if you do kiss him, make sure the Crocodile doesn't see."

The first figure of the quadrille was about to start when the cadet Julia had been speaking of made his way across the rose-scented ballroom. With the charming awkwardness of youth, he bowed from the waist, and asked if he might still have the honor of being Pauline's partner.

With a nod of her head that was all but imperceptible, Pauline allowed the young man to lead her onto the floor, just in time for the French quadrille.

It was only in the fifth and final figure, when the master of ceremonies tapped the floor with his slender ivory stick and called on them to join hands in the *chaîne*, that the cadet spoke, though he did so between clenched teeth. Like Pauline, he'd been warned not to talk during the dances. But now, as the young people moved in a circle of smiling eyes and tightly clutching hands, he asked if she might save him the mazurka, which was to be the last dance of the ball.

"If we had a constitution and a parliament, they wouldn't

treat us this way," the cadet whispered in her ear.

Pauline was immediately intrigued, and when the quadrille came to an end she handed the young man her dance card, where he dutifully inscribed his name alongside the mazurka.

"What happened?" whispered Julia when Pauline returned to the far side of the hall. "What did he say? Oh tell me, Pauline. I can't bear the suspense or I'll faint, I know I will."

Pauline, who didn't even know the young man's name, hid behind a pillar and examined her card. "A. Platonovich" was written out in a small, neat hand.

Julia, standing on tiptoe and reading over her shoulder, said his name was Alexander. "Or perhaps Andrei. Yes, his eyes are like my father's, and he's an Andrei. Andrei Platonovich. Do you know his family name? Wouldn't it be wonderful if he's a prince? But perhaps he isn't. After all, the II Cadet Corps isn't all that fashionable, is it? What else did he say?"

Pauline couldn't help but smile at her friend's excitement. Just as talking was proscribed, so too was taking the same partner for more than one dance. Hoping none of the class mistresses would notice, Pauline heard the red-faced master of ceremonies announce the mazurka and watched the shy young cadet once again make his way across the beautifully decorated hall.

A rose fell from one of the garlands and dropped at her feet. An instant later A. Platonovich snatched it off the floor and presented it to her after carefully brushing off the petals. Caught up in her friend's obvious delight, for Julia was standing nearby clasping her hands to her breast and smiling dreamily, Pauline thrust the rose into her hair and offered A. Platonovich her hand.

She sailed out onto the floor as if she were the princess her mother had always told her she'd become. "Is it Alexander, Andrei, or Arkady?" she asked, trying to speak without moving her lips. "Or Anatole or Artemy? You don't look like an Apollon either, though one can never tell."

"Alexei," he whispered as he gracefully executed the first figure. "And you are?"

"Pauline," she said while she moved in time to the music, listening with one ear to the commands of the master of ceremonies.

"It's terrible how they won't let us talk, isn't it? What do you suppose they're afraid of?"

"A constitution," she whispered with a laugh, only to experience a sinking feeling when she caught sight of the Crocodile who, looking quite grave, was heading right toward them.

Although the history teacher didn't interrupt the dance, the moment the mazurka came to an end she hurried over to where they were standing, Pauline listening attentively as Alexei told her of his plans to enroll at the university after graduation, rather than pursue a career in the military.

"Two dances with the same young man," said Mademoiselle Grushina, all of her enormous yellow teeth clicking angrily as she wagged a finger under Pauline's nose.

"Please forgive me, *mademoiselle*, but Cousin Alex and I haven't seen each other in such a long time," Pauline promptly replied.

Bowing with none of the uncertainty he'd shown earlier, Alexei introduced himself to the teacher.

"Cousins? Indeed?" said the Crocodile.

"Oh yes, ma'am, very close cousins," the young man remarked. "Pauline was just telling me about—" Here he paused and looked at her searchingly, just like an actor who'd suddenly forgotten his next line.

"Petrovka," replied Pauline. "In the province of Orel. Cousin Alex hasn't been there in quite some time."

"That's all very well and good," said the Crocodile. "But I

think it's time you said good night."

"Yes, certainly," agreed Alexei, who now bowed to each of them in turn. "Petrovka, in Orel Province," he muttered.

"Yes," she called after him. "The mail is delivered twice a week."

"You didn't kiss him, did you?" Julia asked when they went upstairs together. "Because if you did you have to tell me everything about it, so that when it happens to me I'll know what to expect. Is it true boys grit their teeth when they do it, or is that just something people say?"

Pauline smiled and told her she hadn't been kissed. She took the rose from her curly black hair, inhaling its fragrance and thinking of the wonderful evening she had had.

"But I wouldn't be surprised if there's a letter waiting for me when I get home."

"A letter," sighed Julia Andreyevna. "A billet-doux."

Pauline laughed. "I'm sure it won't be that. We hardly said two words to each other."

"The language of love defies expression," replied Julia with another languorous sigh. "Yes, I don't think anything else matters, Pauline, not in this world or the next."

Masha had arrived in Moscow for Pauline's graduation, and when she noticed the other women in the hall, she felt self-conscious about her appearance. It had been years since she'd thought of her wardrobe, and years since she'd worn anything even remotely fashionable. But now she was determined to change all that, especially since Henriette had invited her and Pauline to stay at Tsarskoye Selo, the elegant summer resort near Petersburg where the Countess Ignatieva maintained a villa.

We'll stop in Petersburg first and buy ourselves some new clothes, Masha decided as she watched the graduation exercises and listened inattentively to the endless, long-winded speeches of the numerous trustees. No more of this hiding away in corners. I'm going out into society again.

It all seemed very easy, to put aside the last thirteen years as if they'd never occurred, and once again face the world with uplifted spirits and a resolute smile. Although Masha wasn't altogether certain if it would prove as effortless as she imagined, she was anxious to give it a try. What Henriette had told her several months earlier had preyed upon her mind, continually popping up in her thoughts like a jack-in-the-box that wouldn't stay put. That Trigony was still alive, playing the role of rakehell while she'd had to face each day as if it were an insurmountable obstacle, caused her to seethe with rage.

Why did she have to suffer if he did not? Why did she have to give up her happiness while he'd given up nothing? If he was ever to be brought to justice, then she herself must see to it that it was done. To remain at Petrovka for the rest of her life was equivalent to giving Trigony a full pardon, and now she intended to go about righting the wrongs he'd inflicted upon her.

"Pauline Simonovna Belinskaya," announced the head-mistress as the young woman mounted the platform, where she gratefully accepted a Bible in one hand and a diploma in the other.

Masha was very proud of her niece's accomplishments, and a short while later, as they strolled through the Institute's beautifully landscaped grounds, she told Pauline of the surprise that was planned for her. "Your Aunt Henriette wants to hold a ball in your behalf. Isn't that wonderful?"

Pauline lowered her eyes, and a crestfallen expression cast its shadow across her delicately sculpted face. "But I was planning to go back to Petrovka," she said.

"I don't know if your mother's ready for that," Masha said sadly.

"Yes, I know how she feels, Aunt Masha. But perhaps if we saw each other things might change. After all, I'm a St. Catherine's girl now, one of those 'muslin creatures' *maman* always wanted me to become. And I do miss her so. It's been years since we've seen each other. Besides, I won't stay all summer. I promised Julia I'd visit with her for a few weeks before school started. And if I don't see Mother now, I probably wouldn't be able to get away for another year. You do understand, don't you?"

"Which is why," Masha explained when she arrived at Tsarskoye Selo several days later, "your niece isn't with me."

Henriette drew her lips together in a frown. "What ingratitude," she said, irked by the change in plans. "The least she could have done is visited with me for a day or two. After all, how many nieces do I have?"

"Now, you mustn't get yourself upset," urged Countess Ignatieva. "You know how bad it is for you, *ma chère*. Be calm, Henriette, and think of your friend."

Henriette nodded, and a look came over her thin, bony face, one Masha barely recognized.

"Are you in love?" she exclaimed.

"You needn't sound so scornful, Masha. And no, I'm not in love. But I've met the most remarkable man, just extraordinary." Henriette took her by the arm, and smiling almost condescendingly at the Countess, she led her outside onto the veranda, where they might have some privacy.

Here, Henriette told her of Father Gregory, and her experiences at Verkhoture.

"He's changed my life," Henriette declared with the same, wistful, dreamy look Masha had noticed earlier. "A *starets*, Masha, a holy man. And if I have my way, someday all of Russia will know him by name. Why, he can heal you with his touch, just as he healed me. And to think I first saw him in a vision, so many years ago. Just like a dream come true, I

457

swear. Unfortunately, he's thousands of miles away—though perhaps one day he'll be standing right where you are. But what do you think of Tsarskoye? Charming, isn't it? The other day I saw the little Grand Duchess Olga. A precious child, so like her father. They live here all year round now."

"And have you been to see them?" she asked, as if paying a call on the Tsar and Tsarina was simply a matter of inviting yourself over for tea.

"No, not yet," replied Henriette. "But I know dozens of people who say the Palace is not so wonderful, anyway. The rooms are rather drafty, in fact."

"Is that what Colonel Trigony has told you?"

Henriette's sharp gray eyes peered at her accusingly. "Is that why you accepted my invitation, merely to see what he's like after all these years?"

Before she could answer, the Countess began to call out in a vexed and petulant voice. "My lorgnette, I just can't seem to find it, Henriette. Have you been hiding it from me, you naughty girl?"

Henriette smiled patiently and came to her feet, the ruffled bottom of her ice-blue dress trailing across the straw matting that covered the terrace. "One would think she's *maman*, merely reincarnated." She went back inside, leaving Masha alone on the porch wondering when and if she'd meet up with the one person she had come here to find.

It was her stepfather, Rodion Sorokin, who met Pauline at the railway station, where she blew kisses to Julia and her mother as they stood by the open window of their compartment and waved good-bye.

"Now, you promised," Julia called out. "We'll expect you next month without fail. And write every day, Pauline. I'll die if I don't hear from you." She rolled her eyes about just to make certain Pauline understood how important this was, then popped a chocolate into her mouth as the train pulled out of the station.

"Your friend from school?" asked Rodya as he hoisted her trunk over his shoulder and led her in the direction of the carriage.

"Yes, I came down with her and her mother. My, it's been a long time, Rodya, hasn't it? Years and years. But you still look the same."

"Hard work," said the steward, with an agreeable smile that ended in a yawn. "But it's you who's changed, Pauline. Why, I wouldn't even have recognized you if it weren't for that picture you sent us. I never thought . . . what I mean is," and again his lips broke apart in a grin. "Here you've got me all tongue-tied, acting like a stranger when you're not. You're my daughter, aren't you now, my sweet lovely daughter."

Rodya dropped her trunk into the back of the carriage, then suddenly put his hands around her waist and lifted her up in the air, holding her there for a moment and laughing just like a schoolboy playing a prank.

Pauline was a little unsettled by her stepfather's enthusiastic welcome, and begged him to put her down. "You're as strong as ever," she said. "But how is she, Rodya? Has she gotten any better?"

"She's still the same," he replied, his voice low and filled with sadness. "Always the same." He helped her into the carriage, then joined her on the front seat and flicked the reins. The team set off for Petrovka at a brisk and businesslike trot. "Nothing changes, Pauline, except money, of course. Couldn't be helped, I suppose, though your Aunt Irena tried awfully hard. We've had to sell a lot of land these last few years. If old Peter knew, why he'd roll over in his grave, I'll tell you that."

"I remember how Granddad used to talk about the land. He

made it sound like a person, someone he could always depend on."

"Not anymore."

Pauline looked out on the lush fields of bushy rye that grew right up to the edge of the road, a sharp, vivid green that made a brilliant contrast to the pale early-summer sky. Dozens of skylarks rose up from the fields and flew overhead, singing melodiously as they beat their wings. Dandelions and fat marsh marigolds grew along both sides of the road, narrow strips of yellow leading her in the direction of home.

But was Petrovka really home? Pauline didn't know, having been away for so many years that it felt as if she no longer had roots, or any place to permanently call her own.

Her stepfather reached over and wrapped his arm around her, holding her fast until she winced and he pulled his hand away. "I just don't want you to be disappointed," Rodya said. "She's not the same woman she was, Pauline, not most days. At least we've gotten her to stay out of bed. She sits by the window in your grandmother's old room, says she likes to look out." He shrugged his powerful shoulders. "I want to prepare you, is all."

Yet nothing Rodya said could have possibly prepared her for the shock of seeing her mother after so long an absence. When Pauline knocked on the door and let herself into the bedroom, the woman who sat by the window slowly turned her head around as if it were a great effort to look anywhere but out. Her mother's sad blue eyes opened wide, and gradually a spark of recognition began to illuminate her doleful and melancholic gaze.

"I always knew you'd be a great beauty, and so you are. Come, give your mother a kiss. She's waited all her life for this."

Pauline's eyes were wet as she leaned over and kissed her mother on the cheek, unable to reconcile her memories of six years earlier with the realities that presented themselves now that she had finally returned. There was nothing animate about her mother's features, nothing to reveal the vitality of years past. Only her pointy little chin was the same.

Her mother swallowed hard, making a strange gulping sound as if there were something stuck in her throat. "Actually," Vera said, "I'm better than I've been in weeks. Your stepfather says I'm steering an even course, whatever that means."

Pauline tried to kiss her again, but her mother edged back.

"I don't like it when you get too close," Vera said. "It's hard to breathe until I know you better."

"It doesn't matter, as long as I can be with you."

"I didn't want you home, not for the longest time. I still don't. But it's lovely here, isn't it? My mother spent more time in this room than anywhere else in the house. See the thread that hangs down from the canopy? It used to be tied to an angel, a gilded Cupid. See where the carpet is torn near the edge? Her little dog did that one day when your Aunt Henriette forgot to give it a biscuit. She's with me all the time now, poor *maman*. Who would have thought we'd end up being so alike?"

Pauline reached up and touched her mother's hair with the tips of her fingers. It was no longer the bright golden hair she remembered from her childhood, but a coarse shade of yellow like rye dying on the stalk, touched here and there by long strands of gray.

"I was afraid, but now . . ." A faint smile creased her mother's lips.

"Afraid of what, *maman?*"

"That you wouldn't be pretty. I couldn't bear such a thing. To think I'd given birth to an ugly child . . . why, it would be inconceivable. It's just a pity I have to put aside all the plans I made for you. I wanted to give you a proper debut, but there's no money for that, no money for anything."

Pauline put her hand on her mother's shoulder, able to feel her trembling. "I don't need a debut, Mother. Besides, girls don't do that anymore," she lied. "And you've sacrificed so much for me as it is."

Her mother pushed her hand away. "It was your father's money," she said in a gravelly voice. "I merely put it aside, that's all, and didn't spend it when I might have. Now it doesn't matter, anyway. But at least I'm still pretty." Vera looked up, her pale blond lashes fluttering anxiously. "Tell me, isn't your mother still pretty? Isn't she still beautiful, Pauline? And young. Yes, I'm not old, really I'm not. I was the baby sister, the youngest of all of them. How he loved to carry me in his arms, dance me around. If only I weren't so tired all the time." With a loud and self-pitying sigh, she turned her attention back to the window, having already lost interest in her visitor.

That evening, as she sat out on the veranda, Pauline wondered if what had happened to her mother might someday happen to her. Didn't things like this run in families? After all, her grandmother hadn't been well for a long time, too. It was all so terribly confusing. She hadn't expected it to be nearly as bad as this, and now she shook her head, unable to figure out what to do. Then one of the French doors swung back and her stepfather came outside, carrying a tray with a crystal decanter and two chipped glasses.

Rodya poured himself a brandy, downing it so quickly she didn't realize he'd had anything to drink until he poured himself another. Then, after handing her a glass that she held to be polite, he dropped down onto the reed settee where she was sitting.

"Must be difficult for you, isn't it?" her stepfather said, tipping the chipped rim of the glass toward his lips. "Here you come back almost all grown up, and what do you find? A musty old house and a crazy woman upstairs in her room. What's worse, it's not like really being sick, is it? That I could understand. But this other business—oh no, it's different when it's all up here," and he tapped his finger against the side of his head. "Hard on me too, if you know what I mean."

Rodya leaned back, stretching his legs out before him and beating a sharp tattoo with the heels of his freshly tarred boots. He put his hands behind his thickly corded neck, and as he gazed at the violet clouds swirling overhead, he made a sound that was almost like a whimper.

"Awfully hard," he kept saying. "A man like me, wanting to do everything he could for her. I was very much in love with her, Pauline. Maybe you don't remember, seeing as how you were just a little girl. A bratty one, too," he reminded her with a good-natured laugh. "But look at her now. Why, she won't even go down to the bathhouse 'less she's dragged. And after Anninka died, no one else really cared. You loved that old woman, didn't you?"

"Yes, I loved her very much. Granny understood me, even when I didn't understand myself. Oh Rodya," and she swiveled around, the better to see him in the vanishing light of dusk, "isn't there anything we can do for her?"

"Just be glad she recognized you. Some days I go upstairs and she starts to scream, says they're coming to burn the house down, and Senya come quick before they light their torches. And then sometimes she's just the opposite. Hysteria, the doctors call it. She's so wild you can't even reason with her. Says strange things, and runs around the house like she's forgotten something, only she can't find it no matter how hard she looks. Other things too, things that maybe I shouldn't be telling you about. But you're almost a woman now, aren't you, Pauline? And when I tell you how difficult it is for me, 'specially when she's upstairs sitting by that window, not wanting to eat or talk or do anything at all, you'll understand my meaning, won't you? After all, I'm still a young man, Pauline. And she's my wife, no matter what."

Pauline didn't want to talk about such things. It was much too personal, and embarrassed that her stepfather would even bring it up in conversation, she started to get to her feet.

A look of disappointment came over Rodya's boyish, very Russian face. "I thought when you came back I'd have someone to talk to. I have no one here, Pauline, don't you understand? No one. I'm all alone. I'm a man and I'm all alone with a crazy woman who won't leave her room!"

Her stepfather drained his brandy and jumped to his feet, where he walked back and forth, sometimes so close to the edge of the terrace she felt certain he'd fall over the side.

"Alone," he said, "and I don't know what to do about it. It's not right, Pauline, it's just not right. She's been like this almost five years now. Five years!"

"Rodya, please, she'll hear you," Pauline begged, frightened by the way he kept pacing about with short, jerky steps, his boots pounding against the creaking boards.

"I don't care. Let her hear every word. If she wanted to help herself she could, but she doesn't even want to do that. Pauline, I'm lost, don't you see? I'm lost and I'm all alone, and it's tearing me up inside."

Suddenly her stepfather grabbed her up in his arms. As she tried to twist free, she felt his lips against her mouth, and his strong, powerful hands holding her so tightly she could hardly breathe. She pulled her mouth away, but he kept kissing her all the same, rubbing his hands up and down her back. No, boys didn't grit their teeth when they kissed, and neither did men.

Finally she managed to pull free, stepping back until the heel of her shoe got caught on the edge of the terrace. With a helpless cry she swayed back and forth like a blade of grass whipped by the wind, unable to regain her balance. Just when she thought she was going to fall into the stinging nettles, Rodya caught her by the wrist and hauled her back.

His face looked ghostly in the moonlight. "I'm sorry, Pauline. Forgive me, you must. It's just that you're . . . what I mean is, I don't know what . . ." He was so embarrassed he couldn't get the words out, and before she could say anything Rodya rushed back into the house.

It's not his fault, she tried to tell herself. He didn't know what he was doing. It was all that brandy he was drinking. He didn't mean any harm, I'm sure he didn't. Then why am I still shaking?

From upstairs she heard a bell ringing. Then the madwoman who was her mother began to laugh, just like a lonely woodgoblin, the goat-footed *leshi* who used to terrify her as a child.

Three days after she first arrived at Tsarskoye, the elegant provincial town whose heart was the Palace of the Tsar, and whose lifeblood was the gossip that emanated from the court, Masha came face to face with the man she'd come here to find.

The summer quarters of the Imperial Guard, of which Trigony was a regimental officer, were located at nearby Krasnoye Selo, a hot, dusty plain used for maneuvers. Nearly every evening Guardsmen flocked to Tsarskoye, not only to escape the heat, but mainly to partake of the endless round of lavish dinner parties and dances.

Countess Ignatieva was a member of the elite, and having been invited to a dance at one of the aristocratic villas that dotted the neighborhood, she arrived with Henriette and Masha as her entourage. The Countess was much liked, and she and Henriette were known to nearly everyone in polite society. Masha was quite amazed by the numbers of people who came up to them when they made their entrance, all of whom appeared to be on familiar terms with her sister.

"Ah, Mademoiselle Henriette," they would say, the men bending low to kiss her thin, dry hand, the women looking at her searchingly and whispering of their latest visitations, or asking with wide and inquiring eyes if she'd received any word from her friend Father Gregory, with whom they all seemed to be well acquainted.

Meanwhile, the Countess wandered about as if she were lost, bumping into the market baskets that were filled with masses of Parma violets, daffodils, and roses. "I can't seem to find anything," she was heard to complain. "Didn't we come in this way, Henriette? Then why am I heading for the front door instead of the garden?"

With her jet-black dyed hair and blotchy red face, the buxom Countess was an easy target for good-natured tomfoolery. But as Masha observed, it was all done in a spirit of great warmth and camaraderie, and people were continually coming up to the Countess to remind her that her lorgnette was still around her neck, and not back in Petersburg as she kept insisting.

Dressed in a gown of the palest blue, Masha drifted out into the garden, while behind her the strains of a waltz added just the right note of gaiety to the proceedings. Henriette followed after her, as though because Masha was unescorted, she couldn't be left alone, even for a minute.

A brightly striped awning sheltered a long table covered with *zakuski*. Footmen in livery circulated gracefully with glasses of vodka and champagne. A low buzz of laughter and conversation filled the air, while from every direction she heard mention of the Grand Duchess Marie Nikolayevna, whose birth the previous month was viewed with something less than joy, as this was the third girl Alexandra had given her husband. There was talk of the Tsar's younger brother,

Grand Duke George, who at the age of twenty-seven was dying of tuberculosis, and of this one's love affair and that one's indiscretion.

Masha, however, wasn't particularly enamored of what the English referred to as "small talk." Sipping her wine, she moved beyond the awning to stand along one of the ilex-bordered paths that wound through the garden. It was here that she first heard Colonel Trigony's name, and it was here that she first laid eyes on him after nearly thirteen years.

"Eugene Borisovich, you naughty man!" Countess Ignatieva called out. "Why don't you ever come and see us anymore?"

"My dear Countess, what a pleasure to find you looking so well."

"Do you really think so, or is that what you say to all the girls?"

"But of course not," insisted Trigony. "Besides, you're not like all the girls, Countess. I consider you—well, rather special, if you don't mind my saying."

"Special!" squealed the Countess. "Why, you are a devil, Colonel Trigony. Oh, and here's Henriette. You two know each other, I trust."

"Yes, I never forget a pretty face," replied Trigony. "Mademoiselle Petrova, so good to see you again. I understand your brother is causing his usual artistic uproar back in the capital. It must be very thrilling for you to know what a success he is."

Masha, having listened to each and every word, now moved quickly down the path to the *zakuski* table, where Trigony, the Countess, and Henriette were still engaged in polite conversation. As soon as her sister saw her coming toward them, she started to make her excuses. But before she could even get the words out Masha linked her arm through Henriette's and looked up at the Colonel, bringing all of her teeth to bear upon a smile.

She would have recognized him even if he'd gone bald and lost all his teeth. He was still the same swaggering and arrogant figure she remembered from the days when she lived at the Selistchev Barracks, and he was only a captain.

"Good evening," she said with great difficulty.

Henriette pressed her knuckles into the small of her back, as if urging her to excuse herself before anything else was said. But Masha had no intention of turning her back on this pug-nosed assassin who now thrust out his chest like a pouter pigeon, proud of his uniform and the gold aiguillettes that proclaimed him A.D.C. to a Grand Duke.

"Henriette, *ma chère*," Masha said when her sister failed to make the necessary introductions, "are you going to let me stand here and look foolish, or will you give me the pleasure of meeting your charming friend?"

Henriette coughed and cleared her throat. "Colonel Trigony, my sister, Maria Petrovna—"

"Petrova," said Masha before Henriette had a chance to finish.

"These delightful Petrovs are cropping up all over the place," declared Trigony, tapping his tiny nose with the tip of his finger. "A pleasure, *mademoiselle*."

"Masha dear, shouldn't we go back inside now?" asked Henriette. "It's getting rather chilly out here."

"Chilly? Do you find our Russian summers chilly, Colonel?"

"Eugene Borisovich," he said, tilting his head to peer at her more closely. "Actually, I haven't detected a chill in the air as of yet, although my uniform is considerably warmer than your lovely gown."

Again Henriette urged her to go back inside, and again she smiled and declined the invitation.

"I'll join you in a moment or two," Masha said. "I'm sure

Eugene Borisovich has more to talk about than the weather. Isn't that so, Colonel?"

Her long, dark lashes fluttered alluringly, even as something hard and bitter-tasting rose up in her throat, making it difficult to breathe.

"You do look awfully familiar, you know. Are you sure we haven't met before?" he asked.

"Oh Masha dear!" called Henriette from the edge of the terrace. "Do come inside now, *ma soeur*."

"Perhaps we'll meet again during the cotillion," suggested Trigony.

"If not, I shall be sorely disappointed, Colonel." She held out her hand, shuddering to herself when he kissed her.

But she was not disappointed. When the series of dancing games commenced, a high hedge of roses was wheeled into the ballroom. The ladies were requested to stand on one side, and when the signal was given, they all reached over the top of the hedge to grasp the hand of their unseen partner. With a triumphant laugh, Trigony raised his head above the barrier of flowers, slyly admitting that he'd arranged with the master of ceremonies to learn where she was standing.

The orchestra struck up yet another waltz. As he held her in his arms and led her around the ballroom, Masha wondered how she could possibly go through with her plan. To be near this man, to allow him to hold her, was more hideous than she could have imagined.

"You've never been out in society before, *mademoiselle*, have you?" he asked.

"Actually, I've been away for several years, living in the country."

"All by yourself?" The Colonel looked down at her, his narrow lips turned up in an oily smile. "But I do know you, I'm certain. Didn't we meet at Baden-Baden? Or perhaps it was Biarritz."

"Does it really matter, Eugene? The important thing is that we've finally met."

Her forwardness caught him off guard. He laughed nervously, obviously not accustomed to women who spoke their minds. Then, holding her even more closely than before, he asked if she'd ever been married.

"A long time ago," she admitted, trying to sound as nonchalant as she could. "A trivial episode, to be sure. So many men are mere puppies, if you follow my meaning. And then there are those who go after young girls, thinking nothing of bringing them to ruin. I, at least, no longer have to worry about such foolish things."

"Ah, you're still young, *mademoiselle*. And easily the most attractive woman here."

Masha pretended to smile. "It's always a great compliment to hear that from a man as handsome as you, Colonel."

Trigony thrived on her flattery, and sailed about the room as if they were the only ones at the ball. When the waltz came to an end he was unwilling to relinquish his grip on her hand, and hovered by her side, thrusting out his chest and tapping his nose while he told her how enchanting she looked, and how there was something quite magical about being in the company of a woman wise to the ways of the world.

Masha knew exactly what he was getting at, and responded accordingly, joining him when the party moved into the dining room, where dozens of round tables were arranged for the informal supper. Here they dined on sterlet, and white partridge with bilberry jam, while the lackeys continued to make their rounds, serving up small glasses of vodka as well as an overabundant supply of sweet champagne.

Fortunately, Henriette and the Countess were seated at the opposite end of the room, though now and again Masha would catch her sister's eye, trying to calm her with her glance. By the time dessert was served, the Colonel's face was flushed with drink. Emboldened by all the vodka and champagne he had consumed, he now reached under the table, where Masha suddenly felt his hand on her knee, much like a starfish grasping a clam.

She didn't pull away, however, but stared just as boldly into the man's reddened and glassy eyes, as if to say that even though this wasn't the place for such things, she'd certainly be amenable at another time.

Trigony apparently understood the meaning of her provocative glance. He removed the offending hand and leaned forward, whispering in her ear. "May I call on you tomorrow?" he asked as he gave her elbow a little squeeze. "Perhaps then you'll tell me where we've met, because the more I look at you, *ma chère,* the more convinced I am that I do know you from somewhere."

"Such persistence, Colonel," she said, forcing herself to laugh. "But now that I think of it, you do resemble someone I once knew, someone I've dreamed of meeting for many years."

Trigony's chest swelled so that the gilded buttons on his tunic threatened to pop off. "You needn't dream any longer," he announced. "I shall call on you tomorrow without fail."

"Please do," she replied, choking on the words. She pushed her chair back and came abruptly to her feet, gagging now, and knowing that she would soon be sick.

Trigony jumped up, bowing a she hurried from the dining room.

"Masha!" she heard Henriette call out.

Rather than answer, Masha rushed through the empty ballroom and out into the garden, choosing the first path she came to. Only when she was a sufficient distance from the house did she pause in her flight, and bending her head low to the ground, allowed herself to be as sick as she felt.

* * *

The morning following her arrival, Pauline waited in her room until she was certain her stepfather had left on his rounds. Only then did she venture downstairs, where she found Platon the coachman gossiping in the kitchen with Akulina, the freckle-faced woman who'd taken over as housekeeper after Anninka's death. Platon now hobbled about with the aid of a cane, though he was still as fat and merry as ever. She told him that she wanted to drive out to Red Hill, as she was anxious to pay a call on her Aunt Varvara. Then went back upstairs to try to convince her mother to accompany her. But though Pauline begged and cajoled for nearly an hour, Vera had no intention of leaving her room, let alone the house.

The morning was overcast, but by the time they reached Krasnaya Gorka the sun had come out, and the clouds had drifted off to the west. From a distance the little blancmange-colored house looked snug and comfortable, and when Platon drove into the yard the first person to see them was her dear Auntie V.

"You raven-haired little minx!" the old woman cried. "Why didn't you tell us you were coming? We would have prepared a proper welcome for you, my darling. Ardaloshka, look who's come to see us," she called out, her dark eyes shining with excitement as she clutched Pauline to her breast, then stood back to look at her.

"It's your father's coloring, oh yes. And his chin, and his dimples, too," insisted Auntie V., her thick, bold eyebrows darting up and down, and a faint smell of camphor clinging to her black skirts and enveloping her like a cloud.

General Tishin, wearing a voluminous dressing gown of faded Bokhara silk, and red, silver-embroidered Caucasian slippers on his feet, shuffled out of the house. His sleepy blue eyes were suddenly wide awake the moment he caught sight of her.

"What a pleasure! What a surprise! What a delight!" he said in rapid succession, kissing her three times and then stepping back to admire her, much as one might view a work of art in a museum. "A beauty, Varvarushka. A regular Russian *Venus de Milan*—with arms, of course." The General laughed heartily, his triple chin wagging back and forth like a dewlap.

How good it was to see them again, for it gave Pauline a kind of center that was missing when she arrived at Petrovka. Here at Red Hill, their happiness was contagious, and to see both these old people doting on her as they might have doted on their own child made Pauline feel very safe and secure.

Later, they lunched together in a charming little summerhouse that overlooked the river with its broad, panoramic views. It wasn't at all like the moldy summerhouse where she'd spent so much time as a child. Here there was no smell of decay, nor was there a single cobweb to wrap around oneself and disappear. With a canopy of hops, the summerhouse was a cool and shady retreat, and the General took full advantage of the first lull in the conversation to lean back in his chair and close his eyes.

As he drowsed, she and Auntie V. bent their heads together, trying to catch up on all that had happened since they'd seen each other last. Although Varvara Semyonovna was now in her seventies, and the downy mustache over her drooping upper lip had turned as white as clotted cream, her eyes were as sharp and alert as ever and she moved with barely restrained energy.

"I did pay a call on your mother a few months back, the poor child," Varvara was saying, to the accompaniment of the General's winsome little snores. "A terrible calamity, just terrible. Mad she is, and mad she'll probably always be. Now you needn't look so shocked, my dear, because there's no sense hiding from the truth. Incurable, the doctors say, which is very odd, because I always thought that if any of them would go crazy it would be your Aunt Henriette. She was the one who never had anything to look forward to, and always walked around like she'd bitten into a lemon, she looked so sour. I would never have guessed your mother would succumb—not that she had the easiest time of it, of course."

"And my father, what was he like?" she asked, wondering if that wasn't the key to all her mother's problems.

"A very strange man, very strange indeed," replied Auntie V. "As far as I'm concerned, she should never have married him. She had more suitors than you could shake a stick at, but Simon Ivanovich was the only man she paid any attention to. Oh, he was a handsome devil, all right. The women loved him. And he loved the women. But he was a man sorely devoid of principle. Your Aunt Masha was much taken with a young man at the time, and Simon exposed him to the authorities. He had some rather incriminating papers in his possession, and so they carted him off to prison, where he died very young, so I've been told. But why this sudden interest in your father? Had he really cared about you and your mother, do you think for one moment he would have deserted you so long ago? He was a scoundrel, with a gift for hurting others."

How could she tell Auntie V. that she missed him, or at least missed the idea of having a father. Of all the girls at school she was the only one who never spoke of her parents, so that most of the pupils at St. Ekaterina's had assumed she was an orphan.

"Leave it alone, dear," advised her aunt. "Enjoy yourself now, and be glad there are those who love you. I'm afraid it took me too many years to appreciate that."

"And now?"

"Now I'm an old woman, quite content to take care of my big sleepyhead over there," Varvara said with a laugh, one that was so warm and affectionate it made her sound just like a girl.

"Deserters! Murderers!" her mother was screaming when Pauline returned to Petrovka several days later, having decided on the spur of the moment to prolong her visit at Red Hill. "The moment my back is turned what does she do, she runs off, the ungrateful child. Beast, that's what you are, Pauline, a spiteful, venomous beast!"

"It's what I feared," said Rodya when she came into the house. "She thought you were coming back the same day, and when you didn't she started to cry. That's all we heard for nearly two days, just constant sobbing. Then last night she came downstairs and started running around, saying you were lost, and we had to find you."

"The summerhouse, yes," said her mother, who rushed toward her from the drawing room, her hands raised as if she were fighting her way through the air. "I went there and you were gone. Why do they all leave me, Rodya? I only wanted a few nice things, a little happiness for my princess."

Pauline tried to get close to her but her mother jumped back. Her blue eyes were on fire, and a hectic flush completely obscured the true coloring of her face. As calmly and patiently as possible, Pauline tried to explain what had happened, reminding her mother that she'd gone to Red Hill, that the last thing in the world she'd do is desert her.

"I love you," Pauline kept saying, trying to reach out and hold her even as Vera skipped back, determined to stay just out of reach. "I was only visiting with Auntie V."

"That hateful old bitch!" shrieked her mother. "She'd like to see me locked away somewhere. Oh yes, I know that venomous bitch all too well. First she tried to ruin Henriette and now she's trying to ruin me. What lies did she tell you, she and that fat, repulsive husband of hers? I bet she told you how much she hated me, didn't she?"

"No, Mother, nothing like that. She loves you," Pauline cried. "We all love you. Come, can't we go upstairs? You lie down for a bit and I know you'll feel better, I just know it."

It was only with the greatest of difficulty that Pauline and Rodya managed to get Vera upstairs. But at last they reached her room, where Sophia Mikhailovna's enormous canopied bed waited to receive her like the bier it resembled.

"I'm not tired," protested her mother. "I have more energy now than I ever—"

"Just lie down for a few minutes," Pauline begged. "I'll stay with you, I promise. You're right, I should never have gone to Red Hill. I made a terrible mistake, so please forgive me, *maman*, because I love you more than anyone in the world."

Her mother eyed her suspiciously, even as she sat down on the edge of the bed. Her hands seemed to have a life of their own, her fingers constantly curling and uncurling, toying with her lank yellow locks, playing with the edge of a pillow-slip, smoothing out the front of her ruffled dressing gown.

"I don't want you ever to go there again," her mother finally said. "She conspired against me, Pauline. She spread terrible tales, lies about my husband. Senya warned me about her, but I didn't listen."

"Just lie back, rest for a while. I'll be here."

Afterward, when her mother had fallen asleep, Pauline could hardly remember what Vera had talked about, droning on for more than an hour until her mother eventually closed her eyes. Exhausted by the ordeal, she came downstairs to find Rodya sulking in her granddad's study, where he lay stretched out on the old morocco divan that still bore her grandfather's imprint. A glass of brandy was clutched in his hand, and as soon as she entered the room he finished it off, then sat up and poured himself another.

"Now do you understand?" he said.

She nodded unhappily.

"She'll hurt herself one day, that's what worries me. I can restrain her only so much. I can't tie her to her bed, can I?"

"No."

"She'll jump out of a window, or run naked through the yard, I know it."

"And if she does, so what? Who's to see and who's to care? No matter what she'll do, it's certainly better than a lunatic asylum. I've read about such places. Once they're inside they never leave. They die there. All of them. I won't have that happening to my mother."

With an angry scowl, as if this were all Pauline's fault, Rodya began to thump his fists against his knees. "Easy for you to say, my pretty miss. You're leaving here, probably won't be back for a good long time, too. Who's going to look after her then? Me, that's who, the same poor fool who's watched over her since it all started."

"Are you saying that you don't want to bear the responsibility anymore, Rodya?"

Her stepfather picked up the decanter, and when he saw it was empty, he glared at her sullenly. "I'm going out," he announced. "And if she starts to scream that I've deserted her, tell her to shut up and go back to sleep, she's getting on everyone's nerves."

"How can you be so unsympathetic? She's not well, Rodya. She doesn't know what she's doing."

"Aren't you getting righteous," he sneered. "You're not home a week and you're already trying to take charge. Well, I'm still head of this household, young lady, and you'd be wise to remember that."

Having never seen her stepfather so angry, she could only nod her head and look down at her lap. A few minutes later she heard him drive off, the horses galloping down the lime alley and throwing up clouds of yellow dust that hung suspended in the motionless summer air long after they were gone.

Pauline couldn't sleep, and lay in bed listening to the night sounds that drifted in through her open window. Now and again a quail would cluck far off over the fields, and at infrequent intervals the strange, raspy scream of a crane made her tremble, bringing to mind the hideous Baba-Yaga who had stalked through the nightmares of her childhood. Then there was momentary silence, broken by the wind rustling through the trees. The leaves of the limes and the birches murmured solemnly to themselves of things she could never possibly understand.

It was true, there were too many things she didn't know about, the way relationships sometimes got all tangled up like a hopelessly knotted ball of yarn. She might spend all summer setting things right, but then what would happen once she left for the university? Perhaps she shouldn't even be thinking of that. Wasn't it unfair of her to expect Rodya to take full responsibility for her mother, and to continue to live her life as though she had no one but herself to worry about? But Aunt Masha would be coming back, wouldn't she? So it wasn't as if Rodya were going to be left entirely on his own.

That made Pauline feel a little better, lifting some of the guilt she'd carried around ever since her stepfather stormed out of the house. She'd expected him to stagger back hours ago, but he still hadn't returned. Now, as she finally closed her eyes, the faint creaking of carriage wheels and the rhythmic beat of hoofs reached her ears.

"Get up, you old fool, and attend to the horses," Rodya cried out.

Then a door swung open, and a moment after that came a tap-tap-tap. It must have been Platon with his cane, for the next thing she heard was a harsh exchange of voices, first her stepfather's drunken, belittling shouts, and then the coachmen's subdued reply.

"Certainly they'll get water, certainly," Platon was saying. "And a good brushing down, too, Your Excellency."

The front door slammed shut. Something fell to the floor with a crash. Pauline was about to go downstairs to help him when she thought better of it, and remained in bed as her stepfather began to make his way up the stairs.

Tomorrow I'll tell him that I'm willing to stay, she decided. If they need me here, then I'll just postpone going to school. But I won't have them sending her to a yellow house with all the other lunatics.

She felt so good about this, so determined to do her share, that she couldn't help but smile. But then Rodya's lumbering footsteps stopped right outside her door. Without even bothering to knock, he turned the knob and let himself in.

"Did she make any trouble?" He stepped inside, pushing the door shut with his boot.

Pauline sat up in bed, holding the covers close to her neck.

"Now, why're you acting so shy with your daddy?" Rodya snickered, and began to crack his knuckles, popping each finger in turn.

Afraid of waking her mother, she spoke softly. "I was asleep, Rodya. And no, she's been very quiet. Why don't we talk about it in the morning?"

Instead of answering, her stepfather lurched across the room. "You're my sweet lovely daughter, and your daddy's had himself a bellyful tonight." With a loud hiccup he lost his balance and fell across the foot of the bed. He lay there giggling, staring at her as she huddled beneath the covers.

Trying to convince herself there was nothing to be alarmed about, Pauline started to get out of bed to help him when the steward straightened up with a groan.

"It's no use," he said, his glazed brown eyes fixed on the point where the bedcovers met her neck.

"You'll feel better in the morning, Rodya. You've just had too much to drink, that's all."

"That's not all," he insisted. "But you love your daddy, don't you. 'Cause I'm all alone, Pauline. She won't have me anymore. Even if I wanted her, and I do, I still do, she won't have me. But I tried awfully hard, and for a long time, too. No one can accuse me of giving up on her, can they?"

"If you'll go to sleep, I know you'll feel better."

"How can I feel better when tomorrow's going to be just like today?" He sat down beside her and threw a heavy arm over her shoulders. "You'll help me, Pauline, won't you? I should never have yelled at you, I know, but I'm so alone and twisted up inside that half the time I don't know what I'm saying."

Pauline tried to slip free of his arm, but Rodya tightened his grip on her.

"I don't want you to go yet," he protested, whining like a little boy who wasn't getting his way. "You're my daughter, aren't you? Then be nice. You're a pretty one, too. Senya's little girl, ain't that so?"

"Rodya, please."

"No 'please.' I don't want to hear 'please' no more. Just give your daddy a kiss now like a good girl."

Cupping her face in his hands, Rodya leaned forward and pressed his lips to her mouth. It wasn't a father's good-night kiss, and when she tried to push him away, his rough, calloused hands gripped her arms, holding her fast.

"Don't say anything," he whispered. He pulled the bedcovers down to her waist, and when he put his hands on her breasts she shoved him back as hard as she could, threatening to scream and wake the entire house if he didn't leave her alone. But Rodya's response was a drunken laugh. "Your mother'll come in and think it's all your fault, that you invited me into your room. After all, that's how it was with us. Oh yes, she was a passionate woman. That's all she cared about. But now she's all dried up and what am I to do, Pauline?"

He didn't wait for an answer, but threw himself down on top of her, pinning her beneath him. Pauline tried to cry for help, only to feel Rodya's hands over her mouth. Her shouts muffled, he had her nightdress undone before she could stop him. The more she fought and struggled to escape, the more determined he was to have her, kissing her neck and shoulders, then edging lower to nuzzle her breasts with his wet and eager mouth.

When she felt his hand groping between her legs, when he touched her where she'd never even touched herself, it was worse than Baba-Yaga, worse than the day Grandfather had the stroke, even worse than seeing her mother and knowing she couldn't help her.

"I can't stop it. I'm sorry, but I can't," she heard her stepfather say, when a dark shadow reared up before her, and even Rodya froze and pulled his hand back.

Was it Granddad's ghost? the child in her wondered. She slammed her eyes shut, praying this was all a nightmare, and that she'd soon wake up to discover she was all alone.

But it wasn't a dream, because then she heard her mother's voice, sharp and shrill.

"So this is the filth they taught you, is it? Leave the slut alone, Rodya. She tried to steal you away from me, the filthy trollop. I should've known, even from the beginning. She's no daughter of mine and she never will be. She's Senya's little bastard, and just like him she'll burn in hell for her sins."

Rodya staggered away from the bed, looking at each of them but seeing neither.

"Tell her!" Pauline screamed through her tears. "Tell her what you tried to do to me, Rodya, tell her!"

Her mother tossed her head back and laughed, her yellow hair flying from side to side, an imperfect halo for an imperfect angel, condemned to a purgatory of madness.

"Tell her, for God's sake!"

The bedroom door swung shut and she and her mother were alone.

"Mother, it wasn't what you think. He tried to—"

"Liar!" Vera shrieked. "You're just like everyone else. But I won't stand for it anymore, I won't. I'm still beautiful . . . or . . . or pretty. I can have anyone I want. I'll go away from this horrible place, that's what I'll do, and then you can have him all to yourself. Yes, that's what you'd like, isn't it, to steal him away from me and have him for your own."

Before she could answer, or even begin to defend herself, her mother rushed from the room. Pauline ran after her, weeping and begging her to listen. But once inside her bedroom, her mother locked the door and refused to come out.

"Slut," Pauline heard her whispering from the other side of the door. "Vile, disgusting, filthy slut. It's in the blood, and just like me, you'll never change, not even when you're dead."

Three

When Masha came downstairs the morning after the ball, she found Henriette waiting for her in the dining room, clutching her coffee cup as if it were a crystal ball. Without even taking the time to greet her, Henriette launched into an impassioned speech she'd no doubt thought out well in advance.

"Isn't it enough that one of our sisters is mad? Must you make it a family habit, or do you just take pleasure in embarrassing me?"

"I don't care to discuss it, Henriette."

"Whether you care or not isn't the point," replied Henriette. "To speak to him is one thing. But to allow him to touch you like that is another." Henriette shivered dramatically to emphasize her meaning, and as her bony shoulders trembled beneath her kimono, Masha decided she'd had quite enough of her sister's brand of constructive criticism.

She took her coffee with her and went out into the garden, where the dew was still wet on the grass, and a dense growth of Siberian geraniums colored the fence with their delicate pale-pink flowers. Finding a spot of shade beneath a mulberry tree, she sat down on the stone bench and tried not to think of what Henriette had said.

Masha should have known that her sister wouldn't give up so easily, because a few minutes later Henriette came down the steps from the veranda.

"Something terrible is going to come of this," Henriette told her. "And why you'd want to do such a thing to yourself is beyond me."

"Why don't you look into the future, Henriette, and find out for yourself?"

Her sister stiffened.

"I wanted to dance with Trigony and so I did. He's going to call on me today. The least you can do is be civil."

Henriette looked at her in disbelief. A telephone line having recently been established between Tsarskoye and the capital, she now announced her intention of phoning Irena and telling her to come to get Masha and take her home.

"Petrovka is where I've slept all these years," Masha replied. "But it's not my home. It's not anyone's home, not anymore. In fact, I wish Irena would sell it so we could all forget how things used to be. It's a myth, you know, that we were all so wonderfully happy and carefree as children. We weren't, Henriette, not any of us."

"That may be, but it still has no bearing on the subject at hand. If you're so set on destroying your life and hurting your loved ones—"

Unable to bear her sister's self-righteous tone, especially when Henriette was the one who'd first tempted her with talk of Trigony, Masha lost her temper and began to shout. "What do you know about love, anyway? Stepan was love. Victor was love. Did they want me to creep through life like a dog who's whipped and always comes back fawning, just begging for more? Believe me, Henriette, I know exactly what I'm doing. Eugene Borisovich is taken with me. And that's just the way I want it to be."

*   *   *

Countess Ignatieva, having remained in bed until noon, and having just completed her toilette, took Colonel Trigony's arrival as a signal for an afternoon of merriment. But though she rattled off a list of activities, beginning with a picnic and ending with a soirée she promised would be the most amusing of the season, the Colonel smiled good-naturedly and made his excuses.

When Masha and the officer got into the latter's carriage, the Countess went upstairs to her room. Sighing with disappointment, she called on Henriette to come to sit with her, as she was so bored she thought she'd die.

"A harmless fool," was the way Eugene Borisovich described her to Masha, who sat beside him, a rigid smile pinned to her lips.

Having proposed a ride into the countryside, Trigony now set off, patting Masha's knee as if he were exercising *droit du seigneur*. He was in an expansive and affable mood, tapping his nose with every other word as he spoke of the ball, and how he hadn't been able to sleep, just thinking of her. Masha let him carry the conversation as they followed the iron fence surrounding the imperial park, where bearded Cossack horsemen in scarlet tunics kept a watchful eye, lest anyone try to come between them and their sovereign.

As they reached the outskirts of Tsarskoye, a polished rig of English design came toward them at a sedate and dignified pace. It was only when they passed each other that Masha quickly turned her head away, though the elderly woman seated in the carriage had ample time to raise her lorgnette and peer at them inquisitively.

"A friend?" Trigony asked, not having recognized her himself.

Masha continued to stare straight ahead. That she was actually sitting next to him in a pose of intimacy was even more horrifying than what had happened the night before. She had always thought of herself as level-headed, but now it was as if she'd become someone else altogether. This new Masha seemed determined to prove her strength of will, to suffer in silence while she waited for the odious fly who sat beside her to fall into her trap.

"She's General Danchenko's widow," she said at last.

Trigony reacted predictably, jerking his head toward her as if she'd tugged on it with a string. "Not the same—"

"The very same," she said calmly. "And I'm a Danchenko widow, too."

She was fully prepared for him to rein in the horses and come to a stop in the middle of the road, then stare and stare until his eyes popped out of their sockets. Yet the Colonel did nothing of the kind. Instead, he began to laugh, sounding delighted by her revelation.

"Maria Petrovna, and to think I didn't even recognize you," he exclaimed. "It's me though, not you. Because you haven't changed, oh no, not a bit. Still as lovely and impulsive as ever. But why in the world didn't you tell me? No wonder you looked so familiar. But that was—what? Ten years ago?"

"Thirteen."

"Are you going to draw out a pistol, my dearest, and shoot me dead? Or do you have other plans for your Eugene?"

"Of course I have other plans. Why, if it weren't for you, I'd still be—" Here she paused and put her arm through his, leaning her head against his shoulder. "I thought that if I told you I was Stepan's widow, you wouldn't have understood, and might have avoided me. But you see, I've never told you the truth, Eugene. Oh, I wanted to, I assure you. So many times since that day I've wanted to find you and express my gratitude for what you did."

"Gratitude?" said Trigony with another laugh.

Trying desperately to compose herself, and knowing that each word she said would be like poison on her lips, Masha began to explain what she meant. Referring to Trigony as her liberator, she painted her husband as the most villainous blackguard imaginable. Trigony listened attentively, still patting her knee to encourage her, and now and again giving her hand a reassuring squeeze.

"A nightmare," she concluded, dabbing at her eyes with a handkerchief. "You can't begin to imagine how cruel he was to me. And not just mental torment, Eugene, but physical abuse as well. He was ill, deranged, I'm quite sure, for no man in his right mind would have made his wife endure such suffering."

"Yet you never complained?" Trigony asked.

"He would have murdered me in my bed, I'm sure of it. He was ill, terribly ill. A sadist, Eugene, and prey to the most monstrous . . . no, it's too difficult to describe, even now. But he was quite an actor, you see. In front of others he was always a gentleman, as I'm sure even you will testify. But when we were alone . . . no, I've tried to put it all behind me, for what's the use of remembering so much pain?"

Again she pretended to cry, shuddering as Henriette had done at breakfast, and hoped Trigony was completely taken in by what she had told him.

The Colonel wrapped his arm around her and held her close. "You should have left him, Masha, or come to me and told me what a monster he was, instead of subjecting yourself to such torment."

"I tried, Eugene, time and time again. But he always found me out and dragged me back. That's why I wanted the duel to take place. That's why I didn't wait for you as we'd planned, because as long as we kept our love a secret, there would be no way to escape him. When he left to meet you that day, I got down on my knees and begged God to release me from the horror that was our life together. Your aim was true, just as I prayed it would be."

Could Bernhardt have done better? No, Masha didn't think so. This had been a performance she'd waited more than a decade to give. Every nuance, every phrase, had all been carefully thought out. If Trigony failed to believe her, then there would be no point in continuing the charade. But when he stopped the carriage and kissed her, murmuring words he no doubt thought clever and endearing, Masha knew she had succeeded, and that whatever uncertainties he might have felt earlier were no longer in evidence.

"But why did you wait so long to tell me?" he asked. There was something so sincere, and even kindhearted about his expression, that for a moment she almost felt guilty.

"After what he put me through, the years of abuse and degradation, I needed to get away and find myself, Eugene, recover my sanity, if you must. But when my sister spoke of meeting you, it was all I could do not to cry out for joy."

Even as she felt sickened by her words, Trigony let out with a boyish laugh, a whoop of sheer delight that frightened the horses and sent them galloping down the road. Pressing her to his side, he told her that they'd vanquished time, and henceforth they would never again talk of Stepan Danchenko. He was like a changed man, and the arrogance and self-importance he'd formally worn as proudly as his uniform were nowhere to be seen. But his charming manners meant nothing to her. The man was a murderer, and even if he wandered in rags from one end of Russia to the other like Makary the *starets* of Verkhoture, he would still be a murderer, even when they laid him in his coffin.

She eased away from him then, keeping her smile in place as she gazed out on the countryside, the sun red and dripping like the inside of a melon, and the heat rising from the land like steam escaping from a samovar.

"But what of us, Masha?"

If only she could tell him what she wanted from him. But how could she ask him to love her, when that very expression of adoration was the cornerstone of her plan? Yes, she would make him kneel before her, make him profess his undying devotion. And when she had his heart in the palm of her hand, she'd squeeze it dry, leaving him with nothing.

"We must be very discreet, Eugene. His mother is a vicious old woman. She'll spread terrible tales if we're not careful."

"She's nobody, I assure you," Trigony replied. "When one has the ear—not to mention the purse strings—of a Grand Duke, one has absolutely nothing to fear. I run Paul's household for him, see to his family's every need. You needn't worry that you'll be slandered, not by Stepan's mother or anyone else."

They drove into the village of Kuzmino, a double row of wooden cottages flanking the road, each separated from the next by a high fence and a large courtyard gate. Rude perforated woodwork decorated the balconies that filled in the sharp gable end of many of the houses, while the more affluent villagers had white curtains in their windows, and carved horses' heads crowning their rooftops.

Without a word of explanation, Trigony drew up before the inn and quickly jumped down, going around to the other side of the carriage to offer Masha his hand.

"Everything's been arranged," he said as he led her inside, where the innkeeper greeted him in deferential tones and immediately started up the stairs.

Trigony, still clutching her hand, followed after him. Eying the accommodations—a small, clean room with three shuttered windows fronting the streets—he dug a few coppers out of his pocket and instructed the innkeeper to bring them a bottle of his finest wine. Then he sat down on the bed and patted the place alongside him.

"First we'll drink to our reunion," she suggested, stalling for time.

The innkeeper was efficient, however, and before too long he was back with a bottle of sauterne and two glasses. These he wiped clean with his greasy apron, and would have continued like this for some time had Trigony not dipped into his pocket again to pay him for his services. The innkeeper backed out of the room, winking impudently at Masha as he closed the door. Trigony locked it, poured the wine, and raised his glass.

"Had someone told me we'd ever meet again, I would never have believed him. But life does have its share of surprises, Masha, doesn't it?"

"We need surprises, Eugene. After all, think how boring it would be if we knew exactly what was in store for us."

Trigony nodded, drained off half his wine, and quickly unbuttoned his tunic. Masha looked away, trying to enclose herself in a wall of her own devising, so that when he touched her she wouldn't feel anything, and would hardly know he was there. Henriette was right, there was something hideously grotesque and self-destructive about what she was doing. To make love to her husband's murderer, to allow him to paw her, to hear him grunting as he ripped off her clothes, tearing at the buttons in his eagerness to have her for his own, was something so odious as to defy her own ability to understand it. Yet she was unwilling to stop him, and kept her eyes focused above the top of his head, where a cowlick of blond hair waved back and forth like the antenna of a cockroach. He was puffy and soft behind his tightly notched belt, and beneath his cologne a musky, sweaty scent came through.

Was this what she'd waited thirteen years to consummate, allowing herself to be stripped naked, fondled as if she were nothing more than a two-ruble whore? Yet she needed him to love her. She needed to know that she meant more to him than anyone in the world. Only then would the act she planned be fully commensurate with what he'd done to Stepan.

As she lay there on the bed in the inn in the village of Kuzmino, the red melon sun hazy and pulsing behind a jaundiced screen of dust, Trigony pulled her legs apart and rammed himself inside her, as if a vengeful, hammering thrust were the only form of lovemaking he understood. Masha stiffened with self-loathing, and bit down on her lower lip until the skin cracked and a single droplet of blood slowly trickled down her chin. Trigony obligingly licked it off, stabbing into her with short, breathless strokes, knifing her with passion whetted by thirteen years of longing.

Was he being a gentleman when he suddenly pulled back, rearing up before her and begging her to open her eyes and watch him as he reached his climax? Or was this merely the way he functioned, part of the show he put on for his women, the bored wives and daughters who frequented his bed? Masha had no way of knowing, but as she forced herself to stare at him while his seed spurted over her breasts and belly, she understood how truly terrifying revenge could be, not only for Trigony, but especially for herself.

Packed and ready to leave, Pauline stood before her mother's door, begging her to come out and say good-bye. Below the threshold a shadow moved, fluttering like a leaf.

"Go away," said the voice behind the door. "I never want to see you again. Never, do you hear? Never, never, never!"

Having stood there weeping for the last hour, Pauline had nothing left to say. Every argument was exhausted, her mother refusing to listen to her, and shrieking at the top of her voice whenever she began to speak.

"Go away," Vera said again. "Go back to the Presnia where you belong. You're his little bastard, not mine. My princess worships the ground I walk upon, and doesn't invite her step-father into her bed. Was he good, Pauline? Did you like him, you slut? But he wasn't half as good as your father, I'll tell you that. Oh no, that's where you get it from, you little whore."

Even if she stuffed her ears with cotton wool she still would have heard every horrifying word. With a lone and stricken cry, Pauline turned away and ran down the hall. She would go to Julia's, and when they were alone she would tell her friend what had happened, and the two of them would weep that all the promises of childhood were nothing but footprints left in the dust.

When she came downstairs she could hear Platon in the yard, and knew that as soon as she composed herself he would take her to the station. She paused outside the drawing room, wondering what had happened to the ebony-eyed little minx Grandfather used to dangle on his knee, telling her of his youth as if reading from a book of fairy tales.

"And then, when I turned twenty-seven, I acquired the mill. And then, at twenty-eight, the meadows by the river. And at thirty the birch wood, and at thirty-one . . ."

She remembered how gay the sleigh bells had rung that day, and how she'd snuggled against him while Turk and Coco plunged gamely through the snow. They were all dead, and somehow it felt that with their dying her past had died as well. It was something they'd all taken with them, Granddad and Granny, even the ponies, so that she could never retrieve the full share of memories that might have enriched her life.

Pauline went into the kitchen, where there was no one to give her a paper cone filled with gingerbreads, and nothing bubbling on the stove to tempt her appetite. "Have you seen Mr. Sorokin?" she asked Akulina.

"He's down in the storeroom, miss."

Lifting her skirts so she wouldn't trip, Pauline opened the

cellar door and descended the short flight of worn stone steps. Stretching before her was a vast area equal in size to the first floor of the house. Supported by brick arches, and radiating from a large open space in the center, corridors ran off in various directions. All along the walls stood heavy wooden doors like those in a fairy-tale dungeon, many of them bolted with padlocks. As a child she had played here when it was too cold to hide in the summerhouse. During the winter the middle of the cellar was filled with a plot of dried sand in which roots were planted—carrots, potatoes, parsnips, and turnips, just like in a garden. Seated on the sand with her legs sprawled out before her, she recalled making castles, turning the sand into mud with a pitcher of water Granny would give her for just that purpose. She used to stay down here for hours, surrounded by all the stores that made Petrovka self-sufficient. Bags of nuts and dried mushrooms hung from the ceiling so the mice couldn't reach them, while lining the corridors were great wooden casks of salted beef and dried fish, linseed oil, and the sweet, fermented cabbage that was as much a staple as the coarse, dark bread Granny had always baked.

Pauline found Rodya taking an inventory of all this and more, counting off the sacks of flour like soldiers about to be conscripted. At her approach he stopped what he was doing and lowered his eyes, wearing his embarrassment like a tarnished sign. When he finally met her glance his shame had burned itself deep into his face, and his eyes were as lifeless as two bits of glass.

"I'm not an evil man," he said, "really I'm not. When you were just a child, I may have resented you, it's true. But I never wanted you to hate me, Pauline."

"Then tell her what happened, Rodya, because if you don't she'll only get worse, and then you'll have no one to blame but yourself."

Rodya ran his fingers through his hair. He started to crack

his knuckles, then changed his mind, jabbing his hands into his back pockets as he rocked back and forth on his boot heels. "I can't," he whispered, though no one could possibly have heard him. "She'll order me to leave just as she's ordered you."

Pauline shook her head. Despite everything he had done, she felt very sorry for her stepfather. Without Petrovka, he had nothing, and without her mother he had even less than that.

"She won't. She needs you too much. Don't you see, Rodya, you're the only one she has now. And unless you try to help her, she'll be lost to all of us."

Rodya fidgeted uncomfortably, shuffling his feet. Pauline, however, stood her ground, no longer frightened of this sad-eyed man whose sturdy build belied his cowardice.

The musty cellar odor settled over her like ash. "God, everything smells of death," she said. "This whole house is dying, and she's dying with it. All the people who used to live here . . . and now who's left? A madwoman and her cowardly husband."

"You mustn't call me that, Pauline."

"How can I call you anything else? You're helping to destroy whatever sanity she might have left, just because you can't face up to yourself."

"In time, I promise," Rodya said weakly, never once finding the courage to raise his eyes.

"In time there'll be nothing. In time we'll all be dead." Pauline turned away and went upstairs, listening to a snuffling sound that was perhaps her stepfather weeping, or a mouse wrinkling its nose and wondering what next to eat.

So the slut was leaving. So she couldn't get enough of him so she decided to go looking for someone else. Her belly'll swell up too, Vera imagined, and then she'll have no one to blame but herself. I saw girls like that in the Presnia all the time, girls who eyed my Senya like he was the answer to all their prayers.

So the whore was going, was she? Yes, that was her carriage rumbling down the lime alley. But no, I won't go look and peek, because she's probably watching me, hoping I'll come to the window and call her back. Call the slut back? Let her rot in hell with her father, for all I care. You give them your life and they want even more, the bastards. First they took my little duchess and now they turned my princess into a whore, lifts her legs in the air and whinnies like a mare who can't get enough of him.

"Pauline," she whispered in the darkness of her mother's room, the curtains drawn and the shadows crouching low in the corners, where they watched her every move but dared not speak, "why did you do this to your mother, Pauline? Why did you come back when I told you not to? See, they all leave me. Senya, Liza, poor *maman*, even the little bully I hated so much I must have loved him and didn't even know it. But I was young, pretty. They threw gold coins at my feet and said there wasn't a prettier bride in all of Russia. 'Look at her!' they all cried out. Look at her, because in the end the hair turns gray and the waist grows thick, and then what's left for us?

"What?" she asked the shadows lurking in the corners of the room, where the tattered strips of wallpaper met the floor in an uncertain fringe of faded roses and withered bouquets. "Nothing's left for us, that's the answer."

If only it wasn't so dark all the time. If only she had the strength to fight back, to go downstairs and take charge again. But it required more energy and resolve than she could muster. It was much easier, safer too, to lie back against the pillows and think of the summerhouse, and remember the promises they had once made to each other.

But it wasn't his fault, she thought. It was mine. I wanted more than my share, didn't I? Papa warned me about that. He said, "Vera, you mustn't be so selfish, thinking always of yourself." But did I listen? When *maman* died I didn't even come to the funeral, though it wasn't because of the money for the train ticket, which we didn't have. If I'd really cared, I should have walked all the way, even if my feet were bloody sores by the time I got here. It was the going that would have meant something, even more than being here when they lowered her into the ground.

She looked up at the heavy brocade canopy above her head, this stately baldachin from which a Cupid had flown on its slender string. Like so much else, it too was relegated to a memory. But how much easier it was to see things in her mind's eye, to confront them one by one without worrying that they'd answer back. All she had to do was send them away as she'd sent away Pauline, and then she wouldn't have to hear them pleading and telling her to come downstairs, the sun was shining; come downstairs, your dinner's waiting; come downstairs and we'll walk through the orchard to the summerhouse where he touched you here and here and here.

Ever so carefully, as if her bones were too brittle to support her weight, Vera forced herself to climb out of bed. She drew the curtains back, and as the summer light made her blink uncomfortably, she turned and sat down before her mother's dressing table, raising her eyes to confront the woman she had unhappily become.

It was much too terrifying. This wasn't Vera she saw, but a stranger.

Dear God in heaven, why couldn't he carry me in his arms forever, dancing me in the air, higher and higher? What happened to Verochka? She wasn't always like this, was she? No wonder Rodya stays away. It must make him sick to look at me.

She picked up her hairbrush, but it felt so heavy and unwieldy in her hand that she set it down again. What did she need a mirror for, anyway? All she had to do was open her eyes and see before her the reflection of all her memories, an endless, sweeping panorama of her past, as vast and silent as the steppes.

It was no use. Try as she might, she would never make herself happy. Mirrors told the truth, even if people did not. Rodya could say he loved her, and she knew it wasn't so. Pauline could beg forgiveness and do just what she promised not to, once her back was turned. So why lie in bed and wait for the canopy to fall on her head?

"He's never coming back," she thought aloud. "He married me for the dowry, that's all it was. Papa wanted to get rid of me, just like he tried to get rid of Henriette. And now I'm rid of all of them."

She ran over to the window, wondering if it was too late to call Pauline back, to try to explain to her that there was a time in everyone's life when the weight of disappointment was just too difficult to bear. Why live to shoulder yet another burden? Why suffer when you knew it would never end, even if you got down on your knees and prayed for things to change? Nothing changed, once the pattern was set. The stitches were fixed, immutable. The design existed even before you began to catch glimpses of its contours, shaped by forces always beyond your control.

When she heard the bronze clock play its gavotte, she turned back in the direction of the bed. But instead of lying down, she had other plans. Carefully unscrewing the glass globe of the bedside lamp, she reached down and removed the oil pot that fit into its china base. The kerosene spilled over the sides, stinging wherever her skin was chapped and cracked. Sorry she didn't have a spoon to ladle it out, Vera poured the oil over her bed. How lovely the dark zigzagging stains looked against the linen, like something a snake might have drawn as it moved its serpentine coils through the dust.

Satisfied, she reassembled the lamp, knowing it wouldn't do to leave things behind in disarray. It was very stupid of them not to have hidden the matches. There they were, the box just sitting out in plain sight, as if daring her to strike them. Holding the matches tightly in her hand, Vera climbed into bed, leaning back against the soft feather pillows.

"Do you understand why it's time?" she asked the Cupid hanging invisibly above her head.

Seeing it draw its chubby arm back as it got ready to loose its dart, Vera removed one of the wax matches, struck it against the strip of sandpaper along the edge of the box, and tossed it like a flaming arrow onto the foot of the bed.

A flower brighter than any she had seen blossomed and unfurled its stinging petals. She drew in her breath, gasping as the arrows flew every which way, and flowers kept blooming and filling the air until there was nothing but orange and gold and the pain was worse than anything Simon had ever inflicted upon her.

She threw herself off the bed and began to roll on the floor while the flowers raced across her back, igniting her hair and sending her screaming in seach of Pauline. Down the hall she ran until, reaching the top of the stairs, she tripped on the runner and began to fly. Her burning hair like a comet's tail, Vera hurtled through the vast reaches of her imagination, and the dreaded promise of death that was the fulfillment of all her childish fears.

Four

Long before the grown-ups had left, Vera's nephews had been sent upstairs to bed. But neither thirteen-year-old Andrei, nor Sergei, his younger brother, had any intention of going to sleep. Instead, they made a tent beneath the bedcovers, and in the close, hot darkness spoke in whispers, frightening each other with tales of ghosts and fiendish creatures who fed on little boys.

"Do you think she's still here?" Seriozha asked as he stifled a yawn.

"Who?"

"Aunt Vera. Maybe she's watching us. Katya told me that when her mother died last spring everyone knew she was still in the house, that they had to call a priest to come to ask her to leave." He spoke in the same earnest and deliberate manner as his mother, though everyone remarked how he resembled his grandfather more than anyone else. Short for his age, with straight black hair and small gray eyes, Sergei had spent all his childhood trying to keep up with his older brother. Although only four years separated them, Andrei already had fuzz on his cheeks, and walked with a swaggering gait, as if manhood were just around the corner.

When it became too uncomfortable, they pulled the covers back, Andrei putting a finger to his lips and motioning his brother to silence. "They're gone," he said at last, still keeping his voice to a whisper, as Mother and Father were asleep just across the hall. Andrei climbed out of bed, shaking the pins and needles from his legs.

"I'm going, too," announced Sergei. He jumped down and rushed to the door, wanting to be the first one to reach the drawing room.

Andrei, a slim, loose-limbed boy with curly brown hair, looked down at his younger brother and shook his head. "You're too little," he said. "You'll start to cry and then we'll really get into trouble." Having just reached the age when girls were becoming more interesting than tin soldiers, he also found himself less tolerant of his brother than he was when they were younger.

But what he hadn't counted on was Seriozha's determination. With a crafty gleam in his eyes that surely would have looked familiar to his grandfather, Sergei made it very plain that if he wasn't included he'd go across the hall and tell Papa what Andrei was up to.

"Mind you, don't make a sound then," warned Andrei, and he turned the doorknob as quietly as he could, then tiptoed to the stairs.

Sergei was right behind him, following his older brother's nightshirted back. There was nothing Sergei found more exciting than being scared. Now, as he took the stairs as silently as possible, he shivered in anticipation of what awaited them in the drawing room, wondering if Aunt Vera's ghost was watching him, ready to jump out of hiding if he didn't behave himself.

Tomorrow was the funeral, so if they didn't do it now, they'd never again have the chance. But was it wrong? Sergei wondered. How can looking be wrong? he answered himself.

All we'll do is take a peek and go right upstairs.

"Wait here," his brother whispered when they came downstairs.

"Why?"

"So I can see if anyone's still up, that's why."

His brother crept into the drawing room where Aunt Vera's coffin was laid out on a table, with wreaths of pine branches at its foot, and three candles burning at its head. From where he stood he could see the coffin lid leaning against the mantel, and over that a mirror that was veiled like every other mirror in the house. When he asked his mother why the coffin had to remain open until Aunt Vera was buried, she'd looked at him as if he had no business asking foolish questions, saying "custom," and refusing to discuss it further.

Andryushka slipped back into the hall, motioning his brother to follow. The floorboards were cold against Sergei's bare feet, and when he reached the drawing room he was suddenly frightened, not of being discovered and shooed upstairs, but of what might happen when they lifted the cloth of gold that hid his aunt's face and hands from view.

The candles were still burning, while behind the head of the coffin an ikon lamp illuminated not only the casket of yellow varnished oak, but also several dim and ancient-looking ikons, the dark-brown faces peering sternly from their gold mountings.

"I'm scared," he admitted. "Maybe we should just leave everything alone."

"Go upstairs then," replied Andrei. "I didn't want you down here, anyway."

"But I want to stay."

"Then stop acting like a baby. Here, we'll do it together."

Andrei got on one side of the coffin while Sergei got on the other. Each reached down, taking hold of the ornamental cloth that was trimmed with gold braid and numerous heavy tassels.

"When should we do it?" he whispered.

He could see his aunt's feet sticking out at the opposite end, her little pink shoes matching the velvet that lined the coffin. A smell that wasn't very nice drifted toward him.

"How did she burn herself?" he asked.

"She was firing up the stove. It exploded," Andrei said knowledgeably. "Papa told me."

"How come he didn't tell me, too?"

Andrei made a face. "'Cause you're only nine years old, that's why. Besides, you ask too many questions."

"And when I'm ten he still won't answer them." He felt miserable at being excluded from sharing secrets with his father, though now, he realized, wasn't the time to start complaining. "And why hasn't Cousin Pauline come?"

"Maybe they couldn't find her. Are you ready or aren't you?"

With a terrified shiver, Sergei nodded, and at the count of three they both pulled back the heavy piece of brocade. One look was all he needed. The cloth dropped from his fingers and he turned and ran, careering right into his father's arms.

"Papa!" he screamed, as much frightened as surprised.

Volsky demanded to know what they were doing down here when they should have been in bed.

"Seriozha wanted a drink," Andrei hurriedly explained. "He was afraid to go down alone."

"Isn't there a pitcher in your room?"

"No, Papa," whispered Sergei, who kept seeing his aunt's horribly disfigured face, all that terrible blackness without shape or definition that he felt so sick he didn't think he could make it back upstairs.

"Then go into the kitchen, and be quick about it, too. Your mother's trying to get some sleep."

"Come on then, scaredy-cat," said Andrei. Grabbing Sergei

by the hand, he yanked him toward the kitchen, never once looking back.

When Volsky returned upstairs, first setting right the cloth of gold that covered his sister-in-law's frightfully charred face and hands, Irena was sitting up in bed, looking wide awake.

"So young," she murmured, as she had been murmuring ever since they received Rodya's telegram. "Oh Niki, why do such things have to happen?"

Moved by the pain she was trying so hard to conceal, Volsky held her in his arms, so that each transmitted their warmth to the other. He knew her so well now, or hoped he did, that each little gesture she made had gradually taken on a significance all its own Sometimes when he watched her, especially when he was unobserved, he was moved to tears, and always grateful that she'd forgiven him the errors he'd made in the past. That was all behind them now, the foolishness of his vanity, the belief that men were creatures driven not by loyalty so much as by lust. Volsky knew better, and knew as well that intimacy transcended the physical, reaching its highest level only when both partners in a relationship willingly sacrificed their own needs for the needs of the other.

When he kissed her good night and turned away, sleeping on his stomach so that his snoring wouldn't disturb her, Irena remained awake, listening to the cymbals still crashing inside her head. So many questions remained unanswered that even if she wanted to she couldn't have slept. Why hadn't Pauline responded to her wire, and why had she left Petrovka after telling Masha she planned to remain here for most of the summer? Could they have argued, was that it? But Pauline knew her mother wasn't well. Surely she realized that Vera was irrational. Yet Rodya had said his stepdaughter had departed amicably, that even Vera had come downstairs to say good-bye.

And then Vera went back upstairs and set herself on fire.

Irena trembled, huddling there in the darkness with a languid summer breeze stirring the curtains, whipping them drowsily back and forth like the wings of a great pale bird.

But Pauline wasn't the only one who troubled her. As if Irena didn't have enough to worry about, Henriette had taken her aside to tell her that Masha had begun seeing Colonel Trigony, the very same Trigony whose bullet had put a cruel end to her sister's happiness so many years before.

Perhaps she wants to humiliate him, Irena thought. But is a public humiliation in any way equal to what he did to her? Of course not. Then why is she pursuing this, and why did our poor Verochka hate herself so that she wanted to die?

She gazed at Niki, listening to the childlike sounds he made as he slept. Something clenched at the back of her throat, and then the tears broke. She didn't try to stop them, for crying was like a shield against the pain, a watery barrier on the other side of which was terror, and fear of her own mortality.

Afraid her sobs would awaken him, Irena slipped out of bed and stood by the open window. Watching the rays of moonlight refracted through her tear-filled eyes, it wasn't Petrovka she saw slumbering in the waning summer darkness, but the accumulation of images around which a person's character and temperament gradually evolve. Her sisters and brother had shared many of the same experiences, yet each had fixed on one thing and not another. In the end, their differences were often like barriers, too, making it difficult for them to understand the needs and desires of the others.

And tomorrow the youngest of the girls, the baby sister, would clutch a piece of paper in her hand, a kind of certificate from the priest that was like a passport to heaven. Then the coffin lid would be put in place, and the casket mounted on an open hearse. The funeral procession would make its way to the cemetery, where the lid would be nailed down and the coffin lowered on ropes into a freshly dug grave. And just as

Vera hadn't been there to witness these same rites performed for her mother, so Pauline wouldn't be there, either.

The lessons never learned, Irena sadly thought. The mistakes we transmit to our children, convinced that if our own flesh and blood suffer as we have, then surely we've done nothing wrong, and that what we thought was wrong has only been proven right by virtue of repetition.

The first Easter of the twentieth century dawned gray and hazy, the weather strikingly at odds with the joyousness of the occasion. Many-throated chords swelled from the bells of Petersburg's churches, rattling the windowpanes in Masha's apartment. As she looked out, hundreds of pigeons circled overhead, wheeling across the sky. She had read in yesterday's paper that the Tsar was determined to keep them fat and healthy through the winter. Unlike his father, he insisted they were closely related to doves, and therefore harbingers of a peace such as Russia had every right and reason to enjoy.

Watching the frightened birds vanish through the yellow mist, Masha smiled to think that when this was all over she too might fly away. But now, as church bells continued to toll from one end of the capital to the other, echoing the news that Christ had risen, the pug-nosed Lothario who had rented her this fashionable apartment was on his way to see her, not only to exchange the traditional Easter kiss, but also to partake of the lavish banquet her cook had spent the last several days busily preparing.

In the dining room, a table groaned under the weight of all the dishes she had readied to whet the Colonel's appetite. Surrounded by colored eggs, a suckling pig lifted its snout in much the same way Trigony carried his, jabbing his little retroussé nose loftily in the air. There were hot and cold *zakuski*, numerous bottles of wine and vodka, as well as the two traditional Easter dishes—*paskha*, a rich, creamy cheese cake filled with preserved fruit and shaped like a truncated pyramid; and *kulich,* a cylindrical brioche crowned with white icing to form the letters XB, "Christ is risen."

Neither the *paskha* nor the *kulich* had been blessed, though this was not an oversight, as she could easily have taken them with her when she went to the midnight service the night before. But anything Trigony put into his mouth didn't deserve to be sanctified, and so Masha had purposely left both desserts at home.

When the doorbell rang she seated herself in the drawing room that had been decorated to her specifications. Hung with ivory silk, and the latest furniture from Paris—Art Nouveau, they called it—the room had a cool calligraphic elegance that startled visitors unaccustomed to the avant-garde. Only her brother seemed to appreciate her taste, though even he was more concerned about her relationship with Trigony than her choice of décor.

The maid returned with the news that her sister, Madame Volskaya, was waiting in the front hall. Having expected Trigony, Masha breathed a little more easily as she came to her feet, just as Irena entered the drawing room. But though she held out her arms so they might exchange the Easter kiss, Irena busied herself removing her gloves, and with a jaundiced eye studied her surroundings rather than cross the room to embrace her sister.

"How nice to see you in such good humor," Masha said, responding in kind to her sister's chilly glance.

"I didn't come here to trade barbs. But when you never return my telephone calls, when you fail to answer my letters, and when we live in the same city and don't see each other for months at a time, then either I should just forget I have a sister, or else try to shake some sense into your head."

"I've been busy, you know, frightfully busy," Masha replied, still speaking more coldly than she intended.

When Irena declined the offer of tea or coffee, Masha returned to her place, anxious that her sister's visit be as brief as possible.

Irena remained standing, though her severe expression began to soften as she looked down at her sister. "I know why you've avoided me," she said. "You're so ashamed of yourself you can't face me."

"On the contrary. I know exactly what I'm doing."

"Perhaps you'd care to tell me then."

"There's nothing to tell," Masha insisted.

"A woman has an affair with her husband's murderer and there's nothing to tell?" Irena took a seat, perching on the edge of the chair as if she couldn't bear to be here but another minute. "Do you know who came to see me the other day? Stepan's mother, that's who. She can't understand what you're doing, Masha, and neither can I."

"I'm sorry," she said, and she was, genuinely so, "but I'd rather not discuss it."

"But everyone is talking."

"I don't care!" she said, flaring up. "I don't care if the Tsar himself is scandalized. Believe me, there's a purpose to everything. Do you think I enjoy being talked about, having people snicker at me behind my back? When Eugene Borisovich is invited out, the hostess always makes it clear my company is not requested. But that's all right, because it'll soon be over, and then you'll be able to rest easy."

"Do you intend to break this off, is that what you're trying to say?"

"In a manner of speaking, yes."

"But until then you'll continue to be—"

Irena wouldn't say it, but Masha had no trouble uttering the word "mistress," flinging it out like a curse.

"I don't know you anymore, Masha," Irena sadly replied. "I used to think that of all my sisters, you were the one I truly understood. But you needn't worry, because I won't call on you again. If you don't want to listen to reason—"

"You know nothing about this!" she cried out. "I loved him, don't you understand? He was my life, Irena. We were complete together. If I could tell you how I felt, don't you think I would? Is it such a crime to have secrets, for God's sake?"

"No, but it is a crime to take a murderer into your bed." Irena rose stiffly to her feet and started from the room, only to turn back at the last moment. Her voice breaking, she begged Masha to reconsider what she was doing, to at least confide in her as she had in the past.

Masha wanted desperately to tell her sister the truth, yet knew she had no choice but to remain silent. Again she held her arms out, not wanting things to end on such an unhappy note. But as Irena took a hesitant step forward, the doorbell rang, interrupting any hope of a possible reconciliation. Loud voices greeted her as Trigony and several of his officer friends crowded into the vestibule, their faces red from the cold, and their laughter redoubling as it bounced from one wall to the other.

Masha started to introduce her sister, but Irena would have none of it. Grabbing her wrap before the maid could help her into it, she rushed out onto the street.

"Please try to understand," Masha called after her. "If you love me as you say you do, then trust me, Irusha. I swear by all that's dear to us that I know what I'm doing."

"You don't, but you won't believe me, will you? You're as willful as Papa, and just as stubborn." But then, her anger deflated, Irena took an awkward step forward and held Masha in her arms. "We're sisters, Mashenka. You mustn't ever forget that, because I'll always be here when you need me."

And I will need you, Masha thought. But not yet, not quite yet.

*   *   *

Although Pauline had been living with the Volskys since the previous September, when lectures started at the university, she had never admitted to her aunt what had taken place before she left Petrovka. Having expressed her disapproval over Pauline's failure to attend her mother's funeral, Irena hadn't pressed her niece for an explanation. In her calm and deliberate way, Irena's disappointment had been censure enough. But in the months since, Pauline had often thought of telling her what had happened, and just as often had decided to leave well enough alone.

Julia Andreyevna, her dreamy-eyed school friend, was the one who convinced her to ignore the wire summoning her back to Petrovka, certain that if her stepfather laid eyes on her, something terrible was bound to happen. Thus, under the pretext that no telegram had ever been received, Pauline made her apologies and tried to cope with her sorrow as best she could.

More than anyone, it was "Cousin Alex" who helped her through this difficult period. When lectures started the previous fall, Pauline had once again made the young man's acquaintance. Now, with the school term drawing to a close, she waited outside the long row of red-fronted buildings that made up the university, trying to catch sight of her friend. Behind her, the blue waters of the Neva proclaimed spring in no uncertain terms, while students by the hundreds crowded the courtyard outside the main building, talking excitedly of their plans for the summer.

When Alexei Platonovich Annenkov came down the steps, she waved her hand, trying to attract his attention. Aunt Irena had planned a dinner party for them, Julia having already gone on ahead to stop at Ballet's, where she'd promised to pick up some cream tarts for the boys.

"And unless we hurry," explained Pauline, "we're all

going to be late."

A tram deposited them several blocks from the Mokhovaya, and as they walked down the quiet, tree-lined streets, the poplars unfurling their long, slender leaves, Pauline glanced shyly at her friend, enjoying the comfortable silence each shared with the other. The dashing young cadet she had met the year before was now the very picture of a typical Russian student, dressed in a worn gray overcoat, which accentuated his stoop-shouldered walk. Of medium height and build, Alex's one distinguishing feature was the earnest expression that invariably made it seem as if he were scowling. Then a crease would appear over the bridge of his nose, and three lines would draw themselves tensely across his brow, making him look much older than his nineteen years. Pauline knew of his involvement in the political life of the university, yet this was one area Alex consciously avoided discussing, determined that she reach her own conclusions, and not be influenced by what he might have to say on the subject.

But when they arrived at the Volskys, where a breathless Julia was telling Seriozha about all the wonderful desserts Ballet had on display, the talk almost immediately turned to politics. Although Pauline considered her Uncle Niki an enlightened man, and was even inclined to go along with his views on the need for a parliament and a constitutional monarchy, she was shocked by Alex's lack of sympathy for this moderate point of view. Loudly proclaiming his belief that the monarchy should and must be disposed of altogether, Alex was nevertheless rather vague about how this could be accomplished.

"But I still say that until power is placed in the hands of the workers, Russia will never be able to solve its problems. You must attend one of our meetings, Mr. Volsky. Only then will you begin to understand what I mean."

"What I understand is that you mustn't ever let the police

hear you talking like this," Volsky replied with a nervous laugh.

"Alex talks this way only among his friends," Pauline was quick to point out.

As they stood around the *zakuski* table, Julia still going on about Ballet's and describing the various confections as if they were works of art, Irena hurriedly changed the subject, asking Alex about his plans for the summer.

"A tour of the capitals," he said, and would have ended it at that if Volsky hadn't mentioned the large émigré colony in Switzerland, "a nest of revolutionaries," as he termed them. "And what constitutes a revolutionary, Mr. Volsky? There are many people who'd consider your own views rather radical. Yet you think of yourself as a moderate."

"And I am, I am," Volsky assured him, going on at some length about the problems facing Russia, and the need for clearheadedness at a time when many were calling for more extreme measures.

Julia interrupted at the first chance she got, waving her plump little arm in the air. "Why must we talk of politics?" she complained. "That's all you ever hear of these days, strikes and protests and bombs going off. Sometimes I think no one has the time to fall in love, they're too busy worrying about the future of Russia."

Her words were directed at Alexei, who lowered his eyes at the mention of "love," though a moment later he shyly raised them and looked over at Pauline.

Later that evening, when the guests had departed, Irena saw to it that the two young people had a chance to be alone. For a long while they sat in the parlor, Alex holding Pauline's hand but saying very little.

When she saw the three lines furrowing his forehead, Pauline sensed that something was troubling him. "You're not telling me everything about this trip you're planning, are

511

you? You're going to Geneva, am I right? And you're not going to see the sights."

"Who has time to look at the Alps when there's work to be done?" he said somewhat angrily, as if it pained him to tell her the truth. "We can't sit back, Pauline, and let others do the job for us. If the people we go to school with don't have enough to eat, can you imagine how much worse it is for the workers? Yet the Tsar lives in splendid isolation, doesn't he, growing fat on the misery of his countrymen."

She wondered who had put these idealistic phrases into his head, or if he'd come up with them on his own. Julia was right. Couldn't they pretend there was no such thing as politics, and go on about their lives as if nothing were the matter?

"And just live for ourselves?" said Alex. "How can we, Pauline, when we're an anachronism, the only European power—if we dare call ourselves that—whose people are still denied fundamental rights and freedoms, who have no form of representation, and no way in which to air their grievances."

"But why must it be you? Aren't there others with less to lose?"

"If we had nothing to lose, Pauline, then there'd never be any progress at all."

She had no argument with this, and so all she could do was urge him to take every precaution, and be as careful and circumspect as possible.

"I'll be very discreet, Pauline, you needn't worry. I have no desire to spend the next five years in exile, not when I have you to come back to." He leaned forward and kissed her on the lips. When he edged back, his previously thoughtful expression had become one of youthful exuberance, so that he couldn't resist kissing her a second time, and even a third time after that.

*　　*　　*

When Ulyanov spoke, it sounded as if the words came from the very depths of his soul. Sticking his middle finger in the armholes of his vest, he bent forward, pausing with something of an actor's sense of timing until he was certain he had everyone's attention. Then, despite his strong lisp, he would spin the most persuasive arguments, his sharp, hazel eyes taking everyone into their confidence. With his enormous bald head and prominent cheekbones, his appearance set him apart from everyone else who attended the conference held that summer in Geneva.

Listening to each and every word, writing many of them down so he would be able to quote Vladimir Ilyich when he returned to Petersburg, Alexei Annenkov sensed he was in the presence of a natural-born leader, and eagerly followed the round of meetings whose ultimate objective was to found a Party newspaper, *Iskra, (The Spark)*, which was to kindle the flame of revolution.

These were stormy sessions that often lasted well into the night, marked by infighting of the most divisive kind. As one of his fellow Party members, Simon Bazarov, declared, "If we continue like this we'll end up killing each other long before the Okhrana has a chance to do it for us."

Yet Plekhanov, the self-proclaimed father of Russian Marxism, and elder statesman of the Social Democrats, fought Ulyanov every step of the way, determined to hold onto as much control of *Iskra* as he possibly could. As a student representative, and not an actual member of the editorial board, Alex had no vote in these proceedings. But when he was finally given an opportunity to voice his opinions, he made it very clear that he intended to side with Ulyanov. Although the conference ended on a bitter note, Vladimir Ilyich, or "Lenin" as he would soon be calling himself, prevailed.

When Lenin departed for Munich, Alex and Bazarov left with him to help set up the machinery for publishing the newspaper. By the end of August, when it was time for Alex to return to Russia, he and Simon Ivanovich had become so close that not only were they the staunchest of political allies, but also the very best of friends.

As Alexei himself observed on the eve of his departure, "If the only thing I accomplished this summer was meeting you, Senya, that alone would have made it all worthwhile."

"Then you mustn't talk as if we'll never see each other again," replied Simon. "Because we will, Alexei. On that you have my word."

Five

On a night not unlike the night before Stepan had died, Masha found herself bundled in furs, sitting next to Colonel Trigony as a troika carried them to the village of Novaya Derevnya, located on the outskirts of Petersburg in a district known as "the Islands." This was a popular vacation spot, dotted with summer cottages and expensive villas, where Petersburgers could go to escape the heat. But during the winter these outlying islands were virtually deserted, except for the gypsies who made New Village their home.

The narrow road that cut a swath through the forest was polished by sledge runners, marked by hoofprints that vanished as the troika's three horses galloped across them. Four other troikas brought up the rear, and as Masha huddled beneath her sables and sealskins, she could hear the jingling of bells, the drunken laughter of Trigony's friends, and the high-pitched whistling of the runners. There were other sounds as well—a girl's excited scream, the crack of a whip, and the steady thud of hoofs in the frost-bound air. The moonlight, reflected in the silver chains of the harness, was so bright that only when the trees closed in around them did it truly seem dark. But for all the charms of the journey, the fine, dry snow that glittered like sugar, the wind rushing across her cheeks as she peered out from her furs, Masha derived no pleasure from the excursion.

Beneath the heavy bearskin lap robes Trigony pressed her hand, glancing at her and smiling with all the wide-eyed delight of a little boy who's just tickled his nose with the first taste of champagne. When she met his gaze she saw in his features not a reflection of moonlight, but of her own willfulness, this stubborn insistence upon avenging the honor of a man dead fourteen years. If only Trigony were villainous and corrupt, she knew how easy it would be. But he was not that at all, and in the last year had often shown himself to be generous to a fault, amazing her with his tenderness, and even charming her by the obvious pleasure he took in her company.

Perhaps she should go back to Petrovka, lick her wounds, suffer in silence. After all, Trigony was just an ordinary man, no better or worse than most, and certainly no monster masquerading as an officer and a gentleman. Fourteen years had mellowed his outlook, and though he had promised never to bring up Stepan's name in conversation, of late he had, on occasion, expressed his regrets over the mistakes he'd made in the past.

"Yes, mistakes, Mashenka, grievous errors," Eugene Borisovich had declared, tapping his pug nose as if to hammer the words deep into his consciousness. "Between love and lust there's no common ground, is there?"

She hated him for trying to be considerate, for saying aloud what he would never have said fourteen years earlier. She despised him for caring about her, and even suggesting that they should marry, and perhaps retire to the country, where gossiping tongues would have little opportunity to pursue them. But most of all she loathed Trigony for making her realize she had become the very same person he had been when they'd first met, so many years before.

To follow such a reckless course, to fashion her life out of desperation and not inner peace, seemed a far greater crime than the one she had long been contemplating. Yet the course was laid out before her like the pine branches that marked the road to New Village.

When the troikas drew up before a low building half hidden among a clump of spruce, Masha roused herself as if from a deep and disturbing dream. With newly awakened eyes she looked all about, as if expecting Stepan to emerge from the shadows, reminding her of the sin of pride. But there was no ghosts in New Village, only gypsies.

The party tumbled from the sledges, and with riotous cries began to pound on the door until the owner of the establishment hurriedly ushered them inside, where they soon found themselves seated in a big whitewashed room. Masha had barely gotten out of her furs when dozens of gypsies surrounded her, some lighting candles and others bringing out icy bottles of vodka and champagne. A samovar was lit, more wicker chairs were set out around the long table, while Trigony's friends sat their women on their laps, shouting out orders as fast as they could think them up.

By the time everyone's glass was filled, the gypsy women had begun to assemble, taking their places at the far end of the room. Dark-haired and olive-skinned, they wore bright silk dresses, some bareheaded and others with their hair plaited and tied up in gaily patterned scarfs. The older Tzigane women wore black lace capes over their shoulders, and sat in the middle of the group, flanked by the sopranos on one side and the mezzo-sopranos on the other. Behind them stood the men with their guitars, dressed in white-brocaded Russian shirts and embroidered gypsy jackets.

When the singing began Masha sat back in her chair, letting the sad, plaintive chords lull her into a semihypnotized state. The walls of the room seemed to fall away, and the melancholic voices rose up in a kind of morbid ecstasy. There were songs of longing and deep despair, some in gypsy dialect and others sung in Russian. When the gypsies started to dance, Trigony's friends insisted upon taking part, and Masha awoke from her bleak reverie to the sound of stamping feet and frenzied cries, everyone moving to the wild, barbaric rhythm of the music.

Trigony pulled her to her feet and whirled her around, his white teeth flashing as he laughed and called on her to relax and enjoy herself, instead of looking so morose. All around her spun the flushed and drunken faces of his friends, the women shamelessly raising their skirts and showing off their dimpled knees, the men taking off their tunics and dancing in their shirt sleeves. Again and again they raised their glasses in a seemingly endless series of toasts, so that when it was finally time to leave hardly anyone could stand on his feet.

As Trigony was carried outside, his legs trailing behind him and his head hanging limply on his chest, Masha followed after him, picking her way through the shards of broken glass that littered the floor. The moon had vanished, and in the chill, starlit darkness she took her place in the troika and ordered the *yamshchik* to drive them back to Petersburg.

By the time they reached the city, Trigony had sufficiently recovered, though he still wore a rather stupefied expression, as if he were uncertain where he was and what had happened to him.

"Isn't your maid at home?" he said when Masha unlocked the door with her key and led him inside.

"I've given her the week off. Her sister was ill."

"So we're all alone."

"Yes, Eugene. Just the two of us."

Trigony staggered down the hallway, colliding with first a table and then a chair as he tried to make it to the bedroom.

Masha hung up her furs and walked down the hall, remembering how she and Stepan had sat up most of the night, talking in sad, doomed voices as they waited for dawn to break. What had they accomplished but to finalize their pain? But now she was ready to lay her anguish to rest, however irrational that decision might ultimately prove.

It was, she reasoned, much too late to change her mind, to say that Eugene was not the man he had been when, as Captain Trigony, he'd gladly accepted her husband's challenge, eager to prove himself the better of the two. Yes, much too late, she thought, for if I leave him now the disgrace will only be mine, another burden I'll have to live with as best I can.

So she stood there in the doorway, watching him as he fell back onto the bed, a sloppy, childish grin becoming a look of concern when he saw how troubled she was.

"Mashenka my love, what's the matter?" he said, making a cooing sound that oddly enough reminded her of her mother whenever she spoke to her little dog. "Your Eugene had too much to drink, but he still loves you." As if to prove it, he came unsteadily to his feet, falling down again before he managed to stay upright.

Masha, urging him to take a shower bath to clear his head, turned and walked out of the room. When she returned she had changed into a dressing gown, while from the direction of the bathroom she could hear Trigony singing one of the gypsy songs as he toweled himself dry. Still in a playful mood and now somewhat revived, he came out of the bathroom attired in the muslin nightshirt he kept on a hook behind the door.

"Do you know what day it is today?" she asked while he climbed into bed, gesturing for her to join him.

"Not your name day, is it?" he said with alarm, knowing it

would be a terrible faux pas if he'd forgotten.

Masha shook her head, never once taking her eyes off him, and feeling the same uneasy mixture of pity and revulsion that came over her whenever she was in his company. "It was fourteen years ago, this very day," she announced. From the bottom drawer of her dressing table she now brought out a palm-wood case, wondering if he would recognize it.

Trigony eyed her curiously, not certain how to judge her mood.

"Remember this?" she asked, showing him the case.

"Should I?"

Masha sat on the edge of the bed, trying to ignore the way he began to stroke her arm. She opened the box, revealing the weapon that rested against the red velvet lining, a pistol inlaid with mother-of-pearl.

"Remember now?" she said.

Trigony began to look increasingly uncomfortable. "Nasty souvenir, Masha dear. You should have thrown it away the first chance you had."

"But it's not a souvenir, Eugene. I've kept it ready all this time. It's in perfect repair. I only just cleaned it the other day. Do you remember Lieutenant Grinevich?"

"Short and fat, wasn't he?"

"Yes, and loyal, too. He taught me how to take care of it, how to use it, too. Little round Grinevich, such a jolly fellow. How he wept that day. I've never seen a man cry as much as he did. He adored Stepan. Idolized him."

"That's all very interesting," replied Trigony, sounding as if he were trying to humor her. "But it's behind us now, Masha. We can't let our mistakes torment us for the rest of our lives."

"Mistakes?" she cried out, and she removed the pistol from its case and held it in the palm of her hand. "It wasn't a mistake, Eugene. You knew exactly what you were doing."

520

"As Stepan did, too," he reminded her.

"Yes, but it was your doing, never his. You gave him cause. You saw to it that he had no other choice."

"I don't want to discuss it now, Masha," and his finger went tap-tap-tap against his nose. "I'm not feeling very well."

"That's because guilt is so painful, Eugene. I suffer it as much as you do. Everyone thinks I'm your mistress. I'm not. I'm your assassin."

Trigony's eyes opened wide. Then he began to laugh, telling her this was all too foolish for words, some kind of perverse practical joke that having run its course, was best put aside.

But Masha was in earnest. As she tightened her grip on the pistol, she felt like using it like a stone, bringing it down against Trigony's head, again and again and again. Instead, she cocked it and came slowly to her feet, standing alongside the bed as Trigony drew back in surprise.

"This is all too preposterous," he shouted. "Now put that away before I get angry, Masha."

"I'm sorry, Eugene. Maybe you're not the man you used to be. But I'm still the same woman. Fourteen years ago I promised myself this moment, when I'd be looking down at you like this, and you'd understand what terror was all about."

"But I love you, you know that. Surely you wouldn't murder someone who cares about you as much as I do."

"Of course you love me, Eugene. This wouldn't have any meaning if you didn't."

How calm he seemed, even understanding. He made no move to wrest the weapon from her hand, nor did he begin to implore her to reconsider what she was about to do. Fully expecting him to beg and whimper, to throw himself at her mercy, he just leaned back against the pillows, as if refusing to believe she could be so vengeful.

"I wanted to marry you," was all he said.

"I was married once. I have no interest in being widowed a second time."

Her finger gently stroked the trigger, the metal cold as ice. Trigony's eyes grew frantic, and he waved his hands helplessly as if he were swimming through mud.

"No!" he suddenly shouted, and as he threw himself against her the pistol exploded in her hand.

A thin puff of bluish smoke rose lazily to the ceiling. Eugene Borisovich sat there for a moment, looking so amazed he dared not move, his lower lip drooping flaccidly so that saliva began to trickle down his chin. Then he fell back, his entire right side stained red.

Masha remained where she was, the pistol still clutched in her hand, held so tightly that she couldn't uncurl her fingers.

"A doctor," she heard Trigony whisper, his voice like the gaping wound in his side. He made a strange, hollow, leaking sound, and a bright scarlet bubble of blood burst against his lips.

Utterly astounded by what she had done, Masha leaned very close to him now, listening as he tried to shape words with his blood-stained lips. But he couldn't speak, and denied the chance to tell her what he felt, he merely gazed at her inquiringly, his eyes filled with childish reproach.

Unable to accept the tears that spilled down her cheeks, Masha whispered, "Forgive me," and began to weep, as much for Eugene Borisovich Trigony as for herself.

Irena had just finished breakfast when the doorbell gave out with a long, piercing ring. Before she had a chance to come to her feet, Katya hurried into the dining room.

"It's your sister, ma'am. Madame Danchenko."

Irena motioned Masha to a chair, and poured her a cup of coffee, wondering what had brought her here so early in the morning.

Masha's black eyes blinked rapidly, and she fingered the old cypress cross Anninka had given her many years before. She looked as if she were sleepwalking, and the longer she sat there, the more disturbed Irena became.

"What happened?" she said at last. "Is it over between you?"

"Yes," said Masha in a barely audible voice.

"But you're not happy about it, are you? Surely you weren't in love with the man."

Masha made a guttural sound that was like an animal trying to laugh. "Maybe I was. Wouldn't that be funny, Irusha, to fall in love with a man I loathed? Yes, maybe I loved him and didn't even know it. Maybe that's why I killed him."

Certain she hadn't heard correctly, Irena put down her cup and stared inquisitively at her sister. But as she waited for Masha to take back what she had said, the truth clenched at the back of Irena's throat, and the full implication of these horrifyingly simple words came crashing down on top of her.

"Yes, it's true!" Masha screamed. Realizing what she'd done, she pressed a hand to her mouth and began to shake her head.

It's not true, Irena kept saying to herself. She's making it up. She wants to shock me, that's what it is.

"He's still lying there in bed," whispered Masha. "Just lying there with his eyes wide open. He didn't believe me, Irusha. Nobody did."

"Oh my God," whispered Irena. She kept saying that and clutching the table, trying to get the room to right itself. "Does anyone else know?"

Masha shook her head.

"What about your maid?"

"I gave her the week off, the cook, too. There's no one, and he's just lying there, Irusha, staring at me. I waited fourteen years, and now it's done. And now I can't make sense of it," Masha said, choking on the words, and coughing so painfully Irena was afraid she'd spit up blood.

"What will you do?" Irena whispered. "They'll arrest you for sure."

"I'll hide. I'll go away. They'll never find me," Masha replied. She looked wildly about as if she expected Colonel Trigony to burst out of hiding, hideously wounded but still very much alive.

The doorbell rang, and with a look of terror Masha sprang to her feet.

"It's no one, just the stove setter. I'll tell him to come back tomorrow."

Irena closed the dining room doors behind her and saw a man waiting in the vestibule, peering at her inquisitively from behind his spectacles.

"He says it's very important," whispered the maid.

Katya showed her the card the gentleman had given her. PORFIRY NEZVANOV, it read, EXAMINING MAGISTRATE.

So they've found her out, and so quickly, too, Irena thought with a shudder. She told Katya to have the gentleman wait in the parlor and slipped back into the dining room.

Masha was standing by the window, looking down onto the street. As soon as Irena returned Masha spun around, her eyes full of questions.

"What do you want me to tell him?" Irena asked after explaining who had rung the bell. "Shall I say I haven't heard from you?"

Masha shook her head. "I'm not a martyr, Irena. But I won't hide, either. I always knew that anyway, even from the first."

Irena didn't try to stop her, nor did she plead as she would have just a moment before. The sisters embraced in silence, weeping softly.

"No regrets," Masha said in a resolute voice. She drew back her shoulders and took a deep breath. "Because if the decision was mine to make all over again, I'd do it just the same, Irusha, exactly the same."

The murder of Grand Duke Paul's aide-de-camp provided Petersburg with an endless stream of gossip and sordid speculation. Everywhere one went that fall, one heard the names of *Danchenko* and *Trigony* bandied about like shuttlecocks. By the New Year, the capital had split into two opposing camps, those who sympathized with what they called Madame Danchenko's "courageous and romantic act," and those who insisted she was nothing but a murderess, and must be punished accordingly.

For more than two months now, Masha had been interned in the House of Preliminary Detention on Shpalernaya Street, waiting for her trial date to be set. Irena, having learned that the proceedings would begin the first week in March, had gone directly to see Henriette, with whom she had sat for more than an hour, trying to persuade her sister to use whatever influence she had to plead Masha's case.

Although Henriette was utterly appalled at what had happened, and felt that Masha's crime would have a very damaging effect on her social standing, she was ashamed to admit this, either to Irena or to anyone else. Realizing that if she turned against her sister, it would only cause people to think less of her, she agreed to use her connections— actually, the Countess'—to try to get an audience at court. This took much longer than anticipated, and it was fully a month before Henriette had reason to board the train that would take her to Tsarskoye Selo, and thence to the imperial residence at the Alexander Palace.

As she descended from the train early that winter's afternoon, the irony of the occasion did not escape her notice. For years now she had tried to become part of the Empress' entourage, hoping that one day she might receive an appointment that would give her the right to be present at court functions—*demoiselle d'honneur,* for example. But for years, all her considerable efforts in this direction had amounted to next to nothing. Yet now that a murder had been committed, and the gossipmongers were reveling in each and every lurid detail, the Tsarina had finally agreed to see her.

Upon reaching the Palace gates and passing muster with the sentries, her carriage deposited her before the main entrance, flanked by a double row of Corinthian columns. The driver seemed as much in awe as Henriette, and could barely get two words out when she told him to wait for her, as she required transportation back to the railway station.

Once inside the Palace, where the smell of incense and freshcut flowers filled the air, a small army of court servants quickly surrounded her. A footman in a red coat bordered by gold braid with black eagles passed her to a messenger in a black coat and white knee breeches, who in turn saw to it that she was duly handed over to an equerry whose hat was adorned with long red, black, and yellow ostrich plumes. His red cape billowing out behind him, the equerry discharged his duties by summoning a household officer, who began to lead her through the maze of polished corridors and audience rooms. Footmen ran on ahead while at each set of doors a pair of lackeys stood stiffly at attention, stepping aside at their approach. Henriette barely had time to take note of her surroundings as they passed swiftly from one vast room to the next, only the smell of flowers, incense and burning wood remaining constant as she was led to the Empress' drawing room.

This last set of doors was guarded by two young men whose costumes were the most fanciful of all, for red scarfs were bound like turbans around their heads, and fastened with gleaming silver clasps.

"Mademoiselle Henriette Petrovna Petrova," announced the household officer who had taken her through the Palace.

As the lackeys let her pass, Henriette turned to ask him what to do, and what was expected of her, as no one had briefed her on protocol. But the servant was already hurrying down the hall the way they had come.

Left alone in the middle of the drawing room, with only the footmen outside the door to keep her company, she looked anxiously about, wondering if she dared to take a seat, or if she were required to remain standing until the Tsarina made her entrance.

The drawing room was furnished exclusively with Chippendale, the walls and carpets a delicate shade of pale green. Suddenly a page entered, he too wearing his own special uniform—a dark-blue coat with highly polished brass buttons. Informing Henriette that her Majesty was detained, he invited her to take a seat, and asked if she required any form of refreshment.

Henriette was much too nervous to ask for anything, and so she merely shook her head, only taking a seat when the page had departed. Chippendale or not, the chair was most uncomfortable, and whether she leaned forward or back, right side or left, it seemed to be designed to fit a person whose shape bore no relation to the human form.

Although the room was beautifully decorated, there was something rather cold and severe about it, lacking as it did any personal touches, such as photographs or bibelots. How much nicer it would have been had they shown her to the Empress' private apartments, where she would have felt like a confidante and not a humble petitioner.

Far too anxious just to sit there with her hands folded in her lap, Henriette straightened up and began to pace, pausing

before a mirror, where the unflinching honesty of the glass
made her quickly turn away. She had purchased a new pearl-
gray suit just for the occasion, but though it was designed by
Madame Brissac, whose reputation as the Empress' favorite
couturière had made her both rich and famous, Henriette was
certain the woman had gotten it all wrong. Didn't her wrists
stick out too much, exaggerating the bony lines of her hands?
She tugged ineffectually at the sleeves, when the doors swung
open and the same household officer who had shown her
through the Palace stepped inside, moving noiselessly on his
soft-soled patent-leather shoes.

"Her Imperial Majesty," he said in a loud, ringing voice.

As Henriette bent low to curtsy, a small, shaggy black dog
streaked into the room, startling her as it snarled at her shoe,
the dog's carrot-shaped tail held rigidly at attention.

Laska, she couldn't help but think as she heard the Tsarina
call out in French, "Eira, you naughty dog." Asking the
household officer to take the pesky Scottish terrier back
upstairs, Alexandra Feodorovna motioned her to a chair.

As Henriette backed into the Chippendale chair, knowing it
wouldn't do to turn away from the Empress, Alexandra sat
down nearby. Although she had heard rumors the Tsarina
was expecting another child, her tall, slender figure gave no
indication of this, for she was as supple as a willow wand.
Attired in a flowing mauve gown trimmed with lace, with
several ropes of pearls around her neck, the Empress was
much more beautiful then Henriette had imagined. Having
seen her only from afar, Henriette marveled at the woman's
lustrous red-gold hair; her soft, well-shaped hands, upon
which she wore two rings, one set with an enormous pearl,
the other bearing the emblem of the swastika, that ancient
symbol of divinity.

Too late Henriette realized she was staring, had jerked her
eyes away, studying her lap.

"This must be a very difficult time for you," the Empress said shyly, speaking Russian now, but with a strong English accent.

Henriette responded in French, having been told the Tsarina spoke Russian only to those who knew no other language. "A great tragedy," she said, catching the scent of Atkinson's White Rose, and promising herself to tell Irena that the Empress wore the same perfume as she.

"Then let us talk of other things for a while, shall we? I've heard much about your psychic gifts, *mademoiselle*. A member of my suite has spoken of you highly, and has even mentioned your visit to Verkhoture. She says you met a man of God when you made your pilgrimage, a *starets* I believe is the word we use."

How uneasily the Empress said "we," as if she considered herself no more Russian than Eira, her little terrier. But prompted by her interest, Henriette gradually began to relax, and spoke at some length about her meeting with Father Gregory, and how they had been corresponding ever since.

"I've urged him to come to Petersburg, Your Majesty. But he writes that the time is not yet right, that one day he will appear at my door."

"Is it true that he performs miracles?" asked Alexandra, and her gray-blue eyes sparkled with interest.

"He would never boast of such things, Your Majesty. But I've often seen him in my dreams, and know in my heart he is truly a holy man."

"That is very comforting to know. Each week someone tells me of a new 'miracle worker,' yet sadly enough they all prove to be charlatans. To meet a man who communicates with God, who speaks with the voice of the Russian soil upon which we are privileged to walk, would be most extraordinary, Mademoiselle Petrova. Will you express those sentiments for me when next you write?"

Henriette promised to write to him that very day, delighted by the Tsarina's interest and completely forgetting the reason why she had sought this audience.

"But of your poor sister, I'm afraid there's little I can do," Alexandra spoke up, her eyes filled with undeniable sadness.

Henriette was so moved by the Empress' concern she felt like bowing down before her in adoration. Instead, she leaned forward in her chair, wondering if a show of tears would be useful at a time like this. "Yet you know that my dear sister was completely irrational when this happened, Your Majesty. You know of the terrible circumstances surrounding the death of her beloved husband, and how she spent so many years in solitude, driven to near madness by her despair."

Perhaps it was the "near madness" that caught the Tsarina's fancy, for she too leaned forward, two blotches of red appearing in her delicately fair cheeks.

"Yes, near madness," repeated Henriette. "Madame Danchenko is not a common murderess, as some might suggest, but a woman who saw no recourse but to avenge the senseless and brutal murder of her young husband. Would not banishment to our estate be sufficient punishment, Your Majesty?"

"God is merciful," murmured the Empress. "But though you have my sympathy, *mademoiselle*, I must remind you that Colonel Trigony was aide-de-camp to the Tsar's uncle. Grand Duke Paul has personally asked His Majesty not to be swayed by any petitions for leniency. Although your sister may have committed this vile act in the name of love, Colonel Trigony had many powerful friends, and they will not be satisfied until his murderess is brought to justice. Yet I will speak to the Emperor, though it will probably do little good. Please inform your sister that she has my prayers. Perhaps it will make her ordeal a little easier to bear."

The Tsarina came to her feet, signaling an end to the audience.

"Is he really a man of God, do you think? We all need miracles, you know," said Alexandra, half to herself.

"Perhaps with his spiritual guidance and support, Your Majesty, Russia might have an heir."

For a moment Henriette was certain she had made a terrible blunder, speaking of such personal matters and bringing up a subject that surely troubled the Tsarina more than anyone else in Russia. But then Alexandra's expression softened, and she even reached out and patted Henriette on the hand.

"Faith, love, and hope are all that matter, Mademoiselle Petrova. The soul of the holy Russian people will hear our prayers."

"They hear them now, Your Majesty, and will hear them throughout the long and glorious days of your reign." Uncertain if she should back out of the drawing room, or remain where she was until the Empress departed, Henriette glanced at the doors.

The Tsarina, with a sad little smile, opened them herself, surprising the footmen who stood guard outside. Then, without another word, she walked slowly down the corridor, a shy and humorless figure who liked to think of herself as *Matushka*, Mother of the Russian people.

Six

Outwardly calm and resigned to her fate, Masha arrived at court that Friday morning wearing clothes Irena had brought from her apartment, having been given permission to dispense with her prison-issue wardrobe for the duration of the trial. Although she had lost weight during her lengthy period of incarceration, and a hectic flush betrayed the intermittent cough that had plagued her ever since her imprisonment, Masha still looked surprisingly well, and didn't appear to have suffered greatly from her long ordeal.

Three months in a cell ten feet long by five feet wide had given her more than enough time to make peace with herself. But now, whatever emotions had prompted her to take Trigony's life seemed to have little bearing on the proceedings that were about to begin. She just wanted them to be over with, to be left alone, for her family to stop worrying, and for the crowds that thronged the gates outside the prison, and that were equally numerous in front of the District Court where she was taken, to forget there was ever such a person as Maria Petrovna Danchenko, Petersburg's most celebrated murderess.

Even now, the courtroom was packed to overflowing, the

tiers of benches reserved for the public having been filled just moments after the doors had opened. Seated behind an oak railing polished by the hands of those accused of crimes equally as great as hers, Masha glanced over her shoulder, able to see her sisters and brother in the first row of the spectators' section. Gregor winked encouragingly and held up his thumb. Henriette smiled grimly, while behind her someone was complaining that her soaring feathered hat obscured his view. Next to her sat Irena, who, with tightly folded hands, was trying valiantly to look optimistic lest her anxiety communicate itself to her sister.

Masha, returning their smiles, looked away, listening with one ear as her lawyer explained how the proceedings would run, and what she might expect from this first day.

At precisely ten o'clock the twelve jurymen entered from a side door, sober-minded citizens who appeared to be quite pleased with the notoriety they were soon to achieve. Without even waiting to take their seats, they immediately turned their attention to the prisoner, as this was the first chance any of them had to see the woman whose "courageous and romantic act" had so inflamed the public's imagination.

Soon after, an usher stepped in front of the dais and announced, "The court!"

Everyone came respectfully to their feet with a loud scraping of chairs and a round of coughing. Masha too rose obediently as the presiding judge and his two assessors mounted the steps that led up to the platform, where they seated themselves behind a long table covered with a green fringed cloth.

Behind her someone remarked how Masha seemed to be in a daze, while at the front of the courtroom a priest in a brown cassock had begun to swear in the jury, who now crowded around the lectern beneath the ikon. The thorns of Christ's sad mutilating crown thrust themselves out at her, and Masha shrank back in her seat, crossing herself involuntarily.

"I promise and I swear, by Almighty God, on the gospels and the life-giving cross . . ."

The voices, like the drowsy hum of bees on a summer afternoon, gradually faded away, until once again an uneasy silence settled over the courtroom. Then the president of the court, adjusting the gold-embroidered cuffs of his uniform, began a lengthy directive to the jurors, concluding his remarks by calling for a ten-minute recess while the jury elected a foreman.

The spectators, hunched over their seats like children at the circus, munched chocolates, peeled oranges, and generally had themselves a wonderful time. When the jury returned, the gallery buzzed with excitement, now that the trial was finally going to begin.

The judge asked Masha to rise, and then rattled off a list of statistical questions beginning with her name and ending with her occupation.

Following this, the president read off the names of those witnesses and experts who would be called to take part in the proceedings. Immediately afterward, the court clerk stood up to read the bill of indictment. Hearing her name mentioned yet again, and then the damning words "the murder of the nobleman, *dvoryanin* Eugene Borisovich Trigony, late of His Majesty's Chevalier Guards," Masha's quiet and self-absorbed expression vanished, and she clenched her teeth and held onto the railing as if she were afraid of losing her balance.

"Maria Danchenko," said the president, "you have heard the clerk read the accusation. Do you plead guilty to the charges as stated therein?"

Guilty? she kept thinking. Am I really a murderess, as they all say? All the hours she had spent pacing her cell now came back to her. Guilty? But what constituted guilt, after all? Was there no allowance for retribution? Could a man be permitted to go free after taking another's life? Trigony had gone free. Then what make her situation any different?

"Prisoner, I ask you again, do you plead guilty?"

"No," said Masha in a barely audible voice, whereupon her lawyer looked at her in surprise, as this wasn't what they'd agreed upon.

From behind her came a loud murmur of voices as the public discussed this among themselves, none of them having any doubts she'd murdered Colonel Trigony with the very same pistol he had earlier used to kill her husband.

"Then you deny murdering Colonel Trigony?" said the judge.

"No," Masha said, "but I deny being guilty."

"Outrageous," muttered the public prosecutor, who was seated to her right, at the same side as the ikon case.

"We're not here to argue semantics, Madame Danchenko. If you admit to taking the life of Colonel Trigony, please say so, that we may begin."

"Yes, say it," whispered Ilyinsky, her attorney, a stout and imposing figure given to smelling his fingers and smoking cigars.

"Yes," she said wearily, "I admit to taking the Colonel's life."

The president eyed her with something of relief, and after the witnesses had been duly sworn in, he turned to the prosecuting attorney, who called Masha's maid to the witness stand. Although Masha had given her and the cook the week off, the maid had quarreled with her sister, whom she had gone to visit. Returning to Petersburg soon after Masha left for the Volskys, the poor woman had found Colonel Trigony as she went about cleaning the apartment. It was she who'd summoned the police, and they, in turn, had brought in Porfiry Nezvanov, the examining magistrate.

The second witness was Trigony's orderly, who had arrived

at Masha's apartment after the Colonel failed to keep an important breakfast appointment with the Grand Duke. Following his testimony, the prosecutor called a ballistics expert to the stand, who testified that the weapon in question, the pistol inlaid with mother-of-pearl that was labeled *Material Evidence No. 1*, was the same weapon with which Colonel Trigony had been shot. Throughout all this, Ilyinsky, the defense counsel, sat glumly at his desk, offering no objections.

When he was finally given the opportunity to cross-examine the witnesses, Ilyinsky stunned everyone in court by declining, and saying that he was quite satisfied with the testimony so far presented. Even Masha looked surprised, for neither her maid nor Trigony's orderly had actually seen her commit the crime. But the attorney didn't seem interested in pursuing this line of defense, and so both witnesses were escorted from the courtroom, looking rather disappointed that their presence was no longer required.

After a two-hour recess for dinner, during which time the public refused to leave their seats, certain that the crowd assembled outside the court would immediately rush in to claim them for themselves, the trial resumed with the witnesses for the defense. Ilyinsky, sucking the last remnants of lunch from between his teeth, called Dr. Eugen Bleuler to the stand.

Dr. Bleuler was director of the Burghölzli Mental Hospital in Zurich, a facility that was considered the finest in Europe. World-famous for his treatment of psychoses, Dr. Bleuler's reputation had unfortunately not preceded him, and when he responded to Ilyinsky's questions by answering in French, there was such an uproar in the gallery that the presiding judge threatened to clear the court unless order was restored. Although Masha had met with Dr. Bleuler several days earlier, when permission was granted for him to interview her in her cell, she was completely unprepared for the doctor's testimony.

"So it is your learned opinion that Madame Danchenko was not in full possession of her mental faculties at the time this act was committed," said Ilyinsky, turning to the jury so as to include them in his remarks.

"Unquestionably so," agreed Dr. Bleuler. "It is my belief that she has been suffering from severe mental aberration for many years now, no doubt brought on by the death of her husband. A woman of this type, after suffering a prolonged period of melancholia that in turn was replaced by mania at the onset of her liaison with the deceased, would have little conscious awareness of what she was doing."

"Little conscious awareness," repeated the attorney with great satisfaction. "Am I therefore correct in assuming that at the time of Colonel Trigony's death, Madame Danchenko might not even have known where she was?"

"I'd consider that highly likely," said the doctor. "Madame Danchenko was acting on impulses that were completely aberrant to her normal behavior."

"Then you're saying she was insane when all this took place?"

"Very much so."

"Of course she was, the poor darling," cried a woman from the gallery, and all around her the spectators nodded and murmured in agreement.

"So to condemn her for this crime would be like condemning a stranger, certainly not the woman you see before you." Ilyinsky gestured as Masha, who had slunk down in her seat, horrified at the thought that everyone now considered her a lunatic.

"Madame Danchenko acted on morbid impulses of a highly psychopathological nature," said the esteemed doctor from Zurich.

Psychopathological left the gallery in confusion, even those who spoke French. Again there arose a murmur of voices as the spectators conferred among themselves, trying to figure out what the witness had said.

"By psychopathological do you mean deranged?" said Ilyinsky.

"Temporarily so, yes," replied Dr. Bleuler.

Smiling broadly, and bringing his fingers up to his nose, Ilyinsky informed the judge he had no further questions for the witness. The prosecutor then bounded to his feet, eager to begin his cross-examination. Fully as stout and imposing as his colleague, he stood before the witness stand and waited until the courtroom was absolutely silent.

"Is it your opinion, Herr Doctor, that every murderer is deranged?"

"Why . . . yes," stammered Bleuler in confusion.

"Murder then is an act of madness?"

"Of course, certainly."

"Then do you suggest that instead of trying murderers for their crimes, we put them in insane asylums, Doctor?"

The expert from Zurich never had a chance to reply. The spectators began to boo, and one of them even threw an orange, which hit the prosecutor on the shoulder and landed on the floor with a splat. Although the judge, and then his two assessors, loudly demanded order, the spectators refused to quiet down.

"Shame on him, the poor darling," said the same woman who had spoken earlier.

"Killed him for love she did," said the man sitting next to her.

"I'd do the same," said another.

Unable to restore order, the president insisted the gallery be cleared, for which purpose several gendarmes entered the courtroom, leaving the doors open so that Masha could hear the uproar out in the corridor. A man with a camera mounted on a tripod took this opportunity to sneak inside, but no sooner had he disappeared under the black focusing cloth of his apparatus when Gregor hurried down the aisle. With a single well-aimed kick, he sent the camera flying in one direction and the tripod in the other.

So ended the first day of the trial.

The following morning, despite the huge crowds that spilled onto the Liteiny Prospect in front of the court, the presiding judge refused to allow the public access to the gallery. A large contingent of policemen and gendarmes were now very much in evidence, some holding the crowd back while others saw to it that only authorized persons were allowed inside.

When Masha stepped down from the black police wagon that had transported her from prison, a great cheer erupted from the hundreds of men and women who were waiting to catch a glimpse of her. Yet she didn't feel like a heroine, and couldn't even manage a gesture of acknowledgment, let alone appreciation, as a path was cleared so that she might be taken inside.

"We're all praying for you, my darling," Irena called out when she was led into the courtroom, her sisters and brother having been given special permission to attend the proceedings.

"Things are going very well for us, very well indeed," said Ilyinsky, looking dapper and self-confident as he spread his papers out on his desk.

But the jurors didn't mirror his optimism. When they took their seats, Masha could see how uneasy they were, and shrank down in her place as they peered at her with morbid curiosity. Dr. Bleuler, she now learned, had already left for Zurich, and since her counsel had no further witnesses, when the trial resumed the public prosecutor was called upon to address the jury.

Sitting there with her head sunk against her chest, and her eyes half closed, Masha heard him begin.

"Gentlemen of the jury, you see before you not a victim, but a victimizer, not an innocent woman, but a cold-blooded murderess. . . ."

The prosecutor droned on. Words and phrases like "premeditated," "cruel," "vicious," and "let justice be done" came through to Masha's blurred consciousness. Then the defense lawyer stood before the jury. He was equally impassioned, but less in the cause of justice than of anguished love.

When at last she was allowed to speak in her own defense, Masha rose swiftly to her feet, gripping the oak railing and eying the jurymen not as strangers to be feared, but as men who were her brothers. "Yes, it's true, I murdered a man, I took a life," she said in a firm and unwavering voice. "Whether you decide to punish me or not, I'll always have that to live with, for the guilt I bear is profound and lasting. Yesterday, you heard Dr. Bleuler declare that at the time of the murder I was deranged. If that is so, then love too is a form of derangement, and I cannot possibly ask you to forgive me for what I've done. But I can ask for your sympathy, and your understanding."

Trying to keep her thoughts in order, Masha proceeded to explain how she had first met Colonel Trigony, and the circumstances surrounding the duel in which her husband had lost his life.

"How can one defend revenge?" she asked. "How can one understand love? Even before I was arrested I tried to answer those questions. But gentlemen, there are no answers. I've condemned myself. What you choose to do with me now will still leave those questions unanswered. I did what I had to, but I can't even begin to tell you why."

As she slipped down into her seat she heard Irena sobbing at the back of the courtroom. Realizing how she had injured those she loved, Masha too began to cry, and hardly paid attention as the president began the summing up. She had no idea how long he spoke to the jurors, nor if he said anything that hadn't already been said before. When she looked up, it was to see her tear-streaked face reflected in the unsheathed sword of the gendarme who stood beside her.

"Court is adjourned until ten o'clock tomorrow morning," announced the presiding judge. Without waiting for the jurors to withdraw, he tugged at his sleeves and hurried from the courtroom.

The next morning Masha's guards were especially kind, and even knocked timorously on the door before unlocking it and stepping inside. Her jailers, with gold braid on their sleeves like the three judges, spoke in low and solicitous voices, telling her it was time to go. The jury, having deliberated long into the night, was ready to announce its verdict.

When she arrived at court not a sound could be heard as everyone looked anxiously in the direction of the jury room, where at any moment a bell would ring and the twelve jurors would file out to take their seats. When at last it rang, it so startled Masha that she began to tremble. The door to the debating room opened, and one after another the jurors stepped outside, screwing up their unshaven faces and blinking rapidly as if the courtroom were too brightly lit, then dropping into their chairs with sighs of exhaustion.

The president asked, "Is the *dvoryanina* Maria Petrovna Danchenko, forty-two years of age, guilty of having taken the life of the nobleman Eugene Borisovich Trigony?"

The foreman jumped to his feet, upsetting his chair and causing everyone but the presiding judge to let out with a gasp.

"Well?" said the president.

"Yes, guilty," whispered the foreman.

From behind her came a piercing and anguished scream. Was it Irena, or someone else in the gallery? A loud rumble of voices rose up in the air. Everyone seemed to be talking at once. Ilyinsky was gesturing vehemently at the prosecutor who, in turn, was stabbing his finger in the direction of the jurors.

"But Your Excellency, we recommend mercy," the foreman called out.

"Yes, mercy," agreed the jurymen, who were now coming to their feet to make themselves heard.

"Gentlemen, please. Be seated, be seated," one of the honorary justices shouted.

"Mercy, spare her!" a woman cried from the spectators' section.

Masha listened to the uproar as if she were merely an observer and not a participant, having paid the price of admission so that she might sit back and watch the plot unfold upon a stage. Of course she was guilty. But now it was guilt transformed into a judgment, given permanence by the decision reached by the jury. How sad and shame-faced they all looked, these sober-minded citizens who had argued her case all through the night.

The prosecutor, called upon by the president of the court, recommended fifteen years of penal servitude, to which the gallery responded with loud cries and stamping of feet, shouting that it was he who should be exiled, and not the prisoner.

"Court will adjourn to consider the sentence," declared the president. With the two other members of the court taking up the rear, the three men left their seats to retire to the debating room.

They weren't gone but five minutes, and as soon as they returned there was silence, broken by muffled sobbing from somewhere behind her.

Let it be fifteen years, let it be twenty, Masha thought. What does it matter now that he's dead, now that they're all dead?

"The Criminal Court, taking into account the recommendation of the jury, as well as the extraordinary circumstances surrounding this case, decrees that the prisoner, Maria Petrovna Danchenko, be deprived of rights both civil and personal, and is condemned to deportation to Siberia for a period of five years. The prosecutor's motion for penal servitude is hereby denied."

"We'll file an appeal," said Ilyinsky, forced to raise his voice in order to be heard.

"No."

"What?" he said, and he cupped his hand behind his ear, unable to hear her above the clamor of the gallery.

"No appeal," she said. "It's done . . . yes, it's over. Finished."

Seven

"It's these damn agitators," said the chief inspector of the House of Preliminary Detention. "SR's, SD's . . . what does it matter what they're calling themselves, Mr. Petrov, when we all know what they mean to do? Destroy holy Russia from within and without. That's right, from within and without." He said this with a certain degree of satisfaction, as if the phrase had a magical quality to it that bestowed upon him an aura of respectability, since only a man of considerable education could speak in such lofty generalities. "Here, look for yourself," the prison official went on, and he strode across the room, flinging his arm in the direction of the window.

Gregor, determined to be polite, followed obediently after his host, who was pointing toward the Vyborg District on the opposite side of the Neva. A thin plume of greasy smoke discolored the bright May sky, marking the site of the recent riots that had broken out in the industrial section of the capital.

"Yes, from within and without," said the chief inspector. "Yesterday it was the cotton mills—still burning, as you can see. The day before that, the iron works. Thirty-five hundred of them attacked the police, Mr. Petrov. Forty dead, hundreds wounded. I'll tell you this: Put them all behind bars and we wouldn't miss the lot of them. Oh no, not a one."

"Terrible," said Gregor in what he hoped was a convincing tone of voice. "But is she—?"

"She'll be down in just a moment," said the chief inspector, still gazing out the window, which looked down onto the inner courtyard of the prison with its tangle of iron balconies and steep, open staircases.

Having obtained permission from the vice governor to visit with his sister, the chief inspector had kindly offered the use of his office, knowing that any man who was friendly with his superiors was a man worthy of accommodating.

"Where will it end, do you suppose?" said the official, when the door finally opened and the head jailer of the women's division marched inside, clicking her heels together before stepping smartly to the side. Behind her came Masha, wearing a shapeless gray smock with a yellow figure on the back that marked her as a convict.

"Well then," said the chief inspector with a cheery grin, "here she is now. You're looking well, Maria Petrovna. I trust everything is satisfactory . . . not the Hôtel de l'Europe, of course," he added with an unctuous laugh.

"You've been most kind," said Gregor as he stared at his sister with a wistful smile, not having seen her since the trial.

With an obsequious bow, the chief inspector and the guard left the room, closing the door behind them. The moment they were alone, Gregor rushed into his sister's outstretched arms, holding Masha tightly and feeling her frail, slender figure trembling against him.

"There, there," he said, easing back to cup her face in his hands. "It's Grisha, you silly thing. Remember me, your baby brother?" He laughed self-consciously, clutching her slim hands in his, and gazing into her glistening dark eyes as if he might never see her again.

"It's all right, Grisha dear. You mustn't look so despondent. They treat me very well, certainly not like a common criminal. Why, I even have a regular mattress now. Feathers, can you imagine, instead of straw." Masha tried to smile, but her grin wasn't very convincing.

"I have good news," he hurried to say. "No, not a pardon, I'm afraid. But thanks to the Denishevs, the Tsar has issued a special ukase. His edict reclassifies you as a political prisoner, which means you'll get the best possible treatment. You'll be traveling with them when you leave here. They're good people, I'm sure, Masha. They'll take care of you, and see to it that you get there safely."

"A political," his sister said with a funny little laugh. "Wouldn't Victor Romanovich be pleased." She put her hand over her mouth and began to cough, waving aside Gregor's offer of a handkerchief. "The cell is damp, that's all. It's not what you think, believe me. Ostroumov himself examined me just last week . . . see all the privileges I've been granted? It's there, but it's dormant. He said it was. He promised me."

"Yes, of course," Gregor replied, hearing the desperation in her voice.

"So we'll say good-bye and we won't make a fuss," Masha told him. "After all, we all knew this was going to happen. Besides, I'd rather hear about you now. Did you get that appointment you were hoping for?"

He shook his head.

"Because of me?"

"Don't even think such a thing," he hurriedly replied. "We're not royalty, that's why. And you know all the trouble I had with Orlovsky. They certainly wouldn't have chosen me to succeed him. No, I didn't expect to be made Director, and so I'm not disappointed. Larisa and I are working on that portraits exhibit again. I think we'll finally see the project to its conclusion. And other than that . . . ." He shrugged, knowing there wasn't anything else to say.

"But you're happy, aren't you?"

"I don't know," and now it was his turn to pretend to laugh. "Thirty-eight years old and I probably know just as much—or just as little—as I did twenty years ago. Besides, no one knows what happiness is, anyway. They talk about it all the time, but no one has the answers."

"Are you still alone, Grisha?" she asked softly.

He looked down at his lap, ashamed of his solitude, feeling selfish and ill at ease that he had never been able to care about anyone as Masha had cared about Victor and Stepan. But Henriette was like that, too, only when they spoke of an unmarried woman they used words like "old maid" and "spinster," whereas he was just a bachelor, more to be pitied than scorned.

"The exhibit requires a great deal of work," he finally replied. "I'll be very busy for the next year, maybe two, rifling through dusty attics from one corner of Russia to the other, seeing what treasures I can unearth." He looked away, trying to make sense of his feelings, and wondering if she would appreciate his honesty. "I tried, Masha, really I did. I wanted so much from myself, the plans I used to have, the dreams. They're still there, but now they seem less real than ever before. Prince Denishev's even approached me about starting our own ballet company, touring Europe. Gregor Petrov, impresario . . . if only I had someone to share it with."

"You will. Maybe not right away. But someday, Grisha."

"Perhaps," he conceded, hearing the reluctance in his voice. "But now's not the time to sit here feeling sorry for myself. I came to tell you how much I care about you, Masha. Maybe we haven't spent a great deal of time together over the years, it's true. But I don't take you for granted, I never have.

547

I have great respect for you, tremendous admiration." A thick knot of grief rose up in the back of his throat. He tried to swallow, and brushed aside the tears that now began to well up in his eyes. "I don't care if I sound mawkish, I don't care at all. I'll miss you, Mashenka. Dear God, I'll miss you so."

He pressed her close, stroking her hair and thinking of all the things he could have said and hadn't. Yet oddly enough, he was more terrified of his own future than hers. She would survive, he was certain. She had done what she had to, and now she had no regrets. Could any of them say the same? No, they had lived their quiet lives, suffering in silence. But Masha, more than any of his sisters, had demonstrated that rare quality of passion, that commitment to her feelings that had led her here to this terrible place. But was it so frightening, after all? Wasn't an ordinary and uneventful life, cradle to grave and not much more in between, far more terrifying?

The door opened and the chief inspector coughed loudly, embarrassed to see them weeping in each other's arms.

Gregor drew back. "Just five more minutes, please," he begged.

The official nodded, and withdrew.

"I'll come and visit as soon as I can. They say Kirensk isn't such a bad place, Masha. And you won't be behind bars, of course. You'll have your own little house. And who knows, there might even be a valuable portrait stuck away in your attic."

Masha returned his impoverished grin. "Provided there's an attic. But I'll be all right, I promise. I've made my peace, Grisha, and I won't look back anymore." She came to her feet, a slim, dark-haired figure he still saw as a girl. "Be happy, Grisha. And write when you can. And tell me of your exhibits and your plans. I expect great things from you, dear brother. But when they happen, as I know they will, don't start convincing yourself there's no one in the world who's right for you. It's harder for you than most, I know, even if we've never talked about it. But that's no reason to give up, Gregor, because if you do, all your success and good fortune will be meaningless. That's what I've learned more than anything else. The worst punishment is loneliness, Grisha. That's why we need each other, to help make that solitude a little easier to bear."

Masha turned away and walked briskly to the door, her shoulders a trifle too large for her frame, her stride determined and fiercely self-reliant. As she reached for the doorknob she glanced back, a look of keen intelligence lighting up her entire face.

"I'll miss you," he called out, the knot at the back of his throat so painful now he could barely speak.

"I'll miss you, too. But don't worry, Grisha dear. I'm not a bit afraid."

Simon Bazarov, once known as Belinsky, arrived at Alexander Park on the Petersburg side shortly after sunset. Yet the western twilight still lingered among the trees, for this was the season of the "white nights," and not until midnight would it truly be dark. As the moon came up, this purplish half-light mingled eerily with the moonlight, causing the alleys of tall trees to glow with a faint phosphorescence, as if marking the path to the great domed structure they called Narodny Dom, the People's Palace.

This enormous massif of pale-gray stone had opened its doors just a few weeks earlier, built to provide the common people with a place where they could go to enjoy the finest in national music and drama. But as Simon observed when he paid his ten kopecks admission, the ordinary working class was nowhere to be seen. Instead, a well-dressed crowd—the "gray public," as the *petite bourgeoisie* were called—strolled through the brightly lit entrance hall.

Directly ahead were a pair of colossal portraits of Nikolas and Alexandra, from whose private purse had come the millions of rubles necessary to erect this complex of theaters, concert halls, and restaurants. How overbearing and fiercely paternalistic they looked, Simon couldn't help but think as the strains of a popular song drifted through the air, an orchestra playing from the story-high cross gallery just above the Emperor's weak yet handsome face.

Simon edged forward until there wasn't room to move, "not enough for an apple to fall down," as his old nurse used to say. Zubatov should have been here by now, and Simon looked around warily, trying not to draw attention to himself. Zubatov had suggested they meet in the dining room, but Simon was nervous about being seen in such a large open space, and had recommended instead the massive high-relief map of the Russian empire to the left of the main hall. Gradually making his way toward it, and stationing himself directly in front of the freshly painted expanse of a glossy Lake Baikal, he paused to light a cigarette while waiting for his chief.

"Welcome to Petersburg, Mr. Bazarov."

Colonel Zubatov stood alongside him, staring straight ahead so that for the first time since they had met, Simon could see the bright blue of his eyes behind his tinted spectacles. As top man in the Moscow Okhrana, Zubatov had arrived in the capital for a round of talks with his opposite number in the Petersburg division, as well as to consolidate plans with Simon, whose importance to the organization now earned him the previously unheard-of sum of five hundred rubles a month.

As one of Lenin's most trusted aides, Simon had worked diligently to prove his value to the Social Democrats, organizing and coordinating an underground Party network with local committees and factory study groups in nearly every major city and town in European Russia. *Iskra*, the Party newspaper, had already achieved a circulation that was the envy of its rivals, chief of which was *Revolutionary Russia*, the organ of the SR's, or Socialist Revolutionaries. Of late, Simon had openly courted the SR leadership, for Zubatov believed they posed an even greater danger than the Marxist SD's. Terrorism was the backbone of the SR philosophy, and terrorism was what the Okhrana was anxious to combat.

Although Simon had already been able to supply his chief with enough information for the Okhrana to arrest the leaders of both parties, Zubatov felt it made little sense to go after one individual at a time. Instead, he hoped to make the biggest possible haul, so as to strip the SD's, and the far more militant SR's, of all those men and women who threatened the safety of the empire.

To this end, Simon had worked behind the scenes organizing an All-Party Congress, where the leaders of both rival factions would have an opportunity to air their differences and work toward eventual reconciliation, if not outright unification. Now, as he watched the crowds moving through the People's Palace, he told Zubatov how close they were to success.

"Everyone's agreed to meet in Tomsk next month," Simon said under his breath, slipping his hand in his pocket to remove a piece of paper on which he'd written the names of the Party leaders who were committed to attending the conference.

"Annenkov," said Zubatov with satisfaction as he read over the list. "That's the student agitator we've been after. I'll be very pleased when we get our hands on him. Now, if only Lenin decided to slip back into the country we'd end this nonsense once and for all."

"He won't," whispered Simon. "But I wouldn't worry

about him, if I were you. He's a theoretician. Talks a big game, but no one really pays much attention. It's the SR's who'll give us the most trouble. They're organizing a Combat Section, devoted solely to political assassination."

Zubatov looked at him with alarm. "The Tsar?"

Simon shook his head. "But several of his Ministers are making themselves very unpopular with their policies. I'd suggest tighter security in the future."

"And the raid, won't you be compromised?"

"Not if I manage to escape."

Zubatov laughed softly. "I don't think that should prove too difficult. After all, you escaped Butyrky years ago, remember? But why did they choose Tomsk, of all places?"

The Tomsk Detention Center, one of the largest in Siberia, was run by the brother-in-law of one of the SR's leaders. From what he'd heard, even the staff of the center had revolutionary leanings.

"So they think they're going to pull the wool over our eyes, do they, meeting in a prison because we'd never suspect them to convene in such a place? What a surprise we'll have in store for them, Simon Ivanovich. Yes, this operation is going to prove their undoing, and the Okhrana's finest hour. The net tightens, my friend, and you know what happens when you haul a fish out of water."

"It suffocates," Simon replied with a grin. "Quite painfully, too, I'd imagine."

How long ago was it since she'd stood outside a prison, waiting for a convoy of exiles to begin their long journey? Irena couldn't remember exactly what year it was, but as she waited to catch sight of her sister she thought of the cycles imposed on her life, the strange repetition of events to which human beings were often subjected. Had anyone told her years ago that she'd return to a prison to say good-bye to her sister, she would have viewed such a prediction as the height of absurdity. Yet now there was nothing absurd about it, for that was precisely what was about to happen.

"These protracted farewells," Henriette was complaining as she fanned herself with her glove. "Why couldn't we have said good-bye yesterday, or the day before, like civilized people? You know I don't like to mingle with riffraff, I never have."

"You needn't have come if you didn't want to," Irena reminded her. "After all, Masha is only your sister. You could have stayed home and watched everything through your crystal ball."

"How unlike you to be so sarcastic, Irena."

"Not at all," she said in a calm and almost dispassionate tone of voice. "But sometimes your selfishness astounds me, particularly when you yourself are so dependent upon others."

Henriette began to fan herself so vigorously she accidentally slapped herself with her glove. "It's not as if they're going to force her to work in the mines," she said. "They say Kirensk is a pleasant enough little town, once you get used to it."

"If you call being stranded four thousand miles from Petersburg pleasant, then I suppose it is. But I doubt you'd survive even a year there, Henriette. After all, it's so cold that even the spirits don't come out of hiding for nine months out of twelve."

Managing to extricate themselves from the crowd that now began to press close to the gates, Irena tried to convince herself that Masha would be all right, that as a political she'd be given every consideration, placed in the company of men and women whose backgrounds were similar to her own. But when she saw the first group of exiles, the *katorzhniki* whose half-shaved heads singled them out as convicts sentenced to

553

hard labor, a feeling of terror rose up in her breast. She wanted to cry out, if only to give vent to her fears, but knew that her screams would serve little good.

How the ground shook as the convoy of prisoners streamed through the gates, pushed and jostled by the soldiers in their spotless white shirts. Clouds of dust rose everywhere, as if an army were on the march, while all around her, people rushed to get closer to their loved ones, pressing bundles of food and warm clothing into their manacled hands. Above the harsh, biting rattle of chains she heard a more vicious sound, the sharp, snakelike hiss of a lash. Someone groaned and fell to the ground, causing the prisoners behind him to lose their balance and topple like a pack of cards. The guards hauled them to their feet and shoved the men forward, lining them up for the march to the railway station.

The last to leave were the politicals, who wore their own clothes and weren't segregated according to sex. Seated in a tumbrel-like cart, Masha raised her hand and waved.

"You'd think they would have let her wash her hair," said Henriette, using her elbows to steer a path through the crowd. "Here we are, *ma chère!*" she called out, as if to say she wouldn't have missed this for all the world.

Irena reached up and clutched Masha's hand, having already said everything she possibly could. All she could do now was stare into Masha's eyes, communicating without words.

"I've looked into your future," Henriette said brightly. "Something good will come of all this. I don't know what it will be, or what form it will take. But I'm certain it'll be very positive."

Masha smiled faintly, telling Henriette how well she looked, and how much prettier she was now than when she was a girl. "Stately," she said "Yes, Henriette, you've become a regal presence. And is there happiness in your future, too?"

Henriette pulled her glove over her thin, bony hand. "One learns to accept one's place in the world," she replied.

"Indeed one does," Masha agreed. "But what will you do with Petrovka?" she went on, turning to Irena.

"Does it matter anymore?"

Masha shrugged. "Perhaps one day we'll all be there together, and this will just be a memory, something we've put behind us, Irusha."

"God be with you," whispered Irena. "May He watch over you and keep you safe."

"Let us hope He doesn't find Siberia too forbidding."

The cart rolled forward. The crowd drew in its breath. All Irena could hear was the clatter of chains, which echoed like mournful bells in the dusty spring air.

On Vasilyevsky Island, in a nondescript house on a street known as the Eleventh Line, Alexei Annenkov packed a bag, taking as few things as possible. Seated on the edge of a lumpy leather sofa, Pauline watched her fiancé as if he were a stranger. Surely the man she loved wouldn't be going off without a word of explanation.

"I don't want you getting involved, Pauline, can't you understand that?" Cousin Alex said when her reproachful glances finally became too painful. He closed his traveling case, then lifted it up to see how heavy it was. Satisfied that it wouldn't prove cumbersome, he set it down on the floor.

"You share everything with me, Alex, except your politics. Don't you trust me?"

"Of course I do, more than anyone. But the less you know of my activities, the easier it'll be for the both of us."

"Why?"

"Because I don't want you worrying, and I don't want you to have any information that might incriminate you." The crease over the bridge of his nose grew even more prominent than usual, and when Alex looked at her, his expression was so earnest he appeared to be scowling.

"If I don't know where you're going, and if something happens to you, we'll be lost to each other, don't you understand?"

"I'll write."

"And if they don't let you?"

"God, why did I ever fall in love with a girl who had all the answers?" Alexei said, throwing up his hands in exasperation. He sank down onto the sofa that served as his bed, and when he spoke it was as if he feared the sound of his own voice. "Tomsk," he said faintly.

Pauline remained silent for a moment. Then, finding the courage to speak, she said, "What possible reason could you have to go there? It's the middle of Siberia, Alexei."

"There are some people I have to . . . I promised myself I wouldn't discuss it, Pauline."

"But I'd worry about you even if you were going only as far as Moscow. I love you, Alexei. I have for a long time now. And you have to start sharing your life with me. I'd willingly accompany you. I'd leave right now if you let me. So at least tell me what it is you're doing."

It was only with the greatest of reluctance that Alex responded to her plea, telling of the meeting he'd promised to attend.

In the two years they'd spent at the university, Pauline had seen a great change come over him. At times he wasn't even Cousin Alex anymore, but merely a young man spouting rhetoric and waving his fist in the air. How could people be so enamored of ideas, and vague, idealistic concepts? If change was needed to make Russia a better place, couldn't it be effected peacefully? Every day she read of new arrests, secret printing presses closed down, bundles of illegal newspapers seized and burned.

"When will it end?" she asked him. "Why can't we live out our lives in peace, like normal people?"

"But we are normal people, Pauline, that's what makes our cause all the more important." He didn't wait for her to reply, but drew her up into his arms and kissed her.

When at last he let go, Pauline looked at him tenderly. "I want to make love to you," she whispered. "It can't be wrong, not if we care about each other."

How shy and boyish he looked then, how suddenly frightened, too. He touched her with the tips of his fingers, tentative and unsure of himself. Exploring the contours of her face, he traced each dimple when she smiled, and lovingly caressed the extravagant profusion of her raven-black hair. Then he slowly eased her down onto the sofa, hovering over her like a parent watching his sleeping child, till he fell against her with a sob.

In the cool of his shadowy room, she received the shape of his body. Like the children they were, they taught each other as they went along, and the only rule they followed was the expectation of mutual tenderness. Such intimacy was terrifying. It made her realize that having given life to each other, apart they would be forever incomplete.

When he released her, falling back into himself, the fierceness of their desire was replaced by wonder, that each could give so much happiness and pleasure to the other. Knowing this, and still feeling the hard, sinewy curve of his body as he lay against her, Pauline was now prepared to accept the angry catchwords, the glib rhetoric, the stormy banners unfurling against the vast uneasiness of a Russian sky. He was still the Alex she had always loved.

Before she left, he gave her a slip of paper on which he'd written the name and address of a man she was to contact if he failed to return to Petersburg in September.

"Who is he?" Pauline asked, still wanting the nearness of

him, yet knowing she could no longer interfere.

"Bazarov's one of the best men we have, a natural-born leader. He'll know what to do if we're caught."

Caught—the very mention of the word was too horrifying to contemplate. "But why won't he be in Tomsk with the rest of you?"

"The executive committee decided he'd be more useful in Geneva. So if something happens, he'll be able to tell you where I am and how to reach me. But you mustn't worry, Pauline. We've taken every precaution. Nothing could possibly go wrong."

Eight

When Alex failed to return to Petersburg in September, Pauline made discreet inquiries at the university, and then at the house where her fiancé rented a room. The porter, a retired soldier who eyed her suspiciously, had little information to offer. Mr. Annenkov had paid his rent in advance, having informed the landlord he would be away all summer.

"And you've not heard from him since?" she asked.

"No, miss, not a word. But the police came to look at his lodgings. Last week it was, I believe. They didn't take anything though, not unless you count a bunch of old newspapers."

That evening, as she dined with her aunt and uncle, she voiced her fears, not having heard from Alex in more than a month. But when she told the Volskys of his plans, and the trip he'd taken to Tomsk, her aunt seemed more upset by Alexei's political entanglements than by his absence.

Her Uncle Niki, however, was far more sympathetic, even though he and Alex had never really gotten along. "Don't you think it's a bit late to be so critical?" he said to his wife. "After all, I'm a liberal too, Irusha. Alexei's views may not be as moderate as my own, but ultimately we're both working for the same goal."

"Which is why I want to go to Moscow, Uncle Niki," and she hurriedly explained how Alex had given her the name and address of a man she was to get in touch with if anything happened to him. "If the police searched his room, then surely they suspect something. And if they do, I have to find out where he is so I can warn him."

A look of horror came over her aunt's face. "You'll do nothing of the kind, young lady. You're my child now, Pauline, remember that. Your mother's gone, may her soul rest in peace, your father too. We're all you have, and we're not going to let you go off to God knows where."

"But Irusha—" her uncle started to say.

"The answer is no. I don't want her getting involved, Niki. She doesn't even know who this man is, or anything about him."

"But she's already involved. When Alex came to you and asked if they could marry, you gave them your blessing, remember?" Volsky glanced at his niece. "What did Alex tell you about this friend of his?"

"Not very much," she admitted. "But he said if anything should happen to him, Simon Bazarov would know what to do."

"I want to go, too," Sergei said excitedly. "You'll take me with you, Papa, won't you?"

"It gets worse, just worse and worse," her aunt said as if she were talking to herself. "Do you know that every time I close my eyes at night I see my sisters? Yes, your mother comes to me in my dreams, Pauline. Only I don't know what she wants because she never says anything. And your Aunt Masha—it's been months now, and still not a word. Yet you expect me to sit here and say, 'Go to Moscow, look up this stranger, this terrorist friend of his.' I don't want you to go, don't you understand that?"

"She's nearly twenty years old, Irena," said her uncle. "She's not a child anymore."

"Of course she's a child, Niki. She's still a baby. She doesn't know what she wants yet."

"Alex is the man I'm going to marry, Aunt Irusha," she said softly, trying to convince her aunt she wasn't just saying these things because they sounded grown-up. "I want to know where he is, and if he's all right. Surely you can understand that, can't you?"

Her aunt remained silent. Katya, taking advantage of the lull in the conversation, slipped into the dining room and asked if she could clear the table and bring in dessert.

"Do what you have to," Irena said impatiently. "That's what everyone else does, isn't it?"

"Can I go to Moscow, too?" Sergei again asked, excited at the thought of meeting an actual revolutionary. But for all his boyish enthusiasm, his plea fell on deaf ears.

"I'll go with her, Irena," her uncle announced. "So you mustn't let yourself get so upset."

"Mustn't get upset?" shouted her aunt. "One sister dead, another an exile, and I mustn't get upset? What do you expect me to do, Niki, just sit quiet and pretend nothing's wrong?" Before anyone could stop her, Irena flung down her napkin and rushed from the room.

Pauline hurried after her, and when the young woman returned some ten minutes later, she looked at her uncle and nodded her head. "She's given me her permission. We can leave whenever it's convenient for you, Uncle Niki." What Pauline didn't say was that she would have gone anyway, even if her aunt had forbidden it.

Simon Bazarov lived in a modest two-story house on a little side street off the Bolshaya Nikitskaya, not far from Moscow University. Here, in an area of both aristocratic and middle-class houses, Pauline and her uncle descended from the droshky that had taken them directly from the railway station.

The porter, a sullen-looking character whose business it was to know whether or not the occupants of the flats were at home, stood before the freshly painted gate and pretended not to notice them. "Bazarov, Bazarov," he finally replied to her uncle's persistent inquiries. "Now, let me see. There's a Suvorov on the first floor—"

"Bazarov," she said. "Simon Bazarov."

"That would be the second floor, top of the landing. But he's not in."

"When do you expect him back?" asked Volsky.

The *dvornik* shrugged. "Might be today, Your Excellency, might be tomorrow. But his wife's at home."

Pauline didn't wait for the man to hold the gate open for her, but stepped into the yard and went right to the door.

"Shall I announce you?" the porter called after her.

"It's not necessary. The Bazarovs are old friends."

A few minutes later, a rather timid voice asked who it was when Pauline knocked on the door.

"My name is Pauline Belinskaya. I'm a friend of Alexei Annenkov."

The door opened a crack and a youngish woman with lively dark eyes peered out, taken aback when she saw that Pauline wasn't alone.

"This is my uncle," she hurriedly explained. "We just came down from Petersburg this morning. I'm Alex's fiancée, Madame Bazarova. He told me that if anything happened to him, I should get in touch with your husband."

"Yes, of course, come right in," replied the woman. "I wasn't expecting visitors, you understand. Please, let me take your coats. It's turning chilly again, isn't it? I wouldn't be surprised to see snow in another few weeks. My husband just

562

stepped out, but I expect him back before too very long. May I get you some tea?"

Pauline shook her head, following Madame Bazarova into the parlor. It was a small, pleasantly decorated room with a view of the street. On the far wall, which was covered with pale blue paper, hung an oversized portrait of a cavalry officer, his mount rearing up as a bomb exploded at his feet.

"No, he's not a relative," said Madame Bazarova, a small, dark, and intense-looking woman who now smiled for the first time since they'd entered. But then, realizing Pauline's concern, she suddenly frowned and looked away.

"Do you know what's happened to Alexei?" asked Pauline.

"Tea, Mr.—"

"Volsky. No, thank you."

"He's been detained in Tomsk," said Madame Bazarova, trying to break the news as gently as possible. "I don't know how serious the situation is, but my husband had an appointment to see a friend of his this morning, a man who might have more information for us."

"Detained?" whispered Pauline. "Does that mean he was arrested?"

"From what I've been told, the meeting barely got underway when Okhranniks burst inside and took everyone into custody. They say the men put up quite a struggle, though it didn't do them much good."

Pauline pressed her hand to her mouth. But no, she wouldn't allow herself to panic, not until she had all the facts. Besides, even if they'd arrested him, he was still alive, and that was all that counted.

"How did they learn about the meeting?" she asked when she regained her composure.

Madame Bazarova looked at her helplessly. "That's what frightens us more than anything. Someone in the underground must have informed on us. There's no other way they could have found out."

"I think I'll have that cup of tea now, if I may," said Pauline, and when she glanced at her uncle, Volsky looked as grim as she felt.

Madame Bazarova—Anna Abramovna as she insisted she be called—kindled the samovar and brought out a plate heaped with honey buns and poppyseed squares. But Pauline had no appetite, and even making polite conversation was difficult now that the woman had told her everything she knew. Again and again Pauline's eyes strayed to the door, but it was more than an hour before her vigil was rewarded.

Hearing footsteps on the stairs, she came quickly to her feet, standing beside her chair as a key turned in the lock and the door swung open. A tall, solidly built man with graying temples stepped into the entryway, carefully locking the door behind him.

"Anna?" he called out, stopping short the moment he reached the parlor.

"Friends of Alexei Platonovich," explained his wife.

There was something Pauline didn't understand, and as she peered into Bazarov's dark-blue eyes, she suddenly felt very cold, and looked anxiously at her uncle. Volsky was shaking his head, as if he too were confused.

"This is Pauline Belinskaya, Alexei's fiancée," Anna Abramovna was telling him. "And her uncle, Nikolai Volsky. They're both quite sympathetic to our cause, Senya, so you needn't worry."

"My God," Volsky said under his breath.

"What's wrong?" Pauline said, and again she looked at Bazarov, staring at the cleft in his chin, the thick brush of his jet-black mustache as it swooped across his narrow upper lip. The sound of her mother's sobbing echoed strangely in her thoughts. Then she understood, and her legs felt like India rubber, folding up beneath her so that it was all she could do just to sit down in the chair.

"Are you all right?" asked Madame Bazarova.

"She hasn't seen her father since she was a child," said her uncle.

"Father?" said Anna Abramovna, looking at her husband in confusion, and not knowing what else to say.

"And you, Belinsky," her uncle went on, "this must be quite a shock for you, too."

"Belinsky?" said Anna Abramovna.

"Oh yes, Simon Ivanovich Belinsky, my wife's brother-in-law, Pauline's father."

"This is all past history, Anna," Belinsky spoke up. "I never told you because . . . we were estranged, her mother and I. We separated when she was just a baby."

Pauline kept staring at him, unable to say anything.

Father, she thought, the father I always looked for and never found. And now that he's here, I don't know what to feel anymore. Am I supposed to throw my arms around him? Do they all expect me to start weeping for joy? But he's a stranger. I don't know him. He didn't want to know me, either.

"So you're an SR, eh?" her uncle was saying with a bitter edge to his voice. "Since when did you become such a firebrand, Simon? You used to work for the police, not against them."

"What is he saying, Senya?" asked his wife.

Simon Belinsky responded to his brother-in-law's accusations as if they were of little importance. What he had done twenty years ago, he now insisted, had absolutely no bearing on the present.

"But that's not so," Pauline spoke up.

She still couldn't stop staring at him, but even though she'd recovered that part of herself that she had lost, she felt neither love nor loyalty to this man. How could she, when she had never known him? He had fathered her, yes, that was true. But he had taken no responsibility for her upbringing, denying her the kind of childhood she's read about in books, and which the girls at school had all taken for granted, unable to imagine what it was to be abandoned. They were not a happy family, or even an unhappy one. They had never been a family at all, she realized, but for the tenuous link of a common name. So it didn't surprise her that she couldn't even bring herself to call him "Father," not when he'd abrogated that position so many years before.

"I know what you must be thinking, Pauline. But you mustn't despise me. I wasn't the man your mother thought I was. Surely she's forgotten me by now."

"Forgotten you!" Pauline cried out, hating him for knowing nothing of her life. "She's dead. My mother killed herself. Yes, it's true. And when she died she must have been thinking of you, and all the years she wasted dreaming you'd come back."

"I'm sorry."

"It doesn't change things, does it? And Auntie V. said you once betrayed a man to the police. Maybe you've done it again. Yes, that's what happened, isn't it? You betrayed your friends."

"I haven't betrayed anyone, Pauline. What I did in my youth is no reflection on what I do now."

"For some men perhaps, though I seriously doubt it applies to you," said her uncle.

"Did you betray Alex?" she demanded.

"Of course not. Why, the very idea is absurd."

"But why did you change your name, Senya?" said his wife. "You never told me you were married, that you had a child."

"I didn't want the Okhrana to trace me, that's why."

"Or maybe you didn't want the underground to be able to

trace you, too," said her uncle.

"Don't be ridiculous, Volsky. I've worked loyally in the organization for years. Believe me, I'm not the man I was."

"We were going to be married," she told him. "He trusted you. He said you were his friend. No wonder you didn't go with him to Tomsk. You knew they'd all be arrested."

Anna looked at her husband in horror. "But that's true," she said, gazing at Simon as if she too didn't know who he really was.

"It's not the least bit true," Belinsky angrily replied. "We were in Geneva, helping Lenin."

"Yes, but you and I were the only ones."

"We were in Geneva because the executive committee sent us there, for God's sake!"

Anna Abramovna backed away from him, wrenching free when he reached for her hand. "Yes, but it was you who suggested that we go. It was your idea, Senya."

"An hysterical child comes here and you believe everything she says? Where's your trust, Annushka?"

"But I don't know you anymore," replied his wife. "I thought I did, but now everything's coming down on top of me and I don't know what's true and what isn't. Who are you, Senya? What do you believe in?"

Frantic with rage, Pauline glared at her father, wondering what satisfaction she'd derive by throwing herself on him and pounding her fists into his chest. Wasn't it enough that he'd deserted her? Wasn't it enough that when he finally returned, it wasn't because he wanted to take her back with him, or make up for all the years he'd been away? Having denied her a father's love, was he now going to deny her the love she had found to take his place? Alex would never abandon her, and now she had no intention of abandoning him.

"Tell them what he's done," she said to her father's wife,

this small, dark woman whose eyes shone with fear, for surely there was nothing more terrifying than knowing one's husband was a stranger. "Tell them there's a traitor in their midst, an *agent provocateur*. Simon *Bazarov* indeed," and she glanced scornfully at the man her mother had made the mistake of marrying. "Turgenev's Bazarov was a nihilist, a man who believed in nothing except himself."

"Anna knows what nonsense this all is. I've been a good husband. She has no reason to doubt me."

"Perhaps that's true," Pauline said, "though I don't think a man like you could ever be truthful to anyone. But soon the entire underground will know that you're a spy, working for the very people you say you despise. I should like to be there when they confront you with their accusations, though I suppose you won't be there, either. A man as clever and resourceful as you will figure something out. After all, you always have."

Colonel Zubatov removed his tinted spectacles, pressing his thumb and forefinger to the bridge of his nose. He looked very tired, and not at all pleased to see Simon Belinsky sitting across from him, drumming his fingers nervously on the arm of his chair.

"I can't understand why you'd take such a chance," the Okhrana chief remarked. "Don't you realize they have people watching us? They know everyone who goes in and out of here. You could have telephoned if it was so important," and he motioned to the desk set, which stood within easy reach.

"Please don't take me for an idiot, Serge. We've suffered a terrible setback. I'm going to have to leave Moscow as soon as possible."

Zubatov leaned forward in his chair, not at all certain if he'd heard his protégé correctly.

"Bazarov's finished," Simon announced. "Dead and buried."

"What are you talking about, Senya? Bazarov's the best man we have. There isn't anyone else in the field who knows the territory the way he does."

"How good of you to think so," Simon replied, making no effort to temper his bitterness. "But I'm afraid Bazarov has to retire. I had an unexpected visitor this morning, Serge."

Trying to remain as calm as possible, for he was enraged that having steadfastly climbed the rungs of his career, fifteen years of government service now appeared to be so much wasted time, Simon began to explain what had happened.

Zubatov swore under his breath, then hauled himself up from his chair. His knuckles turned white as he gripped the edge of his desk. "You mean to say everything we've been working for is just—" Unable to transform his frustration into words, he snapped his fingers and sank down again.

"At least we netted most of them in Tomsk," Simon reminded him. "As long as we keep them out of the way, the backbone of the organization is crushed."

"For the time being," murmured his chief, sighing so loudly he sent some of the papers on his desk tumbling through the air. "My God, Belinsky, how could you have let such a thing happen?"

"How was I supposed to know Annenkov was her fiancé? He talked about this girl back home. He never told me who she was."

"You'll have to get away, of course. If any of them find you, and chances are they're probably looking for you already, they'll silence you so quickly—"

"Perhaps not," he interrupted. "After all, I'm a wealth of information, Serge. They certainly wouldn't want to kill me until they found out everything I knew. Such as who we have working in the field, and who they can trust and who they can't. Of course, I have no intention of telling them anything, you understand . . . not unless I'm forced to."

Zubatov found this as interesting as Belinsky had hoped he

would, and Simon could see that behind his tinted lenses the man's eyes were blinking rapidly. "Go on, I'm listening."

"You have to help me, Serge. I've given you fifteen years of service. Surely you have a responsibility for my future."

"You're not seriously considering going over to the other side, are you?"

"Of course not," replied Simon, hoping his tone of voice had struck just the proper note of sincerity. "But a man has to eat. A man has to have a place to sleep. I certainly don't intend to return to the Presnia, where you found me. So either you help me get out of the country, providing me with sufficient funds to re-establish myself elsewhere, or else give me an administrative position in another city, where I won't be recognized."

"And if I refuse?"

"But why should you? I know too much."

Zubatov came to his feet, making a slow circuit of his office, his hands folded behind his back. Simon, wondering if he'd been too outspoken, and fearful that he might have overplayed his hand, sat back in the chair and lit a cigarette, trying to act as if nothing out of the ordinary had occurred. After all, his demands were minimal, and it wasn't as if he were asking for a fortune. Besides, he'd been invaluable to the Okhrana, so why shouldn't they go out of their way to be helpful now that he was in need of their assistance?

"We could use a good administrator in Kiev," Zubatov said at last, returning to his desk. "How soon could you leave?"

"Tonight if necessary."

"And your wife?"

"Difficult to say where her priorities lie."

"We could arrest her. Five years where Makar never drove his sheep," meaning Siberia, "is bound to quiet anyone down."

"She's not that important, Serge. They tolerate her

because of me, but no one's anxious to put her in a position of responsibility."

"As you wish." Zubatov reached across the desk and shook his hand. "I'll send someone over later this afternoon with all the information you'll require, funds too, of course. After all, we wouldn't want you so dissatisfied you'd go back to your Party friends and tell them how we operate."

"No, that wouldn't do at all," he agreed with a laugh.

"Besides, you've been extremely useful to us, Simon Ivanovich. I shall be very sorry to see you go."

"These things happen, Serge."

"All the time, I'm afraid." Smiling brightly, and clapping an affectionate hand over his shoulder, Zubatov showed him to the door.

Simon was glad that Anna wasn't at home when he returned. It would have been much too difficult to start explaining, and now all he wanted to do was pack and leave. Who would he be in Kiev? he wondered. Would they allow him to use Belinsky again, or was it time to think up another alias? Perhaps he might call himself Simon Golyadkin, another literary allusion to be sure, for Golyadkin was the hero of Dostoyevsky's singular tale about a man who discovers his double is walking the streets of Petersburg.

Looking up at the General who hung suspended in time on the parlor wall, a bomb forever exploding beneath his horse's prancing feet, Simon found himself smiling, pleased with the ease with which he'd solved his problems. A man, he had long believed, must look out for himself, as no one else in the world would do it for him. But when he thought of Anna Abramovna, so loyal and trusting, so eager to please both in bed and out, he felt an unexpected twinge of remorse. Perhaps he did love her, after all. They had been together for quite a while now, seven years or thereabouts. Yet she'd never really come to know him, had she?

He looked around for a letter she might have left behind, but couldn't find one. A quick examination of her wardrobe revealed everything intact. So she hadn't packed a bag and run off, leaving him to fend for himself. Not that it mattered, because if Zubatov discovered she was with him, there might not be a position waiting when he reached Kiev. No, that would never do, to have the wife of an Okhrannik turn out to be a member of the opposition.

Best to forget about her, he thought as he began to pack his things. At least we didn't make the mistake of having children. One vindictive little bastard is more than enough. Yet she is a beauty, isn't she? I wonder if Anna noticed the resemblance between us.

By the time darkness fell he had everything together, and sat in the parlor, not even bothering to light the lamps. A tumbler of vodka left a ring of moisture on the table near his chair, the portrait of the unknown General glowing faintly in the final light of dusk. Beyond the curtained windows, Moscow's bells sang triumphant, and down in the street he could hear the *dvornik* whistling a melancholy tune. But as he'd often heard people say, Moscow didn't believe in tears, and so he raised his glass and silently toasted his flea-market General, Anna having discovered the painting while haunting the many stalls of Sukharev Square.

Down below, the porter had stopped whistling, the sound of a carriage, hoofs on cobblestones, wheels rattling, and a wheezy voice crying, "Aye, the squint-eyed dunce, the blockhead," breaking the silence of the deserted street.

Someone's heavy, purposeful tread sounded on the carpeted stairs. Draining the little that remained in his glass, Simon went into the entryway to open the door. The carriage he'd heard a moment before was no doubt waiting to take him to the station, where he still might have time to catch the express train to Kiev. If not, the regular train would take several hours longer, though he'd be able to sleep most of the way.

"Yes?" he said in answer to the bell.

"I've come from the Colonel's office. I have your ticket."

Simon undid the locks and opened the door. A short, slightly built man in a moth-eaten gray suit was standing in the hall.

"Simon Belinsky?"

"Yes, come in. I just have to get my bags and we'll be off."

He turned away and started back to the parlor when he heard the sound of gunfire. The floor seemed to drop several feet, and he clawed wildly at the air as if he were trying to fly. Again there was an explosion, though now there was no way he could regain his balance. He tumbled forward, striking his forehead against the smooth, polished floorboards. An astonished "Why?" fell from his lips.

"You should never have threatened Colonel Zubatov," said the man who looked more like a clerk than a paid assassin. "He was very fond of you, Belinsky, spoke of you as a brother. He actually cried when he gave me my orders."

With the next blast of gunfire Simon lay quite still, watching the General and his bomb through glazed, unfocused eyes. Behind him, footsteps retreated, making the floor vibrate painfully beneath his cheek. The door swung shut. The little man in the moth-eaten suit ran down the stairs.

The shame of it, Simon thought, the disgrace. To be shot in the back like a dog.

Except for the slow trickle of blood as it dripped onto the floor, there was absolute silence. The General, Simon observed before he closed his eyes, was smiling.

Nine

She no longer had rose-colored stationery, nor scent to perfume the irises decorating each sheet. The sweet, pale-blue bedroom of her girlhood was relegated to memory, and in its place she passed the hours in a tiny log house divided into three cramped rooms. "Yet I must think of it as home," Masha wrote her sister, "and be grateful for the little I have. I was very sick, my love, but not as sick as I deserved. I really can't remember very much of what happened, for after our party left Alexandrovsk I lay in the bottom of the cart with my eyes on the sky. Sometimes the sun burned so fiercely the sky was white, and sometimes the darkness of night seemed to touch me like a hand against my cheek, but always there was someone beside me to try to comfort me in my pain.

"By the time we reached Kirensk, they say I was delirious, so ill they didn't think I'd survive another week. For more than a month I remained in what passes here for a hospital, until the hemorrhaging gradually stopped and I slowly began to recover. It's a frighteningly insidious disease, tuberculosis. Just when you begin to forget you've ever suffered it, there it is again, eating its way inside you, making the very act of drawing breath seem like an obstacle of major proportions.

"But I'm much better now, Irusha dear, and the cold, sub-arctic air makes me think I'm living somewhere high up in the mountains, the Swiss Alps, perhaps. The money you sewed into the binding of the New Testament you gave me, the one book they allowed me to have when I was in prison, has served me very well indeed. For only five rubles a month I was able to rent this little cabin. One of my fellow exiles, a former gymnasium student who's not even sixteen years of age, comes each day to help me clean the rooms and light the stove. When it's too cold to go out, as it is most of the time now, he manages to come all the same, and brings me food and supplies from town.

"Kirensk is much pleasanter than I ever dared imagine. Situated on an island between the Lena and Kirenga rivers, the town boasts a population of some two thousand inhabitants—most of whom, I've been told, are descendants of convicts. Of course, now that we're in the middle of winter, it's as spellbound as the landscape. But they say that in the spring it's the prettiest town on the Lena, with neat streets, and gaily painted houses. There's an inn, a dockyard, and several fine stores. Why, they even sell talking machines, they're so up-to-date!

"Although they tell me there are police spies everywhere, I've yet to come up against any. I would like to be able to teach again, but unfortunately that's an occupation in which politicals are forbidden to engage, even a 'quasipolitical' such as myself. But the town maintains a fairly well-stocked library, and so I intend to keep myself as busy as possible. With the temperature dropping to forty degrees below zero, I seldom have a chance to go out exploring, although this evening I promised to attend a New Year's celebration—or as much of a celebration as one can expect, given our circum-stances. As news of my 'courageous and romantic act' hasn't reached these parts, few people know why I've been sent here. That's just as well, because I want to put it all behind me. Not that I can ever forget what I've done, and the pain I've caused all of you. But I've learned that it serves little good to keep going over it, day after day.

"I shall write more tomorrow, for it's time I got ready. How odd, though, to look in the little hand mirror I bought in town, and see reflected in its glass a woman and not a girl. Suddenly it all seems to catch up on us, doesn't it? But the wrinkles and the stray gray hairs don't bother me. I rather like this new Masha, and it seems to me as if all her suffering has been of great value. So often we let our lives slip past us, taking each day for granted. Here, with icy winds blowing from morning till night, with a few chimneys poking out of the snowy landscape like currants stuck in a frosted bun, I've come to realize how truly precious freedom is. So many of the exiles are barely more than children, Irusha, banished for reasons that often make no sense at all. Pray for them as you would pray for me. Perhaps more than any of us, they are the symbol of what Russia really is."

In the stuffy, overheated confines of her room, Masha viewed the several closely written sheets with a feeling of satisfaction, then put down her rubber-barreled pen and went into the bedroom to change. By the time she was ready, looking twenty pounds heavier as a result of all the warm clothing she'd put on, the youngster whom she had engaged to assist her had just driven up in a sledge.

"Everyone's coming, Maria Petrovna. Hundreds and hundreds . . . well, not that many, certainly. But everyone I've talked to insists they wouldn't miss it for the world."

The schoolboy, Timofey Gavrilovich, bubbled over with enthusiasm. He was a wiry little fellow who, for all the suffering he had already endured, seemed to have lost none of his spirit or his zest for life. Driving the sledge was an adventure in itself, and as the runners glided over the hard-packed snow, he spoke to the shaggy Siberian pony who dragged at the shafts, clicking his tongue and holding his arms straight out before him, just like a Petersburg *yamshchik*.

Off in the distance, across what appeared to be an untrodden expanse of snow, cinder-black chimneys poured forth their smoke. It was toward the nearest cluster of cabins that Timofey led them, hunching his shoulders like a turtle withdrawing into its shell. A fierce, biting wind was blowing from the direction of the river, sending great stinging sheets of powdery snow swirling all around them. Yet the pony struggled gamely through the deepening drifts, its icicle-strewn mane and long, braided tail tossed this way and that by the gale.

Now and again Timofey would say something to her, though the howling winds made it difficult to hear him. Masha contented herself trying to stay as warm and as dry as she could, peering out from the fleecy woolen shawl she'd wrapped like a bandage around her face, and seeing before her a barren landscape with not even a single tree to add relief to the view.

It took longer than she imagined before they drew up before a cabin, the sides of which were half buried in snow, making it look more like a cave than a dwelling of logs. Smoke rose invitingly from its chimney, and the cheery glow from within lit up the darkness, night having come on so quickly that Masha couldn't even remember seeing the sun go down.

Timofey helped her from the sleigh, urging her to go inside while he attended to the pony, as the sturdy little beast wouldn't survive very long without adequate shelter. As he led the horse to the dilapidated stable at the rear of the house, Masha shook the pins and needles from her limbs and hurried up the sagging porch steps to the front door.

"Ah, here she is at last," said her hostess, a woman who had followed her husband into exile, and with whom Masha had become friendly. "Why, you look half frozen, Maria Petrovna," and taking her by the elbow, she led Masha directly to the stove. "Here, drink this, my dear. It's kümmel."

"Roast mutton—a regular feast, can you imagine?" someone was loudly proclaiming as Masha clutched the glass in both mittened hands, taking a sip of the winy, caraway-flavored liqueur.

"And soup with goose giblets," the same animated voice went on. "It was all quite something, let me tell you. But did you hear what happened to Bazarov? They found him shot to death. His wife discovered the body, the poor girl."

Feeling having returned to her hands, Masha peeled off her mittens, smiling and nodding at the numerous guests who were crowded together in the tiny front room. By the time she took off her coat, a dozen more had arrived, everyone laughing and talking at once as they greeted each other with hearty wishes for the New Year.

In the center of the room, on a plain wooden table covered with a white cloth, a brightly polished samovar occupied the place of honor, bubbling and hissing and clouding the windows with its steam. Clustered around it like a covey of partridges were a motley collection of unmatched cups and saucers. Nearby were dishes with apples and candied fruits, big, coarse cracknels, and several different kinds of cheese.

By Petersburg standards, this was far from extravagant, but for Masha even such simple fare seemed wonderfully gay and festive. How optimistic these people were, despite the privations they suffered. With each new arrival the conversation became more lively, the laughter rebounding from one corner of the room to the other.

Lydia Dmitryevna, her hostess, made sure she was introduced to the guests, so that soon Masha quite forgot where she was, smiling and enjoying herself as she hadn't in a very long time. Again and again the door flew open, bringing yet another visitor bundled up against the cold. Soon the front room became so crowded there was barely space to stand, and the guests began to move into the adjoining kitchen and bedroom, where coats and sheepskins were piled halfway to the ceiling.

"Yes, a friend wrote me about Bazarov," she overheard someone say as she made her way to the samovar, which alternately roared and sputtered, boiling so noisily it sounded as if it were carrying on a conversation with itself.

Wondering who this Bazarov was about whom she'd heard so much talk, she looked over at the two men who were standing with their backs to her at the opposite end of the table.

"Now they're saying he was a spy, an *agent provocateur*," one of them went on. "Still, it mustn't have been a very pleasant way to die."

A stray thought tugged at her consciousness, its very formlessness a nagging reminder of something she'd forgotten. She poured herself half a cup of tea, diluting the concentrated essence with boiling water from the samovar.

"Our friends in Tomsk say his real name was Belinsky. My goodness, Victor Romanovich, have I said something wrong?"

Masha dropped her cup, and as it shattered at her feet and the floor gave way beneath her, she cried out and grabbed hold of the edge of the table for support. Immediately, the two men whose conversation she'd been listening to turned around to see what the commotion was about. The taller of the two, a man with broad shoulders and almost colorless blue eyes set in a pale, mobile face, peered at her curiously, even as his companion insisted it was nothing, and hurried around the table to help her.

Of course not. Only Henriette would think of such a thing.

Buffeted by shapeless thoughts, she clung to the table with its pretty white cloth, terrified that in her loneliness she had now begun to see things that weren't there.

"Only a little bit of water, Madame," said the man who had rushed over to help her. "You didn't scald yourself, did you?"

But Masha couldn't answer. A terrible sensation of falling made her grip the table until her fingers began to ache. She took deep breaths, but it did little good. She knew that if she let go, immeasurable distances would open up before her, and she would plummet as surely as a stone cast into a well.

"Masha?" said the man with the almost colorless blue eyes. "Maria Petrovna?"

She began to weep. It was madness, wasn't it? Yes, it was insanity and nothing more. First *maman*, and then Vera, and now me, she kept thinking. Locked away in that little house of hers, the snow beating against the windows, the wind's howl just another form of silence, she had unknowingly lost touch with reality.

"Here, let me help you," said the man who'd spoken her name. "You look terrified."

But it was worse than terror. Strange and impossible as it seemed, she wanted to be mad, if only to make the moment last as long as she could. When reality would once again intrude, she would at least be left with a residue of memory, a reminder that she had not lost her ability to feel, and to care deeply for those she had loved. But though Masha wanted to tell him that, she couldn't will her lips to move, the fear of disappointment constricting her throat and making it difficult to speak. Yet she wasn't a child anymore, nor a schoolgirl with her head stuck high up in the clouds, the scent of romance and intrigue clinging to everything she touched. Embarrassment replaced fear, and she finally managed to hold herself steady.

"Shouldn't we find you a chair?" said the man she had been told was dead, buried in an unmarked grave.

"I have changed, haven't I?" she said, finding her voice again.

The man looked at her as if she were speaking to someone else. Unable to make sense of what she had said, he was even moved to glance nervously behind him, perhaps thinking her words had been directed to a third party whose presence he wasn't even aware of.

"Why did they tell me you were dead, Victor? I believed my sister when she came to me. God, I believed every word of it, and yet you were still alive."

The man gasped soundlessly, opening his mouth as if he couldn't breathe. "No, it can't be. It couldn't possibly." Yet he reached out and kissed her hands, pressing them to his lips. "But it is you, after all." As much consumed by wonder as delight, Victor Durnovo broke into a hearty laugh, child-like in its simplicity, his habitually earnest expression vanishing so quickly that Masha knew she would never remember it again. "I don't know what to say. I wouldn't even know where to begin. It's been twenty years, hasn't it? Yes. But we were children. And now look at us."

Still children, Masha thought, and now it was her turn to feel giddy, flushed with excitement she had long thought herself incapable of. But did she know who he really was? The sobering thought stopped her short, like an unforeseen barrier one encounters on the road. It wasn't as if she expected him to take her hand and march her into the sunset, where they would live out their lives like characters in a fairy tale, destined for happiness until the end of their days. But perhaps that wasn't as farfetched as it seemed. Maybe there still was room for happiness, and all the time in the world to discover who they had become.

"What a wonderful riddle we've solved, isn't it?" she said,

so overwhelmed by all that she was feeling that she couldn't help but laugh. "I loved you so much, I thought I could never live without you. And yet I survived, just as you said I would."

"I couldn't offer you what you wanted then," Victor replied, his voice quivering with emotion. "I couldn't bear the idea of having you follow after me. I wasn't wrong about that, either. It seems as if I've spent more time here than anywhere else."

Unable to restrain himself any longer, Victor Romanovich broke down and began to weep, clinging to her as if begging her forgiveness. Masha, holding him safely in her arms, thought of how her life had changed because of him, both now and twenty years before. That one man could so alter the pattern of her existence was an awesome and frightening realization. Yet it had happened, and it was done, and now they embraced each other as if transfigured by these visions of their common past, when youth held out its promise with a bright and mischievous grin. There would be time enough to find out what they meant to each other, and if twenty years was too great a barrier to overcome. But now, as a joyous feeling awoke in her soul, she let her tears take the place of words, for she could think of no better way to tell him how she felt.

It was, Masha realized, God's merciful will.

All that summer and fall Countess Ignatieva had not been well. Henriette, fearing the worst, called in specialist after specialist, faced with the terrifying prospect of suddenly being left both penniless and alone. What plans the Countess had made for her in the event of her death had never been discussed, and though there was a great deal of openness, even intimacy, between her and her benefactress, Henriette was afraid to bring up such a delicate subject, lest the

Countess misinterpret her interest and accuse her of being both mercenary and disloyal.

But just when she had begun to lose hope, certain she would soon find herself destitute, the Countess surprised her by drawing up a new will, even consulting with Henriette so that there would be no secrets between them. The woman's generosity astounded her as few things had in the past. In the event of her death her entire estate would revert to Henriette, "my loyal and devoted companion," as the will so described her. The Countess possessed a sizable fortune, with numerous properties scattered in several neighboring provinces, as well as a collection of jewels, which would fetch a tidy sum should Henriette ever decide to dispose of them.

"I'm only sorry I can't grant you my title," the Countess lamented as she lay in her bed, an old-fashioned mobcap covering her hair and concealing the profusion of gray curls that had once been black as jet. "But people still respect you, Henriette, and when I'm gone there'll be no want of admirers."

To this rather unlikely prediction Henriette responded with a sallow smile, ringing for the maid to bring up tea. It depressed her to see her friend so thin and pale and lacking in spirit, and as she sat beside the Countess' bed she spoke comfortingly of the future, promising her a speedy recovery. Yet none of the physicians Henriette had consulted had expressed nearly as much optimism, taking her aside to whisper of clogged blood vessels and failing organs, of complications of such an esoteric nature that even they, the finest medical minds in Russia, were unable to unravel them.

"It's my heart, you know," the Countess would say one day, while the next she insisted her liver was to blame, gingerly pressing her fingers to her stomach and complaining that she had no idea what was wrong with her, except that it hurt.

Having been her mother's nursemaid, Henriette instinctively rebelled against taking such an active role in her friend's illness. But now that she had seen the will with her own eyes, there was no possible way to get around it. So rather than avoid responsibility, she spent her days by the Countess' sickbed, idly turning the pages of *Autour des Indes à la Planète Mars (From India to the Planet Mars)*, a work of theosophical investigation she found much too tedious even to bring up when there was nothing else to talk about.

The Countess' salon had now gone its separate way, as hardly any of the people who had called themselves her friends cared to spend an evening sitting by the old woman's bedside. This infuriated Henriette, knowing how it grieved the Countess to discover that when she most needed them, she had no friends to speak of. It was thus with considerable surprise that Henriette answered the telephone that December afternoon in the year 1902, praying it would be one of their old acquaintances, anxious to come by and pay a call.

"Whoever it is, tell them I'm not up to it," the Countess said fretfully. Though her lorgnette hung around her neck on its familiar black ribbon, she now insisted it was lost, and peered over the side of the bed, upsetting the well-thumbed collection of illustrated magazines with which she passed much of her time.

A vaguely familiar voice, harsh and guttural, came on at the other end. Henriette, holding the receiver tightly to her ear—telephone service in the capital being of notoriously poor quality—looked over at the Countess and suddenly gasped.

Discovering the lorgnette was still around her neck, Countess Ignatieva held it before her shortsighted eyes and returned Henriette's astonished glance.

"Oh, I shall, I shall," said Henriette, shouting somewhat hysterically into the transmitter. "Yes, certainly . . . *Frant-*

zuzskaya Naberezhnaya, the French Quay, that's correct. Of course, of course. We'll wait as long as it takes, Father."

She hung up, and for a moment all she could do was sit there and stare at the Countess as if she'd just seen a ghost—a not uncommon occurrence, according to many who'd attended her séances.

"Father? What father?" said the Countess in a fearful voice. "Surely you're not hurrying me on, Henriette, are you? I may be sick, *chère amie,* but I still don't think it's time to receive extreme unction."

Henriette responded with a dreamy expression, and she rose silently from her chair as if she were levitating.

"I'm not ready yet, I swear," the Countess continued to insist. "When it's time, you'll be the first to know, Henriette, I promise."

"Ready?" Henriette said, coming out of her daze. "Ready for what?"

"Oh Henriette, I don't want to die yet. As God is my witness, surely I still have a few days left, perhaps even a week." The Countess, her blotchy red face trembling with agitation, reached for Henriette's hand, holding it in a terrified embrace.

"Die?" she exclaimed. "But you're going to live, *ma Comtesse!* He's on his way here this very moment. And he'll cure you, my dear, sweet friend. He'll make you well again."

"Cure me?" said the Countess with a look of perplexity. "But I'm sick. Even Dr. Bertenson, who attends the royal family, said there's no hope for me."

"Dr. Bertenson has yet to meet Gregory Rasputin."

The Countess sat up in bed. "Father Gregory!" she cried. "He's here, in Petersburg?"

"Not only is he here, but he's only here because of us. Oh, dearest friend in all the world, he's going to cure you, and cure me, too," Henriette said, clasping her hands together in a paroxysm of bliss. "And then can you imagine what joy it will be when we present him at court?"

"Court?" said the Countess, screwing up her eyes in confusion.

"Why, of course. Don't you remember? The Tsarina said she wanted to meet him. And now she will, without fail."

Then, excusing herself to change, and promising to send up one of the maids to attend to the Countess' toilette, so that both of them would look their very best, Henriette sailed from the room, walking so gracefully one might have thought she was still floating on air.

Pausing before the ikons in her dove-gray room, Henriette sank down onto her knees and gazed at her beloved Redeemer, her sharp, gray eyes now soft and girlish and glistening with tears. At last, all her sorrowful prayers were about to be answered. Father Gregory was coming to see her, had spoken of the tenderness they had once shared, had promised her that he had never forgotten the joyful days they had spent together.

Christ listened in silence, then nodded approvingly.

Yes, at last she could truly call herself *La Belle Henriette.* Soon she would show Petersburg that men could still perform miracles, and that the *starets* whose powers had touched her in Verkhoture was a man that all of Russia might one day love and revere. Yes, that would be her calling, to bring him to see the Empress so that she might experience the blessing of his touch, the spiritual wisdom he would be eager to share with her.

Thank you, she whispered in her prayers. Thank you, my beloved, for bringing him back to me.

But though she said these words, first silently and then out loud, her vision blurred, then brightened, and she saw the gray goat who watched her as he lay in her bed, fondling himself, and laughing that she had so foolishly come to equate physical passion with spiritual rebirth.

"The Antichrist now resides in Petersburg," the Tempter warned her, just as she had been warned more than twenty years before. "But it's too late to stop him, Henriette Petrovna."

"Stop him?" she replied, and turning to face the shape-shifter, the gray goat that sometimes capered in the form of a monk, and sometimes slithered voluptuously like a serpent, she threw her head back and responded with a scornful laugh. "Father Gregory is the source of salvation. He will save us all. He will make Russia the envy of the world."

The serpent reared up before her, challenging her with its coldly menacing eyes.

"Gentle Jesus has brought him to me!" she cried out.

She stumbled back, tripping on the edge of the wax-stained strip of carpet she had brought all the way from Petrovka. But the moment she hit her head against the floor the gray goat vanished, scurrying out of sight like something dark and monstrous that was afraid of the light. Henriette came shakily to her feet, and with a final glance at her Savior, whose sad, merciful eyes once again expressed their approval, she blew out the candle before the ikons and hurried into her dressing room to change.

From that day on, the Countess' health began to steadily improve, and by the following spring she was fully herself again. Rasputin, who was already making a reputation for himself in Petersburg, was rumored to have healed her with his touch.

The Trans-Siberian Express—or *train de luxe,* as it was called—left Moscow every Saturday evening, arriving in Irkutsk eight days later. In the spring of 1903, amid growing signs of unrest within the empire, Irena and her niece boarded the blue first-class carriage that would take them east. Both were tired from their journey from Petersburg, and so as soon as they pulled out of the station, where the admonition "God Save the Tsar" shone in permanent gas illumination over the entrance, Irena rang for a *provodnik* to make up their beds. After the attendant left, having hoisted up the back cushion of the seat to form an upper berth, Irena locked the corridor door, changed into her nightdress, and climbed into bed.

But though the trip down had been very tiring, she was too excited to sleep, and lay in the dark of their compartment, imagining how it would be when she finally reached her destination. Kirensk seemed like the very end of the earth, for after arriving in Irkutsk she would then have to hire a driver and tarantass to take her some two hundred fifty miles north along the Great Lena Post Road. Here, at the river town of Ust-Kutsk, a steamer would transport her upriver to Kirensk.

Nikolai hadn't wanted her to undertake such an exhausting journey, and had, in fact, forbidden it the year before. But when he learned that the liberal party to which he now belonged, the Union of Liberation, planned to hold a series of important meetings in Switzerland, and that he himself would thus be out of the country, his opposition to her plans quickly evaporated. Auntie V., who had recently celebrated her seventy-fifth birthday, agreed to look after the boys, although Andrei, at seventeen, insisted he was old enough to take care of himself.

Pauline would be traveling with Irena only as far as the town of Taiga, where the branch railway would then take her on to Tomsk. She had visited with Alexei the previous summer, and now, despite her aunt's objections, planned to join him when he left with a convoy of exiles late that spring. Although both she and Pauline had hoped Alex might be sent to Kirensk, the authorities had chosen instead a village in the sparsely populated Yakutsk Region, more than two thousand versts farther north. Thus Irena wasn't nearly as happy as she might have been. Even though she knew that in less than three weeks' time she would be with her sister when Masha and Victor Durnovo exchanged their marriage vows, Irena also knew that when she said good-bye to her niece, she might not see Pauline again for many years.

"Are you awake, Aunt Irusha?" whispered Pauline from her berth.

"Yes, there's so much on my mind, I just can't sleep."

"I can't either. I was thinking how much I was going to miss you. You once said that I was your child, and now I know what you meant. You've been a mother to me, and a friend, too. So you mustn't be unhappy about what I'm doing. I have to do it, Aunt Irusha, do you understand? It's not even as if I have a choice. It's a need, a responsibility not to let Alex go off on his own. Surely you can sympathize with that, after what happened to Aunt Masha."

Irena was silent for a long time. She wanted to say something that Pauline would never forget, a universal truth perhaps, a kind of summing-up of her life. But there was still much more of life she was yet to experience, and so all she could think of was love, and how life itself had little value without it. Trying to put that into words, she saw herself and her family, her sisters and brother, her parents before them, as an irrevocable chain of flesh and blood. Denied the ties of kinship, and the roots one put down in defense of one's loved ones, mankind would be like a seed cast adrift on the wind, floating this way and that without purpose or direction. But family, she thought, was like a covenant man had made with his God, the most sacred of all the commandments.

She tried to explain this to her niece, whom she loved as

she loved her sons. "It's all that matters," Irena said with her whole being and the inexhaustible strength of her convictions.

"I never knew you to be so serious, Aunt Irusha. After all, we're not going to die tomorrow," Pauline said with a laugh.

Irena smiled sadly. Someday the child laughing in the dark would be a woman, and then she too would understand.